PRYDE RANCH SHIFTERS

BOOKS 1 THROUGH 5

T.J. MICHAELS

CONTENTS

Pryde Ranch Shifters ©

Copyright 2009 – 2015 by T.J. Michaels
ALL RIGHTS RESERVED.
Second Electronic Printing February 2015,
Bent West Books
2nd Edition Cover Art by Syneca of Original Syn
ISBN: 978-0-9975063-7-2

PRAISE FOR THE NOVELS OF T.J. MICHAELS

Silk Road

"An action packed thriller too hot to miss!" ~Lisa Renee Jones, national bestselling author

"Silk Road twisted and turned flawlessly. The characters were nothing short of fantastic." ~Booked and Loaded Reviews

"SILK ROAD is an entertaining urban fantasy romance that promises to captivate readers as good, evil, and something in between converge in a real page turner from beginning to end." ~R. Barri Flowers, bestselling Harlequin author of MURDER IN HONOLULU and MURDER IN MAUI

The Vampire Council of Ethics Series

"Interesting new world. Hot stuff!" ~Shayla Black, New York Times bestselling author

"CARINIAN'S SEEKER was a highly erotic, thrilling suspenseful, paranormal read that will blow your mind." ~Fallen Angel Reviews

"It had me rooting for their happy-ever-after as much as cheering their kick-ass assignments" ~Just Erotic Romance Reviews

"T.J. MICHAELS has done an astounding job of crafting a steamy hot suspenseful romance—" ~Romance Junkies

---

Spirit Bound Novels

"All in all, [On the Prowl] is a fun and delightful story with spicy sex and great suspense both in the love story and the plot." ~Just Erotic Romance Reviews

"Using heat, danger and tension, Egyptian Voyage will keep you glued to that edge of your seat as you go along for the ride. T.J. Michaels has written a story that will fascinate, horrify and ultimately delight the reader." ~SensualReads.com

---

Forever December

"[Forever December] is a highly erotic, touching and sexy novella that will have you reaching for a tall, cold glass of water and a fan." ~Romance Divas

"Explosive love scenes will curl your toes and leave you fanning. Readers who love a flare for the dramatic with paranormal

elements will certainly become fans of T.J. Michaels."
~Romance Junkies

Jaguar's Rule

"The plot is flawlessly executed and the characters remain true."
~The Romance Studio

"T.J. MICHAELS knows how to write plot and passion in a most memorable way!" ~Fallen Angels Reviews

SPIRIT OF THE PRIDE

$\mathcal{N}$eesia Pryde glanced back and rolled her gaze up to the rain-clouded sky with an annoyed groan. Pinning her younger sisters with a hard glare, she growled right into their minds. They were obviously more occupied with their trip to New York tomorrow than the possibility of getting their asses pounded in a fight tonight.

"Kotara, Koreas, pay attention. Get your heads into this hunt or I'll skin your backsides when we get back to the house."

"Sorry, Neesia," they demurred, their words as identical as their features. Eyes downcast and unmistakably sheepish, the two youngest Pryde twins quietly caught up with their oldest sister.

"Hey, I've got his scent," Niah, Neesia's twin, said as she reached out to her from across the plains.

"Stay put. We're on the way." Neesia moved swiftly out of the thick brush where she and the younglings hid and loped toward the rolling hills where Niah scouted ahead. Without a word, Kotara and Koreas took flanking positions and trailed silently along.

Once they were all together again, Niah motioned to the

spot where the old, almost gagging scent was strongest. *"The scent is strange. I've never smelled anything like it."*

Kotara eased forward, eyeing the grass cautiously. There was no blood, but something had definitely been here. Dipping her head, she took a whiff and jerked her head back in disgust. *"Definitely an animal, but what kind, I have no idea. Whatever it is, it's rank. It reminds me of rabid Were."*

"And," Niah added, *"the scent came from the Clarks' ranch onto ours, then trails off to the east."*

"What the hell?" Neesia cocked her head in question.

"Yeah, my thoughts exactly," grumbled Niah.

This mystery got stranger by the day. Mutilated buffalo carcasses on Pryde lands? And someone or something brought the damned things onto their ranch, drained and half eaten, and left them to rot. This one was a mass of stinking, slimy gore, partially hidden under a thick bush that did nothing to keep it out of the early spring rains.

Neesia looked toward her twin, still stalking silently through the high brush. Ears pricked forward, a low growl emanated from her chest. Niah's edginess was almost tangible. Nervous energy coursed through their bond. If Niah was rattled, that was really saying something. The woman was all logic and reasoning. If it couldn't be parsed or dissected on her computer, it didn't exist and was easily dismissed. But there was no mistaking the flash of concern pulsing through their psychic connection. Niah was worried.

"What do you think? A setup, Niah?"

"It's beginning to look that way, sis. My main concern is that whoever is doing this knows exactly who and what we are. And that just can't be allowed. We've got to find this asshat and put him or her down. Fast."

Neesia sent comforting thoughts along the bond shared with her twin and spoke privately to her. *"Don't worry, Niah. It'll be all right. Let's just do what we do best. Hunt."* The two sisters peered into each other's amber eyes with silent agreement. *"Okay, ladies,"* Neesia called to all three of her siblings, *"let's catch this bastard so we can get on with more important things."*

Together, their locations strategically chosen, four African lionesses stalked across the Wyoming plains.

Damn. Just when he thought he was actually going to get a vacation, the emergency beacon on his secure cell phone lit up. What now? He'd just closed his last case, and was packed and ready to head to the coast for some well-earned relaxation. If the little red light was any indication, he wasn't going anywhere anytime soon. Well, at least not some place he *wanted* to go.

"DiCaplis!"

Damn, his captain had signaled only moments ago. For her to make it down six floors and to his desk so quickly meant trouble. And lots of it.

"Yeah, Cap," Jason replied, packing equipment into his gear bag. Laptop, secure wireless network cards, extra USB storage, mini video cams...

"I want you in my office in ten minutes. Better yet, come with me right now. Leave the rest of your packing for later."

Boy, was *she* in a foul mood. Standing at five-foot-nothing, long black hair pulled back into a severe knot emphasized the blaze in her deep gray eyes. The woman was a formidable shifter, a good leader, and all of her agents respected her. Without a word, he followed behind her small frame, holding his questions. Once behind her soundproofed office doors, the briefing began.

"Cap, what's going on? I'm scheduled for vacation starting in, uh," he looked down at his watch, "about five minutes from now. What's with the emergency beacon?"

"I know, DiCaplis, but this is urgent and it can't wait. When we're done talking, go home, pack fast and sleep faster. You're to be at this address at five o'clock tomorrow morning, ready to work."

Jason took the little piece of paper from Captain Johns. His eyes narrowed with a tilt of his head. What the hell?

"Cap, this is the private airstrip where all the big wigs keep their private jets. What the hell am I supposed to do there?"

"I'll answer your questions after the briefing. Now sit your ass down and don't say a word. Don't breathe until I'm done."

He snapped his mouth shut with a glare. But he sat nonetheless.

"Look at these pictures and tell me what you think," Captain Johns said, switching off the light. A large screen lowered silently from the ceiling and was immediately filled with the most gruesome, sadistic pictures Jason had ever seen. Clamping his lips together, he bit the inside of his cheek and fought the urge to blow chunks.

"Well?" Johns pushed, lips sternly set and eyes lit with anger. Jason took a deep breath and applied his skills at deduction and observation to the photos on the screen.

"Buffalo, slaughtered by a large animal. First guess would be a mountain lion, but the claw marks are too deep, meaning the wounds were caused by something larger. The bite marks are typical of a larger cat, a fully grown lion perhaps." Or a Were. But there was no way in hell he would say so. Not without proof.

"Not bad, DiCaplis. The carcass was found on the lands belonging to Pryde Ranch, but the buffalo is from a neighboring spread. It was hidden, but not well enough to keep from being spotted."

"Who found the carcass?"

"Actually, this is the third. The first two animals were reported lost by the owners, neighbors of the Prydes. The local sheriff found them. The Prydes found the third, but didn't report it to local law enforcement. We found out anyway. We think it's a rogue."

"You really think a shifter or a Were is responsible? Can we be sure it wasn't these Pryde people?"

"The Prydes are two sisters who own a seventy-thousand acre spread in Wyoming. In addition to running a huge estate, they're professionals in their chosen fields of science and technology. They're also bounty hunters."

Jason's eyebrows rose at that little piece of information. "Bounty hunters?"

"Yes, DiCaplis, bounty hunters. For us."

"What?" Jason exploded out of his chair and paced furiously in front of his superior. "We've stooped to using humans? What the fuck, Cap?" he thundered. How dare they endanger the very people they were supposed to protect? The Shifter and Were Armed Tactics, S.W.A.T.'s, sole purpose was to protect humans from rogues, and protect themselves from discovery. In short, no human on Earth should have a clue about the existence of *other*kind.

"Sit. Down. DiCaplis." When he didn't immediately comply, the sparkle and flash in her silver eyes that warned of an impending shift made him sit. After all, the captain was no punk bitch and he didn't particularly want his ass handed to him just now.

"Look, DiCaplis, you're one of the best agents we have. You also have the highest clearance. No one, and I mean no one, is to know the Prydes work for us from time to time. And the Prydes are not to know you work with us at all. Understood?"

At his stiff nod, she held out two black-and-white photos. He practically snatched them from her fingers and froze.

"The first picture is the young lady you'll meet tomorrow. Her name is Neesia Pryde. Twenty-nine years old. Five-foot-eleven. A hundred eighty-five pounds of lethal genius. The technical brain of the two."

A soft whistle left Jason's lips. Wow, what a beauty. Eyes riveted to the small picture, he almost missed the rest of the briefing.

"Neesia is the oldest. Degree in business management and a Master's in marketing. She runs the ranch and does most of her technical consulting from there. The second picture is her younger sister, Kotara, a veterinary scientist and biochemist. She engineered the cure for FIV, a disease similar to HIV but only affects felines and is usually fatal to domestic cats. Right now, she's out of town at a biotech conference in New York."

"So, what do you think this means, Cap?" Jason asked tightly, turning away from the gore in front of him. He'd never seen anything so disgusting.

"What I think, Agent DiCaplis, is you're going to Pryde Ranch and find the rogue that did this. Someone is trying to frame our agents and we can't let that happen considering they aren't supposed to exist."

After the briefing, Jason DiCaplis walked out of S.W.A.T. headquarters shaking his head over this turn of events. Instead of a relaxing vacation, he was walking into the possibility of losing his head on a Were hunt. If he didn't love a good fight every now and then, he would have almost been disappointed.

---

2

*T*he land below took Jason's breath away as the pilot pointed out the beginning of Pryde lands. The land was green with trees, plenty of scrub and grasses that swayed with the wind. The Medicine Bow River wound its way through the property and sparkled under the morning sun as if it the fast-running waters were full of diamonds. He'd never seen such beautifully wide-open spaces. The place seemed to go on forever. In fact, when the jet landed, he had yet to see the boundary marking the edge of the estate.

His face was still damn near plastered to his window as they touched down on the private airstrip. Jason remained seated as the pilot popped the hatch to find a set of jet way stairs already rolling toward the opening.

He grabbed his bag, and headed down. And at the bottom of those stairs stood a goddess.

"Hi, I'm Neesia Pryde. Thanks for bringing this equipment on such short notice."

The woman's voice flowed over him like rich chocolate. The sweet confection was obviously named after her beautiful cinnamon skin, which was clearly visible, compliments of a formfitting white tank top. She was dark, velvety and surely delicious. The thought of tasting her made Jason's tongue dance around in his mouth until he snapped it closed. Lips, full and ripe, had him swallowing hard. And the golden hue of her eyes was simply arresting, like little orbs of the purest honey. The woman was, in a word, fine as hell. Well, that was three words, but it summed her up pretty well.

Jason's prime, a huge sorrel African lion with a full black mane, rolled around beneath his skin. The sensation was so unexpected, Jason heard himself gasp in surprise.

Whoa. Down boy. Deep breath. Deep breath, dude.

Bad idea. That breath brought with it the coconut scent of the woman in front of him. His prime had one thing on his mind—he wanted out, and Neesia Pryde was his sole focus. His mind's eye was suddenly filled with the image of the big cat that shared his mind and body as he licked his rough tongue over Neesia's skin.

It was an insane thought. Besides, judging from Neesia Pryde's strong and fit physique, she'd probably deck him if he stepped up and started licking the side of her neck. Then again, he'd always loved women who were mentally and physically strong. The end result might be wild lovemaking that left his skin scored, scratched and bruised, with a few bite marks here and there, but at least he didn't have to worry about breaking them.

You're such a masochist, DiCaplis. With a mental shake, he reminded himself that he was here to do a job.

"Mr. DiCaplis, right?" Neesia asked, probably wondering if he was some kind of dimwit after staring at her for at least thirty seconds without a word.

"Uh, yes, hi. Sorry, I'm not usually up at dawn and I'm a bit slow this morning," he said with a bright smile. He extended his hand and appreciated the strength in her grip as she firmly pumped it up and down. Thanks to his line of work, it had been awhile since he'd been with a woman. Most of the ones he came across were simpering annoyances. But Neesia seemed far from the sort and damn, he would love to get to know her. And since he wasn't investigating Neesia, there was nothing unethical about tempting the temptress, right?

By the way, had the gods invented blue jeans? Hers fit like a dream. The light blue fabric accentuated a trim waist and a delightfully round ass that tapered down to endless legs. Physically restraining both himself and his animal, he practically shook with the urge to reach out and touch. What in the hell was going on?

Neesia's rich, sinful voice snapped him out of his musings.

"Broglio here will help you unload the crates," she said, motioning to an older, salt-and-pepper-haired man sitting on a small forklift. She held out her hand and jangled something on the end of her long fingers. He looked down at her hand and gulped.

Snap out of it, idiot.

Hell, he was practically slobbering, imagining the feel of those fingers. Mentally slapping himself in the back of the neck, he focused on her words and tried not to look at the yummy lips speaking them. If he kept this up, he'd blow his cover... among other things.

"Here are the keys to the jeep over there," she said, nodding her head toward a sporty-looking four-wheeler parked off to the side. "Just tell Broglio which crates you want brought up to the house and he'll help you get them into the jeep. There's plenty of storage space, but you don't have to take it all up right now. Load whatever you don't immediately need on the flatbed over there and bring it up to the house later. All right with you?"

"Sure, thanks," Jason said.

She turned to walk away and his mind scrambled for something to say, anything to keep her from leaving. What the hell was wrong with him? Certainly he couldn't be this hard up for a female? Hell, who was he fooling? This was a terrible time for his cock to remind him how horny he was.

"Oh, I forgot," she said as she stopped and turned to pin him with her light, tawny gaze. Jason's heart felt as if it would beat out of his chest. "All the wiring and setup for the new surveillance system is going to take a couple of weeks. We told your employer it would be best if you stayed here. Just follow Broglio back to the main house and we'll get you settled, all right? We'll start tomorrow with the grounds around the house, then move out onto the ranch. A schematic is in the jeep for you to study."

"Uh, yeah. Sure. Thanks," Jason mumbled, sounding like some goofy schoolboy as he dragged his eyes away from her smile. And those lips.

Tempting was such an inadequate word.

Waving at the captain who'd come out of the cockpit to help unload the cargo, Neesia called out as she headed back to her own vehicle.

"Thanks for flying on such short notice, Harry. I know your schedule is tight but come up to the house and get a bite to eat before you take off."

The pilot grinned like a loon and bounded down the stairs. "Come on, boys, let's put our backs into it."

But Jason knew the man's eagerness to get the unloading done had more to do with Neesia's invitation to visit the house than a desire to get back in the air.

He couldn't blame the man one bit.

Broglio had been good company. In fabulous shape at fifty years old, the man had known the Prydes since the girls were children. Jason put his subtle interrogation skills to work and learned quite a bit about the family. Originally from East Africa,

Neesia's parents had been killed as innocent bystanders during an uprising in a neighboring village. Neesia and her sister were brought to the States as toddlers and brought up by their grandmother. Good, solid educations, innovative ideas and hard work had paid off big time. Working together, the two women had earned a sizeable fortune for themselves. The huge estate he'd spent part of the morning wandering around was proof of that.

A few hours later, all of the equipment had been loaded, hauled and unloaded in the various supply buildings where it would be easily assessable near the installation sites. Finally, Jason and Broglio made it up to the house, which turned out to be more of a mansion-sized rustic lodge. They parked the jeep in the eight-car garage, and Broglio showed him up to his room, then back downstairs for an early dinner.

When they passed the empty formal dining area, Jason stopped to admire the room. The design was elegant and tasteful. One entire wall was made up of screened windows that allowed the orange glow of the setting sun to fill the room. A lacquered white pine table for eight sat in the center, with little cushioned benches off to the side against the opposite wall.

"This way," Broglio said. "Unless the whole family is here, we usually eat in the kitchen. If you can call it that."

Whole family? Jason pondered the man's words until they walked into an all-white and stainless steel room almost as big as his whole apartment. This was a kitchen? It looked more like chef heaven.

"Neesia loves to cook. She's the head of the family and makes sure everyone is well fed," Broglio said with a proud smile.

Hmm? Strange way to describe a family with only two women in it. Too hungry to pursue the issue, Jason followed the older man past the stove, several industrial-sized refrigerator-freezers, a tile-topped gourmet block large enough to butcher a whole cow, and over to a big bay window.

On top of a quaint country-style table sat a feast presented so nicely, he almost hated to eat it.

There were bowls of steaming white rice, a platter of grilled tilapia fish with a light sweet sauce, a big bowl of fresh greens sprinkled with a light ginger vinaigrette, and a small crock of some kind of clear soup.

Famished, his stomach was immensely grateful as he practically inhaled the meal. With every bite of the delicious Japanese-style fare, he imagined Neesia's exotically beautiful face and her lithe but bountiful body laid out in front of him. During dessert, Jason wondered if she was as succulently sweet as the light lemon cake covered with lemon curd and fresh strawberries she'd so thoughtfully left for them.

His lust was beyond misplaced, but his cock didn't care. Here to solve the mystery of possible rogue Were attacks, the more he thought on how nicely Neesia's full breasts had filled out the tank top she'd been wearing earlier, the more his blood pounded in his ears. He had to see her.

"Broglio, where do you think Ms. Pryde is? Does she always skip dinner?"

"No, the family eats early. Ms. Neesia usually relaxes in the library before she heads up to bed," the older man answered, a knowing, protective look in his eye.

"Which way is the library?" Jason asked, his expression deliberately bland as he gathered his dishes and headed to the sink.

Moments later, he walked into a huge, cozy room filled almost to the ceiling with books. He didn't see a single one. Instead, he zeroed in on his target. Neesia.

Every techno-weenie she'd ever met, with the exception of her twin, was a total nerd. But this "Jason dude" was a hunk and a half with a sexy voice and even sexier body. And so tall! Would she have to get up on her tiptoes to wrap her arms around his neck?

Whoa, where'd that thought come from?

She wasn't supposed to wrap anything around him. The man was here to do a job. There was only one problem...

"Look, Niah," she hissed into the phone. "If I pretend to be you for more than ten minutes with this guy, I'll blow it. You know how important this is. You were supposed to be back yesterday, damn it. You knew this shipment was coming in, along with the tech that's supposed to install it. The goods are here. The tech is here. But you? Uh, not so much."

Always able to play a cool and logical Niah, but not this time. Something about this Jason person had her usually level head giddy and nervous all at once. God, she was a wreck.

"Neesia, will you take a second to breathe? It's not my fault the fugitive gave me a hard time."

"But it's all wrapped up, right?" Neesia asked anxiously, hating when any of her sisters went after a bounty alone. Hated it even more when they were late getting back.

"Yep, wrapped up and tied with a bow. He's in S.W.A.T. custody."

"Good, now hurry up and get here so you can help Jason. He was told we'd help get all the surveillance equipment up and running. Won't he think it's odd when I can't tell one damned wire from another?"

"Oh, relax, will you? I'm on my way. Is something else going on? It's not like you to be so wound up, Neecie."

"No, everything is fine," she lied. After all, how could she answer the question when she had no clue? "And no other carcasses have turned up. Let's hope it stays that way."

"Good. So the equipment guy's name is Jason? What does he look like?" Niah asked.

How about handsome beyond words with dark, golden hair, hazel eyes, the wide-chested body of a god, and a tight ass?

Instead she said flatly, "He's tall, about six-foot-six, brown hair. Why?"

"Since you and I can't be seen together, I'll be meeting him by myself when I get home. It wouldn't do for me not to know him since you two have met."

Thank goodness one of them had some sense right now.

"Look, Neecie, I've gotta run. Harry just got here to fly me home," Niah said around a long, loud yawn. "I'll be in sometime tonight. Don't wait up, all right?"

"Fine, just hurry up," Neesia ground out and quickly hung up the phone as her keen ears picked up footsteps crossing the hardwood floor in the hallway. Seconds later Jason strode into the library.

She looked up from her reclined position on one of several plush loveseats and painted on a thin smile. Her tongue stuck to the roof of her mouth. The tee shirt he'd worn earlier was long gone. Stripped down to a painted on tank top and jeans, the man was all buffed perfection, every muscle movement easily seen.

The man looked like a predator if she'd ever seen one. Hold the door—she *was* a predator, and she knew when she was being sized up.

And he eyed her like a piece of candy.

She should really make a run for it.

Instead, she placed her book on the end table, sat up and tried to appear calm. "How was dinner? Everything okay?"

"More than okay. It was all…quite delicious."

The determined look in his twinkling eyes made her insides quiver. A parched throat kept a reply from leaving her mouth as she tried to figure out what to do with her hands. What the hell was wrong with her? Where was the tough, down to earth and down to business, Neesia?

Garnering her strength, she commanded her stomach to stop flopping all over the place. Just as she swung her feet to the floor to get the hell out of there, her way was blocked by the devastatingly handsome, tawny-haired man. His expression brought to mind something she'd seen on the Discovery Channel about the world's most effective hunters.

And their prey.

"Leaving so soon?" he asked, easing just a tad bit closer.

"Who? Me? Jason, I-I, uh." Well this was new. Neesia at a loss for words? The world must be ending any minute now.

"Neesia, there's something I need," his voice smooth and just shy of deep. Reminded her of Belgian dark chocolate melting on the tongue. And he was even closer now, moving as if he were trying not to spook her.

But his presence didn't scare or creep her out. Instead, something about this man drew her, set her shifter senses ablaze with a fire that had nothing to do with typical heat. No, this blaze was intense, infuriating in its ability to confuse her, and annoying because she should be more concerned with not blowing her cover rather than blowing...uh, yeah.

Change your train of thought, woman.

"Excuse me?"

"I said," he repeated with a half-cocked sexy-as-sin-grin, "there's something I need."

"What's that?" she asked on an unsteady breath.

The next thing she knew the man was on his knees in front of the loveseat, easing his face towards her. His movements slow and deliberate, it was clear he was giving her time to either protest or smack the shit out of him.

Instead, Neesia froze like a deer in the headlights as he leaned into her personal space. The next moment, Jason kissed her like an old lover who'd been away too long. Raising her hands to push him away, her fingers sent a message to her brain that the firm set of shoulders under her fingers felt uncommonly good. The play of solid muscle as he wrapped her securely in his arms and leaned her back against the cushions was even better.

His lips were firm, his kiss gentle yet hungry. And he tasted like berries and cream. She closed her eyes, took in the feel of his delicious mouth moving over hers, and reveled in the blaze of hot ice his touch created in the hollow of her womb. Decadent and devastating all at once, took everything she had, then reached inside her soul for more.

He moaned into her mouth, obviously enjoying the contact as much as she. But when he broke it off so his hot lips could travel along her jaw and nip at the sensitive skin just below her ear, Neesia's world spun as her womb clenched wildly.

Oh, god, it was too much. But why? There was no way she could be this far gone over someone she'd just met. Unless she decided to become a liar, there was no denying the strong attraction between them. But she could—no, *must*—deny the sudden need. There was nothing more important to her than her family, and a liaison with this sexy man just wasn't in the cards, damn it.

Gently, but with firm resolve...oh who the hell was she kidding? Her resolve wasn't any firmer than week-old pudding, but she managed to push against his oh-so-nicely built chest to get his attention.

"What?" he asked, somewhat dazed.

"Jason." Breathless? Since when did she do breathless? "I think I'll go up to bed now. Alone." He backed off and gave her some room.

"What's wrong?"

"I don't usually get intimate with men I don't know. It's just not something I'm into. I'm sorry."

"Well, precious, I'm very interested in getting to know you." He brushed his lips across hers again, this time gently, as if he wanted to ease her. A single finger stroked just underneath her jaw to tease the area near her ear. "I'm going to take a shower and catch up on some work. I'll be back down in about an hour. Maybe we can talk?"

She didn't trust her voice to answer. First off, she had no idea what to say. Second, even if she did, the zing his touch produced from playing near her ear destroyed her ability to think. The moment his head dipped for another kiss, Neesia scrambled from the loveseat and practically ran out of the room.

She couldn't afford to get mixed up with a man right now. Especially a man like Jason—too virile, too male, too much. He wore no façade, was as real as the day was long, and completely honest about wanting her.

And this strange zing between them was just...what?

It didn't matter. She was the oldest female of her family and responsible for her siblings. It was up to her to protect her sisters. She couldn't afford to have anyone uncover their secrets. Besides, what kind of example would she be if she went around humping every beautiful, towheaded hunk that came out to their property? Especially in the middle of trying to figure out who was setting them up for killing off the neighboring herds.

So no matter how much Mr. Jason Gorgeous DiCaplis filled her thoughts and made her body ache and hum, the pride came first. Well, a cold shower first, then the pride.

3

*I*t was so good to be home. Niah had been positively relieved when Harry, after one of Neesia's home-cooked meals, had flown directly to Las Vegas, picked her up, and brought her home. The flight was, thankfully, uneventful after such a long day spent chasing down a nasty rogue Were for S.W.A.T.

From their teens, all four Prydes had been trained in military tactics at the express request of their grandmother. She'd been careful when risking their exposure to S.W.A.T., making sure only two of them were seen at any given time, and only by those responsible for the most covert activities. So far, it had been a decent trade-off. The fact that S.W.A.T. kept their very existence a secret, even within their own organization, allowed them to live as normal "humans". In exchange, the Prydes took down some of the most lethal and dangerous outlaws in the shifter and Were communities.

Niah sighed and slipped further under the water in the deep tub, and winced at the burning sting of the hot scented water over her skin. Lord, she was tired. Glad the hunt was over, now she could do something she enjoyed—installing the new surveillance equipment around the property. Hopefully it would help catch the bastard who had it out for them, or at least let them get a good look at it, whatever *it* was.

After a delicious soak, she dunked her head beneath the suds and washed it clean, loving the squeaky-clean feel after the sweat and dirt were washed away.

This hunt had been particularly nasty. She'd chased that damn Were across California and up through the Sierra Nevada mountains, dodging humans and shifters alike. The whole episode reminded her of a song they used to sing as children, "Over Hill, Over Dale", and something about dusty trails as Niah kept rolling along.

Finally pinning him down near Las Vegas, she'd pulled her favorite weapon, one she'd designed herself—a gas-compressed projectile weapon that fired tranquilizer rounds from an electronic crossbow. Once the Were was secured, she called in the coordinates for S.W.A.T. to pick him up, erased all traces of her presence and disappeared into Sin City. When Harry called her private number and informed her he was at the airport, she'd never been so happy at Neesia's overbearing interference. The woman had sent her a ride home.

Soothed and relaxed by the bath, she dried off with a thick, soft towel. The floor-to-ceiling mirror in her bathroom revealed the source of the stinging along her shoulders and arms—a few bruises and scrapes. Examining the cuts from the earlier hunt, she rubbed her dark skin down with creamy shea butter, noting it was already healing.

She donned a soft, green silk robe, embroidered on the back with the family crest—a fierce lion hunting with his mate at his side. Making her way down to the library, Niah realized she'd never seen nor heard tell of any other lions in the States. No one had. And they were careful to keep it that way. Prolific, deadly and feared for their tendency to completely dominate and expand their territories, news of four strong African lionesses in the States would be cause for alarm. Because of that, even S.W.A.T. wasn't aware of all their secrets.

Picking up her favorite book, *Grimm's Fairy Tales*, she settled down on one of the many loveseats, and tucked her legs beneath her, wrinkling her nose on a wince when the bruise on her thigh throbbed a bit.

The house was quiet, everyone in bed. Now she could relax and try to figure out why Neesia was so anxious about the man who'd delivered the surveillance equipment. Born a few minutes before her twin, as the oldest, Neesia was the glue of their little family. After Grandma died, she'd kept them together, kept them focused, made them all work and study harder. Thanks to her, they'd become successful in everything they'd put their hands to. For Neesia to be shaken by anyone, especially a man, was really saying something. What had she said his name was again? Jason? Yes, that was it.

Her book closed with a snap as she looked up from her seat through her lashes. What was that smell? It enticed her breathing to quicken, her fingers to tremble. It smelled almost as good as Neesia's homemade cinnamon rolls. Like pure male.

Then he was there, his scent preceding him into the room as he stood in the doorway of the library. Her light amber-brown eyes clashed with his hazel ones and her stomach muscles clenched, and remained tight and hard. My god, he looked like walking candy of the Jolly Rancher variety. Beyond yummy in a loose-fitting tank top, she got more than a glimpse of sculpted pecs and rock-hard shoulders, all covered in golden, tanned skin.

His even looser sweatpants did nothing to hide the pole of an erection straining against his groin. Tastefully cut tawny reddish-brown waves graced his head. A strong jaw, with a hint of shadow, made him appear to belong out here in this wild, untamed land near the Rocky Mountains. And damn he was tall, with a heavy frame laden with thick, roped muscle. Good lord, no wonder Neesia didn't want to be alone with him. Men like this stripped away all desire to play nice and just play nasty.

Moving away from the doorframe, he stalked into the room. It was the only way she could think to describe the way he moved. Smooth muscles bunched and released as he made his way toward her, his powerful body a mix of strength and primal grace.

The man was simply overwhelming. An urge as old as time pulled at her typically effortless restraint and overpowered her will. Resisting was impossible. And he hadn't said a word. He'd walked into the room, took one look at her, and the temperature of her body skyrocketed.

Strange, even with all the fluttering and dancing of her nerves, there was no possessiveness to her body's craving. He didn't feel like...hers. But close, very close indeed.

"I'm glad you changed your mind," he said in a silken deep tone. If her breath came any harder, she'd hyperventilate.

"Changed my mind?" she croaked, not sure what he meant, but not sure she cared.

Standing over her he bent down until he was a breath away and inhaled deeply. "Mmm, you smell good. I'm glad you came back down after your shower. Now, how about that talk?"

"Talk?" Niah said, breathlessly. "What talk?"

"I'm with you, precious. Let's talk later," he groaned and knelt on the floor, pulling her to the edge of the loveseat. Her robe fell open as his wide chest settled between her legs as his fingers dove into her hair to pull her into a wicked kiss. Wow, she'd never had the hair on her little pinky toes singed off before.

Her eyes slipped closed as a large, slightly calloused hand caressed her thigh. Right on top of one of her bruises. Ouch.

He must have felt her stiffen, and let out a frustrated groan when he broke the kiss, leaned back on his knees and gazed at her barely clad thighs.

"What the hell happened to you?" he asked, all care and concern, staring at a big purple and blue oval spread across her upper thigh. A bruise delivered via Were-Asshole-of-the-Month.

"It's just a little bruise. It'll be gone by morning." His gentle massage of the sore spot caused her breaths to come out short and fast as a pleasure-pain sensation traveled up her leg and puddled between her thighs. Oh, what a nice touch.

"Neesia, are you sure?"

Niah cocked her head, locking eyes with his. The man thought she was Neesia? Well, duh. Nobody could tell them apart except their sisters. The man was ready to make love to her because he thought she was someone else? Now why didn't that bother her?

His fingers inched higher up her thigh to stroke the skin right where her short cropped curls began. Instinctively, her hips rolled forward, wanting his caress just a little lower. A single finger dipped into those curls and tickled her plumping lips. Niah's mind went blank. His touch was magnetic. Now, if only he'd kiss her again. "This bruise looks nasty," he said, smoothly. His mouth kicked up into a lopsided, very evil grin as he teased her flesh. "Should I get you some ice, precious? I'd be happy to hold it in the right spot for as long as you need."

With her hands full of his hair, Niah took a split second to revel in how soft and thick it was. Okay, time's up. She slammed her mouth down over his, inhaled the inviting scent of his skin and tasted the sweetness of his tongue.

When he settled more firmly between her thighs, the kiss deepened as he tilted her head back for his ravishing.

Niah did something she'd never felt compelled to do with a male, human or otherwise. She submitted.

When he'd come into the library moments ago, he couldn't have been happier to see the woman of his dreams sitting in the exact spot he'd found her earlier. She seemed astonished to find him standing in front of her. Hadn't she believed him when he'd said he would come back down to talk with her?

The urgency he'd felt when in her presence earlier had eased somewhat, but not completely. There was still an unreasonable urge to have her. And, god help him, once he got a good look at her long, shapely legs, barely covered by the delicious, silky confection that was supposed to be a robe, the last thing he wanted to do was talk. Talking was good. Tasting was better.

Kneeling between her legs, listening to her heart run a chariot race, caused his pulse to speed up, striving to match hers. But at least this time he had some semblance of control, and took his time exploring her mouth. Tilting her back onto the loveseat, the soft little pants and moans she made as he wrapped his tongue around hers sent a tingling shiver through his body.

Her hair was damp, the coolness of the blacker-than-black strands contrasted wildly with the heat emanating from her skin.

He groaned with loss when she broke the kiss.

"Jason, listen, you don't know me," she panted. But he'd already heard this song earlier, and didn't particularly want to hear it again. With a single finger over her lovely mouth, he peered deeply into her eyes and met a genuinely troubled expression that pulled on his heartstrings. When her lashes lowered, and a deep blush covered the high cheekbones of her lovely face, he stroked her gently across her lips.

"Ssh, just listen to me a minute." At her reluctant nod, he continued. "I know we've just met but I'm drawn to you in a way I've never experienced before."

"I bet you say that to all the girls," she smiled, her tone light and playful while he'd rather have her breathless and needy.

"Actually, I don't say that to all the girls. I'm being totally honest, baby, I want you so bad I can practically feel my cock sinking into that lovely body of yours. I swear I just can't help it." His words ended on a whisper. Each one brought his mouth closer to hers and Jason literally felt when she gave herself up to his care.

The kiss started out gentle enough, a sweet meeting of the mouths, but quickly escalated into a hot give-and-take. She gave and he took.

Breaking away to remove his shirt, he tossed it aside and unashamedly rubbed his chest against her lush breasts. Licking and sucking a path down her throat, he reveled in the tight clench of her fingers digging into the muscles of his back, holding him tight.

She was burning up, skin so hot it practically sizzled the light sheen of sweat popping up over his skin as he tried to control his need. God, his manhood throbbed and his balls were on fire, but something made him back off just a bit, to give her a little bit of time to get used to his touch.

Her beautiful breasts filled his hands. The warm, swollen globes begged for his kiss as he deliberately rasped his thumbs over the tight, puckered nipples. Unable to resist a moment longer, he lowered his head and wrapped his tongue around one and was rewarded with a deep gasp. Her chest rose and fell rapidly. Her taste and texture exploded in his mouth and were permanently imprinted on his senses for all time. She was all cinnamon and chocolate lust as her strong thighs wrapped tighter around his waist. Jason suckled her lovely breasts until her body undulated with each deep pull.

One hand left her lovely mounds and slid over the trembling muscles of her stomach, then down along her hips to tease her there. Her hips rolled wildly and her words were no longer tentative or concerned, but full of desire.

"Oh, your touch is magic, Jason. Please. Touch my pussy."

"I can do better than that, precious. Much better."

Lifting and spreading her lovely thighs until they were draped over his shoulders, Jason leaned forward and inhaled.

Mmm, she smelled delicious. Her pussy was allspice and cream, a dewy delicious treat just waiting for him to eat it up. A soft breath over her slick heat had her quivering in his arms.

"Jason, please."

Never one to keep a lady waiting, with gentle fingers, he spread her open and dove into her cunt, lapping and sucking on her engorged, sensitive lips until she rode his face with abandon. The wild movement of her hips, the erotic steam of her words, and the sweet nectar pouring from her body seemed to reach into his sweats and pulled on his cock until it throbbed painfully.

But he wasn't finished with her. Not by a long shot.

So sexy, he hummed his appreciation while slipping a long finger into her soaking-wet depths.

The woman grabbed a pillow off the loveseat and slammed it down over her mouth as a spine-grabbing shriek left her mouth. And when his tongue left her pussy lips, encircled her clit and sucked firmly, she just kept right on screaming as a firebomb ignited in her womb.

The sound was pure erotic heaven. And the feeling of her tight pussy muscles clamped around his fingers as he worked in her body while she came was beyond divine.

His cock urged him to lose the sweats and take her this instant, but his mind reached back to the concern he'd glimpsed in her eyes earlier. The words touched his heart and he knew there was more to them than what was said.

Tonight would be for her to learn to trust him with her body, her feelings and her needs.

Easing her down from her climax, he stroked her hair, closed her robe and gently kissed her good night.

Besides, he'd already decided he wasn't going anywhere anytime soon.

4

*S*ix a.m. and the scent of cooking bacon and freshly brewed coffee was delicious enough to get him out of bed. He'd never been an early riser, but he had work to do. A good meal was plenty of incentive to get to it. After a quick shower, dressed in a denim button-down shirt, a pair of black jeans and his favorite work boots, Jason headed downstairs.

The sight of a nearly naked Neesia bending over, half her body inside the fridge as she foraged for something, made his gut clench like someone hit him square in the stomach. He got a good glimpse of strong, long legs where her royal blue robe rode up to just below her tempting backside. It made him smile that her feet were bare.

The wild urgency to take her was back. Shit.

Leaning against the counter directly behind her, he cleared his throat. She kept right on looking for whatever she was after.

"Excuse me?" he called, stuffing his hands in his pocket to keep them off all the cinnamon-colored skin showing.

With her head still in the fridge, she said, "I heard you the first time. Just a minute."

He grinned at the impertinent woman. So she'd heard him,

eh? He'd given her a cataclysmic orgasm in the library last night and she was telling him just a minute? Not.

Pushing away from the cabinet, he walked right up behind her, took her by the waist and settled himself behind her, and nestled his rising cock right in the crack of her luscious ass with a not-so-subtle grinding motion.

Biting his tongue to keep from laughing, he watched her move like greased lightning, bumping her head on one of the shelves trying to get out of that damned refrigerator and away from him.

Eyes wide, she seemed almost shocked that he would do such a thing.

"What the hell are you doing?" she growled at him. Head lowered she watched him like a bull ready to charge. What was wrong with her? Was she suddenly shy now that the sun was up and she stood facing him in the light of day?

"Neesia, why are you shying away from me, baby? Do you regret last night?" he asked calmly, palms up as he walked slowly toward her. After all, he didn't want to make the woman feel threatened if she'd decided during the night that she'd rather not be with him. He'd just have to change her mind.

"Last night?" she queried, at once nervous, then confused, then...knowing? "I mean, about last night. Well, you and me. We, uh, did we...?"

Jason's eyes narrowed. He watched her closely, but was unable to keep up with the barrage of emotions crossing her lovely features. And her scent was a little different, like she'd spent the early hours of the morning eating a sweet fruit of some kind. Last night she'd smelled spicier, like rich vanilla and cloves.

"What are you saying? I left such a poor impression you don't remember last night, Neesia?"

"No, it's just that. I didn't. Oh, hell," she said, slapping the butter she'd dug out of the freezer section of the fridge down on the counter so hard, the rock-hard brick broke in two. Damn, remind him never to piss her off.

"Come here, Neesia."

She didn't move. Just stood there frowning, shifting her weight from one foot to the other while a frustrated growl bubbled up from deep in her throat. Was she upset, embarrassed, or what? He couldn't tell, but whatever it was, he *needed* to comfort her.

"Neesia?" he called her name quietly and moved slowly toward the object of his desire. Holding out a hand to her, Jason released a pent-up breath when she grasped it and went willingly into his arms.

"Jason, I…" she started.

"Sssh, it's all right. Just kiss me." He didn't give her a chance to refuse. Instead, he pulled her into his arms and claimed her lips in a scorching kiss. Moaning at the taste of her—fresh berries and cream—he moved closer, pressing his body intimately against hers.

The response to his nearness affected her as much as it had him. Her arms wrapped around his neck and full firm breasts pressed against his chest as she abandoned herself to the kiss. He could practically feel the round globes swell, burning into his skin through his shirt.

Unable to resist, he slipped his fingers into the neat bun at the nape of her neck and eased the hair tie loose until her hair spilled over his fingers. The soft, black strands were like the most decadent silk. He hadn't noticed it was this long last night.

His free hand strayed down around her ribs to stroke the undersides of a plump breast, weighing and caressing until she squirmed against him, so hot for his touch, she broke the kiss and tilted her head toward the ceiling on a loud moan.

The robe became a puddle on the floor. Jason buried his nose between her breasts, then pulled one taut nipple into his mouth and suckled greedily. She was flame and flood, spicy and sweet. And after he'd tasted her succulent mounds to his heart's content, it was time to feast.

Lifting her by the waist, Jason sat Neesia on top of the gourmet island. He pushed her legs wide, prepared to gorge on the dewy treasure laid out before him. Lowering his head, he buried his nose in that luscious treat. Honey, cream and a hint of spice.

"Wait. Jason, what are you doing?" she shrieked.

"Surely you know, beautiful," he murmured against her clit, coaxing the little bud out of its cowl to play.

"But...oh, dear lord," she gasped as his tongue laved between the silken folds of her soaked cunt. "What if, oh god! What if somebody comes?"

"It's okay, baby. Broglio is already out unloading crates. There's nobody here but us." Her shyness was endearing, but he couldn't accommodate her. Not today. He felt like a damned satyr, an insatiable, lust-filled male in rut.

"Besides, I can't wait to have you, and the bedroom is too far away." With that he buried his face again, reveled in her scent, her flavor. His lips wrapped around the sensitive bundle of her clit and sent her hurtling toward a blistering climax.

Reveling in the pleasure-pain of her fingers yanking at his hair, Jason knew he was tormenting her, pushing her toward another orgasm before she'd stopped trembling from the first one.

The need to mate with her, to bury his painfully erect cock deep inside her sweetly scented core rode him hard. So hard he shook with it. But her pleasure was imperative. He wanted to drive her beyond absolute mindlessness.

"Jason, please, I can't take any more." Breathless and pleading, she pulled harder on his hair, trying to yank him away from her sensitized flesh. She'd never experienced such wild abandon. Damn, her toes tingled from the orgasm—correction, multiple orgasms—he'd wrung from her. But she wanted some good, hard cock. Right. Damn. Now.

Ripping his denim shirt from his shoulders, certain she'd find a few of the buttons in the sugar bin later, she couldn't help but gape at the slabs of flexing pecs and rippling abs. So much sun-kissed skin dusted with the lightest brown-sugared downy hair. The fuzz on his chest was as soft as the hair on his head, enticing her fingers to play in it. But the urge passed the second a jean-covered erection pressed against her soaked core, sending a jolt of pure lust streaking up her spine.

"Do you want me, Neesia?" His voice was tight, gritty and sexy, on the verge of losing control. "Tell me you want me, baby."

"Yes, I want you." Her own words sounded just as raw.

The jeans hit the floor, and his proud cock jutted up to meet her.

Looking down between their bodies, her nerves fluttered at the sight of his engorged shaft. The veined ridges pulsed in time to the beat of his heart. Huge and imposing, it looked almost angry. Hungry. Then a familiar presence brushed against her mind. It flared, leaving an image behind her closed lids as if she'd suddenly experienced a flash of light in the dark of night.

Niah.

Looking out toward the sitting room, Neesia expected to see her sister standing in the doorway watching her do wicked things in the buff. No one was there. What the hell was going on? While she couldn't hear Niah's thoughts, her sister's presence was unmistakably hot and edgy. But why?

Pushing the worry away, Neesia glanced down again. Gaze glued to Jason's strong fingers as they wrapped around his flesh, slid over the velvet-covered steel.

Up. Down. Again. And again.

Finally, the smooth head brushed her clit, then paused, threatening to ease away rather than inside. Suddenly an unexplainable heat bloomed and grew until every cell of her body was aflame. That monstrous cock was to blame, and she wanted it more than anything she could remember craving in life. Craved it more than a midnight run under the stars. More than the thrill of the hunt. Hell, she wanted Jason more than Belgian chocolate! It was like a yearning in her blood, an unexplainable need flowing under her skin from her head down to her baby toes.

Pressed chest to chest now, she kissed him wildly, wrapped a leg around his waist. Hips surged forward, seeking what would satisfy as *she* took *him*.

But nothing prepared her for the feeling of his wide, hard flesh sliding into her body. It had been years since the last time she'd given herself to a man, and none had been as well-endowed as this one. The stretch and burn was quickly replaced by liquid lust. It poured through her aching folds, across her clenching butt cheeks and down the back of her thighs.

Lifting her easily, he balanced her on the edge of the cool, tiled gourmet block. Gaze instinctively lowered to where their bodies joined.

"Keep looking, baby. Look how wet you make my cock," he rasped, moving deeper, then pulling practically free so she could see how she covered him with her dew before easing back inside. "So tight and wet."

His erotic words, combined with the sight of him sliding in and out of her slick core, was the most titillating thing she'd ever experienced. Until she looked up into his face. His eyes gaze burned into hers—how could she have ever thought his eyes were simply hazel. No, the green and amber were now a rich gold that deepened to a smoky brown. With each stroke inside her willing body, his lips parted on a whoosh of breath. His ripped, solid chest heaved. Packed stomach muscles tightened and rolled like the ocean tide.

"Neesia, god. Baby, you feel so good wrapped around my cock."

And he felt more than good filling and taking her. Primal nature lurked just below the depths, wanted to break free and revel in her sensuality until she was mad with pleasure. He seemed to instinctively know, *sense* the wildness, and plowed into her tight depths with firm strokes. Harder. Faster. Deeper.

Oh, yes.

Picking up the pace even more, he laid her down on the gourmet block. The tiles should have been chilly against her back, yet did nothing to cool her off.

"Oh, god, Jason. *Soooo* good."

Strong fingers dug into her hip and held her still for his ravaging until she screamed for more with each thrust.

"Your wish is my command," he panted into her ear, taking her with a force that practically raised her body from the countertop island and threatened to leave her undone.

Jason's eyes were glued to her little pink tongue as it journeyed across her parted, plump lips. He wanted to suck on those lips. So he did just that and leaned forward to capture her bottom lip like a plump cherry. But it wasn't enough.

Grabbing the nape of her neck in a hard grip, he left her delicious mouth and licked the length of her long neck like a lollypop. Shaking his head, he wondered what the hell had come over him. He'd never been rough while having sex with a woman, but the urge to bury his teeth in this one overwhelmed him.

Her thick mass of wavy hair whipped around her head as she panted and thrashed underneath him. When her back arched up off the gourmet block as she demanded he fuck her harder, he couldn't resist. Jason dipped his head and buried his teeth in the soft flesh as he fought to control the urge to shift.

Holy fuck!

The second his teeth made contact, the honeyed walls of

her tight channel fluttered and tightened, milked him, squeezed so tightly, his spine bowed forward as he clenched her neck harder, sucked furiously. After long moments, he released her. Looking down at his handiwork, Jason's chest filled with satisfaction. The skin wasn't punctured, but there was a fat, purple bruise on her lovely cocoa skin. *His* skin. *His* mark.

"*Mine!*" his mind declared as he rode her through another orgasm, and buried himself in her pretty pussy over and over. The actually felt energy gather inside her body, ready to burst forth and bathe them both.

She came again.

The slick, raw heat practically pulled his seed from his balls. He pushed as deep as he could get and threw his head back with a primal roar. One he'd never heard in his own ears before, but would make sure he heard again. With her.

Panting like two over-aerobicized gym rats, Jason laid his head on Neesia's heaving chest and tried to catch his breath. Even in his sated state, he couldn't resist pulling an enticing nipple into his mouth and laved it with his tongue.

She tasted so good. God, he wanted to nibble everywhere. Touch her everywhere. All day. All night. Maybe after he caught whoever was behind the herd killings, he could take her somewhere remote where no one would hear their yell to the rafters.

Damn, for the first time in his life, he couldn't wait to be done with working a case so he could make his way to a woman's bed.

Rising up on his elbows, he took in her dreamy, wistful expression. When she opened her eyes and smiled, pride filled his heart, mind and soul—she was well loved and completely satisfied. A lone finger traced one of her perfect black brows as his lips captured hers in a tender kiss.

"That was beyond fantastic," he whispered. A cheeky grin was her answer as she closed her eyes and sighed like a kitty filled with cream. "Well, I guess I'd better get to work. I'll meet you at the garage after I have my breakfast, okay?"

"Mmm-hmm," she purred, letting him help her up off the gourmet block to stand on wobbly legs. Damn, he'd really laid it on her.

"I didn't hurt you, did I, Neecie?" he asked quietly, gently pulling her robe up over her shoulders. The silk felt nice against his rough hands, almost as nice as her smooth skin.

"Oh, no, you didn't hurt me. It was wonderful," she said softly, traipsing a finger down his sweaty cheek. "Besides, handsome, I'm not that easy to hurt," she sighed, and walked away.

Completely entranced, he watched the sensual sway of her hips as she made her way across the floor, out of the kitchen and through the sitting room before turning to go up the wide staircase.

All the while, he stood next to the large island in the middle of the kitchen, bare-chested, pants down around his ankles and his cock waving after her.

5

*E*nergized by his bout of loving with Neesia, Jason flew up the stairs and hit the shower. Changing into a tee shirt, fresh jeans and a light jacket, he grabbed his utility bag and headed out.

Wow, these Pryde women knew how to pick their vehicles. Standing in the garage, he eyeballed three sport utility vehicles, a military-grade Hummer, the jeep he and Broglio used yesterday and a few luxury cars fit for the stars. For a second, he wondered why they kept their jet at a private airstrip off the property. Surely the garage was big enough for it.

"Hey, handsome."

He turned to watch the woman who'd just screwed him into oblivion walk in the door and across the huge room. And she looked more delectable than she had only half an hour ago. While rummaging through a locked cabinet for the keys to whatever machine they would take out to survey the property, Jason took the opportunity to eye the fit of her jeans. Bad idea.

Stop it, you greedy bastard, he scolded his stiffening rod. *Come on, man, you were just knee deep in that woman and you're horny already? Give it a rest or I'll die from blood loss to my brain.*

"Jason, you all right?" she asked as a perfectly arched brow inched up her beautiful forehead.

Hell no, he was far from all right. Obviously, a taste of her goddess body wasn't nearly enough.

"Jason?"

"I'm fine. Let's just head out already." Geez, his voice sounded tight even to his ears, ears that happened to be burning with embarrassment at no way to hide the growing erection in the front of his pants.

With a shrug of her shoulders and a knowing look, the woman and her tight-assed jeans climbed into the Hummer. Damn, he'd like to wipe that smile off her face, but all he could think about was kissing her again. Hell, it might just work. At least her smart-assed grin would be gone, though in all honesty, he was inwardly smiling at himself.

Tools tossed into the backseat, he hopped into the passenger side and avoided looking at anything that would encourage his wayward cock. But her scent filled the cab of the vehicle. Again, he noticed it was a little different than just a little while ago in the kitchen. She smelled more like she had last night—damned good, and even with the windows down the fragrance swirled around him before floating out into the chilled morning air. Damn, there wasn't a thing he could do about it, except stop breathing. And that just didn't seem to be a viable option.

The vehicle came to a halt at the bottom of a rolling hill. She hopped out, her long legs carrying her a bit further up the rise where they could see the surroundings for miles.

"There's the first tower," she said, pointing to a tall steel structure just on the other side of where they stood. "I want a closed-circuit camera we can operate wirelessly. And one on each tower off that way. They're about a mile apart and enable us to get cell service out here, among other things."

Jason's nose twitched. *What the hell is that smell?* He looked away, trying to find the offending odor. Though faint, it reminded him of old, rotting meat, like something died out here. But he needed to investigate without Neesia on his heels. If a situation arose where he needed to shift, he couldn't allow her, a human, to see such a thing.

"This place is beautiful," he said, stalling. "I don't think I've ever seen this much land in one stretch. You mind if I look around a little?" he asked, sounding merely curious of the layout.

"Sure, have at it," she said, her tone just as calm as his as she moved back down the hill and toward the SUV. Something in his gut screamed that she was more than a little concerned. Did she smell it, too? No, impossible. She would have to be a...

"Shit!" she exclaimed the moment she reached the bottom of the hill. Jason was right behind her. Less than fifty yards from where she'd parked their ride, partially hidden under a scrub brush, was a carcass. A freshly killed carcass.

Damn.

After a quick examination of the bloodied hunk of flesh, they stood together looking down at the mess.

"What do you think did this?" she asked, her face drawn tight with anger. Fists clenching open and closed at her sides, the woman looked mad enough to fight.

"Something big," was all he could think to say. He had other ideas, but couldn't voice them without giving away being more than a simple tech installation guy. "I'm definitely going to look around now. Don't go far. We have no idea if whatever killed this animal is still around," he said.

She nodded her agreement and strode away, eyes alert and shoulders stiff.

As soon as she was out of sight, he walked to the truck, pulled a private frequency videophone out of his utility bag, and spoke into the voice recognizer. Seconds later, Captain Johns' stern voice filled the line.

"Cap, it's Jason. We have a problem. A carcass turned up just now. Fresh kill. Not more than a few hours old. I'd say just after dawn."

"Damn it. He's getting reckless. Find him and take him down, DiCaplis. Today."

"Who is getting reckless, Cap?" When his superior didn't respond, he pushed a little harder. "Cap, who am I after?"

"No need to tell you that, DiCaplis. Trust me, when you find him, you'll know." He knew that tone well enough—take care of the problem first, ask questions later.

"Fine. I'll check in with you *after*."

"Get rid of the body, Jason. The one you found just now, and the one you catch later."

"I'm one step ahead of you, ma'am." With that, he clicked the phone closed, and headed in the direction Neesia had disappeared.

"Hey, it's me," Niah spoke quietly and quickly into the mouthpiece of her wireless headset. "We've got a problem, Neecie."

"Correction. We've got two problems. And one of them is named Jason DiCaplis."

"Aaah," Niah said with sudden understanding. "We've, uh, sort of met."

"Yes, I know you met, damn it. I wasn't even aware you'd made it home last night until I was jerked awake by the sudden feeling of, uh, of..."

"Of hot, wild animal sex?" Niah was nothing if not direct.

"Oh, damn it, Niah. It was disconcerting to wake up to a blistering orgasm and realize I was in bed alone. And I knew exactly who you were with and where. That's never happened between us before."

Niah's logical brain immediately reasoned out what was going on. Neesia had met her mate. It was the only thing that made any sense. Sure, as twins they had a special psychic bond that allowed them to sense each other's feelings. As shifters, the bond was even stronger and allowed them to speak telepathically when in their pelts. But they'd never felt the other making love to anyone before. Ever.

"Deduction says he's your mate. My reaction to him is strong, but yours is off the charts."

Protesting in an unusually loud and shaken tone, Neesia griped. "But he's human. He can't be my mate."

"And how the hell do we know he's human, Neesia? You know as well as I do that you can't smell the shifter gene. Unless a shifter goes rogue, it's damn near impossible to tell a human from one of us. Besides, it would certainly explain the nasty thoughts coursing through my mind this morning while I was in the shower and you were..."

"In the kitchen with Jason. B-but that's just not possible, Ni. It can't be!"

But Niah knew better. All the signs were there—along with something neither of them ever thought to experience.

"Neesia, I think Jason's presence has thrown us into heat," she whispered, trying to look nonplussed while her heart leapt up into her throat at the sight of the sexy man moving up the hill toward her. She shivered with longing and willed her thighs to stop flexing. "I can feel it."

Just then Neesia inhaled sharply. "What are you doing, Niah?" her sister challenged, as if this were all her fault.

"I didn't do anything. I glanced Jason's way and my pussy went haywire." Niah cocked her head to the side, knowing the answer before she asked the question. But logic required her to gather facts, not rest on assumptions.

"You felt what I did just now, just like you felt us last night? Is that why you yelled at me?"

"I did not yell, damn it," Neesia snapped, then backed off with a frustrated "shit" into her sister's ear.

"Shit, indeed," Niah said breathlessly as Jason's scent wafted on the morning breeze and tickled her nose. There was something about the musky clean whiff of pure male that made her insides clench in conjunction with her thighs.

Neesia's firm resolve and even firmer words pulled her out of her musing.

"Look, Niah, we'll figure out this Jason zing thing later. Now, tell me why you really called," Neesia said.

Her sister's no-nonsense tone was like being doused with ice water. With those few words, her big sister's turbulent mood slammed through their bond and delivered an effective dose of self-control. Hell, she'd heard that tone all her life and knew it was time to get down to business. Niah's breathing calmed and her skin stopped burning as she pushed the flaming reaction to Jason's nearness to the back of her mind and delivered the bad news.

"We've come across another carcass. A big buffalo bull, at least fifteen hundred pounds."

"And?" Neesia asked slowly. Niah could picture her pacing around the football field she called a kitchen, eyebrows practically meeting in the middle of her forehead from a deep, fierce frown.

"Claw marks made by something bigger and more powerful than anything naturally roaming this area. The deep teeth marks and puncture wounds obviously made by long canines, a predator. The animal is practically torn apart. Looks like a pack of lions, Neecie. Big, bad-assed African lions."

"But that's impossible," her sister exploded. "The only African lions around here are..."

"Us. Yes, I know." Damn and double damn.

Was there another lion shifter around they didn't know about? If so, they had to find the idiot who risked them all with his stupidity and recklessness. Judging from the size of the bull, the killer must be massive. Niah couldn't think of any circumstance where she or any of her sisters could have brought the animal down without help. Maybe there was more than one?

What fucked-up timing. With Kotara and Koreas in New York, she and Neesia would have to handle this on their own, without involving their potential mate.

"Tonight, we hunt," Neesia said, her voice strong, sure and royally pissed. "Whatever or whoever is trying to set us up is a dead man walking."

"You've got it, sis. Look, Jason's almost within earshot. Gotta run," she gasped, trying desperately to squash the newly awakened butterflies dive-bombing her between her thighs.

"Yeah," Neesia's breathlessness reached through the phone. "Oh, lord, this is insane," she groaned. "Find out what you can and check in with me privately when you get back to the house. I'm going to hit the shower."

"But you showered this morning. Again?" Niah asked.

"Yeah, again, damn it. A cold one this time."

And there was nothing Niah could do to help her sister. She was in the same sorry shape—instantly horny.

---

6

*A*fter a long day of wiring and testing, with yearning just beneath the surface all day, Jason joined Neesia for a late dinner. Feigning tiredness with a very real yawn, he gave her a quick kiss on the lips and rose from the table. At the confused, hurt look on her face, he eased her into his arms.

"Baby, you're the most beautiful, desirable woman on the planet. I want nothing more than to carry you upstairs, strip you naked and dive into you." Nuzzling her neck, he yawned again, exhausted from working literally sunup to sundown. Her reassuring smile warmed his insides as she shooed him off to bed.

His alarm went off at one a.m.

Slipping away from the sprawling house, he headed back to the spot they'd found the carcass, hoping a return to the scene of the crime would get him some answers. And perhaps, an outlaw Were.

They had yet to install any surveillance out in this part of the surround. Glad he wouldn't be seen, Jason prepared for an all-out hunt and checked his weapons before getting out of the jeep —a shotgun with shells powerful enough to leave a hole big enough to drive the jeep through, plus a semiautomatic pistol with several magazines of explosive rounds filled with thermo-gel.

Let's see how the bastard likes being shot, blown up and burned all at the same time.

Cautiously, he surveyed the area, senses fully in tune with the night. Keen eyesight spotted nothing other than the long grass waving under the cooling breeze. But his nose picked up the rank scent of old meat and wet dog—a rogue.

Most shifters and Weres were clean and courteous, typical family members with jobs and careers like everyone else. Other than the ability to shift with strength that would terrify a human, the only difference was they were under the jurisdiction of S.W.A.T. law enforcement instead of the humans' police or military forces. While the average shifter strove to live under the radar, the outlaws of his kind didn't give a rat's ass about fitting into society and were almost rabid. Dirty and filthy were the words of the day when it came to the bastards. Even their scent was different from normal Weres. You couldn't tell a law-abiding shifter from a human. But rogues? You could scent them anywhere.

Quietly stalking through the thick brush on full alert, Jason passed a copse of evergreens and ducked inside for a look around. Nothing in the grass-covered clearing except a hint of pale moonlight. He moved, noting his position at about five miles south of the Pryde lodge, and a couple miles east of where they'd found the last dead animal.

Out here was so still, so quiet, other than the gurgling rush of the river nearby. In fact, too quiet, enough to make him uneasy. And the closer he got to the Medicine Bow River, the more apprehensive he became.

A low, muffled scraping sound caught his attention. So faint he'd almost missed it, even with his acute hearing. Then he caught a scent that made him spin around, draw his pistol with blinding speed and drop down to his knees in anticipation of a long, hairy arm swinging for his head. But no blow came.

He knelt a second, wildly searching with his eyes for his enemy, then eased down on his belly. Crawling through grass so high it almost completely hid his body, Jason made his way closer to the river. Right in front of his eyes, no more than twenty feet, was Devon Lane.

Captain Johns was right—he did recognize the rogue. Devon Lane, number twelve on S.W.A.T.'s twenty most wanted list. Huge, even in his human form, he sat on his haunches, happily crunching the bones of a full-grown buffalo, as at home as he pleased.

Just then a stiff wind blew out of the west. Jason stiffened as the outlaw picked up his scent, turned cold, black eyes on him and charged.

"Shit!" Jason's shot had gone wide and barely grazed the bad guy's ear. The round hit a tree off in the distance and exploded, leaving a big charred hole in the trunk.

The buffalo carcass forgotten, Devon's roar of rage filled the night.

Jason rolled away and a huge clawed foot landed where his chest had been seconds before. His weapon flew out of his hand and landed in the tall grass. There was no way he'd find it in time. He freed the shotgun from its harness and raised it just in time to…

His head exploded with blinding pain as he spun into darkness.

———

"Did you hear that?" Neesia stopped in her tracks and glared toward the eerie sound. *"That's a fucking Werewolf."*

"And it sounds pissed." Niah growled as they broke into a mad dash toward the snarled screams.

Hitting their bellies at exactly the same time, their golden brown coats were camouflaged by the grass and brush. Instinctive hunters, they moved into position for a coordinated ambush.

Neesia lifted her head, got her prey in sight and prepared to take the asshole down. One good look at his ugly maw explained plenty. Devon Lane. A bounty they'd hunted and nearly caught until a freak accident saw him take a tumble off a cliff in the Appalachian Mountains. They thought he'd died in the fall. But here he was, in the flesh. Son of a bitch.

Too much attention on Pryde ranch was detrimental to their very lives. And this idiot had done plenty to shine the spotlight on them. And nobody, *nobody* endangered her sisters.

"Hold, Niah, it's Jason!" Neesia spoke urgently into her sister's head just as the rogue Were landed a staggering blow that sent Jason flying through the air.

"I see him," Niah gasped. *"What the hell is he doing out here?"*

"We'll ask him after we save his ass. Let's go."

The sisters attacked. Neesia's muscles bunched powerfully as she sprang into the air, massive teeth and claws bared. Flying into the rogue Were, she threw all of her heavily muscled bodyweight into the blow. Hitting him square in the chest, she sank her teeth into his throat as Niah plowed into his legs and took him down.

They bit and tore through the thick, tough flesh of the raging beast. Blood loss and severe injuries soon had him face down on the ground, gasping as his lifeblood ran into the dirt.

"Done playing around?" Niah panted with a quirky grin only a lioness could deliver.

"Definitely. Let's finish this." Together they moved in on the downed Were and relieved him of his head. He shifted back to his human form just as his heart stopped beating.

7

*J*ason awoke in the copse of trees he'd passed earlier. His head throbbed, but he was none the worse for wear. No bite marks, no deep gouges. How did he get here? And why wasn't he Were-food?

With a groan, he sat up and froze.

A fully grown African lioness lounged not six inches from his face. Next to the majestic-looking creature was...Neesia? Buck naked? Jason blinked, then blinked again. Were his eyes deceiving him? Maybe he was really asleep—or worse, dead—and imagining all of this?

Then she spoke and her voice had the same effect on him it always did—instant heat.

"How do you feel?" she crooned softly, as her fingers eased gently over his brow.

"I'm fine. Surprised, but fine. What happened?"

"We came up on you fighting a wild animal," she said, matter-of-factly. It was the truth, after all.

"We? You mean you and your sister?" he asked, closing his eyes and sucking in a deep breath. It was all he could do to concentrate on the conversation with her luscious body on display. His mind tried to make him wonder what in the hell she was doing in her bare skin sitting next to a lioness, but he just couldn't make the thoughts stick.

"What do you know about my sister?" she asked warily, but still idly stoking his skin. In light of the fact they'd saved his ass, he didn't see the point in following Captain Johns' order to keep his affiliation with the Shifter and Were Armed Tactics agency a secret. He owed them his life.

"I'm S.W.A.T., Neesia."

"What?" She stiffened and started to move away. His hand shot out, grabbed a wrist and held fast while he spoke even faster. He needed her to understand, needed her close, and he hoped like hell not to get bitten by the now-growling lioness who, even now, was showing some wicked-sharp teeth.

"I'm not supposed to tell you this, but I was sent here to find the rogue that was setting the Prydes up as the ones trying to wipe out the other ranchers. S.W.A.T. didn't want attention on you or your sister, Kotara. And I know all about you working for us from time to time."

"So you weren't sent here to investigate my family?"

"No, precious, I came to take down a Were. But seeing I'm still alive, someone has already taken care of it. What happened?" he asked, rubbing the hard, sore knot on the side of his head.

"We took him down, and dragged the body to the edge of the property. We'll send the coordinates to S.W.A.T. when we get back to the house. They'll fly in and do a snatch-n-grab. They never see us. We never see them."

"I don't like S.W.A.T. using humans to take down Weres, Neesia, but in this case it seems to be a nice arrangement."

"I don't much care for it either. You could have been seriously hurt. I don't even want to consider the worst case scenario, Jason."

The breeze ruffled the soft curls that lay against her neck.

Her scent filled his nostrils and his self-control slipped. Unable to resist, he released her wrist and lightly scraped his nails up and down her arms until goosebumps appeared. The second her perky nipples tightened and puckered in the chill wind, Jason had to touch. The backs of his fingers rasped over the luscious peaks and Neesia's subtle shudder delivered an achy jolt of awareness straight to his balls.

He wondered why in the world she was naked way out here, then his mind went blank when she straddled his body and settled in his lap.

The heat of her sex seeped through the crotch of his jeans, seared the flesh down to the bone. A wild craving slammed through his blood with the potency of rare, aged rum. And neither of them was immune. He felt the answering blaze in every flutter of her stomach, every clench of strong thighs that tightened around his hips. God, he wished he could touch her everywhere all at once.

His mouth fell open when the rest of his already torn shirt was suddenly shredded from his body. The woman urged him backwards until the cool blades of grass caressed the heated skin of his back. Raising herself back up, she turned until his only sight was her flawless ass. Then she spread her legs and Jason's shaft throbbed fiercely as he watched her soaked pussy release sweet nectar down the inside of her thigh.

Deft fingers unbuttoned his pants. He swore his cock yelled, "Free at last!"

All breath left his lungs when his woman's smooth cheek brushed against the rigid length. The thing bucked uncontrollably from sheer anticipation of what she would do next.

Neesia shoved his pants down around his knees and plunged her luscious mouth over him so fast he shouted into her pussy at the same time his eyes crossed. Her talented tongue wrapped around the swollen head of his cock and pulled with a delicious suction. Then she took him to the very back of her throat with a low moan of satisfaction that vibrated through his sac. That hum worked its way from the base, up the shaft and tornadoed around the sensitive tip until he was dizzy with pleasure. Damn, the woman knew how to suck a cock!

As she worked him over with her tongue, Neesia's creaming center was a few scant breaths from his face. Jason gently spread her swollen lips and the scent of her coral channel made his mouth water. He wasted no time and thrust his tongue deep, swirled his tongue in and around, lapped up every dewy drop.

God, he wanted to gobble her up, eat her until she became a part of him, inside and out. He slipped a single finger into her tight channel and was met by a gasp and a sensual swivel of her hips. So he slid in another and reveled in the smoothness of those strong inner muscles tightening hungrily, grabbing at the digits as they slid in and out of her soaked flesh. Each pull of his tongue on her unhooded clit was answered with a maddening vibration around his cock, compliments of Neesia's hungry moans.

His wild need for Neesia had him in such a lust-filled haze, he'd completely forgotten about the big cat lying just out of reach. The lioness growled deep in her chest, eased closer and lowered her large tawny head. Fear of losing his man-parts was quickly replaced by curiosity as he prepared to embrace the change in case he had to protect Neesia.

The beautiful creature didn't bite him. Instead, she licked the sweat-slick skin on his thigh as if she were...grooming him? Jason waited to be repulsed by the animal's tongue moving over his skin and...

Wait? What was an African lioness doing in Wyoming?

He had no idea why, but the combination of Neesia blowing his cock, the scent of her drenched sex, and the rasping groom of the lioness's tongue against his thigh, felt so good he gritted his teeth and tried not to explode.

Protesting with a whimper when his woman eased away

from his face, Jason reached up and tried to pull her hips back to his mouth. Agile and quick, Neesia evaded even his fast reflexes. Placing the entrance to heaven over his iron-hard shaft, she plunged down and took him fully inside with a single stroke.

Threw her head back and screamed as grabbed her by the hits, grit his teeth and went to work. She might be on top, but he was more than up for meeting her thrust for thrust. Anything to please this woman who'd wiggled her way into his heart, his head, and thankfully, his bed.

"Oh yeah, baby, ride me," he growled. Yes, this is what he needed. To be buried inside her, to blast her full of his seed, to make her his in every way.

With a hand buried in her wavy locks, he pulled Neesia forward until they were practically nose to nose.

"As of this moment, I'm claiming you as my own. You're mine, Neesia. Now and always. Mine!" The urgency he felt while claiming her took him by surprise. But not as much as the need to mark her.

With a subtle shift of his grip, her neck was bared to him. Biting down on the sleek muscle between her neck and shoulder, he sucked and nipped as she bucked on top of him, moaning her pleasure in breathless gasps.

Fingers dug into her hip and held her to him as he plunged deep, filler her until he bumped against the firm knob of her cervix.

"Oh my god, yes. Fuck me," she demanded, cried and yelled as he pummeled into her welcoming body. And he gave it to her until she was a trembling mass of delicious woman and her pussy tightened around him in a death lock. She fell apart in overwhelming orgasm followed swiftly by another shock of pleasure.

He snarled as he hit a wall of need so powerful his body shattered, then went up in flames. The blood boiled in the thick veins along his shaft and he wondered if he would survive it. One final, long stroke inside her addictive pussy and his full sac pulled tight against his body. Come erupted the length of his cock at light speed and burst through him with violent velocity. Jason saw stars, and they weren't the ones filling the pre-dawn sky overhead.

Not until she sprawled in a boneless heap across his body did he release her neck.

"Damn, baby, that was beyond wonderful," he whispered into her hair as she lay on his chest, her warm wet channel still wrapped around him.

Abruptly, she sat up. Steady fingers smoothed her hair behind an ear as she gifted him with an unsteady smile.

"That was good, Jay," she crooned, "but there's more."

"More?" He wasn't sure he could take any more.

"Oh, yeah," she grinned, easing off his semi-hard cock with a hiss. The exquisite slide of her juicy sex against his sensitive cock pulled a raw groan from his throat. He sat up, fully intending to reach for her again.

When Neesia joined the lioness lounging in the grass, both females pinned him with a serious stare. He sat frozen to the spot—out of self-preservation or sheer curiosity, he wasn't sure.

Suddenly the lioness's body shuddered. Powerful shoulders twitched and shortened. The unmistakable pop of bones crunching and rearranging was heard in their little tree-surrounded haven.

Before him stood Neesia and…Neesia?

"Wait a minute," he gasped, "you mean, there are two of you?" Hell, one Neesia was almost more woman than he could handle. But two of them? He was going to die, he just knew it.

Jason sat there shaking his head, a silly lopsided grin on his face. How the hell had he missed something his agent's training should have caught on day one? Now it all made sense. This explained why her scent seemed different from time to time, because she *was* different. Hell, not just different, but two different people! And S.W.A.T. had no idea their secret bounty hunter had a secret of her own—practically a damned double.

"So, which one of you is really Neesia?" he asked, wondering aloud.

The woman who'd sexed him up moments ago stepped forward and his libido went off the chart. His skin was suddenly too tight and his body shivered from head to toe, cock instantly on alert. And not from the cool breeze off the river.

Gently running her fingers through his hair, her wicked pink tongue slid over her lips as she whispered, "I'm Neesia."

She moved back as the other woman approached. She too let her hands play in his hair. Her touch rang his bells, but the skyrockets didn't fire. "And I'm Niah Pryde. And you," she said with a smile, "are my sister's mate."

A completely naked Niah returned to her equally naked sister's side and remained quiet. They were both so beautiful, Jason's cock began to sing their praises. He was, after all, a very lucky man.

He understood the insanely strong reaction to Neesia. While his attraction to Niah was definitely there, it wasn't as frantic. The ridiculous urge to fuck Neesia from sunup to sundown made sense. She was a lion shifter. And his mate! And since Niah was her twin and part of the pride, it was normal for him to be attracted to her. But Neesia had his heart.

"I can see in your eyes that you understand what's happening," Neesia said quietly, waiting.

Jason nodded his head, but his mouth remained closed as he tried to unglue the tongue stuck at the roof of his mouth in shock. Incredulous? No doubt. But he was also so damned happy he could barely stand it. His mate was a strong, shape shifting, fine-as-hell woman! And he'd thought her to be human?

Yep, words were impossible just now as his blood-starved brain ran to catch up.

"I never expected to mate since there are no male lion shifters in the States," she said easing back towards him. "And I certainly never expected to mate a human. But you are mine, so let me make one thing clear. I don't share, Jason." Her tone was so sultry it damned near singed the hair off his body. Jesus!

Hips swayed seductively as each word brought her closer to his itching fingers. "And yes, I know about that night in the library, but you've only made love to me. Now, I'll gladly share with my sisters under, shall we say, special circumstances?"

"Sisters, plural? What the hell are you talking about?" he asked impatiently. The closer she got the more he wanted to jump up off the ground, grab her by the waist and drill her silly.

"Yes, three. Niah, you've met. The other twins, Kotara and Koreas, are out of town," she explained.

God, please let her hurry up and finish talking so he could sink into her luscious body, he whispered to the sky as both women stalked, their looks hungry and determined. Then another thought popped into his head. Was Niah's loving as sweet as Neesia's? He'd tasted, but damned he'd love to feel. And there were two more he hadn't even met? The thought just made him hotter.

"So what are the special circumstances?" he asked.

"Your presence has thrown us into heat, handsome," she purred.

Oh, so *that* was the special circumstance she'd alluded to? Heat? Shit!

Yes, it was crystal clear now—twins plus heat equaled off-the-charts horniness for all.

"So, what are you gonna do about it?" Niah asked, eyeing him like a perfectly cut, rare filet.

His wayward cock became a ramrod. Yep, he was definitely going to die. But he'd die fucking happy!

But not before he sprang a little secret of his own. The two beauties stood over him while Jason toed off his boots and kicked his pants from around his calves. Rolling over onto his stomach, he allowed the change to ripple through his body. Limbs stretched and pulled. The familiar sound of a body rearranging itself hissed and crackled in the peaceful copse of trees.

Jason tossed his head and looked up at the two women, who were now speechless with mouths gaping. The unmistakable roar of a fully grown, majestic male lion echoed in the dark hours of the morning near the winding Medicine Bow River in Wyoming.

The women joined him in the change, shifting right away. The second they were in their pelts they tried to play hard to get, but Jason was a determined male in his prime and resisting the call of the wild beauties in front of him was impossible.

Without warning, he pounced. Neesia, immediately captured under his big body, growled with pleasure as his cock slammed home. Jason's sharp canines clamped down on her neck as he took her fast and fierce while Niah padded restlessly on silent paws. When his woman lay licking grooming her claws, sated and content, Jason turned blazing eyes on Niah. She sprung away and evaded him for all of six seconds.

In heat? Well, he was the man to put out that particular fire. After all, caring for his pride was his number one concern from this day forward. And if that meant seeing to their pleasure, he was all in.

Literally.

NIAH'S PRIDE

This book is dedicated to my family, without whom I would be...actually, I'm not sure where I'd be. They love me no matter what, support me without fail, rip me a new one when I need it, and tell me the truth no matter what. Wink and Maito, it's all about the true-true! I love you!

To the Raven authors, ya'll are my girls!

1

"*More!*" Niah yelled to the diamond-studded heavens.

Finally, she was having sex. Very good sex, by the way, under the night sky with no strings attached. Yes, this was exactly what she wanted. After all, the life of a part-time S.W.A.T. bounty hunter was a dangerous one. Niah Pryde and her sisters never knew when a request might come in from the handlers of the Shifter and Were Armed Tactics agency. They could be called out on a hunt at the drop of a hat.

The Pryde women had only one rule—they worked alone or only with each other. Period.

So why hadn't Niah been more pissed off when she'd discovered that the boneheads at the agency had sent in a backup hunter without her knowledge? Didn't have a thing to do with the expert swivel of said hunter's hips as he plunged into her soaked heat just now. Her lack of disgruntled feelings couldn't be chalked up to the instant zing of ridiculous horniness she'd felt the second he'd walked into her camp days ago, announcing he was there to help her. Nor the number of times she'd been distracted by the play of muscle all over his perfect body, in both human and shifter form, as they'd stalked their prey.

While it wasn't like her to sleep with a man she'd just met, something about this one, this Ryland Lee Lewis—Lou, for short—and his damned southern drawl, called to her. Mmm, he was just so...

Back up. There was no way Niah was going to waste this first, awesome roll in the sack fighting with herself over what was and wasn't. Their bounty had been taken down, wrapped up nicely and already delivered. This was her last night sleeping in a tent in the Rockies at ten thousand feet. Niah was headed home in the morning, and more than likely would never work with Lou again; especially after she tore a chunk out of the idiot who'd chosen to break the one and only rule the Prydes held with S.W.A.T.—their utter and complete secrecy.

But that would come later. Right now, she was going to enjoy this.

Settling into a fierce rhythm that sent her channel rippling around his cock, Niah sucked in a wild breath and let it out with a moan. Yep, definitely good. Better than rare-steak-on-the-barbie good. Better than chocolate-fondue good. Put-a-swivel-in-your-hips-and-make-a-girl-faint good.

"Damn, you feel like heaven, Neesia."

A twinge of guilt tapped at Niah's forehead, along with the temptation to tell him her real name, to hear it on his lips as he filled her. But it quickly passed when Lou's words were followed by a deep penetration as he hissed between his teeth. Strong fingers sank into the flesh of Niah's hips and held her in place while he pumped furiously.

One hand eased down along the sensitive flesh of her inner thigh and traced a path straight to her center. Niah bit down on her tongue to stifle a scream when a talented thumb stroked the slick bundle of nerves expertly. It all came together in a perfect symphony of lust that rang a high staccato deep in her womb.

As she neared completion, a deep inaudible *something* rang like a gong in her soul, as if the pieces of a Lou-shaped puzzle snapped into place. But no, she wasn't going there. She was simply feeling vulnerable at the moment. This was a physical act of a mature woman of breeding age, nothing more. She might be one of very few African lion shifters, but other than that, there was nothing out of the ordinary about what she was doing just now.

So...why did it feel as if the male working behind her had just eased a bit of himself into the little corner of her head where only her sisters had always dwelled?

And with that thought, the orgasm dancing just within reach put on a pair of skates and headed in the other direction. Fast.

"You still with me, darlin'?" Lou asked.

Eyes scrunched closed against the argument with her common sense, Niah pictured her lovely orgasm in her mind. The thing had exchanged its skates for a wispy ghost-like shape and floated away faster and faster as she ran after it as it sang, *'Over hill, over dale as we hit the dusty trail...'*

Damn it.

Then, to make matters worse, the expert tool sending her pussy up in flames stopped adding fuel to the fire when the body attached to said tool went completely still.

"What is it? What's wrong?"

The firm hand on her thigh both soothed and annoyed her all at once. The former because it seemed to belong exactly where it was, sliding against her skin in a lazy pattern that relaxed rather than stimulated. The latter because it shouldn't be so comfortable, as if it were meant to be there. It wasn't logical. And Niah didn't like things messing with her logic.

"You seem a bit distracted, lovely."

What a fucking understatement. God, she'd let her brain talk her right out of what would have surely been an awesome climax.

Without warning, she was flat on her back, staring into the gem-green eyes of a determined male shifter obviously intent on handling his business.

"I can't have you unsatisfied in my arms, woman."

"It's not you. It's just that...see, I, uh." Well, this was a first. Niah Pryde, unable to explain her side of a situation? It was unheard of.

"Considering I'm the only man in this tent, it's most definitely me. So, let's see what we can do about whatever is on your mind, other than my cock, of course."

Lou slid his sweat-soaked body down her curves and settled his wide chest between her legs. She looked down and gasped at the golden glow of his skin cast by the lantern. In fact, his eyes, his flesh, his tastefully cut hair...everything was aglow. And this would be the only time she would behold such beauty in a man.

The rush of panic that kicked up in her gut at the thought of not seeing him again almost sent her scrambling. Squashing the jarring emotions, Niah instead allowed herself to slip deeply into the pool of need Lou drew her down into.

Her heart flipped over as her knees were pressed into the sheet covered canvas of the pallet.

Then the flat of his roughly textured tongue plundered and explored every dip and sensitive fold of her sex. Unable to keep her hips from seeking more, Niah gasped when a sharp nip caught her unaware.

"Keep still, darlin'."

Was he crazy? There was no way to keep still when he devoured her like she was his last meal ever.

"Lou, that feels so good. I have to move."

"Then let me help you." Two fingers dipped into the honeyed dew at her entrance, then pushed inside.

"Yes, more."

And, God, did the man oblige. Those fingers whipped her

into mindlessness as his lips closed over her clit and sucked. Hard.

"Oh my God!" came out on a rush followed by a bout of wild panting as the ever elusive orgasm swept back into view.

"Mmm, you taste so good. I could eat you all night." The deep throaty bass of his words vibrated through her flesh, setting her ass a-tingle.

But Niah was quickly passing the 'eat-me' stage and approaching the 'fuck me like an animal' stage. A flick of his wrist sent her passion off the charts and she tumbled over the edge.

"I'm coming!" Toes pointed so hard, the bones cracked like the glowing coals burning in the fire ring just outside.

"You drive me insane. I swear when I'm near you the need to fuck you blind rides me hard."

"Then please do. Please fuck me." Niah needed nothing at that moment as much as she needed this man buried inside her.

Without preamble, Lou flipped her over again.

"Ass up. Head down," he ordered. Then he was on his knees, pushing his ready length back into her willing body. He drove deep and delivered exactly what she'd asked for. Tossed headlong into another orgasm, Niah reached back with one hand and held tight to Lou's tense, muscled ass as he joined her in the ultimate pleasure.

Had anything ever felt so good? Hell, not even her sister's home cooking compared to this. Wrapped in the warm embrace of her Mr. Right Now, Niah fell into a deep peaceful sleep.

Early the next morning, while the moon was still high, Niah sighed as she slipped from underneath the heavy arm that lay across her waist. Muscles deliciously sore, from both the hunt and the wild bouts of loving during the night, Niah stood and silently stretched. She dressed quickly, eyes straying time and again to the sculpted back of the man who'd shared his bed with her last night. Warm blankets bunched just below his butt. He snored lightly. Hair the color of dark chocolate was tousled all over his head. She almost wished he'd wake so she could look into his eyes, an unusual jeweled jade that was such a contrast to his deeply tanned skin and dark hair.

Beautiful. Male through and through.

God, she wished he was hers. But Niah had never been one to pretend reality was anything but what it was. She was a single woman, and single she would remain.

After all, as much as her sisters looked forward to the day she found a mate, Niah didn't share their sentiment. Her whole life had been work, hunting, and family. It was all she could depend on.

With some wonderful memories and a quiet sigh, she packed up her gear and hiked out.

Lou had done nothing but dream of Neesia Pryde since the day she'd left him up in Rockies after a successful bounty. Working with her had been pure torture of spirit, soul and body. Anytime she was close, his need to touch her had him gritting his teeth. It had been a relief to finally make love with her on their final night together. In fact, after the toe bending climaxes she'd wrung from his body, Lou had practically collapsed with relief that he'd worn her out.

But that relief hadn't lasted long.

Shortly after their wild joining, Lou had experienced something so profound, there'd been no mistaking the soul-stirring connection that snapped into place and warmed his heart. Practically plugged her into his heart, eased her consciousness underneath his skin. It had knocked him so off-balance he'd allowed himself to slip into sleep rather than stay awake and face it. Face her.

But when he'd awoken, Neesia was gone. In fact, Lou had

slept so deeply, so peacefully, he'd snored through what would have typically woken him...like the sounds of a woman packing all her gear and hiking down a mountain. Yeah, that had pricked his pride, all right. In fact, not only had she been gone, when he'd rolled over and felt the coolness of the blankets, the faintness of her scent, he knew she'd been absent for several hours.

Hours, damn her.

Some hunter he was. A female, *his* female had flown the coop. It had taken him three weeks and some creative hacking into the S.W.A.T. database to find her, and 007-type planning to get onto Pryde Ranch undetected.

He'd better make this count. Besides, after this stunt, he might be fired, considering he'd managed to snag details on shifters with clearance so secret he wasn't sure anyone other than the current director had a clue of not only who the Prydes were, but *what* they were.

He'd tracked her on her own land for several days now and had come up with nothing. Suddenly, there it was—Neesia's scent. The moment he caught it, Lou had to fight the need to chase the woman down, pin her to the ground and demand her submission. But she was a lioness, not a wuss. Having no idea how the woman would react to his uninvited presence in her territory, Lou was careful to stay out of sensory range as he dropped to his knees and let the energy of the change wash over him.

Amazing how the faint, juicy smell of her body wash remained even when she was in her pelt. But it was her underlying natural scent that made him grit his teeth against arousal. Neesia wasn't alone. It would be stupid to give away his position and end up corralled by a group of bad-assed African lionesses. There was a reason the lioness was the most lethal hunter of all the felines. And there was no way he would become an example of how to *get dead*, not when he was this close.

He had less than ten minutes to make it to the huge, main

house before all the cameras he'd disabled automatically came back online, along with the noxious gas dispensers he'd discovered at various points. Two nights ago, he'd learned the hard way that whatever the hell was in the stuff affected the shifter nervous system. When inhaled or in contact with skin, it caused a bout of dizziness severe enough to incapacitate even the strongest specimen for up to twenty minutes. Tripping a dispenser also set off a silent alarm. He'd just recovered and gotten the hell out of there before the unmistakable crunch of tires tearing over gravel had sounded in the distance.

It was a brilliant deterrent actually, one he'd barely escaped. The only upside to the experience was that the smell of the gas had masked his presence.

Sticking to his tactical plans, Lou headed downwind to make sure Neesia caught his *scent* without catching *him*. At least not until he was good and ready to be caught.

2

O n the way back to the house after an invigorating run in their fur, two African lionesses stalked across a shallow bend in Wyoming's Medicine Bow River. Once on the other side, the race home was on again.

Niah's claws dug into the dew-soaked ground, sending clumps of moist dirt and grass flying into the air as she skidded to a dead stop. Her sister followed suit and turned caramel-brown eyes on her.

"Hey, you smell that? It smells like L...uh, nevermind." Niah cut off her thoughts mid-sentence. After the explosive roll in the proverbial hay, she'd know that particular scent anywhere. But she hadn't told any of her sisters of the decadent down-time she'd spent with a very special hunter after her last job.

Ryland Lee Lewis was more than a sex god. The man was both hunter and lover extraordinaire. Just from the single take-down they'd worked on together, Niah knew he could track an ant over a field of rocks in the burning desert and never lose its trail.

But she'd left him a state away, and *way* up in the mountains. She was sure she'd made a clean getaway, right? So there was no way that man was here in Wyoming at Pryde Ranch. Not possible.

Yet still...her nose didn't lie.

Niah took another deep sample of the air. Whiskers twitched as the clean, masculine scent hit her olfactory system again. Pure prime male with a hint of rich soil and golden sunshine. It was definitely him, damn it.

Lou was here.

But why?

It had to be a business call, because up in those mountains as they'd rolled around their tent, he wanted the same thing she had—a quick fuck without getting stuck. At least that's what Niah had assumed he'd wanted. As for herself, it was all she could afford.

Neither had expressed undying love on their one and only night beneath the stars. She'd neither asked for, nor given, any promise to stick around. So why had she suddenly contracted a sudden case of guilt-itis at ducking out on him?

Neesia nipped Niah's ear with sharp fangs, just enough to snap Niah out of her musings.

"Earth to Niah."

"I'm not zoning out, damn it."

"Good, because whoever you picked up, I smell them, too. It's definitely not a rogue, thank God. Whoever it is," Neesia said, *"hasn't been on this property before. I never forget a scent. I wish we could tell if a person was a shifter by scent alone."*

Most shifters and Weres were just like anyone else—kind and courteous, with families and jobs. Their human skins looked just like everyone else's and unless a shifter revealed their true nature, it was impossible to tell they were more than human.

Niah growled back. *"Yeah, rather than just the ones gone over to the dark side."*

But once they went rogue something in their physiology

changed, became rank and...wrong. It permeated their cells until even their scent was disgusting, like a roll of old bologna left to rot in the sun.

"I agree, young Skywalker."

"Oh shut up, you," Niah chuckled, though she was far from amused. Not only was she angry that they had an uninvited guest-stalker, she was pissed off that her stomach had started doing the "gimme-some-hard-and-fast" mambo because she was going to see Lou again.

"Damn."

"What?" Neesia asked.

"Sis, I've got something to tell you. Just promise not to bite me in the ass after I'm through."

"Puh. I'll promise no such thing, young Jedi."

Niah flopped down in the high prairie grass with a loud groan and spilled her guts about the hunt, and the one-nighter that had apparently decided to reappear.

———

Lou sat on the steps that led up to the huge wrap-around porch of the main house on Pryde Ranch and waited. It was a beautiful structure, more of a mansion-sized rustic lodge than a house. He'd left enough clues as to his whereabouts that he was sure it wouldn't be long now before Neesia, or someone, showed up. Of course she'd want to know what he was doing here, and how the hell he'd gotten onto the estate without passing through any of the heavily monitored gates.

Of course he couldn't tell her he'd hacked the estate's security network remotely, found the connect keys for all the hubs and routers, broke into one of the system password files and reset the cycle time on the motion sensors on a far-off fence. With that done, he'd walked right through the temporarily unprotected entrance in a rarely used corner of the vast property.

While scouting the place he'd often wondered why Neesia and her sister, Kotara, needed such tight security. The vast acreage the estate sat on should have been enough of a deterrent for any bad guy, yet he'd had to squeeze through a tight web of electronic controls. It hadn't been easy.

She was going to kill him. The thought brought a grin. God, he couldn't wait.

The land in the immediate vicinity was cleared of anything that could hide an intruder, so if he could see from here out to the rolling hills, then he could also *be* seen.

And here they come. There was no sound other than the whip of wind through the trees, but knew he was being closed in on like so much fresh meat. No surprise. In fact, it's exactly what he would have done if he were in her shoes.

Finally, two lionesses stalked out of the brush in the distance and calmly approached from off to his left. Bearings regal and heads held high, they moved like the queens they were. Even the unusual sight of weapons strapped to their muscular feline bodies didn't detract from their beauty.

The two cats halted at the bottom of the stairs. One of them immediately shifted out of her tawny pelt with a blast of energy that nearly knocked him to his knees.

And there she was—Neesia Pryde. God, the woman was breathtakingly, deliciously naked as she stepped forward, armed with a weapon that was uniquely hers—a titanium automatic incendiary projectile crossbow with self-reloading bolt cartridges. Lou had become intimately familiar with it during their short time together.

With fire in her amber eyes, and predatory intent in her ready stance, Neesia was vibrant, and so fucking gorgeous it stole his breath just as it had the first time he'd laid eyes on her. And every time since.

As he stood and took the first few steps towards his woman, Lou literally led with his cock.

Steps halted at the *cha-chink* of shotguns being cocked. Two more women dressed in lab coats and sporting shoulder harnesses flanked him along with a pissed-off male. Yes, Jason-goddamn-DiCaplis stood not fifteen feet away with a pretty cool-looking high-powered rifle aimed at Lou's chest.

Shock didn't describe the flash of emotion at the sight of the other male. What the hell was DiCaplis doing here? And why was he stroking the shoulder of the lioness that had arrived with Neesia? A lioness who chose that moment to shift at stellar speed, bringing with her yet another unexpected fact—Neesia had a twin. Amazing how they looked so much alike, but Lou could tell the difference. For starters, the long-limbed grace in the way his mate shouldered her weapon was just a bit different from this other woman. The cool intellect of his woman's gaze versus the warm, no-nonsense expression of her sister. But most importantly, it was all in her sweet, natural fragrance.

"So," the twin asked. "Who do we have here?"

Neesia answered the question for him. "Ryland Lee Lewis. Lou for short. The one I just told you about. He worked my last case with me in Montana where those rogues had been terrorizing that little town south of Long Knife Peak a few weeks ago."

"And *what* do we have here," Jason DiCaplis snarled.

Lou slowly sat back down on the beautifully-crafted cedar porch steps and smiled. "Lion shifter...just like you, and you know it. How are you, Jason?"

"You know him?" Neesia sputtered.

"Yeah. Unfortunately," Jason said, brow furrowed and jaw ticking madly.

"So is he friend or foe?" Neesia's mirror-image posed the question with a smile.

The response of a caramel apple blush on his woman's cheeks told Lou that her sister knew all there was to know, in spite of her seemingly innocent question. Lou smiled. Couldn't help it.

"I'm definitely a friend, ma'am," he said to the sister, though he kept his gaze on his woman and ate her up from her toes to her nose. Her blush deepened, but she never took her eyes off him. Not even when he extended his arms and said, "You have my word that I'm a very good friend indeed."

The twin said, "Well, in that case I'm Neesia Pryde. These are our sisters, Kotara and Koreas. And that guy you already know as Jason is my mate."

Lou looked from one to the other and back again.

"You're not Neesia. I'd know my woman's scent anywhere. No offence, ma'am, but you're not her. Very close, but..."

"She *is* Neesia Pryde, Lou," said the woman he'd spent weeks chasing, whose scent was imprinted on his brain and reached for him even as she spoke. "My real name is Niah. Niah Pryde."

"Your real...what? You gave me a false name?"

Niah, not Neesia as he'd previously believed, simply shrugged. Then the light bulb went on in Lou's head. "Wait, there are four of you?"

Now *this* he hadn't seen even in their secret files. There were two pictures on record—one of the real Neesia, and one of the younger twins. Lou wondered if anyone other than the people standing here knew that the two Pryde bounty hunters listed in the S.W.A.T. covert files were really four different women.

Two sets of African lioness twins in the U.S.? It was unheard of. African lions were fiercely protective of their prides, and were known to expand and hold their territory ruthlessly. A single male, if left unchecked, could take over one hundred square miles without a challenge. Five lions could wreak havoc if they chose.

Unfortunately, reputation alone could sometimes be enough for a few cowards to push for eradication of them all. In fact, the only known male African lion shifters in the entire country worked for S.W.A.T. and were closely monitored. But the number of lionesses publically recorded in the States? Zero.

No wonder Jason DiCaplis' file listed him as single. He could never "officially" be mated to a Pryde. And if Lou won Niah over, neither could he.

This absolutely had to remain a secret.

"What do you want to do with him?" Jason asked, the words as cold as the chill rolling onto the prairie with the late afternoon fog.

"Do with him?" Niah asked, sounding alarmed. "What do you mean, do with him?"

"He can't be allowed to leave here with this knowledge, sis. He could endanger all of us. Nothing personal, Lou." This from one of the younger women—Kotara, he thought. Her words were firm and she clearly meant business. But so did he.

Arms out to the side, Lou slowly rose again from his spot on the porch, moving into Jason's space until his left pec was almost flush with the very cold muzzle of the rifle. "I came for Niah. I have no need for secrets. My only need is to make her happy. If shooting me is in Niah's best interests, then put a bullet through me."

Jason lowered the weapon and said, "Look, we all know lions in the wild are territorial, and I can't help but want to protect my pride. But shifters, being also human, have the ability to reason and understand. Why would I stand in the way of Niah's happiness?" Then Jason turned to Niah, stepped close and snarled in her face, "If you want this fucker, that is."

Four sets of perfectly arched eyebrows flew upward. Mouths

dropped open in shock, while others curled in snark-filled grins.

Jason stepped back. He had the decency to blush as he settled the rifle on his back, and jammed his hands into the pockets of his jeans. "Sorry. It just sort of slipped out."

Lou'd had enough. He sensed that Niah was getting more and more upset the longer they stood here bandying words.

"Listen, I know my showing up here is unexpected. I didn't tell the agency or anyone else where I was going. I have nothing to hide and my intentions have been made clear. I want that woman right there," he said nodding towards Niah, careful to keep his hands at his sides. "My gear is in a copse of trees five miles southwest of here. You'll find my S.W.A.T. ID, an agency-issued camping kit, and my weapons. You'll have to use your eyes because you won't be able to find it by scent. I sprayed my stuff down with scent hormone to mask my presence."

"Well, that explains how he slipped by us," Koreas said quietly. The look in her eyes made it clear that she was already considering how to fix that little problem. Shouldn't be too much of an issue considering that the Pryde labs had created the stuff to help the agency hunt rogues.

"I can't believe you planned all this," Niah said.

"Niah, sweetheart, why are you so shocked? I'm a bounty hunter just like you. Would I roll into another's territory without a plan *knowing* they were shifters?"

All the sisters were damn gorgeous, and carried curves and confidence wrapped in the most luscious maple sugar skin. Intelligence, and a mischief they just couldn't hide, shone in light brown eyes, and strength was evident in the way they handled their weapons with ease.

And if they were anything like his Niah, they were equally lethal in their human skin as they were in their pelts. Speaking of Niah, the woman looked as if steam would start to blow from her ears any second now.

"You don't have to be a smart ass about it." And now her crossbow was pointed at his naked groin.

"Well, this isn't going well," said Kotara and Koreas in unison. One of them looked amused, the other concerned.

"Niah, I came here for you. I've been looking for you since you left me up on that mountain."

"Well," Jason snapped, "if she left you up on a mountain isn't that a clue that she expected you to *stay* there?"

"Not happening. She's my mate."

"No I'm not!" Niah gasped.

"But how do you know, Ni?" Neesia asked quietly.

"How does *he* know?" Niah growled back before turning on Lou. "You can't just roll in here and make claims like that and expect me to, to..."

"What?" Considering he hadn't asked for anything Lou wondered what she thought he would demand from her. "Expect you to what?"

She said nothing. Just looked at him as if he'd morphed into a puzzle that she couldn't decide whether to figure out or throw against the wall.

She was turning that alarming shade of caramel-apple red again, only this time she wasn't blushing. She was pissed, but that was just too bad. He wasn't moving off course. Not in this lifetime.

"I believe I've been pretty clear, Niah. I suspected there was something between us the first few days we hunted together. But after we touched, I knew it without a doubt. And I plan to win you, woman. Hands down."

With a very unladylike snort, she walked away just as the staff filed out the front door with several plush robes.

"So, Lou," Neesia asked, pulling on and belting a thick, light blue garment before handing him one. "Where are you from?"

"I was born in Lincolnton, Georgia, but my family relocated

to the big city when I was a cub. Didn't last long. Too hemmed in with all the concrete and glass."

"Is that where the drawl comes from?" Koreas asked.

"Drawl?"

"Yes, that whole 'southern charm' thing you have going on." This from Kotara.

"I guess I'll always be a country boy at heart." Lou gave her a genuine smile. At least now he had something to help him tell the younger women apart. Kotara was the straight forward one and Koreas was the quiet one.

Neesia began walking towards the porch. "How long are you with us, Lou?"

"Officially, until after I recover from the, uh, terrible sickness that caused me to have to take some time off." A few faked coughs and groans earned him a smile and a nod from the woman who was clearly the matriarch here. "Unofficially, for as long as it takes."

"Well," Neesia said, looking off in the direction Niah had stomped. "Guess I get to show you to a guest room, eh?"

"Hell no." Jason DiCaplis—royal pain in Lou's ass right now. "I'll take him."

"We'll both go. I can't have you biting our company. It's bad manners."

Lou tied his own robe and then held out a hand to Jason. Head dipped just enough to acknowledge the other man's authority as alpha of this pride, Lou simply said, "Thank you for the hospitality."

He breathed a bit easier when the guy finally shook his outstretched hand and nodded in turn.

With that, they all headed into the mansion-sized lodge in the middle of several thousand acres of prime prairie and rolling hills—Pryde Ranch, home of the deadliest creatures in the shifter hierarchy, bar none.

3

*N*iah was more than a little rattled at Lou's appearance. The last thing she wanted to do was admit he'd knocked her off-kilter, even though he had in a major way. She'd spent weeks convincing herself that her reaction to him, to his very scent, had been a total fluke and was due to a bone-dry spell in the sex department. But Lou's arrival blew her theory out of the water and she was barely holding herself together.

Now his scent lingered, caused her skin to feel too tight, too hot. Scenes of their one night together played in 3-D in her head, bringing with them all the wicked and wild emotions she'd felt as they'd rolled around in that tent.

Unsettled was a word that hadn't been in her vocabulary since she'd been a teen, yet here it was, live and in living color. In short, Niah Pryde was...unsure. It was unacceptable, but right now it was all she had.

Thankful didn't describe what she'd felt when Broglio had offered to drive with her to retrieve Lou's things. He'd been with them, managed their property, and anything else they needed him to, since the Prydes had been little. He, a human, had been their Grandma's right hand, and now he was theirs. For all intents and purposes, Broglio was part of the pride, too; and he was just as perplexed and concerned as everyone else.

Rolling at top speed along one of the private, graveled roads in Niah's favorite Jeep, she and Broglio covered the five miles to Lou's camp in short order. A one-man tent and other agency-issued gear were bundled up, hidden in the brush, in the exact spot he'd said they would be.

Tossing the stuff into the backseat, Broglio huffed, "Honestly, Miss Niah, if that damn lion shifter...no offence..."

"None taken."

"...breached our security, who else could manage to get this close to our family?"

Niah shook her head and kept her mouth shut. After all, Broglio was only saying what she was thinking. At first she'd been flat-out disbelieving that Lou had tracked her down, but now she was both pissed off and impressed at how he'd waltzed onto her family's property and sat his naked ass—correction, perfect-for-bouncing-quarters-off naked ass—down on her front porch as if he did this every day.

Back at the house, she found her sisters preparing for dinner in Neesia's pride and joy—an oversized, professional, stainless steel-everything, football stadium-sized kitchen.

She dropped Lou's stuff on the floor near the ginormous gourmet block and rounded on her sisters.

"I'm responsible for network security, you guys. How the hell did he get in here? How did he do it?"

Lou chose that moment to poke his head through the entrance that led into the space from the hallway.

"I'm sorry to interrupt, but can someone loan me..."

Niah's eyes caught his and the man's speech faltered as a smile spread across his lips. And that's when she felt him—it was just an inkling but there nonetheless. Lou was *happy*.

Simply happy to be here. And she could give a rat's ass right now.

"Tell me right now, or I'll have to kick your ass."

Lou's warm smile faltered. A lot. For a split second she actually felt bad that she'd been mean, but as quickly as his hurt washed over her, his determination was on its heels and overtook it. And she felt *all* of it.

"Niah, you're overreacting," Lou said firmly.

"Overreacting? Fuck you! It's not your family at risk here, is it?" she snapped and stepped forward. A black, tempered-steel machete cleared the sheath strapped across her back with a *schnick*. She knew he was trying to reassure her, but all it did was piss her off more. She'd never failed her family like this. Ever.

"Niah, if you get blood on the grout in my perfectly tiled kitchen, I swear you'll wear a black-eye for a week," Neesia said calmly, not even looking up from the bowl of batter she was mixing. K and K both looked on quietly. Kotara sported her typical snarky-looking half-grin that said she knew more than she was letting on and Koreas looked back and forth between Lou and Niah before returning her interest to the stack of reports she was reading.

Niah's lips peeled back from her teeth in a snarl. Lou held her gaze, clearly anticipating what she'd do next. She growled louder, tempted to see if she could take him down before he knew what hit him.

But Neesia wasn't having it. She'd always been the one with manners, damn the woman. "I mean it, sis. Blood on my kitchen floor equals you and me scrapping in the front yard like when we were little. And I win."

Damn.

"Fine. If I can't carve him up, then I'll go wash. I'll be back down later to help prep the sides for dinner."

"No worries, I've got it," Neesia said. "I think you need a

minute to relax, given your uncharacteristic departure from your calm, logical self. I'll press your lazy ass sisters into service."

"We are *not* lazy," Kotara and Koreas declared together.

No, they weren't, but if you used the words work and kitchen in the same sentence, the twins found a way to get scarce in a hurry.

"Anyway," Neesia said as she tossed a piece of cabbage at the younger girls' heads, "Trouble One and Trouble Two will help me in here, and Jason is outside on grill duty. We're all set, so both you and Lou can take a minute to decompress. It's been an interesting day. Dinner in an hour. We'll eat in the dining room tonight instead of here at the breakfast nook."

Neesia set down her bowl, strolled over and kissed Niah on the cheek. Without an ounce of shame, she said, "Girl, if he's your mate, he can't be all bad. I'll be happy for you if he is, but if he's not, we can all sit around and whip his ass for stressing you out, 'kay?"

Niah laughed, hugged her sister, and turned her thoughts towards a nice, warm shower. She felt Lou's eyes on her as she crossed the kitchen and headed for the swinging door of the dining room...away from him. His feelings followed her like a specter chanting, *"I hate to see you go but I love to watch you leave."*

Perv. She managed to hold her chuckle back enough that it was more like a snort. Niah scooted out the door with what sounded like Lou's laughter, both inappropriate and illogical, echoing in her head.

Fresh from the shower, Neesia walked out of the bathroom and dropped her towel on the floor at the foot of the bed. Batting away Jason's hands, she side-stepped him, grabbed a bottle of cocoa butter oil from the night table, and proceeded to lotion herself down with it.

"Okay, Jason, tell me the deal between you and this Lou fellow?"

"Deal? What deal?"

Neesia smiled as her husband continued to reach for her with eager hands.

"Jason DiCaplis, if you think I didn't notice that there was a bit of tension between you and our unexpected guest while you had a loaded rifle pointed at his chest, then you must think you married someone else. Someone *not* me. And no nookie right now considering we're already late for our own dinner. "

"God, such lovely skin. And you know I love it when you flash your tits at me after a shower. Tension? Really, sweetheart, because I can't seem to recall any tension outside of me wanting to get my hands on you just now."

"Don't even try it. You may as well spill it now, in the privacy of our bedroom, rather than have Kotara or Koreas coax it from either you or Lou at the dinner table. You know how the two of them can be when there's a juicy mystery to solve. There's a reason they're the research science experts, remember?"

Nosey didn't begin to describe the younger Pryde twins. Neither did ruthless, persistent or down-right pushy. God, she loved those girls.

Jason's lips lifted in a devilish grin. "Lou has no idea what he's in for at dinner, does he?"

"Not a clue, so tell me now, or I'll just sick 'em on Lou during dessert."

Yes, she was being totally evil just now.

Neesia made a deliberate show of shimmying into a comfy pair of black yoga pants and a knobby short-sleeved sweater Jason had given her for Christmas. It was the same maple syrup brown as her eyes, and the perfect weight for springtime.

Jason shook his head at her naughtiness. "Marvelous doesn't begin to describe my mate."

"Uh huh," she said with a grin. "You just like my ass."

"Damn right."

"And the offer still stands, stud. Me...or the girls at dinner."

Heh. Let him squirm.

As she brushed her curly locks into a poofy ponytail, she noticed that Jason's hair was a hot mess from him dragging his fingers through it as he stalked around in circles trying to come to a decision.

Finally he said, "Fine, you win, woman. At times like this I'm glad the bedrooms are soundproofed against people with awesome hearing, otherwise I'd never hear the end of how I totally gave in just now. I know Agent Lewis from a long time ago. In the early years, we worked for the same department in the agency. Competed for a special project with S.W.A.T. We were trying to go after a notorious group of Were rogues that were slaving out young shifter females to humans."

"Who won the competition?"

"Neither of us. We went at it so hard, we were totally beat up by the time the tests were done. We were both out of the running, and down for the count, for almost two weeks. Our boss just shook her head, told us we were idiots, and then sent someone else out on the case."

"Oooh, so this is a rivalry thing?"

"Look, I don't have anything against Lou."

"Uh huh. I'm buying that, love. Really. I am."

Jason eased up behind her, clasping the necklace she held out to him 'round her neck before wrapping her up in his embrace. God, she loved the way it felt to be held by this man. He was her rock in every sense of the word, her true partner. If he was the alpha male of their little pride, she was the alpha female just as she'd been before he arrived. When they'd mated, rather than take over, Jason had complemented Neesia. His presence filled a hole she hadn't realized was there until Jason occupied it.

Neesia felt like the luckiest woman in the world. And she wanted this same specialness for her sisters.

"You do know you'll pay for that snarky shit later, right?" He lifted her hair and dropped kisses at the base of her neck until her toes curled into the plush carpet under her feet.

"Pay?" she purred. "I'm counting on it," she said, turning to raise up on tip-toe. But instead of kissing him, she feigned left and scooted out the door.

Lou walked into the elegant dining room and was immediately directed by one of the staff to a chair across from Jason and Neesia. Neither sat at the head of the table, but side-by-side instead. Lou couldn't blame them—the view was spectacular, given they faced a wall of screened glass with an unimpeded view of the setting sun on the vast horizon.

The table was set with elegant silver-lined china, dainty tea cups and crystal wine glasses. Lou appreciated Neesia's attention to detail when he noticed the sturdy glass beer mugs among the delicate stuff. The second he sat down, Lou's mouth watered. Neesia Pryde appeared to be quite the chef. The smells wafting from the uncovered dishes were absolutely delicious and set his stomach to rumbling. It was pretty impressive considering the woman had managed to whip up many of his favorites with no warning of his visit at all.

And then Niah was there. The huge, white pine table sat eight with room for more, and his woman had waltzed in and sat her pretty self clear at the other end. God, she seemed practically a world away.

Patience, Lou. Patience.

Turning his attention back to the table, Lou wasn't sure what made his stomach grumble more—the huge spread in front of him, or the scent of that lotion stuff Niah used on her skin that made him think of sundaes—warm, sweet syrup poured over something fruity...with a cherry on top.

Neesia started the dinner off by passing the first dish around. When Lou was done piling his plate, his inner country boy shouted a big *yeehaw*. He had a pile of hot water cornbread, mustard greens doused in what tasted like homemade spicy chow-chow, and a mountain of macaroni and cheese—and the stuff was made with real cheese instead of that orange, plasticky stuff. He lifted his fork and then paused a moment when the staff brought in yet more food.

This time, his inner-lion lifted its head and took notice—buffalo. Huge pieces of rare, perfectly cut buffalo steak that had been grilled just long enough to add a hint of smoky flavor to the meat. Lou turned towards a smug Jason. "Really?"

Jason simply grinned, and leaned in to kiss his smiling mate. "Yep, that's how we roll, isn't it honey?"

"Damn right."

As a shifter of one of the predator species, his body required huge amounts of protein to stay healthy, and this was a close to heaven as a carnivore could get. He didn't care that all eyes were on him as he dove headlong into the grub. There was very little Lou loved more than good, southern cooking...other than Niah in his arms, of course.

There was very little talking during the meal as they all stuffed their faces. Lou was glad to see none of the women did that dainty shit where they just pushed the food around on their plates. No, these were lions dressed in designer jeans—beautiful killing machines who took their food seriously.

When the dishes were cleared, cold beer was poured and set in front of Lou along with a baked dessert—bread pudding with raisins and pecans. Mmm, one of his all-time favorites. He took a bite and moaned his appreciation.

That's when the grilling began...only this time it wasn't a buffalo on the barbeque feeling the heat this time.

"Just spill it already. What do you know about us?" Kotara demanded.

Without hesitation, Lou laid it all out for them. "I can tell you that the S.W.A.T. database shows that you and Neesia are the only sisters on Pryde Ranch. Neesia is the technical whiz and you're the scientist. There is no hint, and I mean not even a sniff of a hint, that there are really four of you. There's no mention of Jason being here either. They've gone through a good deal of trouble to muddy the waters of your true origins, and your current location."

"Anything else?" Koreas asked.

He took a deep draught of his beer, thankful for the cool, bubbly brew. It was the height of spring and the air was cool outside, but like most big-game shifters, he ran hot all year 'round. He set down the stein and wiped his mouth with a soft, sturdily-woven napkin.

"Other than a bogus address, there were a few contracts between you and S.W.A.T. that guarantee the agency gets first crack at the vaccines and medicines you all discover. There were also some old training records, but they only show that two of you came into the program under an agreement with your grandmother, now deceased. You're marked as classified and off-limits to anyone below the director level. A special code is required just to see the names of your files, and that code doesn't even allow the files to be opened."

"That makes sense," Neesia said. "All four of us were trained in military tactics at the express request of our grandmother, as you said, but she was careful when risking our exposure to S.W.A.T. Gran made sure only two of us were seen at any given time, and only by those responsible for the most covert activities. So far, it's been a decent trade-off. In exchange for keeping our existence under wraps, we take down some of the most lethal and dangerous outlaws in the shifter and Were communities."

Cutting to the chase, Niah threw a question Lou's way after Neesia was done talking.

"So how did you do it?"

He knew exactly what she meant.

"I hacked in." Lou took another long pull on his beer, then scooped up a spoonful of bread pudding. Huh. Never expected the two would taste so good together. "Through several layers of encryption, plus some interesting tracing programs that I had to keep confused so they wouldn't track back to me. It took weeks. "

"Weeks? Either you suck or the encryption is out of this world," Jason sputtered.

"Trust me, Jason, it's that second one."

"Okay, no pissing contests allowed, guys, so don't even start. I mean, damn, I get that you're both alphas but don't they sometimes get along in the wild?" Niah grumbled.

"Are you insinuating that we should be in the wild?" Jason snapped.

"Well, we live on plenty of acreage," Neesia said, then turned to the younger twins. "Hey, didn't we install a dog house out on the prairie last summer?"

Kotara and Koreas both nodded and grinned but said nothing.

Jason glared at his mate, who smiled back at him. But damn if it wasn't the most feral showing of teeth Lou had ever seen.

Neesia left the dining room and headed to the kitchen.

Lou leaned towards Jason. "Your wife is scary."

Now it was Jason's turn to grin. "Yeah, she is. Actually, they're all kind of scary in their own special way."

Kotara rolled her eyes and Koreas stuck her tongue out.

Niah stared as if they'd all lost their minds, then she burst out laughing as the "scary wife" returned with a strawberry shortcake so huge it looked more like a tower than a confection. And nothing said "tough woman" quite like the whipped cream on Neesia's cheek.

4

"That was a fabulous meal, Miss Neesia. Thanks so much for the hospitality. It's rare to get a good home-cooked meal being a combination bounty hunter and bachelor."

"Did he say *Miss* Neesia," the entire table wondered aloud.

"It's a southern thing," Lou said, wiping his mouth on his napkin and folding it neatly on the table. "My ma raised me to respect those in authority. Neesia is matriarch of this pride so I hope you all don't mind me calling her miss."

"Mind? Is he serious," Neesia whispered to Niah, though nobody missed a word given they were all shifters with their animals' acute ability to hear. "He can call me whatever he wants in that sexy-ass drawl of his."

Laughter circled the table at Jason's growl and Neesia's very un-lion-like squeak when her mate nipped her on the ear. Even Jason couldn't hold back a chuckle. It was, after all, very cute to see the couple interact.

Now if only Lou could get his own mate to open up a little, but her shell was closed tighter than a clam's ass. She barely looked at him, let alone spoke to him.

As the meal concluded Niah muttered, "I'm headed for a shower before you guys use up all the hot water."

The second she was out of the dining room and up the wide staircase, Lou looked around the room. All eyes were on him. The women were a mix of sisterly concern and mirth, while Jason was a mix of alpha aggression and male understanding...which seemed like an oxymoron now that Lou thought about it.

"So," Lou asked quietly, "any of you buy that whole 'use all the hot water' thing?"

In addition to the fact that she'd already had a shower, the snorts and snickers from her family told him what he already knew—Niah was running. And running from a predator was the last thing any sane person should do.

Luckily he was a patient man. In fact, he spent a whole twenty minutes chatting with her kin and listening to funny stories of their growing-up years. After he hit the shower in his suite up on the third floor, he made his way back down to the family room just off the dining room.

"The meal was delicious and the company even better. But it's time for me to see if I can win myself a mate. Good night, all." With that he bowed to Neesia, shook Jason's hand and waved to the younger twins.

Back in his room, he lay with his hands behind his head on a big, comfy bed, thinking about Niah. About how she moved when hunting, all smooth grace and deadly skill. How her smile lit up the night as they'd celebrated their success. And how smooth and supple the skin on her back had felt under his hands as he'd taken her from behind.

Suddenly his thoughts shattered as something hit him so hard in the gut he jumped up with a very audible, "holy shit," while looking for whoever had belted him.

"What in the hell was that?"

It felt as if his heart was being ripped out through his

nostrils. His chest tightened, his gut quivered...and he had to suddenly fight back the urge to cry like a fucking baby?

He sat down on the bed, closed his eyes and tried to nail down exactly what he was feeling.

Heartbreak. Fear. Loss.

And none of it belonged to him.

Without a second thought, he was out the door and headed to the source of a pain so god-awful that he practically shook with it.

When he finally stood outside Niah's door, the sound of her muffled sobs broke Lou's heart.

Lou was in her house sleeping up on the third floor. Well, Niah hoped at least one of them was getting some rest, considering she lay in her bed counting uncooperative sheep, wide awake. Even with her door firmly closed, and six paperwhite-scented candles burning in the holder across the room, the faintest hint of Lou's scent still tickled her nose. And it was just enough to make her skin feel prickly and a hair too tight, while a low burn heated the sensitive mound of her sex.

Yet her heart lay in a million pieces. God, the sorrow was bone-deep and planted solidly in the pit of her stomach as if someone had sunk a rock into her and then stood on top of it. She couldn't make up her mind if she wanted to bawl her eyes out and let the tears flow freely or continue to put all her energy into holding them back. To give the impression of a woman in complete control of her life and everything around her. To keep up the pretense that the fierce loneliness that gnawed daily at her soul was nonexistent.

She tried to push the utter despair and feelings of worth-lessness down into the bottoms of her socks, where no one knew about them but herself. But for Niah there was no escaping the knowledge that she was only good enough to be used by others. And once they had what they wanted, achieved their innermost desires, she was no longer needed or desired. Tossed aside like a used dishrag that wasn't worthy of being laundered.

Unworthy of notice, attention. Or love. Besides, why care for the rag when you could toss it and get a fresh one? And she resented the assholes that pulled her strings.

Her family was safe only because they served S.W.A.T.'s purposes. They were the best damn bounty hunters the organization had, their record of capture-or-kills unparalleled by any other team.

And the agency constantly used them all in exchange for keeping their existence a secret.

Now the tears flowed unchecked the moment she admitted to herself that she only had a shell of a life. A shell worn so thin it was practically see-through, so fragile it had begun to crack with Lou's sudden appearance.

Just as Niah lost control of the typically tight reins she kept on her emotional baggage, thoughts of her sisters came to the rescue. They were her life. Her only true friends. The only ones who had never betrayed, used or abandoned her.

Her parents and grandmother had left her. Though it was no fault of their own, leaving was leaving even if the reason was death.

So where did that leave Lou? What did he really want from her? Was it more than she could give? What if her biological instinct was wrong? Sure, it had been spot-on when both she and Neesia had recognized Jason as Neesia's mate. In fact, she and her twin had been thrown into heat, something wholly unexpected, as a result of Jason showing up at Pryde ranch.

The whole thing had tossed quite a wrench into the covert mission he'd been on at the time.

"That's what he gets for showing up here pretending to be

our network fix-it-guy," Niah whispered into the darkness with a chuckle at the memory.

She cocked her head and considered what was happening now. The same heat burned in her blood now, but that didn't mean the flush that lay just beneath her skin meant anything more than a strong attraction to Lou.

Liar.

She ignored her own admonishment because it didn't matter that she'd felt as needy and out-of-sorts upon meeting Lou as she had upon meeting Jason. Made no difference that this was seven times worse. Nor did it matter that the need, the bone-deep ache, had flared to life when the wind carried his scent to her out in the brush earlier today, then blazed wildly at that first sight of him sitting on her porch in all his naked perfection.

But she was no cub. None of them were. Niah's career was well established, and she was perfectly content to run her part of the family business. The temporary satisfaction of a short-term lover held no appeal, but that was all she would ever have —a short list of few-and-far-between boyfriends she could never share her true self with. Besides, she and her sisters were safer that way.

So why did the thought of *not* being with Lou make her feel as if someone had stolen her puppy and then run over it with a field mower?

Sigh.

Startled by a knock at her door, Niah bolted out of bed and called a muffled, "Coming!" as she blew her nose and snatched on her robe. Who the hell had the nerve to knock on her door at this time of night? After a few grumbles and a mad-dash for the bathroom, she gave up splashing ice-cold water on her face. The puffy bags underneath her eyes persisted, just like the tapping on her door.

Six steps from the threshold, the hand she stretched towards the knob froze in mid-air.

Lou.

She knew, simply *knew* it was him who stood waiting for her to open up.

Could she smell him through the door? No. Hear him in her head? Nope. Yet something in the very essence of her being screamed that her mate was on the other side of that door.

But could she do it? Twisting the knob was more than showing common courtesy to the person that knocked. It was deeper, symbolic of opening a larger door. A door that was three feet thick, made of steel, and hadn't expected anyone to have the combination. Ever.

But have it he did. Her heart knew this was it. This was the man made for her, created for her. But her head didn't want this. If the risk didn't involve chasing down bad guys, it just wasn't her thing.

So, instead of opening the door, Niah yelled through it.

"Who is it?"

"Niah, you know it's me. Stop playing games, woman. Open this door and tell me what's wrong."

What's wrong? How the hell did he know she was in here wallowing in her tears like a big baby? Turning away, Niah stifled the urge to sniff, quietly wiping her still runny nose and teary eyes in silence. A few deep breaths later, she asked, "What do you want?"

"Is that a trick question?" Lou asked with that smile-inducing southern drawl of his. If shifters were cowboys, Lou would have been the poster boy for them. "Open up, darlin'. If we're going to talk, it's going to be face-to-face and not through this damned door."

Decisions, decisions. God, what to do? Her forehead met the solid wood while her hand reached for the knob of its own volition—well, it wasn't quite true, but that was her story and she was sticking to it.

Instead of throwing the door wide like her body and heart

wanted her to, her head won out. She cracked it just enough to get a quick peek at his bare chest and towel-shrouded hips.

Mistake number one was opening the door at all.

Mistake number two was breathing rather than holding her breath and shooing him away. One lungful of his earthy, scent and her legs threatened to spring into action in hopes of landing wrapped around his waist.

"Oh. My. God." The words were a strangled whisper as Lou gently but firmly shoved against the wood to make enough room for his big body to ease through and into her domain.

His piercing, green gaze took her in, then his arms were around her, soothing, comforting and giving.

And she lost it yet again, gave in to the gut-wrenching sobs that she'd barely managed to stop only moments ago.

Her head was tucked beneath Lou's chin as he gathered her up, eased her into bed and held her tight until she'd exhausted her tears.

"Aw, darlin', don't cry. It just breaks my heart to know that something has you so sad. Especially if that something or someone is me."

"No," she sniffled. "Not you. Well, yes you, but not really."

Okay. Good thing he'd read that Mars and Venus book or he'd be really confused right now. Instead of trying to immediately fix her problem, Lou just rocked her gently and waited for her to tell him what was on her mind.

After what felt like forty years, she finally gave him what he needed.

"I'm so drawn to you, Lou, but I can't be with you. I just can't."

"Niah, listen, we'd be good together. You're a woman I know

I could care for. Be a mate to. A woman I could love. I know you feel it, too."

"I absolutely cannot be ruled by my hormones, Lou. Besides, I'm the rational Pryde. The calm one. The logical one, damn it. I don't *do* this kind of stuff."

"Mating is normal for us, Niah. Your sister is mated, for cripes sake. And I'll let you in on a little secret, I don't do this either. In all my years of working for S.W.A.T. I've never been compelled to mate with another agent, and I've never slept with another agent—neither on a hunt, nor off duty. Ever. But you call to me, darlin'. On every level I can think of. You're the one, Niah. You're it. You deserve to be happy, to be loved. And I can give that to you. Just let me."

Niah tried to think of the last time she'd been punched in the gut. Hard. Surely it had felt something like this, right?

So he could make her happy, eh? Arrogance, thy name is Lou.

So...where was her mad? Why wasn't she telling him he was full of week-old, dried-up horse shit?

"I won't leave you, Niah." He paused and grinned. "So you may as well scoot over."

"You won't leave me? How in the world can a mere mortal make such a promise?"

Besides, it wasn't as if they were wolves who mated for life or anything. In fact, she'd had no idea what his animal side was until after they'd been on the hunt for a few days; they'd needed their larger, shifter bodies to bring the final rogue down. Until that moment, he could have been a damned beaver shifter for all she knew.

Then an image of Lou with a round, pea-shaped head and long buckteeth popped into her mind. The image made chompy noises as it gnawed on a piece of wood in the middle of an imaginary river.

"If I weren't so sure of myself, I would be offended about you chuckling after I've declared myself, woman."

"It's not your wanting to mate with me that made me laugh. It's...uh." She giggled and sniffled some more. "Just something else that teased my brain."

"Care to share?" He nipped her ear and let the light-heartedness of his nature be heard in his voice. Lou nuzzled the side of her neck as he gently maneuvered her into the center of the big bed.

"Share? No way!" Her giggle became an outright laugh as he tickled her until she squirmed and cackled like a hen rather than a lioness. During their play, he'd eased himself over her body until he was settled firmly between her thighs.

"Wanna use my towel to wipe your face?" he teased. A growing bulge hardened underneath said towel. And then he snatched the towel away.

All she could do was gasp when the steel heat of his sex lit up her body as his bare skin touched hers.

Grinning like a mischievous boy, Lou wiped the salty tears from her face in the same rhythm as his hips moved against hers.

And just like that, Niah went up in flames. Sadness and pain were forgotten, replaced by a heat so thorough, it burned away all her apprehension. When Lou lowered his head to kiss her, she held his face in her hands and looked at him. Really looked at him. His eyes said everything his words couldn't.

The green gems deepened and flecked with gray as she watched him watch her. Thick, mahogany hair, still damp from his shower, was a mass of glossy, loose waves. A one-sided grin told her he knew exactly what she was thinking, feeling, as she let herself fall under his spell.

And she did indeed *feel* him. Felt the sincerity of his need and desire for her, along with something deeper than sex or lust. It was care and concern. For a mate. *His* mate. The knowledge that he saw her as more than a lay at the end of a hunt stoked the fire until it burned higher and hotter.

Damn.

"So, let's cut to the chase, Niah. Can I have you, love?"

"You mean right this moment, or forever?"

"If right now is all you can give me, I'll have to be satisfied with that while I work on getting you to give me the rest."

"And what if I won't?"

"You will."

"How do you know?"

"Because we male lions always get what we want. I thought you knew that by now." With each word he'd eased his lips closer to hers until they were sharing the same breath.

"I'm waiting, Niah."

She sighed in response to the press of hard male flesh against her core.

"Yes. God, yes." *For tonight.*

And the man sure could kiss. Mouth settled gently on hers, he teased a bit and then slipped his tongue in to tangle with hers. Overwhelming? No, he cajoled her into the dance. And when she was fully engaged, *then* he plundered, taking her under until waves of need crashed over them both.

Finally he slid his thick cock inside, a bit at a time. The second he was fully sheathed, he pistoned through the quivering muscle of her slick walls and rode her into oblivion.

Niah decided she liked oblivion.

For tonight. Just for tonight.

5

*D*uring dinner, Niah's sadness had been palpable. The pain had been so acute that Neesia had to stop herself from wiping her own eyes even though there were no tears there. She was sure they were all worried about Niah and the impact this new development was having on her.

The staff had finally finished clearing the debris left over from dinner. Neesia had kissed her mate as he headed out to do the final nightly security check on the estate, and then she'd sent the younger twins back to the labs to finish up some tests. Now she could check on Niah alone, rather than have them all converge on the poor girl.

The house was quiet as Neesia made her way upstairs. Down the hall from Niah's room, she slammed to a halt.

"Holy shit!" She sucked in an unsteady breath. Knees locked as her womb went up in flames for no apparent reason. Her gaze flew to her sister's door. What in the world was Niah up to? Of course it was a rhetorical question because the ever-increasing burn burrowing into her belly gave a pretty good indication that Niah was engaged in activities of the carnal sort.

It reminded Neesia of when Jason had first arrived. The man

had sensed that Neesia was what he called "fucking awesome mating material" after he'd come to Pryde Ranch on a covert mission for S.W.A.T.

The moment she'd accepted Jason, both Neesia and Niah had been thrown into a full-blown feline heat from hell. So intense, they'd felt each other's arousal when one or the other was in Jason's presence. It had been in-fucking-sane.

Kind of like now.

Here in the hall, Neesia was awash in heat to the point she squeezed her thighs together just to remain standing.

When sweat began to bead on her upper lip, she moved. Fast.

Get to your room, get to your room, get to your room.

Gasping, she flew over the threshold, breathing so hard she was sure she'd blow a lung.

"Jason!"

Thankfully he was back from patrol and came running out of the bathroom still covered in soap from the shower. "What? What's wrong?"

Without a second thought, Neesia tackled him.

"What the...?"

They became a wild, wet tangle of arms and legs, kisses and bites, teeth and growls.

When they finally made it up off the floor, they were both too tired to do much more than drag themselves to bed. But they were smiling as they hauled the sheets over each other and fell into oblivion.

Niah kicked the tire of the Jeep she'd be taking out on the property. She'd told her sisters she wanted to check on some cables that appeared to have come loose during a recent storm. A low priority, that danged thing had been needing repair for months, but she just had to get the hell out of the house for a bit.

What a frustrating, completely impossible man. Ugh! Niah wanted to roar at the moon while taking a bite out of Lou's stubborn, though nicely firm, backside. Maybe with her teeth planted in his ass he'd finally get what she was trying to say—they couldn't have a mating. A fling? Sure. But a permanent, do-you-take-me type of mating? Not a chance.

But had he listened? Noooo. Lou was everywhere, in everything, talking to everyone. Personal space meant absolutely nothing to him. Funny nobody else seemed to mind, damn it.

Fine, I've got a fix for that, she grumbled. The urge to drop into the change and take off running in her pelt rode her hard, but if she did so she'd have to come back to the house tonight.

Not a chance.

So instead of letting her lioness out to play, a tent, sleeping bag and camping stove were tossed into the back seat along with a small cooler.

Lou was a prime specimen, but mating just wasn't for her. The ridiculous notion that she might have found someone perfect for her pricked the buried longing of her subconscience. She squashed that longing like a bug on a windshield and tossed it out the window of her mind. It didn't matter that her older sister had mated, and that her younger siblings were looking forward to finding their own true loves. Didn't mean that she had the same fate in her future, did it?

Besides, the thought of leaving her family sent a very real panic streaking through her soul. No more Neesia—a twin linked to her by more than just blood. No more Kotara or Koreas, younger sisters who, in spite of their identical features, sported personalities so different they threw people for fabulous loops. The very idea of leaving Pryde Ranch left Niah practically breathless with fear.

If she admitted it, which she wouldn't in a million years, being without her family had been her biggest fear since she was a cub. After their parents had been killed and the Pryde sisters were sent to live with their grandmother in America, Niah had always feared losing her sisters. There had been a close call all those years ago. All four Pryde girls had been so very, very close to death. In the moments after the murder of their mom and dad, Niah had lain in her hiding place not knowing whether her sisters were safe or not.

With her fist jammed between her teeth, she'd huddled in silence, too terrified to move, to dig out of her secret spot to see if they were safely in their own hidey spots underneath the house. Too afraid to even take a deep breath. She'd been still for so long, tears and snot had dried on her face, clogged her nose and crusted her lashes partially closed. But there she'd stayed.

It had seemed like hours before Neesia, covered in balsam, had come to fetch her from underneath the house. It wasn't until after they'd retrieved the younger twins that Niah allowed herself to throw up from a combination of fear and the cloying smell that had saved their lives. Her parents had been geniuses to make their home among a stand of balsam trees. Their mom had also stashed pots filled with a paste of the smelly stuff in each hidey hole so the scent coming from under the house would be attributed to having so many trees on the property. None of the marauders had even considered that Laila Pryde had used the scent to mask her babies' natural smell. It was a brilliant plan to keep her daughters safe from other lion shifters. Unfortunately it hadn't saved her own life.

After moving to the States, it had taken Niah years to let even one of her sisters out of her sight. She recalled bursting into tears at the thought of going off to school and leaving Kotara and Koreas at home with their Grandma. Then, when the younger twins were old enough for kindergarten, Niah led a one-girl mutiny after learning that the school she and Neesia attended didn't have a kindergarten program, and that Kotara and Koreas would have to go to the one around the corner.

Her family was everything.

With that thought weighing heavily in her mind, Niah set off for the western-most part of the property. Considering they owned seventy-seven thousand acres, she had a nice number of "get lost" places to choose from.

So why was there a lingering sadness in the back of her mind at the thought of missing some of Lou's funny "Jason and the old days" stories over dinner?

Or the way Lou closed his eyes and moaned as he appreciated a good meal? Or the way he drawled the word *darlin'* when he spoke to her? Or his sharp wit and bossy-guy tendencies?

Pushing the thoughts away, thoughts that clearly didn't want to go anywhere but 'round and 'round in her head, Niah headed out with a loud, annoyed sigh.

Lou stomped into the kitchen feeling quite petulant. It was an emotion he had no experience with, and he wasn't quite sure what to do with it.

He dropped into a chair at the oversized breakfast nook, sat back and sighed. He hadn't managed to get Niah alone since that first night they'd made love. Damn woman.

Neesia's root beer gaze landed on his. "So what's wrong with you?"

"Your sister is what's wrong with me." The woman had the nerve to grin, but damn if Lou could blame her. He was sure he looked absolutely pathetic.

Broglio, who was thankfully a bit friendlier now, picked up his plate. "I can see this is going to require some privacy. Neesia, I'll send Solie to you for her accounting task in about an hour. If you'll excuse us." And with a wink he strolled out as Kotara and Koreas appeared in matching lab coats streaked with various interesting colors.

They smelled like a mix of cucumber and ammonia, and

managed to make it seem as if this was totally normal. Then again, he guessed it was normal for them as scientists. They sat down to dig into bacon, eggs, some huge beefy-looking sausage, and rare buffalo steak cut into thin strips.

"Well," said Kotara, "given that our boy Lou here could care less about this lean, juicy steak I'm dangling in his face, I think this might be serious."

"Oh, good grief," Neesia grumbled while Koreas elbowed her twin and said, "That was just terrible, Tara. I mean...really?"

Ignoring the banter that should have actually been funny to him, Lou laid out his case.

"Niah's like a fucking ghost around here. I know she's here, but the moment I hone in on her scent, she's gone again. And forget trying to call her on her cell phone. The damn thing goes right to voicemail. She's avoiding me."

"You don't say?" Kotara said, which pulled a chuckle from the quieter Koreas. "Knowing how much Niah likes to keep up with all of us, I'd be inclined to challenge you forcefully on the cell-to-voicemail assessment...if Niah used a cell phone."

"What do you mean if Niah used a cell phone? Of course she uses one. I snagged the number out of the S.W.A.T. database. I even created and then killed a fake mission to send her out on 'cause it was the only way to get at the data."

All of their eyebrows rose, then three, very unique voices all burst forth as they laughed at him. Lou didn't appreciate being the butt of any joke, especially one that involved his wayward mate.

"Oh, stop growling at us, Lou," Neesia said with a bright smile. "None of us have cell phones. We only use satellite phones, Lou."

Kotara sniffed as she tried to control her giggles. "So, yeah, I think she's avoiding you."

"Stop it, Tara," Neesia snapped with very little authority, considering she was biting her lip trying not to grin. "Lou, the contact details we provide to the agency are phantom numbers. I'm sure you'd understand why we do that. It's kind of a glorified call-forwarding, untraceable. They ring wherever our network engineer wants them to ring, no matter where we are."

"Then who's the network engineer?"

All three women paused and then burst out, "Niah!"

"Fuck!"

Jason shuffled into the kitchen, looking like something the cat dragged in. Literally. After a huge yawn, he sprawled in a chair and leaned his head back. The man's neck had to be spring-loaded with the way it snapped back up when Neesia presented him with a big mug of black coffee.

Lou couldn't resist. "A cat that likes black coffee? That's just wrong. No sugar? No cream? Come on man, where's your pride?"

"Right here," he grinned as he patted his wife on the backside.

"Mmm, one point for Jason." Neesia dropped a kiss on her mate's forehead then moved away to fetch yet more food. God, lions ate a lot.

She set a platter of what looked like pancakes with a big bowl of fresh strawberry compote on the table.

"These are specifically for you, hon," she said, handing Lou a plate.

"Pancakes?"

"Nope. Hoe cakes."

"What? No way. Made with bacon drippings? Miss Neesia, the southern cooking almost makes me feel better, considering your sister is practically running from me with rocket boosters strapped to her ass."

"So," Neesia said, sitting down next to Jason. In her hands was a plate piled with so much protein Lou was almost speechless. "I believe you when you say Niah is your mate because I know what that feels like. Between you and me, I have no doubt that she's feeling the pull of a mating, but if you tell her I said so, I'll deny it, track you down and skin you where you stand."

"Agreed," Lou said, feeling the first thread of hope in the two weeks he'd spent here. "I can say that my strategy of chasing Niah around Pryde Ranch isn't working. Kind of hard to find a lioness on seventy thousand acres if she doesn't want to be fucking found."

"No doubt. So, how can we help you two? I want my sister to be happy, Lou. And if you think you can help her with that, I'm all in." Neesia winked at him and Lou decided that she was going to be the best sister in the world.

"I know I can get her to see reason if I can just get her out of here for a little while. Perhaps a vacation of sorts?"

"Are you saying that *we're* keeping you and Niah from mating?"

"No...uh, Koreas, right? Still trying to tell you two apart. But, no, I don't think you're keeping us from mating. *Niah* is keeping us from mating, but the stubborn witch is using you all as the excuse."

"Excuse me?"

"She thinks that the only semblance of family she could have can only be had here," Lou said. "An outsider doesn't stand a chance. And I, unfortunately, happen to fall into the outsider category."

"She...huh?" Koreas said. "I don't follow."

Neesia spoke, her voice laced with sadness. "Think about it, you guys. Niah must really believe that mating isn't for her. I mean, she's said as much before, but I didn't take her seriously since she didn't have any prospects at the time. But if you think about it, her life is work, work, and more work. I know she's resentful about how S.W.A.T. basically blackmails us to keep our secrets, but she honors the deal that Grandma made for all our sakes. On the other hand, she's perfectly happy to do whatever it takes for our family, including pass up her own happiness, no matter how much we tell her that she deserves more than that."

"Yes," Lou cut in, "but I need her to see that she can have it all. If she, and you all, will accept me, that is. I know it will take time, but hell, I can't even get a running start without Niah finding some task or another to do."

"Let me guess, every time you want to speak to her she's got to go run some fiber optic cable..." Kotara said.

"Or rekey the security, or pull a network cable or..." Koreas picked up where her sister left off.

"Yes, all of that." Lou didn't bother to keep the grumble out of his voice.

"Wow, I almost feel sorry for you, Lou. Even as tough as it was breaking into the family, I had more of a head start," Jason said between gulps of steaming coffee. "I came here on a bogus assignment, undercover. That at least got me through the gate and into my lady's good graces long enough for us to realize that Neesia and I were meant to be together. I don't envy you, dude."

"Gee, thanks, Jason."

"You're welcome. No offense, but Niah can be a tough nut to crack even when you *are* in her good graces. But I know you can do this. Besides, she needs this and if there is one thing our genetics does well, it pairs us with what we need. Might not be what we want at the time, but definitely what we need."

"Well said, husband. Now, how are we going to get Niah to go along with it?" Neesia asked as her fingers stroked her chin in devilish concentration.

"That's easy," Koreas said. "Order her to do it. You know, like you order us to do everything else. You are the oldest, even if it is only by a few minutes."

"Keep that up and you'll be on poop patrol in the buffalo pens," Jason promised.

Kotara burst out laughing until Jason *and* Neesia pinned her with a "you, too" raised-brow glare. With that, the younger Pryde twins gathered up their dishes, dumped them in the sink and hightailed it out of there, muttering something about correlations and control charts or some such.

Jason and Neesia began to plot, and the more they spoke, the wider Lou's grin became. Yep, he was going to love being a part of this pride. Now, all he had to do was convince his mate that he belonged exactly where he was—with her.

hen Niah awoke, she remained completely still and took stock of her body and surroundings. She wasn't in her bed, and she definitely was not at home. No bruises or cuts ruled out any violent situations. The sounds and pressure she sensed were something she was intimately familiar with—someone had the balls to stuff her in a sack and put her on a plane.

But how the hell had they done it? She'd returned last night from her temporary escape to the prairie just in time to have dinner with her sisters. After dessert and a drink, she'd gone up to bed early. Niah was a light sleeper, lived on a property with the most sophisticated security systems money could buy, and had gone to sleep in a house surrounded by five, count 'em, *five* African lion shifters.

How the hell had anyone gotten the jump on her, damn it?

And why a sack? There was nothing more stupid than putting a cat in a bag. Cats had claws. Very sharp ones.

She didn't hear anyone moving around but she knew there was no way she was alone. With a quiet but deep breath, she weeded out the various scents carried through the recycled air of the circulation system. Ah, there it was, or rather there *he* was.

Ryland Lee Lewis. She was going to kill him good and dead. Maybe twice for good measure.

Oh, you just wait until I get out of this bag, you son of a bitch.

She threw herself into the change, uncaring whether the force and speed of the shift alerted her captor to the fact she was now fully awake and spitting mad.

Fuck!

The material was shifter resistant!

She should have known, given she was playing with a bounty hunter as skilled as herself. The smooth material expanded with her body, accommodating her larger lioness shape with ease. And the stuff didn't shred under her super-sharp claws either. All she got for her escape efforts was tired.

This material might not shred, but the skin on Lou's ass will.

"I think I actually felt that thought, Niah. I should check to see if I have claw marks down my left butt cheek."

Back in her human skin she growled low in her throat. "Laugh now, country boy, but you just wait. And if you've made my family worry, I will absolutely kick your ass, up one cheek and down the other."

"Niah, don't you even want to know what's going on here and why?"

"Hell no! I can figure that part out later. You know, *after* you're bleeding."

She couldn't see his smile given she still had a bag over her body, but she felt it down to her bones. And, God, it felt like so much sunshine spilling over the eastern plains as the sun rose in the morning. Then he laughed as if he was truly delighted.

"But I am delighted, love."

Oh, hell no!

"Get out of my head, Lou."

"Not a chance, darlin'."

They were already picking each other's thoughts out of the air? Damn, but it shouldn't have been possible yet. That kind of closeness was only possible with family and a mate. The end.

Lou definitely wasn't family, and Niah had decided long ago that she wasn't going to have a mate. It didn't matter how much this man made her skin prickle with awareness, or how much she swore she could feel what he was feeling. Or how much she craved him, skin-to-skin, pelt-to-pelt, or however she could have him.

Nope. Not happening.

But Lou's strong presence continued to storm into her head even as he started to speak aloud once more.

"Though you're not the least bit curious of where you are and why, I'll tell you anyway. You're on *your* jet and we're going on vacation."

"You're serious?"

Lou unzipped her temporary prison just enough to bare her head. Then he called up to the cockpit and put the system into conference mode. Her mouth fell open when a familiar voice filled the cabin.

"Hello, Miss Niah."

"Harry, is that you?" She didn't bother keeping the incredulity out of her voice.

"Yes, ma'am. I'm under orders from Miss Neesia that no matter what you say, I am not allowed to turn around and take you home."

"B-But you've been our pilot for ten years! I can't believe..."

"Not his fault, Niah. Even though I was totally involved, I did get your family to buy in to my crazy idea. Can you imagine anyone saying 'no' to your sisters after they've put their mind to something? Poor Harry didn't stand a chance and you know it."

Lou's words made too much sense. She ignored him and asked a question instead. "Where are we going and how long was I asleep?"

"We're over the Pacific Ocean. Kotara administered a dose of something that was supposed to keep you asleep for twelve hours. Guess you were tired, though, because you were actually out for a little while longer than that."

"But how? Wait, she roofied me, didn't she?"

Lou grinned again.

Ignore. Ignore. Ignore. She was supposed to be mad, damn it, not fall under the spell of that gorgeous, bright smile.

"I knew I shouldn't have had that damn cranberry vodka thing she offered me last night. Or this morning. Or whenever. Just wait until I get home. I'm going to kill her twice over."

Harry's voice filled the cabin again. "We'll be landing in about three hours, miss. The crew will bring you a snack whenever you're ready. We're on the larger jet so you can shower. There's a change of clothes in the bedroom, too, if you need it."

"Thanks, Harry."

Then reality became crystal clear. She was on a plane. With a man she wasn't supposed to want. Going who-knew-where. And her sisters had done this to her. Why? Sadness washed over and through her.

"Why is my family turning on me?"

"Niah, no one is turning on you. They love you. In fact, they love you enough to risk your absolute and total wrath if it means that you'll be happy in the end. You're my mate. I know you feel it. Even *they* know it. Time to stop running and give me a chance. Give us a chance. What's the worst that can happen?"

That was a question for another day. *God, just let me get through today with my pride intact.*

First, she needed to stop thinking that her family didn't love her. It was far from the truth and she knew it. And given the fact her sisters were part of this grand scheme, well, she couldn't really be pissed with Lou, if Neesia and K-and-K were the actual perpetrators. Sometimes it was a damn curse to have four genius feline scientists under the same roof.

Family. Loving, loyal, nosey-as-hell family.

"Can't live with 'em and you just can't shoot 'em," Niah grumbled.

"I thought those words were from a song about men?"

"Yeah, them too."

"Can I cut you loose now, or are you still determined to challenge me? Believe me when I say that when we have it out, you will not be shaking off the effects of any sedative, nor will you be winded from trying to escape. We'll be face-to-face and on equal footing. I trust you'll be a graceful loser?"

"I'll be a what?"

And then she was free. Lou quickly wrapped her in a thick, warm robe, for which she was grateful, considering she'd shredded her clothes during her bag-wrapped shift to her lioness form. Once she'd settled into a comfy but cool leather loveseat, Lou lovingly stroked her wrists, though they'd not been bound.

He must have sensed she needed just a bit of space, because he eased back and away, sitting across from her while dismissing the staff.

"You heard me, woman. You'll be a graceful loser."

"Fuck you, Lou."

"I'm counting on it."

"God, you're such a perv."

"I am. But so are you. My equal in every way, and I couldn't be happier."

Her mouth fell open for a split second. When she regained her semi-composure, she fired right back. "Are you saying I'm on horny toad overload?"

"Yep. Well, except for the toad part. You're more of a wildcat in the sack, though I must admit that last encounter in your bed wasn't nearly recent enough."

"Oh please. You should have had enough sex to last you a

year, the way you camped out between my legs as if you hadn't had dinner that night."

"And I'd gladly do it again. Hell, woman, I'll even bring the marshmallows to that particular campout. But don't forget, my beautiful Niah, after I had my fill of feasting, you begged for my cock. In fact, when I asked how much you wanted it, you said, 'Like a fat kid needs cake.'"

Lou's words made Niah shiver, but there was no way she was backing out of this conversation, not without the last word, damn it. But all she could manage was a petulant, "So fucking what." Then she flipped him the bird.

His response was a sadistic grin that made her reminisce.

Skin heated at the memory of how he'd instinctively grabbed a handful of her hair, pulling it to position her the way he'd wanted...not knowing it was exactly what she'd needed. Everything she'd always desired but hadn't ever bothered to ask for in a lover. Besides, why go through training a guy when she'd had no intention of staying with anyone?

Now along came this man who read her like a book and still liked what he saw, though some of the pages were fragile and stuck together.

At the same time, Lou gave her only as much space as he wanted, and took no shit from her, while remaining a gentleman. Well, a gentleman-jerk-asshole-bossy-gorgeous-cowboy-shifter-hunter when out of the bedroom. In the bedroom, he'd been...in charge. Stroked up and down her spine. Sunk his teeth into the areola around her nipple and sucked until she'd squirmed with delight. Took her from the front, the back. Hell, even sideways. Basically, he'd *handled* her.

As they continued to squabble, the heat ratcheted up in her belly. Maybe she was demented to get so turned on by a verbal spat? Her cat was scratching to get out, and it had nothing to do with sinking her claws into Lou's butt. Okay, wait, maybe it did, considering she'd done just that the last time he'd laid into her with smooth, skillful, sure strokes of his cock.

It was in this moment Niah realized that the lioness had no problem recognizing her need for him. So why was the woman being such a bonehead?

Perhaps because you're always in control and you don't know what to do with a man like this.

"Oh, bullshit." Stupid conscience.

"Excuse me?"

"Nothing. I'm talking to myself."

He raised a brow, but didn't ask her if she was nuts.

So now back to the issue at hand. Niah had had no problems believing Jason belonged in their family after he'd arrived at Pryde Ranch, so why was she having such a hard time accepting Lou?

Well that was the rub, wasn't it? Jason wasn't her mate, so she'd truly given him nothing but a bit of hot sex once and her loyalty. She'd given up none of her heart. None of her soul. None of her*self*. In fact, there was no requirement that she even like Jason for him to be part of the household. Every family had relatives who didn't get along, but that didn't mean they weren't kin. It only made them a pain in the ass.

However this Lou situation—this was different. Mating with this man, this dominant shifter, would mean letting him truly inside. She would be able to hide nothing from him. And frankly, the thought both terrified and relieved her.

She wasn't ready to reveal all her fears, her hopes and dreams. Yet at the same time there were times when she felt so alone, she simply locked herself in one of the outbuildings on the ranch and cried while imagining what it would be like to have someone to hold her at night.

Yes, Niah loved her family. Loved her life. Her work. All the fun times with her sisters. Yet there was, without a doubt, something, *someone*, missing—a mate.

But if she was honest with herself, he really wasn't missing. Not anymore.

Just then she looked up into a pair of summer-green eyes and felt Lou's caring concern. There was nothing ambivalent about what this man carried in his heart for her. The question was—why? Why her?

"Lou, you don't know me. How can you even begin to think you want to be with me permanently?"

"Are you still expecting me to play the human man, Niah? To pretend that I don't know what I want, or need, or fail to recognize what you are to me? Do I know everything about you? No. Do I expect us to have smooth sailing just because I decree it?"

"Well, you may as well say a big, fat yes to that one," she scoffed.

"I'm a dominant male, Niah. And I won't apologize for it. But I'm not stupid, and I do believe that for me to expect you, an equally dominant female, to give me no problems, ever? That would be the dumbest set of expectations known to man. All I'm asking for is a chance. If you don't choose me back, I'll walk away. Clean break. The end."

The thought of not feeling Lou's presence sent her gut into free-fall, as if she'd just jumped out of the airplane. It felt...foreign. Wrong. Which was the exact opposite of what she'd expected to feel considering she'd just gotten her way. Hadn't she?

"Come on, Niah. You're thinking too hard. Just take the next couple of weeks and just...be."

"Fine."

With a huff she stood and headed for the shower. Niah washed and dried her skin and tried to ignore how sensitive it was. It was as if she held a low-grade electrical wire and the voltage made the fine hairs on her arms and legs stand at attention.

God, this is all too much, too soon but instead of hiding in the bathroom I'll just try not to think so hard.

Yeah. Good luck with that.

Back in the main cabin, she sat next to Lou. While she enjoyed a glass of sparkling wine and a light, but protein-rich snack, he showed her the resort they were headed to.

Niah had to admit, it was a beautiful looking place. But it didn't stop her stomach from flipping around at the thought of being alone with a man she wanted to run from and to at the same time.

A few hours later, they landed at the airport on Bora Bora. The trip from the plane to the transfer boat, and then to a luxurious, floating bungalow passed in a blur of sight and sound.

Numb, she stood on a private dock and watched the boat depart.

"They'll be back tomorrow, Niah," Lou reassured. "For now, you're all mine."

But even as Lou grasped her hand and led her inside, she couldn't help but think that he would eventually leave just as the boat had. It's why she worked so hard for her sisters. They were committed to her, and she to them. They would never leave her. She had to do her best by them knowing that even in death they would be with her. Always.

So why can't a mate be as dedicated to you as you are to your family? As dedicated to you as Jason is to Neesia?

Nope. Not going there. Mainly because she didn't have an answer.

———

Eighteen hours after her abduction, Niah found herself enjoying a delicious dinner of fresh Skipjack tuna with citrus, with sides of steamed yam drizzled with butter and fresh-cut starfruit with the lightest dusting of sugar on top. The dining area was nothing more than an elegant, frosted, round glass table in the middle of the floor near the kitchen. She loved that there were no walls in this lovely space, and that the only thing that delineated between the kitchen, dining room and living room was the furniture arranged atop large, brightly woven rugs. The warm wood floors underneath them made paths of sorts through the room.

As they enjoyed their meal, the only light came from the candles on the table and the luminous moon that was just taking the place of the setting sun.

Lou pushed their plates aside and disappeared into the luxurious kitchen before returning with a treat—a light, fruity wine he swore had not been visited by Kotara.

With a smile, he poured them each a glass, held his hand out for hers and they retired to the living room. A cream-colored sofa, draped with red and green throws, faced a wall of glass that looked out into the lagoon. She could see the ocean on the other side of the reef separating them from the Pacific. The sight brought a measure of both awe and contentment Niah was sure she'd not experienced away from home before. Ever.

Usually when she was not at Pryde Ranch, she was chasing a bounty. It was adrenaline-inducing, hot, sweaty, dangerous work with her shelter being anything from a grove of trees to a shoddy motel. There were no cool ocean breezes. No fabulous cuisine. No relaxing. But this evening, here she sat in the Leeward Islands with her feet up as she lay against her mate.

On the next breath, Niah found herself sitting in Lou's lap. The wine glass slipped from her fingers and something small and cool took its place.

"What is this?"

She flipped it over and cocked her head at the sight of her cell phone.

"I want you completely comfortable, so you're calling your family."

"I'm not some little kid that needs to check in with mommy, Lou." She almost laughed at herself knowing good and well she'd just been thinking about calling home. After all, the last thing she wanted was for her family to worry.

"You're calling just the same."

She was sure her glare was nothing short of mutinous, but seconds later, Niah smiled as her sisters ribbed her about how she'd been trussed up in a shifter-proof bag and hauled off to Bora Bora with her mate.

Lou had kept his arms wrapped around her through the entire phone call and good-naturedly poked at her right along with the rest of them. The snorts and giggles were endless, so by the time it was over Niah had a cramp in her side from laughing so hard.

After the I-love-you's and see-you-soon's, she clicked off the phone and finished her wine on a wave of nervousness.

Okay, time to stop being a wuss. You want him, so put on your big girl panties and own up to it.

She'd been alone with Lou before. Had made love with him more than once, in fact. But this time she couldn't pretend this was just a fling or a one-time lay. If she went through with this, there would be no more running or avoiding this beautiful specimen of a man while clinging to her loneliness the way Linus from *Charlie Brown* clung to his blanket.

She watched Lou's eyes take her in as she rose from his lap and moved closer to the windows that led out to the deck. Turning her back to him, Niah set the empty glass on a side table. The highly polished wood floors were warm underneath her bare feet as she peeled off the loose tunic she'd donned on the plane.

Slowly, ever so slowly, she turned and let the garment fall into a silky pool at her feet.

Lou stood.

Niah shivered.

He walked towards her and her thoughts scattered with the exception of one—*my, what a big* everything *you have, said Little Red Riding Hood.* Only in this scenario, the light of a lion stared back through Lou's eyes rather than a wolf. Niah took a deep, calming breath and was met with sweet, clean air laced with the salty Pacific and a hint of Ryland Lee Lewis.

The man had moved into her space until her ruched nipples almost brushed the linen of his shirt, but he didn't come close enough to actually touch her. He simply stood there, took her in, seemed to roll against both the woman and the animal.

Nerves began to set in at his stillness. Had he changed his mind? The look in his eyes said he was still with her. The heat rolling off of his muscular body said he was as interested as ever.

Then suddenly she was pulled into his kiss until she couldn't tell where he ended and she began.

She moaned into his mouth as his fingers traveled over her skin, exploring, learning. This thing with Lou was still something new, yet it felt as old and comfortable as her favorite fluffy slippers.

Her fingers unbuttoned his shirt and pants. She then eased them down his arms and legs as she forced herself to slow the pace. When he was naked, Niah took her time tracing the lines of his body. Lou was all hills and valleys of solid muscle and raw power. His tanned skin made her think of caramel kisses, and her body remembered how it felt to have all that warm flesh against hers.

Then Lou took over, pressing his lips to hers he wrapped her up in his embrace. When he broke the kiss, her name was a whisper so full of need it raised gooseflesh on her arms. God, she could almost see the beast within staring back at her through those beautiful green eyes.

Her lioness responded with a soft roar even as she mentally lowered herself to her haunches, belly to the ground. She waited, willing and ready. Dew had gathered, thick and hot, at the entrance to her sex and she was more than ready to receive this man.

Niah raised a hand to touch him, but he backed up so fast he was gone before her fingers were in position to tease the soft curls on his chest.

"Lou?"

He swallowed. Hard. Then took a deep, determined breath before making clear his demands.

"Tell me what you want, Niah. Tell me, or this stops before it even gets started. God, even if it kills me."

"Tell you...? What? Why?" she asked quietly, forcing herself to meet the intensity of his gaze. "Why do I have to say it?"

"Because I have to know that you really want me. There is no way I can go forward unless I know that you won't regret it later. I can whip the biggest, baddest, rogue Were out there in a hand-to-hand fight, but when it comes to you, baby, you have more power over me than anyone or anything."

"Why?"

"Because you can hurt me, Niah."

"But..."

"No buts. Rejection from my woman, from you, would cut me off at the knees. It's...uncomfortable, being this vulnerable, but it is what it is. Now, tell me."

She opened her mouth, but the words were like dried kelp stuck to the mucous membranes in her throat.

He backed up another step. Panic filled her chest and spread down into her gut until it felt as if her entire upper body was being dive-bombed by something out of the Boeing catalog. Fucking 747s, perhaps.

The words tumbled out. "I want you, Lou."

He cocked his head and waited. She knew what he wanted. Could feel it in her bones.

So...she gave it to him, knowing that she was being honest

and truthful. "I want you, Ryland Lee Lewis. As my lover and my mate."

Then Lou was behind her, pressing her hands against the cool panes of the sliding glass doors. The light of the moon was fully upon them now and filled the room with its glow. The brilliance of it made her think of how Lou's presence lit up her soul, made her glow from the inside out.

Lou tucked his engorged cock between her thighs. Her sex pulsed in anticipation, but he was nowhere near inside her. Heat radiated from the smooth, tender skin of his erection, setting her core ablaze.

He tugged and teased her nipples, until the globes of her breasts were swollen and heavy. The delicious sensation of him twisting the little berries, combined with the weight of his cock between her thighs, disintegrated what control she had left.

"Oh, please. Please, Lou. Inside."

"God, I thought you'd never ask," he growled into her ear as he repositioned himself with a swift move, then surged up and into her ready sex.

She'd died. She must have...because this was pure heaven.

7

*S*he was awakened by the shifting of a heavy arm draped over her ribs. Niah sat up and looked out into the darkness. They'd left the curtains drawn when they'd fallen into sated sleep. Now, the sky was just beginning to lighten from the deepest black to a beautiful, deep blue. A deep breath and a stretch of the person attached to that arm told her Lou was coming awake. She turned her head, taking a moment to simply watch him. Watching the muscle of his forearm flex just a bit as he tightened his hold on her. Watching dark auburn lashes slowly raise as his sleepy emerald gaze landed on her face. Watching one side of his mouth lift in a sexy half-grin as he rolled over and took her with him.

Niah found herself draped over a very awake Lou, if the pole of flesh pressing into her groin was any indication.

"It's barely five a.m. but you're ready for sex?" She tried to sound annoyed. Really. She did. His chuckle made it clear she'd fallen awfully short.

"What can I say, darlin'? You have it like I need it, Niah."

"And my being naked, lying skin-to-skin has nothing to do with it, eh?"

The man was smart—he didn't answer her question. Instead he grinned, raised his head and nipped her playfully beneath the jaw as his hands went on a journey from shoulder to butt and back.

God, he had such nice hands. Big. Strong. Work-roughened. Just enough to rasp over her bare skin without scratching yet left no doubt he'd been there. He made a trail of barely-stinging bites as he kissed along her neck.

And then he hit *that* spot and she gasped aloud.

"Oh, I found something, didn't I?" he asked with a dose of mischief in his tone.

When she didn't respond, he nipped her there again.

"God!"

"So, tell me about this spot, Niah."

Not a chance. It was the one, very small, and precise, area on her neck that could send her up in flames.

This time instead of using his teeth, he latched on and sucked until she panted, squirmed and gasped.

"Oh God!"

Then she was hissing and writhing, trying to get up on her knees to get Lou's morning erection where she really wanted it. Let's face it, she was far from wanting it. She *needed* him. Right now.

Damn the man. He held her tight and exactly where she was until she was pushing against his chest trying to move, trying to press her hips to his. Trying to...anything!

Finally he let up on teasing her and said, "I think you just told me everything I need to know about that spot, except one thing."

"What's that?" she panted.

"Do you have one on the other side?"

But instead of giving her time to respond, he feasted. The answer? Yes, that damn spot had a twin on the other side of her neck, barely an inch and a half from where neck met shoulder. And he zeroed in on it like a precision weapon.

The second his hot tongue lapped over the skin, she lost it. Only, this time, he let her move, let her position herself with a knee on either side of his waist, breasts plastered against his chest as he continued to lick and suck at her tender skin.

Hands slid down her spine, slipped down and around until fingers were parting her. She should have been embarrassed at how slick and wet she was, but with Lou she was always wet.

"Mmm, just the way I like you, soaked and ready for me."

And she was definitely both of those things. And he was moving too damn slow.

"Inside. Now. Please."

He nuzzled her ear and said, "Oh, it's like that?"

"Yes." No hesitation. No second thoughts.

"In that case," he growled as the fingers poised at her entrance sank deep inside. In seconds, Niah's soft pants became needy moans.

"Oh yes. More. Please."

He never let up on the attention he gave that sensitive area on her neck as fingers pumped furiously inside now. Thighs trembled. Breath soughed in and out of her lungs. Sweat gathered behind her knees. Close. She was so very close.

"I feel you tightening on my fingers. Ready to come, darlin'?"

She couldn't talk. Couldn't get her brain to form the words. All she could do was gasp, roll her hips to the rhythm he set with his fingers as they slid in and out of her body. Then his thumb came into play and nudged the bundle of nerves at her core.

Niah tumbled into an orgasm so powerful, the ability to think past the pleasure was impossible.

Lou finally released his hold on her neck and sat up as he kissed his way down to her breasts. He inhaled the scent of her skin as he moved deliberately and oh-so-slowly. He breathed her in and then slowly let the air leave his lungs. Niah trembled as the small puffs passed over her sweat-dampened skin.

Her head fell back when his lips finally latched onto a ready nipple. Tongue and teeth played with one berry while thumb and forefinger twisted the other.

"You taste and smell so good, Niah. I could eat you all day."

He'd never get a complaint out of her on that score. But the heat that had been cooled by her first orgasm was quickly reigniting.

"Lou?"

"Mmm...?"

"Please. I need you..."

It was as far as she got before she was flipped onto her stomach and arranged to his liking, which happened to be her liking as well—on her knees with a cheek resting on the cool sheets of their bed, and her ass up in the air with Lou's hard cock pushing inside. The plum-like crown breached the tight ring of muscles, eased along by the dew of her arousal.

Fingers gripped her hips and Lou pistoned into her. And it was just what she needed. She'd had a lovely orgasm courtesy of his fingers, but now she needed him to fuck her like only a mate could.

Teeth found their way back to her shoulder and clamped down on *that* spot again. Pleasure was a momentary flash of pain that whipped through her nervous system as Lou plowed deep. His teeth held her in place as his velvety-steel cock tapped the entrance to her womb as he rode her from behind.

In moments, they followed each other over the edge of that fantastical cliff of lush bliss that surpassed that of mere lovers.

When she lay lax in his arms, his very simple, "Good morning, darlin'," filled her with a contentment beyond words. So instead of responding, Niah drifted back to sleep with a smile and a soft sigh as Lou gathered her up against his body.

"It's almost noon. Ready to get up?" Lou asked, nudging the jaw of a sleepy Niah with the tip of his nose.

"Mmmmnnnhhh."

Snore.

"Does that mean, no?" He laughed. Niah after fantastic sex, but before coffee was an adorable but disgruntled pile of lazy flesh and bones. "Come on, hon, let's get you into the shower."

Lou shook his head when the only response he got was a pillow to the face as Niah yanked the covers back over her head.

But there was more than one way to skin a cat. So he ducked into the bathroom, flipped on the shower and then returned for his mate, whom he literally dragged out of bed—blankets, pillows and all.

When they climbed out of the oversized shower, Lou pulled on a pair of shorts, left Niah to dress and headed to the dining room where an impressive spread waited for them. Today they had beef tar-tar—a fancy way of saying thinly sliced, raw steak —with an array of peeled fruits, including three kinds of citrus and cubed breadfruit. There was also, he noticed with a smile, a full pot of strong black coffee for Niah.

The caretakers of this little hideaway did not disappoint— they'd better not, since Neesia had actually selected them from their staff at Pryde Ranch, but he wasn't going to tell Niah that. Besides, she was an intelligent woman with the keen, logical mind of a superior hunter. Lou was sure she'd already figured it out.

He sat down at the table and a moment later the object of his desire walked into the room.

Grub? Check. Coffee? Check. Niah dressed in the sexiest bathing suit he'd seen on a woman? Definitely double check.

And boy did he have plans for his formerly-reluctant mate today.

After they shared a quick meal, he stood and said, "Just leave the dishes. The staff will take care of them for us."

"Funny, but I haven't seen anyone but us since we got here."

"That's the point, darlin'. You're not supposed to see them. We're supposed to feel completely alone so we can enjoy our time together. But no shifting."

"What? Why? Look, I haven't seen anyone but I know what, or rather who, I smell. The staff is from Pryde Ranch. They know what we are."

On vacation or not, they never stopped being shifters. Their sense of smell was so keen, Lou was sure that while half-asleep Niah had been totally aware of who'd been preparing their meal while pillow-bashing him on the way into the shower an hour ago.

"True, but I promised to keep your family secret. As long as we're away from home, no shifting. Period. I don't want to risk you being seen by anyone."

Niah's grunt of understanding was welcome. He didn't want her to think he was hiding her away, even if that's exactly what he was doing.

As they headed out the door and towards the boat waiting at their private dock, she asked, "But what if the staff is perving? You know, watching us when we think they're not? Kinda like when we're at home?"

She was kidding, of course, and they both laughed at the thought as they headed out for some post-brunch fun.

Contrary to popular belief, cats were very good swimmers and Lou couldn't wait to get Niah wet. The woman had a body like no one's business—curvy, lush, and strong. Beautiful, caramel skin was set off by the orange-coral color of her two-piece swimsuit. He liked that the top was more of a tank-like thing rather than a couple of bits of string that bared her goodies to the world.

Thick, curly hair was pulled back into a neat ponytail and

showed off the light amber of her eyes and those feline cheekbones she couldn't quite hide even in her human skin.

Such a lovely female, his Niah. But what the woman didn't
do nearly enough of...was play. So that's exactly what they were
going to do even if it killed them.

Up on the rear deck of their boat with her face lifted to the early
afternoon sun, Niah closed her eyes a moment and enjoyed the
whoosh of the warm breeze as they cut quietly through the
water. This place was beyond beautiful. The difference between
the lighter turquoise of the water near the lagoon's edge and the
deeper blues of the ocean was quite marked. Welcome was the
humidity that clung to her skin and the scent of brine that
tickled her nose. The scents and sounds reminded Niah that she
was more than an accomplished geek—though geeks ruled the
world, of course. But in this place, she was also a creature of
nature, both nurturing and primal.

The sudden urge to play with her mate in her pelt had her
smiling, even as she forced back the change and kept her human
skin on.

The boat was a large, powerful craft, at least forty feet long
for sure, with cabins below and a raised navigation hub. It cut
smoothly through the sea towards their destination, wherever
that was.

After watching the blue of the water go by outside the reef
for about a mile or so, Niah shifted in the arms of her man and
turned to look up at him.

Her man.

Wow. Words she'd never thought to say, let alone mean. But
there was no use denying it—Lou was, indeed, hers.

"What's on your mind, beautiful? Ah, now there's the smile I
love to see."

And it was something she rarely gave anyone but her sisters because at home was where she was truly happy. But it was a relief to learn that Lou could also make her happy if she only let him. It might not seem logical but it didn't make it any less true.

"Just wondering where we're headed."

"No need to wonder. We're here."

"Uh, but there's nothing here. I don't see anything but water."

"That's because water is all you need for this activity."

Then she looked up to see some of the crew emerge from the cabin with stuff she hadn't laid eyes on since her growing-up years.

The man had taken her fishing! Sport fishing of all things.

"I know I have Koreas to thank for this. There is no way you could have known that I love fishing! Haven't been in..."

"Too long, Niah. We both know you're overdue for some relaxation."

Wasn't that the truth?

"God, you're such a sweetie. Stop making me think about stuff," she grumbled while choosing which station she was going to fish from. Thankfully, the poles were large enough for big fish and could be mounted on the railings so she didn't have to worry about losing one in the water if she got a bite while she was distracted.

"What do you mean, Ni?"

Ni? Heh, she liked that. Only her sisters had ever used her nickname. So a nickname from a guy? *Her* guy? Too cute. Anyway...

"I was thinking about how long it's been since my last vacation and realized that my sisters have been physically hauling my ass off of Pryde Ranch for the last ten years. Basically, they *made* me take time off. And even then, I'd find something that needed fixing, or doing, or whatever. It was easy to lose myself in work."

"Why is that, Niah? What's with the work, work, work?"

"It's all I've ever done. Never had a reason to turn it off. I work with my sisters, whether it's on a hunt for S.W.A.T. or at home. I'm good at it. And it's what I do to take care of my family. Family is all I've got, Lou. And I want to take care of them. It's important to me."

"Yeah, but there's more to it than that. I can feel it."

This mate stuff was going to tell all her secrets, wasn't it? Damn it. But she kept her mouth closed, pretending to look through the little booklet that showed the different kinds of fish she could catch.

"Okay, since you're not talking, I'll talk. Stubborn woman. You deserve more than working all the time. Your family wants you to have a life. I want you to have a life. Too bad I had to kidnap you to prove it to you. Then again, you in that swimsuit is a lovely sight I'm sure I'd never see in Wyoming this time of year. Bottom line is, there's no reason why you can't have your sisters and a mate, Niah."

He'd hit the nail on the head. Several nails actually.

"Of course I hit the nail on the head," Lou laughed.

Smart ass.

"I think I'm going to like this mating business," he teased, then kissed her playfully behind the ear.

"Well, just remember that this shit works both ways." And she was amazingly happy about it, which was totally illogical. "You're lucky I've experienced this mate stuff when Neesia met Jason, otherwise I'd chalk this giddy-goofy-emotional stuff up to a case of bad takeout, stud."

"As long as I'm *your* stud, it'll be no hardship. I like knowing what you need, Niah. I want to give it to you. And if you think about it, or *feel* about it, you want to let me."

Jerk.

"I felt that, too, darlin'." Followed by another kiss, this one on the neck as he eased her towards a large, leather chair. "From here you can cast your line, sip sparkling water, eat like a cow...er, lioness, and settle into the company of your man."

And Niah totally enjoyed herself.

In fact, she squealed like a little girl when she caught a tuna, even though it was only big enough to throw back into the ocean. Luckily, Lou snagged a Mahi Mahi that could feed a small army and she looked forward to enjoying it for dinner. If they'd been in their pelts they could have devoured it on the spot. Then again, the thought of maneuvering around all those little bones gave her pause. There was a reason why lions preferred big game.

They were almost back to the bungalow when Lou slipped his arms around her waist from behind and gave her something she couldn't resist—a challenge.

"We're almost home. Race you to the dock?"

"Tempting. What do I get when I win?" she asked with a cocky grin.

"You win, I'll rub you down with some of that coconut stuff in that toiletry bag your sisters sent with you. What do I get when you lose?" he asked, sly intent written all over his face.

"Lose?" she scoffed. "I won't lose."

"Really? You sure about that, darlin'?"

"I'm so sure I'll win that you can spank my ass purple if I don't."

She bit back a belly laugh at the way his eyes lit up and his brows flew upward on his face. And then he was moving at top speed, stripping off his shorts as he went. Bare-assed naked, Lou stood at the ready...in more ways than one.

"Can you swim with that cock of yours weighing you down?"

He flashed a grin that was nothing but the baring of canines as he called the captain via intercom.

Niah couldn't take her eyes off of him. He knew exactly what she was thinking and his grin—along with the erection waving at the fish—grew as she stared.

"Captain, you can stop and drop anchor. We're going to swim in from here." Then he covered the mouthpiece and asked if she wanted to fish again tomorrow. At her eager nod he continued, "Please deliver the staff to their bungalow after we disembark. We'll see you in the morning for another go at the marlin that escaped us today."

"Will do, sir. See you in the morning."

The engine cut and the boat slowed, then drifted a few moments before finally halting.

Lou was at the back of the boat, ready to dive.

God, the man was just too damn gorgeous for words. Packed muscle flexed on his chest and back as he readied himself. His ass, which was pure perfection, flowed down to sculpted thighs. Hell, even his feet were pretty.

A breeze ruffled unruly, dark brown curls just as he snapped her out of her ogling.

"Come on, woman, hurry up. I have a spanking to deliver."

She laughed, stepped up next to him and stuck out her tongue. Without another word, she dove into the water and swam for it.

---

8

*N*iah had learned on her last bounty assignment that Lou fought dirty. A gorgeous hunk of male perfection, cunning and relentless when in pursuit of a goal, but his ruthlessness had never been directed at her. So when he'd challenged her to a race from the fishing boat to the bungalow she'd expected to simply swim for it and let her sleeker body give her an advantage in the water. Kind of like pitting a nimble seal against a killer whale. Nine times out of ten, the seal would win the match by out-maneuvering his opponent.

It was a great strategy...and she'd quickly found its flaw.

The man had used his stronger legs to dive farther away from the boat, then when she'd caught up to him, he'd grabbed at various body parts to keep her from pulling ahead. In the end, he'd played so dirty she came up sputtering and laughing at the absurdity of it all. When she'd finally stopped coughing and giggling, Lou was sitting on the edge of the dock in front of their thatch-roofed bungalow, grinning.

Finally up the ladder of the pier, she walked past him without a word and headed inside, where she stripped out of her wet bathing suit and hit the shower to wash off the salt of the ocean. Wrapped in a damp towel and still inwardly beaming at the genius of her mate, she headed into the living area and spied him pouring wine in the kitchen.

She dropped the towel.

The wine stopped mid-pour.

Once at the loveseat, she bent over the back of the couch, bared herself and waited. After all, a girl was only as good as her word.

"Mmm, look what the cat dragged in," Lou drawled. His swim trunks hit the floor and he walked around her like a shark circling a juicy meal. Hmmm. Maybe she should have reconsidered her analogy—seals had a pretty good survival rate against killer whales...but against sharks? Not so much.

Damn.

Lou's warm hands traveled up her back and the scent of coconut filled the air.

Mmm, his fingers felt heavenly as they spread the oil over her damp skin. "I thought I only got a massage if I won the race," she sighed.

"I don't recall saying that was the only way to get a massage. Besides, by the time I lay my hand to your beautiful ass I want you begging for it, not tolerating it because you lost."

"Cocky son of a...oooh."

Lou's fingers sank into the flesh at her shoulders and soothed a particularly tight muscle. God, that felt good. She started to move so she could lay down on the loveseat rather than over the side of it.

"No, no. Stay right there. Head down, ass up. Perfect position for a massage, don't you think?"

He continued to rub the coconut oil from shoulders to knees, careful to avoid her butt while touching her everywhere else. Her thighs trembled from the sensual torture of his hands sliding up and down, from the front of her legs around to the back only to dip into the hollow below her ass cheeks so he could tease her sex with his fingers. Then, as he made each round, he began to deliver small smacks to her ass.

"Just warming you up, hon."

Lips and teeth met her skin, sucked on *that* spot on her neck. Moved along her spine. Kissed each rib.

Now the smacks on her ass were firmer. The sting left behind was just this side of pleasure with the slightest edge of pain—exquisite though diametrically opposed. It made her so wet and needy, her body pulsed. And then Lou got down to work, spanked her until her skin was aflame under his hand and she did exactly what he said she would—she begged for it.

Squirming, trying to get closer while trying to get away, Niah cried out for more. And then those cries became demands for his cock. When he didn't give it to her, she turned, growled at him and then let the change bubble up just enough to elongate her fangs...which she promptly snapped in his direction.

"Oh, I think you just earned a punishment, darlin'."

Niah didn't care. She needed him inside like she needed coffee in the morning. Like a scuba diver needed air. Like...like... God, was there anything that could truly compare to her hunger for this man?

No. Not anymore.

She pictured the last of her doubts being swept out of the bungalow on a late afternoon breeze to drown in the ocean outside their door. And then Niah let herself fall open to Lou.

The second she surrendered, Lou's need flashed into the little corner of her mind where he'd begun to take up residence since he'd waltzed onto Pryde Ranch.

The man was a worthy mate. Her lioness rolled against her skin in acceptance. There was no need to go through hell and high water before she finally acknowledged that nature had indeed given him to her.

After all, her own family had set her up for some alone time with Lou, and there was no one she trusted more than her sisters...except for herself. Instinct and the newly forming bond said he was hers, with all his heart and soul.

His desire flowed into her head, thick and sweet, yet raw, kind of like new honey. His body was hard as his damn head—stubborn males of the world unite—and his skin was as warm as his heart.

And the man was on fire with longing, just as she was.

"Lou, please. I need it."

Without another word, he tucked himself against her gate and sank inside.

"God, yes," she yelled, uncaring of whether the people on the other side of the island heard her or not. Besides, Lou riding her from behind was a glorious thing, meant to be shared with the world.

From the loveseat, to the floor, to the bedroom, Niah took all he had to give and gave back in turn. They made love until they were both little more than worn-out dishrags.

Her last thought as she drifted off to sleep in Lou's arms was how much she loved worn-out dishrags.

After a lovely late afternoon nap, complete with sex-and-humidity-induced sweat and a bit of snoring, Niah looked out the window and sighed. She was content to just gaze out at the stars as they hung up in the black. Amazing how dark it got out here without the contamination of artificial light from nearby cities. The pale glow of the moon reflected off the dark waters and practically lit up the room with its brightness.

And she was...happy. Happy to lay next to her mate. Happy to breathe the fresh air wafting in through the wall of screened windows. Happy to wince as she sat up and discovered her ass was on fire. Lovely, glorious fire where Lou had taken his time turning it to what must surely be a lovely shade of red.

Rustling sheets said Lou had come awake. The mattress shifted under his weight as he rolled over and pulled her into his arms so she could lay her head on his chest.

And with her acceptance of him, their bond was solidifying, joining them together in a way reserved only for mates. They would always be able to find each other, speak privately to one another, and know each other's needs and desires.

"*Something wrong, sweetheart?*" he asked sleepily, gliding his hand over her tender skin. And she so liked the way his firm fingers felt easing over her ass.

"*No, nothing wrong, but that's the last time I offer up my ass as the prize for any bet. In fact I'll never bet you again that you can spank me if...hell, screw ifs. Never again.*"

"*Spoilsport much?*"

"*Uh...*" No comment. Besides, he knew she'd enjoyed receiving it as much as he'd loved dishing it out.

Lou laughed out loud. The sound made her happy through and through. However, the next sound? Not so much.

"Can't you change that tweeting to a normal ringtone or something? Who is calling you this late anyway?" She grumbled as she rolled over and snatched his cell phone off her nightstand —what was it doing on her side of the bed anyway?—and tried to kill the angry bird that was supposed to be a ringtone.

"Stop smacking it. Just pass it to me already." Cell in hand, he answered, "Lou here. Oh, hi, Neesia. Yep, she's right here. Just a moment."

Niah sat up in a rush and grabbed the phone. "Hey, Neecie. What's up? Everything okay?"

"Yep, everything is fine but life is intruding on your little Shangri-La. Bounty just came in, and it happens to be on your side of the world. Harry can have the jet there in the morning to pick you up. You game?"

She looked over to Lou and grinned as he said silently, "*Whatever it is, I'm game as long as we can do it together.*"

"We're in," Niah replied with a lot more pep than she'd expected considering they hadn't had dinner yet at almost midnight.

"We?" Neesia questioned. Niah caught the bit of snarky humor in her twin's voice. It was nice to hear. Nice to be proven wrong in regard to her take on "that mate business". Nice to be loved both here and at home.

"Yes, *we*, Neecie. Besides, I'm pretty sure Lou's sick leave is up anyway."

"Hey, how did you know about that?" Neesia squeaked through the phone as Lou's mouth fell open in disbelief. "Lou only told me, Jason and the twins about that. You were deliberately left out of that particular loop, missy."

"I'm a genius, remember? Now, what's the bounty?" Niah asked her sister as Lou whispered into her mind, *"I can't wait to hunt, live and love with you, woman. I simply can't wait."*

And just like that, Niah Pryde's life became as perfect as perfect could be.

PURSUIT OF PRIDE AND PLEASURE

---

1

*H*air still damp from the shower, Jason DiCaplis walked into the football field his wife called a kitchen. And there she stood, the apple of his eye. And she was a total wreck. Instead of greeting her with a playful nip and a hug from behind, as was his habit, he wisely kept his mouth shut and stayed out of biting distance. Given her current mood, he'd just grab a quick snack and a cup of hot coffee and get out of her hair.

He yanked open the doors to one of the huge stainless steel refrigerators when a sting radiated across his left butt cheek.

He cocked his head at his wild-eyed mate. "Ow, woman! What the hell are you thinking?" He hopped back in time to avoid the tip of another expertly snapped towel.

"This is a big deal, and you're moving too slow. Clear out so I can get on with... God, I don't know how I'm going to have everything ready by the time they get here. I haven't even finished all the prep and the staff are all doing other tasks so I don't have any one to *mise en place* for me and..."

Really? Neesia had them all in the kitchen late last night slaving away over the ingredients she needed for the clan-sized meal she'd planned. All four of the Pryde sisters, plus himself and all the household staff had been called in. Even their pilot, Harry, had been recruited. They'd sliced, diced and cut both themselves and the mountain of veggies, fruit, seafood, and whatever else Neesia cracked the whip about for this week's visitors.

"Neesia, we did food prep for at least a hundred people just last night. I only have four friends coming."

"But the scientists coming to work with K and K…"

"Rescheduled, remember? We'll have a total of ten people, not a whole malnourished rugby team. This is fucking ridiculous, Neesia. I don't like it when you worry this way."

Oooh, wait a minute. Said bustling woman wore the little green silk robe he loved, the one that fell just below her hips and left most of her thighs bare.

Forget breakfast. Neesia looked good enough to eat.

With one hand, he rubbed the welt forming under his shorts while trying to wrap the other around the frazzled female bustling about the kitchen.

"Jason, stop it. I'm nowhere near done and they'll be here this afternoon. Damn it, damn it, damn it."

"Neesia?"

No answer. She'd wiggled out of his arms and buried her head in the freezer.

"Neesia?"

A bag of frozen prawns and some carrots crashed to the floor as she snatched and tossed various items in a flurry of movement. Okay, enough was enough.

"Neesia!"

"What!"

He eased her back and away from the fridges, freezers, and anything else that was stainless steel and involved with cooking.

"Look, these are my friends. My family. You don't have to go through all this stress. They're going to love you."

"But they're important to you. Cooking for them is a big deal, damn it! I want it to be perfect!"

"Neesia, you're yelling. And your hair is all over your head from running your hands through it. If you pull any out, I'm telling you now, I'm going to be very upset with you. If you're going to be bald, it should be all over rather than just one spot in the top of your head."

His words earned the chuckle he was after.

After all, Jason understood where she was coming from. Cooking for her family was important to her. It was an expression of love into which she put her all, but this was fucking nuts. The woman was wearing herself to a nub over pleasing his friends. And while Jason was flattered that she cared enough to go to these lengths simply because these people meant a lot to him, he was not pleased that she was weirding out over it. Nobody, not even the James boys, were worth risking her sanity. And if Jason prided himself on anything, it was taking care of his mate.

When she wouldn't stop squirming and trying to get back to the damned fridge, his patience slipped. A deep feline growl pushed its way past his throat and reverberated around the stadium-sized kitchen. Neesia immediately stilled and cocked an eyebrow at him.

"Are you growling at me, Jason DiCaplis?"

"I'm going to do more than growl if you don't stop this madness. Relax, or else." The firm grip he had on her shoulders eased as the tips of his fingers traipsed down to her wrist to hold her still. Leaning in, he inhaled his favorite fragrance—the natural scent at the nook of her neck. God, the woman smelled so good. And it always drove him wild. Especially when the aroma of her sex blended into the mix.

And he knew how to make her cream in record time. Knew exactly what she liked and how she liked it.

"Damn it, Jason. Not now," she semi-demanded and tried to

push him away, but her fingers flexed on his bare chest and then played in the sprinkle of hair there.

"Now is the perfect time. I think you're overdue for a bit of stress relief."

Cradling the back of her head, Jason held Neesia in place as he gently kissed her lips. Well, it started out gentle, anyway, but in mere seconds, the attempt at seduction grew into flat-out raunchy need. The need to devour rather than simply taste. The need to rut rather than distract. Bottom line—Neesia simply brought the freak out in him.

"I love this robe. Especially if you're naked under it." Because when she bent at the waist, her pretty pussy was fully accessible and the silk was light enough to allow full stimulation of her breasts without her having to be completely nude given they were, after all, in the kitchen.

Roughly tonguing the dense muscle at the juncture of her neck, Jason bit down and couldn't suppress the moan of pleasure at his mate's gasp. Neesia's fingers stilled then plucked a tight male nipple. He returned the favor, tugging and twisting on her tightening berries until she leaned into him for more.

Neesia's breasts were perfect, weighty and her Hershey Kiss peaks were extremely sensitive and as responsive as the rest of her. Occasionally, Neesia liked her love play gentle and sweet, but the majority of the time she was a wildcat in the sack. His goal right now was to bring kitty out to play.

With a deft move, Jason had her turned around, her chest pressed down to the gourmet block in the middle of the kitchen. His fingers slid up her thigh to palm her fabulous round ass, while the other eased around her front to play in the short cropped curls between her legs. The silky smoothness of her skin sent his inner beast rolling around inside of him, eager to get out.

"Jason, you're trying to distract me." Her breathing deepened as fingertips curled against the granite tiles of the counter top.

"Yes, I am. Is it working?"

Another gasp, accompanied by the little swivel of her hips when he ground his engorged cock against her beautiful backside, said what her mouth would not.

After a few deep breaths, she finally said, "No. It's not working." Then her hips pushed back against him as her eyelids slipped closed. "What about Niah and…"

"All three of your sisters are across the estate in the labs. Niah's doing an upgrade on the servers, and the twin mad scientists are hard at work in anticipation of their fellow mad scientists' arrival which, may I remind you, has been postponed," he said. Easing his shorts down over his erection, Jason almost groaned with relief when cool air caressed his flaming hard on.

"But what if Broglio walks in here? I, oooh…" she purred. "God, how do you always manage to drive me nuts? You get under my skin so much I can't ever stay mad at you, even when you deserve it."

Shorts in a heap on top of his feet, Jason slid back and forth against his wife's slickening folds. He hissed between his teeth at the contact—the heat, the gathering of warm dew at her gate. "Broglio went out early to get some last minute maintenance done around the property *and* get away from you for a while. As for nuts, mine could use some relief. We drive each other crazy, agreed?"

"Oh, yes. I totally agree." With that she reached down, spread her own slick cream over her sex and welcomed him inside.

Not one to pass up such a delicious invitation, Jason slid slowly home in one long, deliciously agonizing stroke. Then he stayed until his woman was good and relaxed, and purred like the good little kitty she was.

"Damn it, Tara, can you talk to Erin again? She left a sample in the pre-bio lab again. Shay found it this morning when he went in early to clean the tanks. Luckily it was nothing toxic to either species." Meaning shifter nor human was in danger. Luckily.

"Are you kidding me? Again?" Kotara replied. "I'm seriously shaking my head here. I know she's the absent minded professor type, but I'm tempted to ship her off to the other side of the labs to sweep up skin cells with a toothbrush or something just to keep her out of trouble."

The Pryde labs were state of the art research and development facilities full of brilliant human scientists—some of which were also a bit on the goofy side.

After making a note to smack Dr. Erin around for being so careless, Kotara Pryde turned to her spitting image, Koreas, and tried for the four-hundredth time to convince her of what she needed. Though she was the eldest of their twin set by only five minutes, it still made her the oldest. And as such, it was her duty to try and see her sister happy. Koreas' love life needed some serious assistance and Kotara was determined to give it to her, whether she liked it or not.

"Kory, we should go out salsa dancing tonight."

"What are you, crazy?" her sister responded with barely any inflection. "We have scientists flying in from Japan in a few days. We haven't even finished arranging all the samples or running the control charts on the data. Thanks to a certain someone." Koreas looked over her shoulder to Niah Pryde, whose head was buried in a rack full of computers, cables and wires.

"I heard that, cub," Niah said around a very bored-sounding yawn. "I'm working as fast as I can. Don't like it? Do it yourself."

"Damn it, Kory, don't you dare piss her off," Kotara replied, not bothering to keep her voice down. Besides, Niah would hear her anyway. Every lioness had exceptional hearing. "It's nobody's fault that our last bounty took longer than anticipated and we're all running behind. If Niah doesn't finish upgrading the database and statistical computation servers, we won't have the bandwidth to finish crunching the numbers in time."

"Hmmpf," was Koreas' only response.

"Come on, let's go out tonight. We haven't been out of these labs in forever. And yes, while I love my work, I also love shaking my ass on the dance floor. I could also use a good hard run in my pelt and an even harder bout of raunchy, toe curling sex."

Koreas gave a snarl in response.

"What?" Kotara demanded, head cocked to the side.

"What'd you have to go and mention sex for, Kotara Ann Pryde?"

Koreas had called her by her whole name? *So* not good.

"It's all I can do to keep my head on straight since Neesia mated. She walks around reeking of sex all the time now. And Jason is no better. Not only is he gorgeous, but he smells like her. She smells like him. It drives me nuts."

They both ignored Niah's muffled chuckle.

"All the more reason to get out tonight," Kotara said. "We obviously both need it considering just the sight of the two of them together, knowing they've been screwing like bunnies, er, lions makes me horny half the time, and jealous the other. Don't get me wrong, I'm happy for our big sis, but all of us are well past the time when we could take a mate. I'm so ready for a mate. I want to smell like some-fucking-body, too."

"Oh shut up already," Niah laughed. "You two sound like nymphos during dry humping season."

"You should talk," the younger Prydes said in unison. "You got to fuck Jason when you were in heat."

"You know it was one time, and only because it was biologically necessary." Jason's arrival at Pryde Ranch had thrown both Neesia *and* Niah into heat all at once. "Look on the bright side."

Kotara raised her eyebrows. "And which side is that, exactly?" She knew she was being snarly but she just couldn't help it. Niah had just come home from what turned out to be her honeymoon. Her new mate, courtesy of a well-executed, family arranged kidnapping, was Ryland Lee Lewis—Lou for short. Niah had been so convinced that Neesia's mating had been a fluke that she'd almost missed out on her own dude. Since she hadn't believed that Lou could possibly be hers, the man had plotted with the Pryde family to whisk Niah away long enough to convince her that she was being boneheaded.

The result—Niah was happily mated to the sweetest, cutest, most stubborn, country-bred, corn fed lion shifter in all of creation. Who'd have thought that lions and cowboys could inhabit the same body? Charm didn't begin to describe Lou, and the way his dark hair and deeply tanned skin set off his bright green eyes was just too much. He was, in short, a stunner.

It also meant now they had two couples in the house...and more sex hormones floating around. Gah!

"At least we know there are mates out there somewhere for you. Before Jason and Lou, we were all resigned to remaining alone because we had yet to meet anyone genetically compatible. Admit it, before those two legends of hotness, we didn't even know there were other lion shifters in this country."

Well, couldn't argue with that...but she didn't have to like it.

All three heads swiveled around when the thick glass double doors to the inner labs eased open.

"Hey, ladies."

Kotara and Koreas groaned aloud. Why? Jason's potent scent, layered under coconut lotion, wafted into the space courtesy of their sister, Neesia. Shit. It didn't matter that she'd undoubtedly showered after her recent romp, pheromones just didn't wash off. They lingered. Perhaps they could bottle the stuff and market it as Instant Horny. The four sisters were already worth millions, why not add to the family legacy?

"What the hell is wrong with you guys?" Neesia asked.

"Nothing." Two identical synthetic grins appeared as Kotara and Koreas took shallow breaths and tried their best to ignore their current circumstances. Niah was immune now that she'd mated. Lucky bitch.

Neesia shook her head at them and gave a "you guys are so weird" frown as she said, "I just came to tell you that Jason's friends will be here in a few hours. Can you guys come on up to the house and meet them?"

"I'm all done, so sure, I can come," Niah replied with a grunt as she stood, dusted off her spotless jumpsuit and hefted her gear bag full of tools and wires and crap over her shoulder.

"Kotara and I aren't quite ready for the arrival of the scientists from Japan. We're just going to push through a few more tasks tonight and we'll meet up with you all in the morning."

"Oh, didn't you get the message?" Neesia asked.

"What message?" asked Kotara and her sister, in sync.

"The project parameters changed. I spoke with the procurement department of the firm we're doing the analytics for and they said the drug didn't get approval. So, we'll have to do the modeling on another drug, which means…"

"Yeah, we know," said Kotara. "Start from scratch with negotiations, redo the contracts and put together a new proposal. Blah, blah, blah."

"Yep," sighed Koreas. "Well, let's finish up anyway, then we can take a break starting tomorrow. We may be able to use some of these protocols for whatever bio compound we work up for them on the renegotiated project. Work for you, Tara?"

"Yep. Okay with you, Neesia?"

"Sure. I know this is important so I'm not going to bug you about not coming to meet Jason's friends right now. By the way, one of them is a shifter. A female jaguar. She's mated to Aaron James."

"Wait, I thought Jason's best friends were human. The jaguar is mated to…a human?" Koreas wondered aloud.

"Yep. All three brothers are fully human. There's Aaron, of course, then there's Anthony and Austin James, both single. I met them on web chat with Jason the other night. Good god, they are so damn hunky it's not even funny." Neesia rolled her eyes up to the ceiling and offered a kiss to God in appreciation of, as she called them, "those James boys."

"I'll explain your absence, though they know you're working on a project right now. And just be comfortable around them. They've known Jason forever and they know all about our kind because of that friendship. I don't have all the details but they're aware of our origins."

Kotara tilted her head in curiosity. "They must be the epitome of special if Jason trusts them with such knowledge." Most humans were terrified of what they didn't understand, and because of that, S.W.A.T.—the Shifter and Were Armed Tactics agency—made sure that they all kept a low profile. Even when hunting weres-gone-bad, discretion was required. Yet these humans knew Jason was a lion and hadn't exposed him? They must be *beyond* special. Suddenly, meeting Jason's friends became a lot more interesting. Perhaps they might be able to fit in some fun sooner rather than later.

"I'll send Broglio down with some dinner for you. See you in the morning?"

"Wouldn't miss it, Neesia," Kotara grinned as she looked over to her twin, who seemed ambivalent at best.

Not a cheek was missed as the four sisters exchanged kisses and hugs. Neesia and Niah left the inner labs together. Kotara stood and listened for the almost undetectable whir-click that indicated the activation of the security system and automatic locks. The occasional light clink of Koreas handling the delicate glass vials containing their test specimens was the only other sound. Though they were alone, she didn't quite relax until the clunk of the double locks sounded as the steel hanger doors that led out of their state-of-the-art scientific sanctuary closed with a muted bank vault-type *kung*.

And still, the scent of sex and mating lingered.

Kotara's amber brown eyes met those of her twin, a woman who'd appeared to be working so diligently only seconds before. Now, both breathed deeply, let it out on a whoosh, screamed out their frustration to the rafters, and then laughed like loons.

Yes, they definitely needed to get out more.

2

*R*eya Daines-James sat across the large dining table from her mate, sipped a cup of delicious buttered rum and thought on the events of the day.

A few hours earlier, she'd hopped out of the SUV that had picked them up at the Pryde's private airstrip. The moment her feet hit the ground, Reya had taken a moment to stretch before twining her fingers in her husband's offered hand. Aaron had pulled her into a hug and said, "I can't wait for you to meet them, sweetheart. They're going to love you and you're going to love them."

Uh huh. Lions and jaguars weren't the best of friends in the wild, so Reya had hoped the human side of herself allowed her to make friends with these people. Aaron had then dropped a kiss on her forehead before his long legs ate up the distance across the front drive as he pulled her along.

She tried not to gawk but the main house they'd pull up to was quite impressive. It was the largest log-style chalet she'd ever seen. Three stories of light reddish-brown wood and huge panes of glass seemed to stretch out forever, all illuminated by the afternoon sun and framed by manicured lawns. The place had a certain peace about it that had seemed to welcome Reya personally.

And then at the foot of the wide stairs leading up to the wrap-around porch, Reya had come face to face with the matriarch of the family—Neesia Pryde.

The woman's dark-streaked auburn hair had been pulled up into a poufy ponytail with wisps of long natural curls framing her face. Dressed in jeans and a tank top, Neesia's smooth-looking skin reminded Reya of melted caramel.

"Welcome, all of you." Reya had taken the offered hand and shook it as she'd met Neesia's gaze. They were of similar height and build, but where Reya's eyes were a deep crystalline gray, Neesia's were like looking into pure amber of such a clear and light brown, they were mesmerizing. In a word—gorgeous. And on Neesia's left had been an exact copy of herself.

"This is my sister, Niah Pryde. Kotara and Koreas are working late in the labs so they'll be along in the morning."

Niah's smile dazzled as she'd nodded in greeting. The only way Reya could tell them apart was that instead of jeans and a tank top, Niah had worn a pair of black shit-kicker boots, a blue and gray plaid lumberjack shirt and black jeans laid over by doe-skin chaps the same whisky color of her and her sister's eyes. A totally dangerous geek, though the combination should have been an oxymoron.

"Hey, old man," Aaron had called out to the man standing alongside the Pryde women. "You're looking good in your old age, dude!"

"Get your ass over here so I can show you how an old man whips a younger one into the dirt," Jason said, all smiles. "Anthony, Austin, you, too."

Then they'd been a tangle of arms and legs as Aaron, Anthony and Austin James all tackled Jason DiCaplis on the front lawn at Pryde Ranch.

After the enthusiastic greetings and being shown to their

rooms for quick wash-ups, here they sat at dinner like civilized folks, rather than the most deadly creatures on Earth.

And within an hour of arrival, Reya Daines was ready to run for the hills. Any hill. In fact, the rolling prairie grass-covered ones just outside the nearest window would do quite nicely, thank you very much.

Reya wasn't sure what she'd expected, but this wasn't it. Given her brush with a crazy infanticidal father as a cub, followed by a lifetime of hiding her origins, *this* was extraordinary. Quite frankly, Reya just didn't know what to do with it. So she sat, enjoyed the meal, watched and listened.

In fact, some of their veterinary discoveries was the reason that Reya had recognized the Pryde name the moment her mate had mentioned it. But that was where her knowledge of this remarkable family ended.

She'd actually never met another shifter outside of her family. As a child, her aunt protected her by teaching her how to blend into human society. As an adult, she'd spent her years in the jungles of Belize building a successful bed and breakfast and medical facility. Until Aaron and his brothers, Reya's origins had remained a carefully guarded secret to all but her two closest friends. Even the rangers of the Cockscomb Jaguar Sanctuary didn't know she was one of the jaguars they were protecting.

So to walk into a house where everyone was a shifter, with the exception of the staff and her mate's human family, had Reya a bit on edge. No one threatened her or anything, but no one hid what they were.

At. All.

Occasional partial shifts with threats to bite one another in the butt seemed totally acceptable. Unpolished, perfectly manicured nails occasionally elongated in playful jabs—literally—at each other. Sure, her dude had told her the history of Jason and the Pryde family, but *hearing* about their normalcy as a pride of African lions and *seeing* it were two different things.

"Neesia, that was an awesome meal. I'd say I'm really sorry that your other sisters couldn't come up to join us, but it meant more food for me, so I'll just hold that thought," Austin said.

"Thank you. Anyone for dessert?" Neesia asked.

After lots of head nodding, she disappeared through a swinging door at the back of the room. A few moments later, a man named Broglio brought in a huge tray with a number of different beverages. Neesia was right behind him with short-cake, strawberries and whipped cream, as well as warm chocolate chip cookies with, of all things, strawberry bits and pecans in them.

The woman returned to her seat next to her mate, pecked him on the cheek and dished out the nom-noms. Reya didn't think there was room in her stomach for a single bite of anything more, but dessert smelled so good the traitorous organ seemed to stretch to accommodate the sweets.

The moan that followed a bite of a cookie was unavoidable. They were just so damn good. Even the blush that heated her cheeks from Aaron's wink in reaction to her moan didn't keep her from doing it again.

After a cookie or five, chased down with some strong hot coffee, Reya wiped her mouth with her napkin and sat back with a sigh. "God, these are so good, Neesia. I'm not much of a baker but I'd love to have the recipe and give it a try."

"I'm happy to share the love, hon." Neesia's smile was nothing short of devilish, and rightfully so. Thank god for an accelerated shifter metabolism because there was no doubt this entire meal would head straight for her hips.

"You know," Reya began feeling like a bit of a fan girl. "I've been wanting to tell you that you all have saved lives that you're probably unaware of."

"How so?" Niah asked before taking a big bite of shortcake smothered with fresh fruit and cream.

Reya thought about trying some of that cake. Instead of reaching for a slice, she asked, "You all discovered the cure for FIV, right?" FIV was the feline version of the HIV virus. "I oversaw the administration of that medicine to the entire jaguar population in the sanctuary park in Belize. Those cats who had the virus were cured. The rest were inoculated so they'll never get sick. At least not with FIV."

The sisters wore genuine smiles but said nothing. In this instance she could almost tell them apart. Neesia was the sweet but firm one so her smile was warm and welcoming. Niah was the logical geeky one and her grin was more of a "well, of course, just doing our job" sort of grin.

"Niah, I understand congratulations are in order?" Aaron added and lifted his mug in salute.

"Yep." And that was the end of the discussion. No one else seemed to think Niah's one-word response was odd behavior so Reya just rolled with it.

"Where's your mate? I hope to meet him before we go," Austin said.

"He's out on a bounty."

"Bounty?" Reya gulped, almost choking on her coffee.

"Yep. He's a hunter like the rest of us. Geez, Aaron, didn't you tell her anything?" Niah scolded.

"You mean other than you're a family of African lion shifters with the last name Pryde? No, not really. I figured you'd tell her what you wanted her to know. It wasn't my place to spill all of your business."

"Well, thanks, I guess. Anyway, my mate, Lou, is on a hunt for S.W.A.T. It's the Shifter and Were Armed Tactics agency. Basically we see to the needs of known shifters and hunt down the ones that go rogue."

Reya's head was suddenly so full of questions, she felt it tilt to the right and stick. "There's an agency for us? Are you seri-ous?" As realization dawned, she turned to her husband with a snarl. "And you knew all this time?"

Without an ounce of remorse, Aaron nodded, raised his mug and sipped. Reya sputtered and knew she sounded like an idiot but she just couldn't wrap her head around what she'd just learned. "How many people know about this agency? How many people know about you guys?"

Neesia set down her coffee, pinned Reya with a no-nonsense gaze and said, "Most shifters in the more populated areas know about S.W.A.T. but it's not an international agency. It's just here in the U.S. As for who knows about us, our family, specifically? Our mates and the people on this property. No one else. So for Jason to allow you to come here means we're trusting you with our lives. I'm okay with that because I trust my mate. The end."

Reya held that firm gaze. Understanding passed between her and the matriarch of this small but strong pride. After a moment of companionable silence with only the sounds of pouring coffee, crunching cookies and the clink of forks meet-ings plates, Reya asked another of about ten thousand questions she now had about a world she'd never known existed.

"But if S.W.A.T. takes care of the shifter community, why do you keep your family situation a secret?"

"The same reason we'll keep your existence a secret."

"But I don't have any secrets..."

"Yes, you do. Because in this country, jaguars are as tightly controlled as lions are," Niah replied. "It's because of our instinct to acquire territory. All the male lion shifters are closely monitored. In fact, they all work for S.W.A.T. in some form or another. As for the number of recorded lionesses, that would be zero."

"But how do you work for an agency that doesn't know you exist?"

"Our grandmother cut a deal with the agency when we were

little. In exchange for training and silence, we'd work for them and they would keep our names off the rolls. It was in their interest to recruit us. We were the only known lions at the time and there is no class of shifter with the natural hunting instinct of our class. In their records, they show Neesia and Kotara Pryde as hunters, and only the highest officials within the agency even know that much."

Ah, so the rest of the Pryde's were completely in ghost territory. Brilliant, actually. Reya found herself a bit envious that their grandmother had taken so much care with their futures by protecting them in such a manner. Her aunt had done her best, but Reya's life had been considerably more sheltered as she hid in plain sight. It wasn't a bad thing...just different. It had allowed her to go to medical school and do an internship among humans. She'd become a doctor, and a damn good one. Such a thing might not have been possible if she'd been known to an agency that policed her kind.

"Jaguars are rare here." Niah continued, "Pound for pound, they're third in line on the shifter scale, after tigers and lions. Even as solitary creatures, you're much too powerful to just let roam at will. You're free, sure, but you'd be watched. Very carefully. Probably recruited to hunt for S.W.A.T. whether you wanted to or not. Well, if you had the skill for it."

"Yeah, but that's like asking if elephants had the skill to lift their trunks, you know? Hunting is something that feline shifters are naturally good at," Neesia said. "So our secret is your secret and vice versa, Reya."

"Sounds good to me." And Reya genuinely meant it. "Do you guys ever run in your pelts?"

"Oh lord, yes," Niah laughed. "This place is pretty secure. No one gets in or out without our knowing about it. The only one who's ever achieved sneaking into Pryde Ranch is my husband, but he's one of the best bounty dudes that S.W.A.T. has. Also, we have thousands of acres. Plenty of room to run. If you want we'll show you around after your food has had a chance to digest, or we can go first thing in the morning. You've had a long flight from Belize, so whatever works for you."

"Fabulous!" Reya squealed and, to her own surprise, actually clapped her hands. "I've never been in a place where I can just... be. In the jaguar sanctuary, I could go for a run in my fur, which was awesome, but I couldn't allow myself to be seen shifting. I had to sneak, you know? Oh, and the only other shifter I knew tried to rape me and kill my mate, so needless to say we aren't friends anymore since he's kinda dead now."

"What happened to him?" Niah asked at the same time Neesia gasped and said, "Excuse me, but say what?"

"Aaron, Austin and Anthony disappeared him."

Neesia and Niah looked at each other, then back at Reya. "Good."

Yes, it was *all* good...except for one thing—Reya was on fire with a case of instant-horny from out of nowhere.

It had started as a low hum in her belly at the beginning of dinner. She'd chalked it up to having so much testosterone in the room. Aaron James, hunk extraordinaire, husband and mate, along with his two brothers, Anthony and Austin—equally as hot. Then add Jason to the mix and *dayum*. She was surrounded by alphas, both human and shifter, who were sinfully delicious. Who wouldn't have a physical reaction to that, right?

But as the evening had progressed, the low hum had flared into what felt like a full-body erection of the female kind. The energy of the shift percolated just below the skin. The cat was clawing to get out. Reya's scalp tingled as if she'd licked a bazillion volt battery. She expected the curly strands on her head to start standing on end any second now.

Then a flash of heat radiated from the inside out. God, her blood was on fire, and trying to boil up out of her pores.

Oh my god!

"Uh, I think I'm going to head up to bed and let the fellas

have some time. A soak in that big tub in our bathroom seems to be calling my name," Reya said and hoped someone would buy her reason for bowing out.

"No problem. It's getting late and Neesia will be up early puttering around in her ginormous kitchen, making enough food to feed all of Wyoming."

"Oh hush, Niah." But the words were void of heat and full of affection. "Reya, I've been meaning to tell you that you have the most beautiful eyes. Such a pretty gray."

Reya heard herself respond to the compliment but her mouth seemed to be the only part of herself that wasn't flipping around like a jumping bean. She was overwhelmed. Overloaded. Over-horny.

"What's wrong, sweetheart?" Aaron asked, rising from the table to follow her from the room. She waved him away and prayed like hell he'd stay behind.

"Just tired. Long day. Going up now. Goodnight, everyone. Neesia, Niah, it was fantastic meeting you. I really look forward to getting to know you. See you in the morning."

Then she ran for it while trying to look like she wasn't. After a hot bath and the help of the toys she knew Aaron packed in her toiletry bag, Reya planned to at least have her libido under some semblance of control by the time he came up for bed. Hopefully. Maybe? Who was she kidding? If Aaron showed up in the next thirty minutes, he was going to take the place of those toys. She had no idea what the hell was going on with her hormones but...

"God, I hope I don't kill the poor man," she whispered to herself.

Giggles met her ears. The lionesses must have overheard her prayer.

Damn shifter hearing. Then she took the stairs three at a time, trying to outrun her hormones.

3

"Well, since Reya's gone up, I'll do the same and let you guys catch up. I won't be here tomorrow. I'm flying out early to help Lou finish up his mission." Niah rose, grabbed an extra cookie and headed toward the door. "Oh, wait. Who's on schedule to do security tonight?" she asked.

"Jason's turn," Neesia replied. "So with that, I'll say good-night, too. Breakfast tomorrow at nine. See you James boys in the morning." She rose and planted a quick kiss on Jason's lips. "K and K are still in the labs, sweetheart. See you upstairs later."

The second both women left the room, Austin James let his little green monster out to play.

"Jason DiCaplis, you live on a hundred and twenty square miles of some of the prettiest land on God's green earth with beautiful women everywhere. Where's the justice in life?"

"Do I detect a hint of jealousy, my old friend?" Jason prodded with a smile so big, Austin was sure he could see all thirty-two of his friend's teeth, including the fucking wisdom teeth. Asshole.

"Hell yes! I'm not even sure I want to meet the other set of twins. There's only so much gorgeous I can take at one time, man. So unfair. I was the studious one in school. I was the good one growing up."

"Yeah, and see where that got you?" Aaron flew out of his chair and out of punching distance. Austin snarled when his fist met nothing but air a scant inch from his little brother's chest. The chuckles that filled the room became outright laughter. "That's okay. The night is young, you fuckers. I will get even."

"Well, let's head out." Jason pushed back his chair and walked over to an intercom on the wall. "Broglio, we're done in here so the staff can come on in and clean. I'm headed out to do the security check. I'm on close-in duty so surrounding buildings and acreage only."

The response came back, "Yes, sir. I'll be on my way out to the western side."

Jason pulled out his smartphone and started punching buttons. "I've just logged into the system and my GPS is turned on. I'm taking Niah's Jeep and my guests are coming with me. Roger?"

"Roger, that. I'll log my time when I return, sir."

"Good man. See you in the morning. By the way, breakfast at nine, says Her Royal Highness."

Broglio's response was a chuckle and a simple, "Yes, sir. Goodnight, sir."

"Come on, let's went." But Austin didn't want to go tooling around. He wanted to go to his room and fantasize about being Jason. The lucky bastard. "Since Austin here seems to need a cold shower, I'll do you all one better."

At Austin's quizzical expression, Jason elaborated.

"Skinny dipping in the Medicine Bow River, dude. We've got a good stretch of it on this property and the weather is perfect. We'll stop there after I'm done checking Niah's handy work."

And Niah's handy work was impressive as hell. By the time they finished inspecting all the wireless security, satellite, heat signature and camera doodads, Austin wondered if he was in the wrong line of work. With military grade everything, it was obvious all this high-tech network stuff was lucrative. According to Jason, Pryde Industries was often called upon to design and deliver some of the most sophisticated security and defense protocols in the nation.

Luckily, Austin and his brothers made a more-than-generous profit designing swanky buildings for their international clientele, otherwise he'd be asking Niah Pryde for an apprenticeship.

Stripped naked, Austin swam out into the river. His feet shifted on the gravel bottom as he pushed off. The depth was such that he could still wade, but the current was good and strong with just enough pull to give Austin's muscles a challenge without the concern of drowning. He was a big boy—all of them were—and while his brothers were content to chill on the bank catching up with Jason, a good workout was just what Austin needed. The night sky was clear and the air crisp and clean. Being in the middle of nowhere had its perks, namely the ability to see stars that he was sure he'd never set eyes on before.

Sound carried in the quiet and Austin listened to his brothers poke fun at Jason over the goo-goo eyes he'd been making at his woman over dinner. But Austin wasn't in the mood to tease. He wanted to punch something.

Problem was he had no idea why.

He felt...twitchy. Out of sorts. Anxious. Yet he wasn't angry or upset with anyone in his present company.

Weird.

Maybe he was stressed about something that required a bit of introspection? Perhaps he'd come back out here during the day and do some angling. Nothing helped him work through issues like a good bit of fishing.

The wind picked up. Gooseflesh raised on his wet skin as he cut through the ice cold water. Damn. He hadn't meant to come this far out. Halfway back to the other side of the river, Austin went still. Or as still as he could while treading water against the current of the Medicine Bow.

Something watched him from the thick stand of trees just behind where the guys lay on the bank relaxing. Austin didn't have the senses of a shifter but his instincts were buzzing off the charts. He knew someone was there.

And that someone peered clear down to his soul. Touched a piece of him that made him want to stay where he was, yet chase them down at the same time.

Mind made up, he swam with everything he had. The second his feet touched the bank, he headed straight for the brush.

"Hey, where the hell are you going?" Jason called behind him. "If you're headed back to the house, it's quite a walk from here. Besides, you forgot your pants!"

Shit.

For the second time in as many minutes, Austin went still and looked down. Bare feet. Bare chest. Bare ass.

And his cock waving in the wind.

Maybe his dick knew what he was after because, for the life of him, he didn't have a clue.

Koreas had just shed her last article of clothing and tossed it into the back of the truck when her cell phone vibrated. It was a text message from Neesia.

"So? What's up, Kory?"

"Dinner was a fabulous success. She and Niah were headed to bed, along with the cool jaguar shifter. Name's Reya. Aww, man."

"What," Kotara asked, tossing her shoe into the passenger side.

"We're having breakfast early tomorrow. Nine o'clock. Damn, I really was looking forward to sleeping in."

"Nine o'clock *is* sleeping in, you crazy scientist," her sister laughed. "But at least we finished running the analytics so we don't have to look at it again tomorrow."

"Amen to that. Let's go already."

Together, Koreas and Kotara dropped into the change and let the energy of their inner-beasts wash over and through them. Sense of sight and smell, which were pretty sharp in their human skins, now roared to the forefront.

After a wild and exhilarating run across the prairie, the twins found themselves in one of their favorite places—a copse just off the river. It was a place where you could relax naked, even in broad daylight, because the little meadow was completely enclosed by a thick stand of trees and brush.

Remaining in their pelts, Kotara and Koreas flopped down in the grass and enjoyed simply being. They'd been working like dogs on their current project only to learn it was delayed. But such news didn't stop the work, it just meant their attention moved on to the next deal. It was like shifting one's weight from one foot to the other—the same amount of weight was still there, it was just distributed a little differently.

Koreas had been grooming herself when she heard splashing and voices. *"Hey, Tara, I hear Jason. The other voices must be his company."*

On their haunches, they stalked to the edge of the small meadow and peeked through the brush. Lioness vision let them easily pick out three shapes laying on the shore. One was Jason. The others must be their company.

"So, those are the James boys, eh?" Kotara said. *"And look at the one swimming against the current. Man's got a serious pair to get in the river this time of night. Neesia wasn't lying when she said the three of them were damn gorgeous. They're all big and hunky. And all that dark hair. I wonder what color their eyes are."*

But Koreas only had eyes for the man in the water. As dark haired as the others, this one seemed to have a direct link to

Koreas' brain, which seemed frozen in place at the moment. Maybe it was all that tanned skin laid over heavily defined muscle. Or the way the eyes that she couldn't really see from here still seemed to drill into her, bringing an awareness that didn't quite make sense.

And suddenly he was moving. Straight for her.

"Whoa. Do you think he can see us, Tara?"

"Not a chance. Neesia said they were all human."

"Then why is he swimming straight for us like his life depends on it?"

"I don't know, but I think that's our cue to get back to the house. Past our bedtime anyway."

"Very funny, Tara."

"Yeah, I know. I'll be here all week."

oreas, shadowed by Kotara, shuffled into the central space that made the huge house feel like home. Unlike most families that spent time together around the television, the Prydes hung out in the kitchen. It was as natural as breathing for them to talk business or pleasure as Neesia stirred, kneaded, whisked, chopped, and diced. Everyone sampled the nom-noms-in-progress, though there was always the risk they would be commandeered into giving a hand in the cooking, which was much less of a chore than they made it out to be.

Koreas mumbled a greeting to no one in particular and then made a beeline for the coffee pot. She poured herself a big mug, complete with real cream and a dash of sugar, and then leaned back against one of the counters with a loud sigh. Yep, this spot held true warmth of the non-physical kind. When thoughts of her pride filled her head, they would always be accompanied by images of a big gourmet kitchen with stainless steel everything, and filled with love and laughter.

"Koreas, Kotara, this is Reya Daines-James. She's mated and married to Aaron James." The hint of mischief in Neesia's voice caused Koreas to lift her gaze for a moment. Bright eyes and a wide smile made it clear that her sister genuinely liked the jaguar shifter. "Reya's been helping me get breakfast together this morning. She's pretty good in the scrambled egg department."

The woman was a real beauty, with high cheekbones and eyes in an unusual shade of gray that reminded Koreas of the luminous streaks in black mother of pearl. The shape of those eyes were common among their kind—feline to the bone.

"Nice to meet you, ladies. I've been looking forward to it," Reya said.

"Nice to meet you, too, Reya," Koreas and her mirror image said in unison.

"Reya is medically trained. In fact, she runs a medical facility in one section of her bed and breakfast in Belize. I think that alone gives you three something to talk about. Oh, and she's a ranger in the Cockscomb Jaguar Sanctuary," Neesia said.

There was nothing Koreas enjoyed more than sharing ideas with a fellow medi-geek, but she was so wiped out that her hip probably had a permanent indent from the counter as she continued to lean heavily against it. Eyes closed again, Koreas sipped her oh-so-good-but-not-quite-caffeinated-enough coffee. After the third yawn, she hoped that the present company hadn't noticed that she was quieter than her usual quiet self.

She heard Neesia, Reya and Kotara head off toward the country-styled breakfast table at the nook that looked out toward the prairie. Judging from the number of trips the other women made back and forth to the table, Koreas was sure a mountain of scrumptious awaited her. She inhaled deeply and smiled. There was no mistake as her mouth watered at the smell of smoked meats, fresh fruit and...was that waffles? Belgian? With bananas?

Oh thank god!

Her stomach rumbled loudly from so many scrumptious smells. Man, she couldn't wait to eat, but at the same time, she wasn't quite ready to move from this spot either.

Koreas sighed at the feeling of safety that wrapped around her mind just before a gentle hand caressed her cheek.

"What's wrong, baby girl? You okay?"

Koreas lifted her lids and met eyes the same whisky brown as her own.

"I'm fine." She gently rubbed her cheek against her sister's. "Just tired, Neecie." Her jaw stretched to horror movie proportions around a jaw-cracking yawn. "The long hours spent on the now-postponed project caught up to me is all." She tried to smile reassuringly but her lips felt kind of rubbery. "One night of good sleep and I'll be fine."

"Well, let's eat, sweetpea."

Her body followed Neesia toward the food, but Koreas' mind was stuck on the fact that she'd flipped and flopped all over her mattress until the early hours of the morning while images of a man she didn't even know played through her head on the "repeat" setting. It was one of, as Neesia called them, "those James boys," but Koreas didn't know which one. God, she hoped it wasn't Reya's husband—that would just be awkward.

Her dream dude had swam against the current of the Medicine Bow with ease as he'd made for shore. Once he'd climbed out of the water, Koreas' eyes had been drawn to muscled chest and thighs. Beautifully tanned skin was wet and illuminated by the moonlight. So damn beautiful to look at—not just in face or stature, but something else radiated from the inside out.

Koreas picked up her fork and just barely remembered her manners. Sitting the utensil down again, she looked around. "Jason and the guys joining us this morning?"

As the last word left her lips, in they walked. All of them. And the ginormous kitchen now seemed a tad too small with four giants in it.

Oh my god.

Jason DiCaplis was a gorgeous man, no doubt about it, but right behind him was the man of her literal dreams.

"Oh good," Jason said. "Kory and Tara are already here. Koreas and Kotara Pryde, meet my best friends since forever. This is Aaron." Aaron gave a nod of his head and a friendly smile, and then took a seat next to Reya and planted a kiss on her lips.

"This one's Anthony." Again, another polite nod and a rogue-laced gentleman's smile. "And the grumpy one there is Austin James."

Oh. Austin James. No nod of greeting. No smile. The man went completely still the moment his eyes met hers. Yet even in his stillness, he projected a flash of energy that she could practically see behind her eyeballs.

Coming face to face with Mr. Late Night Swim was a completely different experience from seeing him at a distance. Correction, at a *safe* distance. Last night, he was just a guy out for a swim with a somewhat attention-grabbing look. Today, this man, this *human*, felt like a riptide that grabbed her by the ankles and tugged her under.

"Breathe, Kory. He's just a guy, albeit a very hot guy," Kotara whispered into her head.

As twins, they had an unshakeable connection, just like Neesia and Niah did. At times that connection could be a pain in her ass. Like now. Kotara had obviously noticed...

"Of course I noticed. Your dumbstruckness is out there for all to see."

"Dumbstruckness? Really, Tara?"

"So what if it's not even a word. If the shoe fits, chicklet."

"Hush, Kotara. I'm fine."

Actually, Kotara's made-up word did indeed fit. Perfectly, in fact. Koreas was taken aback to the point where her typical snarky comeback had left the building. In its place was a sex-starved, shell-shocked-at-meeting-Mr. Midnight Swim, mush brain with not a single smart-assed comeback at the ready.

Snapping her gaze away from Austin, Koreas concentrated on her orange juice.

"If you're fine, then answer the man's question," Tara insisted.

Question. Uh...what question? Fuck.

"He asked if you were out in the grove last night. Guess he did see us."

Koreas looked up into a pair of eyes that brought to mind the clouds over a stormy sea—deep gray and enchanting...and exactly the same color as Reya's. Interesting. That's when she noticed that all of the James clan were blessed with those enchanter's eyes.

Koreas felt her tongue attempt to glue itself to the roof of her mouth. Abandoning the orange juice, she took another sip of hot coffee. What was better for glue than something hot, right?

"Ever the scientist."

"Hush, Tara. If you make me snarf my drink I'm going to bite you on the ass in front of company."

The knots in Koreas' gut unraveled as she shared a private laugh with Kotara. It was all she needed to shake herself out of the speechless-by-gorgeous-man state she'd been in for the last few moments.

She turned her full attention on Austin and replied with a polite smile.

"It's so nice to meet all of you. And yes, we were out running last night, Tara and me. You saw us?"

"No," Austin responded, scooting in to sit next to her. His nearness set off an instant buzz across the skin around her mouth, like she'd licked a battery or something. And wanted to lick it again. Weird. "I just kind of felt someone was there. It was too dark to see but..."

Jason cocked his head. "I didn't know you two were out last night, Kory."

Huh. Austin James had known someone was there, but Jason, a shifter and experienced bounty hunter, hadn't? Interesting. And unsettling. Almost as unsettling as Austin's presence.

"Kory, what are you doing?" Kotara hissed into her brain.

"What do you mean, what am I doing? I'm sitting here trying to eat my breakfast, thank you very much."

"Oh dear god, Kory, dial it back."

"Dial what..." she protested even as her skin flushed. Muscles twitched as Austin tried to engage her in what was supposed to be casual conversation, but the way he watched her set her on edge. Not in a *"I veel keel you"* kind of way, but more of a *"throw me over your shoulder and take me to bed"* sentiment. Which made no sense considering she didn't even know the man. And he was human on top of that.

Kotara surged to her feet. "Excuse me. I'm, uh, not really feeling well. I think I'm going to go lay down awhile."

Koreas almost felt sorry for her twin when Neesia pinned her with that all-knowing gaze of hers. The matriarch missed nothing. Ever. Kotara avoided their elder's eyes, scooted away from the table and tossed down her napkin.

"Kotara, do you need something? Are you sick?" Neesia asked. "Reya was hoping to tell you and Kory about some of the solutions she's been able to implement in regard to the health of the jaguars in Cockscomb. Some of it is because of your and your sister's research."

"No, don't need any meds, Neesia. And sorry, Reya. Promise to sit down with you. At. Another. Time."

Each word was bitten off as if Kotara were trying to keep the lioness inside her skin.

"Tara?" Neesia called as the other woman practically fled the kitchen.

Koreas stared after her twin, determined to ignore the

reason Kotara had torn out of the room as if her ass was on fire. But if Koreas was being truthful, her *sister's* ass was on fire because *her* ass was on fire. And it made no sense whatsoever.

"A whole lot of fire going around at this table, damn it," Koreas grumbled to a retreating Tara.

"Don't snap at me. I don't know how you're still sitting there! I couldn't take another second of feeling that arousal. Yours was bad enough...not to mention kinda odd considering the air-tight, water-proof, nuke-resistant lid you keep on it. But add Austin's lust to the mix and I just couldn't stand it."

"What about breakfast?" She couldn't face this without her sister. There was just no way. Correction—no way in hell. *"Tara, don't you dare leave me here. Where are you going?"*

"To shower, Kory. Where else, damn it. Who'd a thought your mate would be a human?"

"Mate? Human? Nu-uh!"

"Yes, uh-huh," Kotara insisted. Hissed, actually. *"Now, get out of my head for now. My toy and I need some privacy."*

"Toy? What—"

"The one that runs on double A's and remains charged at all times. That's what toy."

"Oh? Oh! Shit. Never mind."

"Yeah. Now scoot already."

When Koreas turned her attention back to the table, she noticed that everyone seemed a bit twitchy. Neesia and Jason shared a quick look that must have accompanied some naughty thoughts. A heated blush traced across Neesia's cheeks from the laser-like focus Jason gave his mate.

Reya's eyes were glazed over and Aaron was gulping water like he was as parched as a man who'd ridden across a desert for three days.

Anthony's brow was furrowed in confusion.

And Austin? My god, his eyes were glued to Koreas as if she held the key to some long lost secret that involved pirates and buried treasure…and he was Cap'n Jack. He was speaking to her but she couldn't make out the words past the pounding of her heart in her head. It was like standing in a flooded tunnel with her ears full of water. Then the man lifted a piece of fruit to her lips and it didn't even cross her mind to refuse. His gaze drifted lower as he took in the way she chewed and swallowed.

Quietly, he laid down his fork, his gaze both intent and dazed at the same time. Then he spoke her name, said something about wanting to know her.

Yep. Definitely under water. In fact, she was in over her head and drowning in his presence. It was almost tangible. Deliciously so.

Which made no damn sense. And things that didn't make sense pissed Koreas Pryde off like nothing else.

Time to go. Politely, of course.

"Excuse me," she said as she stood and pushed back her chair. "I have a few things to attend to. See you all at lunch, perhaps?" Kory had no intention of getting anywhere near this particular James brother at lunchtime or any other time—not until she understood what the hell was going on.

For now, she was out the door.

She almost smiled when behind her, Jason and Neesia made their apologies and headed out a side door at the same time Aaron and Reya got scarce through the swinging door to the dining room. All of them were kissing, smooching and touching as they went.

Perhaps this particular affliction of Instant Horny was contagious?

If so, she was headed straight to the labs to find a goddamn cure.

Then again, screw the lab. Kory needed a drink.

And it's only ten o'clock? Geesh.

*a*aron stepped into the bedroom he shared with Reya.

He cracked the bathroom door and stuck his head in. "Hey, beautiful," he called out. "Sorry it took me awhile to get up here. I ended up talking with Jason. Didn't realize a couple of hours had passed until Neesia stepped into the library, literally grabbed him and hauled him outside. We're planning a shopping trip in a few days. Niah and Lou should be back by then, so we'll all go, okay?"

"No worries. Be right out."

Moments later, she opened the bathroom door and the plentiful steam from the shower spilled into the room, bringing with it the coconut scent of the girly stuff she washed with. He knew it would fade shortly and he would be able to bury his nose at the crook of her neck and inhale the sweetness that was simply his woman.

"I thought you showered this morning," he said.

"I did. I just took a cold one, then turned on the hot water for a few to knock off the chill."

"You sick?"

"Nah. At least I don't think so."

Covered from neck to knees in an off-white silky looking, flowy robe, she walked into his arms without hesitation. With her head tucked beneath his chin, he enjoyed standing there in the middle of the floor and simply holding her.

"You know, the last time we were able to hang out with Jason was three years ago. It's pretty cool getting to come here and see him in this new life. I mean, we've been friends since we were little tykes. The day he landed the job with S.W.A.T., he called me and told me that he was an agent for them. That man has worked his ass off for the agency, but he was always by himself, you know?"

Reya nodded.

Aaron really didn't have to ask that question. He was well aware that his feisty mate used to have an intimate relationship with loneliness and was well acquainted with it. If not for her longtime friends in Belize, Dr. Matons and Bethsaida, and her occasional visit with her Aunt Sulu, the woman would have gone plain batty by now. Her jaguar might be a solitary animal, but her human half definitely was not.

"Aaron, you know I won't mind if you want to soak up as much time with Jason as you can. In fact, I can dress and head out onto the property or something. I'm sure one of the Pryde females wouldn't mind..."

"Not a chance." Aaron nuzzled his wife's neck, then loosened his hold on her just enough to turn her around. Then he wrapped his arms right back around her lush body and pulled her close until her back was flush against his chest. "I absolutely require some of your time and attention just now. Perhaps some special attention?"

His hands began a slow downward trek, passed over her hips, then made the journey back up her body to caress the underside of her breasts.

"You are such a horn dog," giggled Reya.

"Are you complaining?"

"Not a chance," she murmured as she turned to face him and raised up on her toes to plant a kiss square on his lips. He loved how uninhibited she was, how free and giving. And not just in the bedroom, but in every aspect of their relationship.

Aaron smiled to himself. It was a quietly kept man-secret that right after he'd married Reya, Jason had told him to read that Mars and Venus book and promised that his world would rock sideways. And the man had been right. In fact, that little paperback had saved Aaron's sanity because lord knows he hadn't understood a single thing about women prior to reading the thing. And his woman noticed that something was different. Noticed that he made an effort to let her talk his head off if that's what she needed. Noticed that he was aware of her natural cycle, and how the ebb and flow of all those female hormones affected her moods. Noticed that he had chocolate for her at the right time of the month, and was always ready to sex her up during the other times.

The result of his efforts meant that Reya showed her appreciation. Loudly. Enthusiastically. And often. Why? Because she knew she could trust him not to invalidate her feelings. To care for her like only a mate could. Allow her to let down her walls and simply let him love her.

Aaron knew her deeper and more intimately than he could have otherwise. And he knew something bothered her.

"So what's up, Reya? What's really going on?"

She pushed out of his arms with a sigh and walked over to their bedroom window. It was beautiful here. At mid-spring, the rolling prairie was covered with tall green grass out in the distance. Trees full of brand new blossoms dotted the entire estate and the beautifully landscaped parts of the property had containers and pots full of plants everywhere.

Neesia had told him that they didn't use cultivated grass on Pryde lands, only the grasses and plants that were native to this area. As he looked out toward the sweeping prairie he felt...at home. The tall drifts waved like stately little soldiers under the light rain that had just begun to fall. The windows were open and fresh air swirled into the room, bringing with it the scents of sweet grass and dew.

A swift gust of wind lifted Reya's damp hair from her shoulders. God, his woman was so damn beautiful. Too beautiful to have concerns like the one that sat heavy on her brow just now.

"Reya, I asked you a question. Now tell me what's wrong, baby."

"It's...I just don't understand what's happening. I feel...weird."

"Weird like how? Sick weird, uncomfortable weird, crazy weird?"

"I don't know how to say this so I'll just spit it out, though I feel like total shit." She took a deep breath, closed her eyes and let fly. "Okay, here goes. I'm attracted to Jason and I have no idea why I feel this way."

Aaron chuckled but Reya obviously didn't see what the hell was so funny.

"Do share what you're laughing at. Cheeky bastard."

He laid a kiss on her lips and wrapped her back up in a hug. "It seems I know a bit more about shifter physiology than a shifter. It's just funny to me, that's all."

"Well, it's not funny to me at all," grumbled Reya. "What do you know? Spill it before I shift and bite you in the ass."

"First, let me say that the only reason I know this is because Jason and I have been friends for so long, and he went through something like this when his mate and her twin were unexpectedly thrown into heat at the same time. His sisters-in-law, being scientists, explained it to him and he explained it to me. What you feel is the result of something biological, sweetheart. Not a lack of loyalty or passion for me, so stop worrying."

"I still don't get it."

"When Jason first came into the change in his early teens, we shared blood."

She remembered this story. Jason had been a late bloomer, hadn't thought he'd change at all and when it came, it was at the most inopportune time—at school one day while in the middle of being picked on by a bully. Even though Aaron had befriended Jason when they were in second grade, he'd had no idea his best friend was a shifter until he'd helped a half-shifted Jason make quick work of the bad guys. Aaron then dragged Jason—who couldn't walk because of his half-done state—to a broom closet, where he'd safely completed the change. Aaron sat with his buddy through that agonizing first shift. They'd done the whole "let's become blood brothers" thing and had been lifelong friends since then.

"While you were growing up, Reya, you were never human. Always a shifter. Your body replenished your blood supply every twenty four to forty eight hours, but nothing affected your shifter genes. But the change that took place in my human cells as a result of mingling mine and Jason's blood didn't get washed away or undone. It became a part of me, just like it's a part of you."

"Okaay?" Reya cocked an eyebrow. She looked a lot like Mr. Spock just then. Only he dared not laugh because he liked his balls exactly where they were—intact.

"Jason's blood, though it was only a little, changed a small bit of my DNA, and mine changed his. Kind of intertwined us together so to speak. As my mate, you feel a natural, though slight, attraction to him because of my connection to him. I suspect that my attraction to his mate is due to the same thing."

"You're attracted to his mate? You wanna jump bones with Neesia?" She stepped back in a rush and the temperature rose in the room in spite of the cool breeze flowing in through the open window.

"You're adorable when you're riled, you know that?"

She hissed in response.

"Reya, I only wanna jump your bones. No different than you feeling horny towards Jason but not really wanting him. In fact, it makes you uncomfortable, am I right?"

She nodded truthfully.

"I want you. No one else. So…come back over here and let's get to jumping."

After a few tense moments, she was back in his arms and all was right in their world. Especially after Reya's robe hit the floor.

It was a good thing they had so much room here, otherwise the growls and snapping would have surely alerted someone by now.

The tawny lioness bared her teeth at the male advancing on her. He was a beautiful specimen—fully grown, sleek and powerfully built. His pelt was a perfect dark gold, and his eyes of hazel and green. Muscles bunched and stretched as he stalked her until finally, she simply turned and ran…directly to the spot Kotara and Koreas referred to as "The Coochie Copse."

They tumbled onto the fresh smelling grass, arms and legs in a tangle. The second their bodies hit the ground, the energy of the change rippled through them both, vibrated in the air and around the surrounding trees. In moments, they were skin to skin, chest to chest. Lip to lip.

Neesia moaned as her husband's mouth left hers to lick and suck a wet path to the sensitive skin of her neck. The breeze did little to cool the rising temperature at her core. If all the man had to do was look at her to make her cream her panties, then his touch against bare skin was fifty times as potent. Made her fifty times as hot, fifty times as needy.

His hands were everywhere at once. Fingers tugged and

pulled on her nipples. Nails gently, and then not-so-gently, scratched along her waist. Pads dipped into the swelling flesh of her sex as she squirmed to get closer to the touch that was driving her mad.

And then Neesia was flipped onto her stomach, hips pulled back toward the prime male on his knees behind her. His cock, hot and smooth, nudged at the opening of her channel. The cooling breeze played over her sweat-dampened skin and made her aware of just how wet she was. Wet and ready.

And Jason wasn't moving fast enough.

She opened her mouth to demand what she so desperately needed when her man slid deep. Gasped on that first deep thrust. Moaned on the next. Went crazy on the one after that.

Urgent whispers tumbled from Neesia's lips. The things she said to him as he rode her from behind, the demands of what she wanted and how hard she wanted it, spilled out in an endless torrent. She couldn't help it, and she knew her man didn't want her to help it. At all.

Their bond hummed with their combined desire—his reaction to her erotic demands and her reaction to his skillful fucking. Soon, he was pounding into her and the more he gave her, the more she wanted.

"Greedy woman...for which I am eternally grateful to the whole fucking universe."

God, she loved Jason DiCaplis, mate extraordinaire.

The smack of slick skin meeting skin filled the space around them and she grew practically drunk on the scent of their loving.

"Touch your clit and come for me, Neesia."

Her gut tightened at the thought of what was coming. It was something she'd experienced countless times with her husband, but that didn't dim the anticipation in the least.

She was going to come. And she was going to come *hard.*

Balanced on one elbow, she reached back between her legs

and tapped the swollen bundle of nerves. Oooh, it was fantastically good, but not quite enough.

Cued without words, Jason slid his fingers into that sensitive space and gently spread her flesh so her clit was fully exposed. A few well-placed rubs and the spring coiled tight in her belly snapped free. The scent of sweet grass filled her nostrils as she inhaled, pressed her face into the grass and screamed out her pleasure.

When they were totally and completely spent, they laid out under the baby blue sky. Some particularly persistent blades of grass stuck to her legs, her arms, stomach, and calves. Sunlight filtered through the needles of the white fir evergreens. Neesia and her mate lay amidst a wash of color, budding green and bright red bracts of Indian Paintbrush. The air was rich with the scent of moist earth and hot sex.

"Holy hell, woman, you have worn me out, thank you very much," Jason said. Neesia laughed and picked a few pieces of dandelion fluff out of Jason's hair—hair that stood on end as if he'd just rolled out of bed. Well, technically, she guessed he *had* just rolled out of bed, in a manner of speaking.

"It's a good thing I know why you're more of a horny toad than usual, otherwise I'd be worried. Good thing only shifters have such acute senses," Jason said on a yawn.

"Why?"

"Because I smelled your arousal all during breakfast, Neesia. That shit smells better than bacon. If I knew they'd caught your scent, I'd have to shank my friends in the neck with a pencil." Jason laughed until the corners of his eyes crinkled and the already high color that filled his cheeks bloomed even more.

"Oh please," she teased. "You knew good and well that I'd feel some attraction to...wait, you said friends, with an 's'? Why? I thought you only shared blood with Aaron all those years ago."

"True, but Aaron has two brothers who I'd also have to

tackle, hence the 's' on the word 'friend'. Those James boys have always run together. Mess with one, you mess with them all."

"So how come you didn't share blood with all of them?"

"Aaron was the only one that actually saw me change that day. We've been best friends ever since. Anthony and Austin didn't learn my secret until later."

"Makes sense," yawned Neesia.

"Oh, no you don't. No yawning."

"Why not? I didn't tell you not to yawn thirty seconds ago when your jaw cracked from how wide it opened."

"Are you saying I have a big mouth?" he teased. "Never mind. Don't answer that. Anyway, yawning is contagious," Jason said, forming the words around another jaw-cracking yawn of his own. "See, I told you. And we can't start yawning because yawning leads to sleeping. And sleeping would lead to us being late for lunch…a lunch you're making."

"I made it this morning. Broglio will see that it gets laid out properly." Neesia rolled so her back was to Jason's front and he automatically pulled her close and wrapped his body around hers as they spooned.

Neesia folded her arm and let her cheek rest on her elbow. Barely-brown eyes slipped closed. "Besides, we're technically on vacation while your friends are here."

Surrounded by waist high sweet grass, two lions in human skin slumbered peacefully beneath a blue spring sky.

6

"*H*ey, are you here by yourself?"

Koreas jerked her head towards the owner of that totally-male voice—Austin James.

Damn it.

She'd managed to pretty much avoid him from the moment they'd formally met at breakfast a couple of days ago. Other than a polite greeting in passing and group conversations over dinner, she'd kept her distance from the man.

She bit her lip to keep her mouth from falling open. It just wouldn't do to let the man see her drool. Her stomach fell down into her socks as she pretended not to look her fill. Austin James was a feast for the senses.

Smell—his natural scent was lightly layered by an earthy, spicy cologne that made her think of walking in the woods after a spring rain. Her heart rate ratcheted up and it was all she could do to keep her nose from twitching.

Hearing—the man's voice was smooth, not too deep but not too…squeaky was the only word that came to mind. She almost laughed but the intensity of his gaze brought her up short and her gut began to dance again.

Sight—ruggedly gorgeous with a body to die for. She'd gotten a good look at him as he'd stormed up out of the river and could practically recall in vivid details exactly how many water droplets shone under the moon. But more than that, his physique was evident in the fit of his clothes—the way the short-sleeved tee fit around his biceps, the stretch of fabric across broad chest, and the fall of denim from hips to feet.

She took a quick gulp of her ice cold drink and refused to fan herself as she wondered just what Austin's touch and taste would be like.

And yet again, he'd asked her a question that hadn't made it past her ears and into her brain.

"Koreas?"

"Yes?"

"Are you here by yourself?" Crystalline gray eyes twinkled as he spoke and out of left field, her "mad" showed up. How dare he get a kick out of her temporary bout of goofiness.

"Why?" she snapped, then tiredly raised her glass for a sip.

"Mind if I join you?"

Koreas hated when people answered a question with a question. It was time to cut to the chase, though why she was so eager to be rid of him, she hadn't a clue. She just knew that he knocked her off kilter and she appreciated her kilter exactly where it was, thank you very much.

"What are you doing here, Austin? Neesia isn't going to appreciate that you skipped afternoon tea."

"But you're missing it, too, I reckon?"

Another question with a question. Bleh.

"Yes, but food is always laid out and we swing through and grab it when we can. Pryde Ranch is a busy place. No one expects us to always make it back to the main house in the middle of the afternoon."

"Then why would I be expected to make it to a formal tea?"

"You're a guest. You're on vacation, not working, so of

course you would be expected to attend meals provided by your host. I thought all you country boys had manners."

Rather than get offended, Austin tilted his head and regarded her with a very naughty smile. Damn. There her kilter went again—way off to the left somewhere.

"I do believe that would be the mannerly thing to do, of course. But for your information, Miss Beautiful, lunch was indeed laid out for us. It was delicious, in fact. However, our gracious hosts, Neesia and Jason, were conspicuously missing courtesy of their note that they'd see us this evening. When I asked your twin about it, she said something about a Coochie Cove or Coochie Copse or some such."

Koreas' face was instantly on fire. A total hot hunk of a man that she wasn't well acquainted with was in her face discussing…coochie.

Oh. My. God. Just kill me now. But the earth didn't open up and swallow her nor her mortification.

She opened her mouth with a retort, but the moment her lips parted, said retort dissipated into dust. Instead, she shook her head and grumbled.

"Wow. I've got nothing."

Her tormentor of the moment sat down at her table wearing a shit-eating grin that rivaled one of Kotara's after she'd pulled off the ultimate prank on one of their sisters. But just now, Koreas didn't quite feel like being laughed at. She let her introverted shy self take a back seat to the powerful feline inside. And the feline burst forth so strongly, it was all she could do to control the sudden urge to shift and bite Austin in the ass.

Strange. She had no reason to care if this guy was getting his kicks at her expense but for some reason, she did care. A lot.

"Are you laughing at me, Austin James?" The words were squeezed through bared teeth and a hint of the lioness bled through into her voice.

Wow, that's a first.

"Me? Laugh at you?" His full-out grin dialed down to a lop-sided one, but the sparkle in his eye said that whatever he thought was funny hadn't diminished at all. "Not a chance. By the way, you sound really sexy when you get all growly like that."

Sexy? She wasn't sexy. Sure, all the Pryde women were attractive, but that didn't make her sexy by a long shot. She walked around spattered in various foul smelling concoctions. Half the time her head was buried in a book, and the other half, her eyeballs stayed stuck to a microscope. Numbers and potions were her friends. Sexy didn't even come visit, let alone take up residence.

That made Austin James a beautiful liar.

Speaking of beautiful, he'd referred to her as beautiful and sexy in less than five minutes. She wondered if he'd meant it, but no way in hell was she going to ask. Instead, she turned back to the drink in front of her that she'd barely managed to sip. And why? Because she'd been sitting here thinking about the very man next to her, that's why.

Speak of the devil and in he walks, right? Shit.

"So what are you having?" he asked.

"It's a Long Island Iced Tea…without the Long Island part."

"Oh. In other words, a Coke."

Koreas laughed. She couldn't help it. He was a mix of devilish and handsome—desirable and adorable—as he teased. And the instant attitude that had reared its head when he first arrived was losing ground to his charm.

So she let it go. Besides, her grandma had taught her better as a child. Koreas could hear that woman's voice, see her face as she smiled sweetly before taking a doll from her hands—a doll that she'd snatched from Kotara. "Hug your sister and tell her you're sorry," Grandma used to say. "You lose nothing by being nice, Koreas Pryde. And you'd be surprised at what you can gain." And it was the truth. What could possibly go wrong by simply showing courtesy to this man?

"You're a beautiful, intelligent woman, and I'd really like the chance to get to know you, Koreas."

Okay, she took it back. A lot could go awry by being nice! He wanted to get to know her? First, he'd declared her sexy and beautiful and now, he wanted to *get to know her*? Holy shit.

"Uh…"

His one-sided grin became a full showing of teeth. And he kept right on smiling until finally some words came to her obviously-tired brain.

You're not tired. You're googly-eyed over this handsome hunk of perfection that you don't have time to mess with.

Or at least that was her story. And she was sticking to it.

"Get to know me? Don't see how that's possible. You're going home in a couple of weeks, Austin James."

"Doesn't mean I can't come back. Better yet, one of the perks of running my own company with my brothers is that we each call the shots for ourselves. My schedule is my own and I can work from anywhere."

Okay, this all sounded a bit bigger than she could handle right now. Bigger and faster and scarier because the man was dead serious. And drop-dead gorgeous, to boot.

Rather than answering his question, she sipped her Coke. Austin obviously picked up clues quickly because rather than press her, he ordered a snack for them to share along with his very own Long-Island-Iced-Tea-Without-The-Long-Island. Then he did the one thing that Koreas had always hoped would happen during a conversation with a man—he asked her about her work and then actually *listened* to the answer without his eyes straying down to her boobs.

Then he did the unthinkable—he recognized that while her life was pretty damn awesome, it was far from perfect. He said,

"I do realize that what you do is important and while you enjoy your work, it seems to me that you do it entirely too much. So if your projects were all caught up and you had a month to just relax, what would you do?"

Wow, the man has some serious discernment because lord knows I'm tired as all get out, and ready for some down time.

They swapped ideas and stories, and Koreas found that for the first time in a good stretch, she wasn't paying attention to the time. And the moment she realized what she *wasn't* doing, she stuffed her hand in her pocket and fished out her phone.

"Oh my god," she gasped. She yanked her sweater off the back of the chair beside her and pulled it on. "I hadn't meant to be gone so long. The stability charts should be finished rendering by now. I have things to do. And I missed dinner!"

She quickly shot off a text message to all of her sisters at once and let them know she'd derped out on the time and that she was with Austin in town. The quick responses said that her check-in was appreciated and there would be something in the fridge for her if she got hungry later.

Her hurrying should have been obvious but Koreas had learned years ago that common sense was damn near a super power these days. Needless to say, it was a relief when Austin actually caught the huge hints she was throwing out with her bustling and waved his hand for the waitress to bring the check.

But when he paid her tab without asking, Koreas frowned.

"What?" he asked, clearly perplexed.

"Why did you take care of my bill?"

"Because that's what gentlemen do." He was serious. Huh. "And it's what a smart man does if he's trying to woo a woman."

Woo? People still used that word? It was old fashioned and quaint. Koreas decided that she liked quaint. Strange. How could she like something so much yet want to run from it at the same time? It was like having the urge to wear rocket skates and an open parachute at the same time.

Something about Austin James made her twitchy. Not in a nervous, scary kind of way, but in a way she didn't want to ponder just now.

Austin stood and held out his hand.

She took it and allowed him to help her out of her chair. She pulled on her sweater, grabbed her purse and opened her mouth to say goodbye.

"Can I walk you to your car?" he asked.

"I, uh, didn't drive." *I rode shotgun with a big ass lioness.*

She didn't finish the sentence because she really didn't want to lie, but she couldn't quite tell the truth either—especially not in a pub full of nosy people. Thankfully, he latched onto the little bit of information she'd provided, filled in his own blanks and gave her a discreet wink.

"Oh, okay. Guess you could always call one of your staff to come and get you, but since I'm here already, how about you let me give you a ride back? I'm borrowing Niah's jeep while she's out of town hunting with her husband."

"Sure. Okay."

The miles passed in a weird slushy mix of companionable silence, nervous anticipation and flat-out annoyance. She was getting back to work so late and it was all his fault. If she hadn't been sitting there pondering over Austin, who then chose to show up and delay her even more, then she would have been back to the labs a good two hours earlier. It just wasn't like her to be so sidetracked.

Didn't matter that she totally enjoyed his company. And some of the tales he'd told her over a trough of french-fries— very funny "growing up" stories that Jason had smartly managed to keep to himself. She couldn't wait to see Tara so she could spill some of those hilarious beans!

"Just drive on past the main house. I'm going to the labs."

"You guys call it 'The Labyrinth,' right?"

She glanced his way and nodded. What a fabulous profile.

Strong jaw, stylishly short black hair, devilish smile with features that were all symmetrical and stuff. Koreas dragged her eyes away and stared out the window into the black. She still couldn't believe it was so late, but she admitted to herself that the annoyance was at herself and not at the present company.

"I understand you and Kotara spend quite a bit of time there. Mind if I see?"

"We don't usually allow hu…" Holy shit, she'd almost said 'humans'. A mental picture flashed in her head of her walking outside of her laboratory and introducing her forehead to the nearest tree. Repeatedly. "We don't usually allow visitors inside. Some of the proteins and viruses we work with aren't good for you. We take precautions and the place is sterile, but we still would rather not take chances."

"No problem. Maybe next time, then? I don't even mind putting on one of those bunny suit things to get a tour from such a lovely scientist."

Oooh. Again with the charm.

The vehicle came to a stop. Austin hopped out, walked around to her side and opened the door for her.

When she swung her legs around to exit the car, Austin didn't move back. Instead, he eased forward until her knees were almost flush with his groin.

He leaned in. And because it wasn't in her nature to retreat, she let him.

"Koreas?"

"Yes?"

"I'd very much like to kiss you goodnight."

Yes, she wanted him to kiss her. Wanted it so much it was baffling. Koreas craved companionship as much as her sisters wanted her to have it. One-night-stands weren't her thing, but there wasn't time for a relationship either. A part of her wanted to run and bury herself in her work, as always, yet something about this man drew her in. And it wasn't just a subtle tug, this was more of a swift yank that left her hurtling toward the sun.

So should she burn? Or remain in the cold alone?

Koreas wasn't so much of a scientist that she had a hard time accepting things that science couldn't explain...such as why she was letting Austin James lean into her space and take what he wanted.

She had no reason whatsoever to want this fabulous hunk of a man—hunk of a *human* man—to lay a lip-lock on her. None at all. But the closer he got, the closer she wanted him.

It was almost a relief when he finally placed his lips against hers. But instead of the peck she'd expected, it was a lingering of mouths until they shared the same breath.

When he finally let her gather her own air, Koreas was light headed, giddy and wearing a truly feline smile.

Austin took her hand and helped her from the jeep. It wasn't until he'd walked her through the front door that she realized he'd brought her home rather than dropping her at her lab.

Austin had only known Koreas Pryde for mere days, yet he already understood two things about her without a doubt—one, she worked too damn much and two, the woman caused a zing in his gut like he'd never experienced before.

He and his brothers had been quietly aware of shifters since they'd met Jason when they were kids. They'd never met another shifter since so imagine their surprise when Aaron, the youngest James boy, met and married a jaguar shifter, Reya, after she'd rescued him from a plane crash in Belize. While they knew that shifters and humans were mating compatible, Austin hadn't expected to find himself insanely attracted to Koreas or anyone else.

Luckily he was open minded, otherwise he'd be offended.

When he took a woman for his own, he wanted it to be because they loved and cared about each other, not because some chemical or hormone threw them together.

On the other hand, nature seemed to know what she was doing. If Aaron and Jason's accounts of their relationships were any indication, their wives were women they would have chosen for themselves even without the help of the whole genetic insane attraction whammy thing.

So here he stood, barely able to keep his hands off of her. And it wasn't just the physical need she evoked in him, but an emotional one as well. He wanted nothing more than to talk to her until neither of them had anything else to say. But when he looked her way, Koreas had asked him to drop her off at the series of buildings built into the side of a hill. He hadn't been inside the labs that the Pryde's lovingly called "The Labyrinth," but given he was the geekiest of both his brothers, Austin would find a way to arrange a visit.

During a heated, yet hilarious, debate about the best childhood Saturday morning cartoons and worst Seventies disco tunes, Austin deliberately drove through the front side of the estate closer to the main house rather than around the back and past the numerous research buildings and labs.

Keeping that woman's sharp mind occupied while he took her where she hadn't asked to go had been a delightful challenge —one in which he'd been wholly engaged given he'd done little except observe and think about Koreas since they'd arrived at Pryde Ranch. His conclusion—the woman needed some down time, and she was going to get it. Austin wasn't sure why he felt so protective of Koreas, and to be honest, he didn't care why. He'd learned over the years to follow his instinct, and those instincts told him that this woman needed him as much as he needed her.

And right now, what she *didn't* need was to work all through the night...again. And he'd certainly noticed, just as he'd noticed she'd been avoiding him for the last couple of days. Thankfully, she had a family who thought he was plenty good enough for Koreas and they were willing to allow him to pursue her in his own way.

So this afternoon he'd gone after her.

And now that they were at the main house, Austin knew the moment Koreas realized he hadn't taken her where she'd asked to go. She wore puzzled and disgruntled well. The little wrinkles between her brows as she scrunched up her face in challenge were adorable. Austin was no fool. This woman may be a nerd extraordinaire, which was extremely attractive to him, but she was no pushover, and not because she was a literal lioness. Something about her whispered to him that in spite of her quiet nature, designer glasses and stained lab coat, Koreas Pryde was an alpha chick on the down low.

Even with all the funny stories he'd heard about the childhood years of the Pryde sisters during the family meals, no one had provided this kind of insight into the woman before him. But he knew down to his bones that if he pushed her, she'd push right back. And if he tugged on her sensual nature, she'd go all out.

Right now, she didn't believe he wanted her. Wasn't sure what he was after. But she would soon. He'd make sure of it.

"I love this room. Love the way it fills with light from the moon and stars on clear nights, like this one." The longing in her voice touched a chord inside Austin's chest.

"The view of the sky is nice, but I'm much more interested in the star right next to me."

"But you don't know anything about me."

"You mean other than the fact that you're brilliant, you love your family, you're gorgeous and sexy and geeky and beautiful?"

"I...uh. Well..."

"And there is something indescribable about you. Something I'd like to explore very much."

"Explore?"

"Well, maybe that didn't come out quite right, but I think you get my meaning."

And without another word, Austin took her hand and raised it to his lips before pulling her into his arms.

7

*S*he loved nature, the outdoors. Loved her family. Her work. She had everything a girl could want...except a mate. Both her older sisters had African lion mates. Neesia's Jason and Niah's Lou had been totally unexpected and complete surprises.

But Koreas didn't believe in the whole "three's a charm" thing. What were her chances of finding a mate in the shifter community given the scarcity of her particular breed? It wasn't a trick question, either. She was a statistician and had actually run the numbers. The result—damn near nil.

The thought that she might never find love was fucking depressing. She hadn't shared as much, but she knew her family felt her loneliness. It was one of the reasons no one bothered her about how much time she'd been spending in the Labyrinth or her reluctance to go get her groove on, out dancing with Kotara.

But tonight, she had to admit she'd had a total blast just talking with Austin. She hadn't seen that coming, nor had she foreseen the fierce attraction she felt toward him.

The man was just that—a man. The sudden urge to jump

him didn't make any sense. She'd expect such a thing from the pheromones put off by a shifter, but a human? Not so much. Like her sister, Niah—though not quite as anally retentive as that particular Pryde—Koreas was a logical person, moved by numbers and analyses. And there were no reports or calculations she could use to explain any of this "Austin business."

So, for now, maybe she'd take a cue from yet another sister and do what her twin had been poking at her to do for years— just go with it.

So she allowed Austin to kiss her and keep on kissing her until she was damn-near drunk on her own arousal.

It began as warm and coaxing, sweet and melty, like dark chocolate held in your hand until it began to pool in the palm. Her stomach danced around as the lioness beneath the skin rolled against her consciousness. In her mind's eye, she could see the beautiful cat rolling around like a young kitten playing in summer grass.

His lips left hers as he moaned deep in his throat. His mouth pressed against the skin just beneath her ear. A trail of kisses, damp and steamy, dotted a trail down the flesh of her neck, eased across her collar bones and up the other side.

She sighed in pleasure as fingers tangled in her hair. Pins hit the carpet with dull pings. Her scalp tingled just shy of pain. And she wanted nothing but *more*.

So she asked for it.

Then, when he found "that" spot along her trapezius muscle, she stopped asking...and begged.

And the man did not disappoint. He kissed her until her head spun, then he picked her up and everything else began to spin, too.

Koreas didn't bother trying to keep the little "squeee" of fun to herself as they turned. It wasn't until she opened her eyes to see Austin headed out of the room did she realize that it wasn't the room spinning. Austin had pivoted sharply on his heel and was literally carrying her off.

"Where do you want to go, beauty? Your room or mine?"

Whoa. Had she wondered aloud where he was taking her? Koreas didn't think she'd opened her mouth. And a moment later, she didn't care because he picked up where he left off—sucking on her neck as he walked. The combination of that lovely bit of suction, a nip here and there with sharp teeth, and the strength of his arms around her sent her up in flames.

It was so very nice to have a man pick her up as if she weighed nothing, given she was a solidly-built woman with a two hundred forty pound alter ego.

Two flights of stairs later, Austin stopped.

"Koreas?"

She knew what he was asking, but she didn't have the answer. And if she was honest, she didn't want to make the decision. She spent the majority of her days investigating, analyzing and deciding which road their research would take. Medicine was tricky business that could result in life or death. All it took was one ingredient gone wrong and...

"Koreas, come back from wherever your head went just now."

"Uh, right. My room."

Up one more flight of stairs and halfway down the wide hallway, Austin stopped and set Koreas on her feet. The moment her feet touched the carpet, she wanted to be right back in his arms. Raising up on her tip toes, she planted a kiss on his jaw and let her fingers play in the soft black waves on his head. "I don't usually kiss on the first date, but with you I just can't help it."

"I'm not asking you to help it. Not at all," he chided, hands on her waist. "And if you invite me in, I promise not to bite. Well, not unless you want me to."

She buried her face in his chest and laughed, but didn't hesitate to reach out and open the door.

A sudden shyness overtook her as the door closed quietly behind Austin. She, Koreas Pryde, was alone with a hunk of a man. In her room. After what was essentially an unplanned first date?

And good lord, she was uncharacteristically a-flutter.

Koreas turned away from her present company, kicked off her shoes and padded over to the window. A smile spread across her lips when strong arms came around her from behind and wrapped her in warmth. A shiver spread through her body as the evening shadow of whiskers raised gooseflesh on the sensitive skin of her neck.

Austin inhaled deeply.

"Mmm, I love the way you smell, Koreas. And I want to know you, learn you. Learn what you like and how you like it."

His hands joined his mouth in the game. Kory nibbled the inside of her bottom lip as Austin stoked the kindling of arousal. Just as it began to flare, it iced over. Suddenly, she was all nerves...and not the good kind.

Maybe they were moving too fast? Then again, perhaps this was normal for mating heat, if that's what this was. Tara seemed to think it was and Koreas had a feeling her sister was right. But what if she wasn't right? What if she got all excited and expectant just to find out she was wrong? What if...

"You're thinking too hard, so definitely no dick for you, Miss Kory." One arm banded beneath her breasts and held her tight. The other slid through the curls at her nape and brushed them aside to bare her skin more fully. "I need to spend a little more time with you before I allow you to take full advantage of me. I want you to be completely into it, so we'll go slowly."

And just like that, the roaring flame was back, brighter and higher than before. All because Austin managed to be bossy *and* considerate? Oh yes, he'd just pushed all the right buttons and Koreas needed, really *needed* to be touched now. Austin's suggestion of slow was bullshit. Fast had replaced it on the menu.

As if he'd read her mind—which he might just have done, given the *ker-chung* of the connection that had slammed into place today as they spent time together. Her attention was caught by a nip of teeth, followed by the most delicious suction over the tendon on the right side of her neck. The nip became a sensual bite that sent a tingle down her body, from her scalp to the curve of her ass.

"ERMAGERD!" she gasped.

Austin chuckled but never lost contact with her skin. Instead, he continued to kiss a trail of bliss across the back of her shoulders. The arm across her ribs eased away just long enough for a hand to slip beneath her top. Fingertips skimmed back and forth across her belly until the muscles twitched and tightened.

Breath wafted across her ear and she ducked her head, trying to get away from the tickle.

"So, beautiful," he said. "I think after I know you for, oh say, at least ten minutes, you can take whatever advantage you want. Just sayin'."

She laughed and said, "Way to take the pressure off, Austin James."

"Well, I'm not sure about that, but I do want to take this at your pace."

The erection he tried not to press against her ass said otherwise. Then came a brush against her mind. Tara? No, Kotara had a different "feel" to her when she used the little pathway into Koreas' head—a pathway worn smooth and comfortable by a lifetime of use. It wasn't the older Pryde twins either.

This was someone new. Fresh. Unused to peeking into someone's mind, *her* mind, if the hesitance and wonder trickling through to her consciousness were any indication.

Austin.

And while hesitant, it was deeply intimate. As intimate as the kiss that Austin James was currently giving her. Lip to lip. Breath to breath. Just...wow.

But it didn't make sense. Sure, attraction could indeed be explained through science, but what didn't make sense was why she was into, and in tune with, a human.

Nothing against them, of course. She worked with humans both in and outside of the lab. Pryde Ranch was home to several of them, all of whom had been caretakers of some sort for years. In fact, Broglio, their facilities manager, used to walk all four of the Pryde sisters to elementary school and was companion to their grandmother. Though that particular woman had long left this earth, Broglio still loved her going on at least forty years now.

Koreas had always fancied herself falling for a shifter—whether he was her own or another species made no difference to her. Growing up, her fantasies included her and her mate running out on the prairie, rolling in the grass and swimming in the Medicine Bow, her in her pelt and him in whatever his animal skin was.

This, as delicious as it felt, just wasn't what she'd...

She looked up and froze.

Kisses no longer trailed the line of her neck. Hands weren't roaming her back, skimming over her waist nor kneading her shoulder muscles. The warm little light of consciousness that had wrapped around her own like a sensual smoke was gone.

The slate gray of Austin's eyes held a chill. Dark brows pulled down into a deep frown and marred the handsomeness of his face.

"What?"

"Is this going to be a problem?" he asked.

"Is what going to be a problem?" Koreas blinked, unsure of what he was talking about. After all, her thoughts had passed so quickly, she'd all but forgotten the last thing she'd been thinking on.

"Me being human. I had no idea you considered human men beneath..."

"Whoa, whoa, wait a minute. You may have gotten a glimpse into my thoughts but don't think that you know me so well that you have a clue what just went through my head."

"I all but felt it, woman."

"Felt what, exactly? And if you're honest, you'll admit that it was such a rush of emotion you don't know what's really in my heart, versus what was just fleeting thoughts."

"Really?"

"Yes, really. Besides, you couldn't possibly have me figured out when I don't even know what the hell is going on." She delivered that last with a shy smile.

"Okay, you've got me there. So, why don't you tell me what's what, Koreas?"

"I will if you'll wrap me up in your arms again while I talk to you."

"You'll never have to ask me twice to hold you, darlin.'"

"God, you sound just like Jason. I swear he tells Neesia that kind of stuff all the time. So sappy."

"And you like it."

"I like Jason's sappiness?" A gust of cool wind through the partially open window had her burrowing back into Austin's warmth. His arms encircled her again as if it were the most natural thing in the world to do. And perhaps it was.

Koreas inwardly shook her head at herself. Confusion and half-guessing wasn't something she was acquainted with.

"You know what I mean," he said as he nipped her ear. "But I will gladly hold you some other time. Why don't you go shower."

"Shower? Why?"

"You worked in your lab all day, then sat in the pub with me until just an hour ago. It's getting late, you missed dinner and frankly, you look all done in. Beautiful, but done in just the same."

The man was clearly joking, but Koreas swatted at him anyway. He danced out of reach with ease and winked at her as he backed toward the door.

Koreas had already planned on hitting the tub tonight, but rather than saying so, she chose to address the issue at hand—Austin was giving her an out, a chance to walk way.

And she had no intention of taking him up on it.

"I know what you're doing."

"I'm being a gentleman," Austin replied, hand on the door knob.

"You're giving me a chance to be alone. If it's all the same to you—"

"I want no regrets between us, Kory."

His hand twisted the knob and Koreas' anxiety shot off the chart. And with a speed born of her kind, she was across the room and face to face with Austin James in less time than it took him to blink.

Huh. Interesting. Kotara was the pushy, non-shy half of their twinset. Yet here she was, itching to jump a man she only *thought* might be hers. Yet now, for a man she'd barely shared fries, beer and a kiss with, Koreas wanted so much more. From him. With him.

The thought of being alone after having tasted Austin made her gut dance with angst. Bottom line—she liked him in her space, whether it was here in a physical sense, or the tentative little touches of his conscience to hers. He fit. Perfectly.

"You promised to hold me if I tell you what's what. And I expect you to keep your word. So..."

She took his hand and was grateful that he allowed her to pull him back toward the swath of pearly moonlight that streamed into the room.

"I still want you to shower and relax, Miss Pryde. You work as hard as a one-armed ranch hand and I want you to shower and relax."

She looked at him sideways, trying to decide if she was offended or not. "Of course I work hard. Luckily, I love what I do and not everyone can say..."

"Doesn't change the fact that too much work is never good for anyone, darlin'." He ignored her disgruntled expression and dropped a kiss on her forehead. Kory scrunched up her face, then scrunched it up some more when he laughed. "Scowling gets you nowhere, now scoot. I'll be here when you come out."

"Well, just because you kiss good doesn't mean you get to tell me what to do," she stated resolutely.

He didn't answer. Instead, Austin ran his hands up and down her arms and asked, "You cold?"

"Not right now. But it's still early spring and gets a bit chilly at night."

"Well, whaddaya know. I'm one of those skilled men who can actually start a fire. In the meantime, you, into the shower."

"Not sure if starting fires and being bossy go well together," she grumbled under her breath. His response was a simple lopsided grin that charmed her right down to her toes. "So, pushy and charming all in one package, eh? Well, a fire sounds lovely. And since I'm wearing my latest style of lab goop, a shower does, too. Ten minutes?"

"Take your time, beautiful."

She stripped off her lab coat and dropped it into the separate laundry basket reserved for her work clothes. She tried to stomp off to the bathroom, but she couldn't really pull it off—something about being a lioness who naturally walked soft. The thought that she pouted because Austin was trying to take care of her made Kory shake her head at herself as she flipped on the warm water in the bathroom.

She tried to go slow and take her time under the rainfall-styled shower. In fact, she tried really, *really* hard, but even after she'd washed and exfoliated, Koreas' feet hit the fluffy rug that covered the cool tiles of her oversized bathroom at exactly five minutes. She wondered if the warming rack had even had enough time to heat up the soft fluffy towel she'd laid over it.

And the entire time she stood there amidst the steam, Kory had a bad case of Austin James on the brain. There was no doubt that this particular hunk of hotness called to her, and she was mature enough to accept that fact. However, she also acknowledged that the quiet-but-stubborn part of herself wanted to yell "screw your ten minute shower decree", tear out of the bathroom mid-shift and go off to play in the prairie grass. The other part wanted to make him work just a little bit, then lay in his arms for more of those toe-curling kisses she'd been enjoying for most of the evening.

That second part won…barely.

So Koreas slathered on the moisturizers that she would typically skip all together, clipped her nails and brushed her teeth. Twice.

At exactly ten minutes, she exited the bathroom with a swirl of steam chasing behind her. A few steps into her large room, her feet rooted themselves to the thick plush carpet.

The bright ceiling light she'd clicked on when they'd first entered was now off and every candle she owned was lit. The small flames set a lovely glow around the room as they flickered from nightstands, bookshelves, the dresser and little curio cases.

Austin had started a small blaze in the wood burning fireplace just large enough to compliment the romantic ambience. And the brilliant man had even drawn back the floor length curtains, raised the blackout blinds, and cracked the window a bit so it wouldn't get too warm for her. The scent of pine and wood smoke tickled her nose and though it was only spring, the scents brought to mind her favorite holiday—Christmas.

And Austin James was her type of Santa Clause...a present she wanted to unwrap, minus the oversized belly and red suit.

Koreas managed to close her gaping mouth as she took another look around. Her pulse kicked up when her gaze landed on the talk, dark and handsome man sprawled on her bed.

"You like?" he asked.

Did she like? Hell yes! In fact, her stomach was doing the twirl-a-whirl with anticipation of whatever else Austin had in store.

He was laid out on top of the covers. So tall, his feet practically hung off the end.

"Come on over here, gorgeous." He patted the space next to him.

As she approached, he pulled her favorite fluffy throw from the foot of the bed. She climbed onto the mattress and he wrapped her up in the blanket.

"Comfy?"

"Mmmhmm," she whispered on a dreamy sigh as she snuggled in. His natural scent filled her lungs and Koreas found herself inhaling again and again just to get another deep whiff.

"Yes, definitely comfy. A bit turned about, but comfy."

He dropped a kiss onto her forehead and she waited for him to push for an explanation of what she'd meant by "turned about", and was grateful that he didn't. The truth was her skin was on fire and her libido was headed for the moon. And all because this particular man held her in his arms. In his rock hard, Mount-Olympus-Zeus-sized, fabulously defined arms.

"What's wrong? You just went all tense?"

"Laying in my bed with a stranger isn't something that's normal for me. I barely know you."

"Uh huh. So what's really wrong, Koreas?"

Okay, so he'd seen right through that, eh? And he was right —his being a supposed stranger had nothing to do with her sudden tenseness. After all, she'd met him days ago, avoided him for just as long because of the way he seemed to waltz beneath her skin as if he belonged there. No, this sudden tenseness had more to do with the fact that Kory knew what he was to her, but didn't know if he was aware of just how connected the two of them could become.

After all, he was human, through and through. And she was *so* not. What if he didn't want her the way she wanted him? Sure, he knew what she was, what her entire family was, but that didn't mean he wanted a mating. And Kory would not press any man into a relationship with her. Period.

"Well, I think we've had enough companionable silence since my last statement. You gonna 'fess up as to what's going through that beautiful head of yours, Kory?"

"I was being honest." Sort of. "I don't know you, Austin."

"Well, we could know each other better but you've been somewhat scarce the last few days. Ah, she blushes," he said. "And such a pretty shade of caramel apple. Or at least that's what your skin brings to mind. Smooth. Pretty. And sweet."

"How do you know it's sweet? You haven't tasted—"

"Kisses don't count? I'm pretty sure I got a nibble or five. It was definitely pretty tasty, Kory. And back to the subject at hand, darlin'. I am very well aware that you've been avoiding me, though I'm not sure why. I will say that I plan to keep right on chasing you."

"But why?" She raised her head from his chest and pushed up on one elbow so she could look him in the eye. Part of the blanket and towel slipped down just enough to give a peek at the swell of her breast.

Now she really blushed as Austin's gaze unabashedly followed the path of skin down to the darkening ring that gave a hint at the color of her nipple.

Then his gaze rose up to meet hers.

"Why do I want you? To be honest, I've felt a ridiculous attraction to you since before I met you. That night near the river, I know that was you I sensed in the darkness. I'm not a shifter, but something pulls me to you and I want you like crazy."

"So you're interested in just a piece of ass?"

"Not even close. You're a brilliant woman, and I love talking to you. You're beautiful inside and out and I love the dynamic you have with your family. Plain and simple, you're my kinda girl, Koreas Pryde. And unless you think I'm a total douche canoe and not a suitable match, I intend to woo you, woman. The end."

The combination of her flushed cheeks, the blanket and towel, and being all wrapped up in Austin's burning touch set Kory on fire. And his declared intentions had her downright giddy.

Wow. A lioness, one of the most deadly creatures on the planet, was giddy?

Didn't stop her from giggling, though.

"Thank you for laughing. I'd rather you think I'm corny than not serious. In fact, thank you for laughing at all my jokes for the last several hours."

"You're welcome. Austin, listen, I'll just be honest with you. I don't do one night stands."

"Good, because that's not what I want from you, darlin'."

"I'm drawn to you, too, but it isn't something I expected. Ever. Maybe it's just biological, but it doesn't change the fact that I want you."

"And here I was thinking you were the shy one," he chuckled.

"I *am* the shy one. God help you if you'd fallen for Kotara." His chest rose and fell with his laughter and lit something light and airy inside of her until the rest of her words just bubbled on out. "This still isn't logical, but I understand biologics enough to know that it doesn't always make sense." After all, she could change into a fully-grown African lion and speak perfect English mind-to-mind with her family while in cat form. Nothing in the universe could explain that.

"You mean my human dude mojo isn't what's got you hooked? No? Well, thank you for laughing at my joke."

Well, he really was funny. The dimple on his left cheek winked at her as he smiled, and those smoky-gray eyes, so much like his brothers', were alive with mischief. And ropy, defined forearms, all thickly veined and solid? Kory wasn't even going to go there.

Finally, she caught her breath, lay back down with her cheek on his pecs and said, "I don't know about the mojo, but you're ridiculously handsome and I've totally enjoyed you this evening. I even appreciate that you had a Long Island Iced Tea without the Long Island just to make me feel comfortable while we hung out at the pub."

"No worries. It was the best Coke I've ever had, darlin'."

"I don't think we know each other well enough to say where this is going, but I can say that I like you enough to just enjoy your company while you're here and let things work themselves out."

"And that, right there, is exactly what I like about you Pryde women. You don't fuck around and play coy. You tell it like it is and don't make us poor males guess what in the hell is on your mind."

"Well, I flunked mind reading in the second grade and never quite recovered, so I figured it wasn't fair to expect others to have aced that particular class either."

He laughed, deep and rumbly beneath her cheek. Though her eyes were closed, she could practically see the sparkle in his eye as he smiled. He was the eldest James brother, just like Neesia was the matriarch of the Pryde's. It was a lot of responsibility to lead a family—she'd watched her oldest sister do it for more years than she could remember. But during her conversations with Austin, Kory learned a lot about this man. She liked that while Austin took his familial responsibilities seriously, he wasn't a broody, grumpy man. He knew when and how to turn off his serious side and let his inner kid out to play.

In fact, now that she thought about it, according to her twin, it was something Koreas totally sucked at—turning off the responsibilities she had to her family and her career, and relaxing long enough to enjoy life.

"Enough thinking. Kiss me, Kory. Worry about the rest of it later."

Finger beneath her chin, Austin lifted her face to his and dove right in. No teasing, coaxing or playing around, the man kissed her fully, thoroughly. Took her mouth with skill and purpose.

And she loved it. Wanted more. And without her having to ask, he gave it to her until she threw her head back and invited him without words to take things one step further.

Austin eased her onto her back and nibbled his way down one side of her throat, across her collarbone and up the other side. When he bit down on the tender flesh of her neck, Kory sucked in a breath and let it out on a needy moan.

"Oh my god," she mumbled, barely able to put the words together as her whole body went taut. Then her hips joined the dance, moved against him restlessly. Arms entwined around his neck and held tight. Legs rubbed against his. Hands explored the hard planes of his back.

And her mouth hung open as she tried to keep breathing.

But good lord, the man did indeed steal her breath. Wow, it was like zero to bonfire in six seconds flat.

"May I?" he asked with his hand poised over a towel-covered breast. He still managed to seek her consent even as his breath soughed in and out of his lungs with the same wildness as hers.

"Yes. Please."

She lay on her back and allowed him to unwrap her as he spoke.

"I'm clean, by the way. Can you even be affected by human disease?"

"Certain things. For example, I can catch a cold from you, and certain viruses. But no, I can't catch any serious sexual cooties. As far as felines go, I'm clean, too."

He smiled and Kory kept her gaze glued to his face as she tried to shake off what she assumed was natural nervousness. Sure, she had a nice body, but to be honest, she hadn't really worried much about what anyone thought of how she looked. But in this moment, she really wanted to please this man.

She'd had a few boyfriends over the years, but if she was honest, she'd never felt as connected to them as she did to Austin. Even the one guy she'd dated for a year didn't light up her hormones like this man.

As her skin was revealed, Austin's eyes took on an indescribable gleam, and what she couldn't quite define in his gaze, she almost felt, *heard*, in her head.

Beautiful. Perfect. So passionate.

Really? But rather than dwell on something that should be impossible, given the fact that he was fully human, Kory pushed it away and decided to live in the moment. And right now, the moment consisted of Austin as he yanked off his shirt and Kory found herself face to face with the most perfectly chiseled chest she'd ever seen. This man was cover model gorgeous, complete with eight pack and the perfect amount of sinfully dark hair sprinkled across his chest.

His skin was deeply tanned. Nipples, dark, tightly drawn and inviting, were proudly displayed in the center of lush breasts and firm pectorals. Just...wow.

She was completely naked while all he bared was his chest. And what a magnificent chest it was, too.

When Neesia had told their family that all "those James boys" were hunkalicious, she hadn't been kidding. But now Kory had the privilege of seeing beyond the ruggedly dark good looks and disarming charm. This was more than business acumen and brains. This was fucking gorgeous, buffed body to boot!

Austin laughed.

"I heard that, sort of. Unless I'm crazy and just imagined I heard you say I have a gorgeous buffed body."

Nope. Not his imagination.

"You heard me? Can you describe it?"

"It was like a wisp of a warm breeze across my brain."

Now it was her turn to laugh. "Warm breeze across your brain? I didn't know you were such a poet, Austin James."

He gave her hair a sharp but playful yank. "No laughing at the big buff man."

She laughed harder.

"Well, I guess there's only one way to get you to stop laughing at me. Actually, there are probably at least twenty good ways, but tonight we only have time for one."

Finally, he removed his belt and Kory almost panted in anticipation.

Then, to her surprise, he lay back down and pulled her into his lap.

"This is as naked as I'm getting, beautiful."

"But—"

"No buts. Tonight is for you. You work like a damn dog—no offense considering you're a feline and all—and I want you to enjoy tonight without worrying about whether you should or not."

Austin went to work.

Koreas' giggles became moans, groans and lots and lots of "aaaah's".

As she straddled him, Austin pretty much moved her where he wanted. He kissed his way down her stomach until her entire belly was one quivering mass of muscle and flesh. His mouth was magic, and his hands were fire to her kindling as he pulled and twisted her nipples until she arched and ground against him with abandon.

She lifted her hands to sink them into his hair, but Austin was quick. The second her fingers touched the black silky waves, she found them captured in one of his as he looked up at her.

"Hands over your head. Hold onto the headboard."

"But I want to touch you, Austin."

"I know, but you can't. Not until I say so."

"Yep. Definitely bossy," she growled but couldn't hide the bit of amusement laced within the words.

"Hey, I'm the oldest, so of course I'm bossy."

And his grin was disarming as hell.

Then ever so subtly, the inner Austin bled through her haze of lust. She *felt* him. Felt his need mixed with an uncertainty that matched her own. As unreasonable as it was, she wanted this man to know without a doubt that this thing between them was right. Even if she wasn't sure herself, it hit one of her insecurity buttons to know that he was just as nervous.

Just another damn thing that didn't make any sense.

"Stay on task, Kory, or I'll have to spank you."

Whoa, wait. What?

She looked down her body and right into Austin's beautiful crystalline gray eyes. He looked awfully good with a sheen of sweat covering his face and neck.

Koreas couldn't decide whether to argue with him or just bathe in the sensual sensations he caused in her body and mind.

"Don't even try to look innocent, Koreas Pryde. Your mind wandered. In fact, it took a side trip right into mine. It's not freaking me out because, after all, I grew up with Jason DiCaplis and I understand shifters, to a point. But let's be clear, woman. I'm plenty sure of what I want. My uncertainty is that you may not want me back."

"Really?"

Oh, that single word managed to drag with it a nice dose of saucy-with-a-side-of-sarcasm. She hadn't meant it to come out that way, but a part of her geeky scientific brain had checked out, and the me-must-challenge-big-bad-hunky-dude part had popped right out.

His brows rose as he quietly said, "Challenge, eh?"

Damn it. Had she said that out loud? Hell no, she hadn't. Crap. Looked like this connection of theirs definitely worked both ways.

And just like that, Koreas Pryde found herself face down over Austin's lap.

"Though I don't usually respond to challenges this way, something tells me you're going to like this."

Koreas hadn't had her ass spanked since she'd been a little girl. And that wasn't by some hot guy that she wanted to fuck silly. How dare he presume to spank her! He had no right to...

The first slap landed on her bare ass.

After a swift intake of breath, her protest came out as a breathy, "Oooh."

Okay, now that was a surprise. The light smack was followed by sweeping delicious passes of his hand over the warming skin. Then another easy blow, followed by more caresses.

When her body took over and began to squirm, the spanking got more intense.

And so did the pleasure. The amazing edge of pain and bliss pushed at her tolerance until she stopped trying to figure out why she liked it so much, and simply let it happen. Finally, as she squirmed and panted with need, Austin's fingers dipped down between her thighs and found her dew thick and hot. His answering moan of appreciation stoked that fire higher.

"Mmm, you're so wet. And you smell so good. Time for a taste, Kory."

Back in their original position with Koreas straddling Austin as he lay on the bed, he said, "Now, let's try this again. Hands on the headboard."

Kory shook her head at him…and then she did exactly as she was told. She wrapped her fingers around the slats of her headboard as Austin pulled her up onto his face.

And the moment his mouth touched the drenched folds of her sex, strong hands wrapped around each thigh and spread her wide open. Koreas was sure she'd never been so exposed.

The wet heat of his mouth swept over her drenched folds—back and forth, up and down. Round and round. His whole head was in on the action as he made sure that no part of her juicy sex was untouched. He lapped, sucked, slurped and ate her like she tasted better than the big batch of fries they'd shared at the pub earlier. And he'd confessed that fries were his favorite snack.

Each lick, each tug as he pulled her clit into his mouth sent her arousal up yet another notch.

Kory held on to the solid wood bed for dear-fucking-life.

When Austin slipped a finger into her body, she gasped and ground down on him. Then another finger joined the first and he worked her into a frenzy.

"Please, more. Oh, god, Austin."

Those fingers sped up just a bit more just as he pulled her

distended clit into his mouth and worked the tip of his tongue back and forth over it.

"Yes, oh my god!"

Then he hummed.

Kory came so hard her eyeballs crossed, breath stuck in her throat and she almost fell over sideways.

But Austin was relentless. He held on and pushed her through another orgasm that made it clear her first one was simply a warm up.

When her breathing returned to normal, she lay on the bed in a boneless heap.

Austin arranged her over his body and simply stroked her hair.

The only sounds were their combined breathing, the quiet crackle of the wood in the fireplace and the evening breeze that blew in through her window and cooled her sweat-soaked skin.

Kory spoke into the comfortable silence.

"Yep. Cowboys for the win."

Austin's chuckle warmed her from the inside out as he gathered her closer and dropped a kiss on her brow.

About an hour later as she dozed, Austin gently roused her, said goodnight and gave her another kiss on her cheek, her forehead and her neck. "Goodnight, beautiful. Sleep well and dream of me."

With his scent on her skin and on her sheets, Kory whispered, "Night, night," rolled over and did just that—dreamed of rolling around in the spring sweet grass in her pelt with a gorgeous dark-haired, gray-eyed man at her side.

---

8

*B*y now, Kory would typically have her to-do list for the day categorized and ranked in neat little columns in her notebook. Two or three of those tasks would already be completed, but she'd been in the labs for at least an hour, yet accomplished absolutely nothing.

There were two large desks—one for her and one for Kotara —and an oversized work station with equipment for research and plenty of room for the twins to collaborate. Kory straddled a stool in a completely unladylike fashion at the workstation and let the events of the previous afternoon-into-evening wash through her as she poked at some proteins growing in a glass flask. A wave of mixed emotions filled her chest and exited as a quiet sigh. Spending time with Austin had been wonderful. Period.

On one hand, she wished the man was down in the Labyrinth right now talking to her about his life and just stuff in general. On the other hand, she was glad he was nowhere near because she'd never get anything done, and gawking at his über hotness didn't count as a task.

Down here there were no windows, hence no sunlight, yet

heat radiated from her skin in all the places that Austin had touched the night before. And there'd been a *lot* of places. It was as if she'd bathed in him, and he'd left his impression on her just like when she lay out under the brilliant rays of the sun and soaked up their warmth.

Sure, the night had been fantastic, but Kory was practical. And that meant she had no expectations other than what she'd put forth last night—enjoy Austin while he was here and let the rest sort itself out.

Just as the thought cleared the ether of her mind, the hair on the nape of her neck began to dance.

A shadow out of her peripheral vision had her twirling around on her stool.

"What the hell are you doing in here?" Kory snapped and then clamped her lips closed. An instinct as old as time made her aware of the shifting dynamic between her and the too-damn-gorgeous-for-words male standing in the doorway.

"Well good morning to you, too, Koreas," Austin said. And there stood the literal man of her dreams. A dark blue plaid shirt peeked through the partially zipped leather bomber jacket he wore to help ward off the early morning Wyoming spring chill. A pair of worn black denims fit as if they were tailored and showed off muscular thighs and a perfect ass. On his feet were soft leather boots—to her surprise they weren't cowboy boots but a pair of custom dyed Dr. Marten's. It still amazed her that this country boy and his brothers were sought-after, world class architects of some of the most expensive and exclusive buildings in the world.

She watched him closely but it really wasn't necessary because he didn't bother to school his features. The expression on his face morphed from a hint of surprise, to curious, to completely *not* amused. In fact, he'd gone from happy to see her to downright pissed in just a few seconds.

Something whispered against her mind, told her that he

knew exactly what she'd just been thinking. And he was not pleased. At all.

It was true that Kory expected nothing from Austin past last night. It didn't matter what he'd said—talk was cheap. Kory had learned over the years to have no expectations when it came to relationships outside of her family. That way she couldn't be disappointed, right?

"Wrong." Austin's voice was a whip in the silence of the room.

Whoa.

For a moment, the man looked just as taken aback as she was, considering that she hadn't said anything out loud. Kory was so surprised that her growing connection with Austin had made it from her bedroom last night and into the light of day, she hadn't noticed that they weren't alone.

"Uh, so, are you two cool or what?" Kotara spoke up with her no-nonsense tone firmly in effect. And Kory knew that her twin had missed absolutely nothing.

"Uh...yeah. Well, I...Yes. I'm fine, Tara. Thanks, sis."

Austin's frown morphed into a smile that seemed to grow in direct proportion to Koreas' level of discomfort. Bastard. Considering he'd come into her domain uninvited, she had no idea what the hell was so damn funny. So she repeated her original question with a bit less rudeness.

"So, Austin, what brings you here?" she asked quietly, yet not bothering to keep the annoyance out of her voice. Question was, what was she really annoyed about?

Are you irked because he's here when you expected him to hit and run, or because you're busted because he obviously picked up on the fact that you didn't believe his words last night?

Damn conscience. She wished it would just shut up and go crawl into a corner somewhere.

"I brought him in, Kory. He's been asking for a tour since he and his brother's got here. And you're going to give him one. Right?"

Koreas resisted the urge to roll her eyes at the pair staring at her as if daring her to say something they didn't like.

Kory was the down low Pryde, the introvert, the quiet one, but the ball busting part of herself that she kept under wraps had started to wriggle free with Austin last night. And right now, with Austin looking at her as if she'd kicked his horse, it wanted to rebel. Loudly.

Said male eyed her closely as he cocked his head to the side with an expression that growled, "Who the hell do you think you're talking to like that?" when she hadn't actually uttered a word. But rather than speak, he simply pinned her with a look that told her they would be talking about this later. And that talk would be intense...and might lead to some physical deliciousness just as intense as the verbal sparring she knew was coming.

For the barest of moments, Kory was amazed she knew all this about a man she was just coming to know. Just because she had an idea *why* she had such insight didn't change the wonder of it all.

Shifter mates began to develop a bond of sorts. But Austin wasn't a shifter so surely the dynamics of mating would be different between them, right? Besides, biogenetics or not, mating was still a choice, damn it, and she might just choose to tell him to go suck wind.

Thoughts and questions swirled through her head, and just as suddenly, they fell to the ground of her mind like a kite with no wind. It was a total a-ha moment—Reya was mated to a human male. Maybe the jaguar shifter with the dazzling gray eyes would share her experience? God, she hoped so because Kory had no doubt that Austin James was hers, through and through. But she had no fucking idea what to do with that knowledge considering he was fully human.

Then again, perhaps it wouldn't be an issue considering the man was seething and might not want to stick around anyway.

"After the tour, meet me in the library, Kory. We're going out to lunch," Kotara said, breaking into Kory's whirlwind of thoughts. "Oh, and Austin?"

"Yes, ma'am?" he replied politely as he turned to fully face Tara.

"Since my sister seems a bit put out with you right now, you piss her off further, we'll be planning your evisceration in great detail. Friend of Jason's or not. Just sayin'."

Koreas let gooey warmth flow over her. It was a feeling she always got whenever her twin subtly took up for her—or in this case, not so subtly. Her sister might be outwardly threatening the very large man standing in their private labs, but deep down inside, Tara was thrilled to her toes.

Kory should probably be annoyed at Kotara's declaration of promised pain to Austin, but she honestly couldn't muster enough irritation at the person who loved her the most. Sure, all her sisters doted on her, but Tara shared a unique connection that no one else ever would—with the possible exception of the man standing across the room.

So rather than being pissed that her twin had just threatened a world of hurt to her not-quite-claimed mate, Koreas grinned, smacked her sister on the cheek with a sloppy kiss and then burst out laughing at Tara's wry expression.

"See you in the library, sis." Tara walked over, kissing her on the cheek. "Better yet, let's just meet back here. I've got to go lay the smack down on Erin, she left another sample laying around. I may have to bite her in the ass to jog her memory. Later, Austin." With that, Tara walked toward the frosted glass double doors, which automatically slid open for her and then *snicked* closed after she crossed over the threshold.

Seconds later, Austin moved at near-shifter speed and had Kory off of her stool before she could form her next thought.

Her back met the nearest wall and Austin plastered himself against her front as his emotions exploded through her head.

Oh my god!

So *this* was how he felt about her? He *needed* her—to touch her, to hold her against him, to meld into her until there was no way to tell where one began and the other ended. On the tail end of all that desire was anger.

She hadn't believed him last night when he'd expressed his hunger for her. This anger of his wasn't male pride. It was hurt. Plain and simple.

His hands were gentle, even as he plundered her mouth with his kiss. It was as if he tried to brand her, make her his, make her see how much he wanted her.

When he finally let her up for air, Kory had partially shifted under the passionate onslaught. Her claws were exposed, had shredded through his leather jacket and sank just the slightest bit through his shirt and into the skin of his pecs.

Just as she'd come to her senses enough to be mortified, Austin sucked in a hiss. "Oh baby. God, that's hot."

Hot? She'd just cut him with her claws and he was making "gimme some" sounds? *Da fuck?*

"You're like one of those secret agents on television. Gorgeous geek by day, hot as sin, kick ass agent by night." He swiveled his hips and leaned in closer, causing her claws to sink in just a bit more. "And you blooded me. I think you've ruined me for all other women."

"You're a deranged masochist." Then again, the way he'd delivered that spanking last night, maybe he was a sadist. Maybe both. The thought sent a serious thrill up her spine and a rush of wetness down her thighs, but she held her mask of calm together. For now. "I've ruined your jacket, but I don't think I've ruined you for any other woman."

She wouldn't tell him that as irrational as it was, the thought of him with another woman made her want to sink those claws just a bit deeper.

"You doubting me again, Kory?" he asked, and then he nipped her on the chin with sharp, but very human, teeth.

Still holding her off the ground and against the wall, Austin nibbled and licked her skin as he ground his thick erection against her core. Kory's head fell back on a moan and hit the wall with a thud. Good thing she had a thick skull.

"Listen, woman, I don't care that we're newly acquainted. I know what I want." Kiss. "I'm not some kid or boy playing grown up." Nibble. "I'm a grown ass man who knows a good thing when I see it. I need you to know right now that I say exactly what I mean, Kory. It comes from raising two bone-headed brothers. So when I say I want you, that's what I mean. Period. Got me?"

Austin pumped his hips forward again, letting her feel exactly where his head...both of them, were at the moment. So was he thinking with his dick? Or did he really mean it?

"Stop it. I can get sex anywhere, Kory."

Wow. He'd cut her thoughts off at the pass again. She wondered if he was this good at roping cattle or whatever other cowboy architects did.

"I don't rope cattle, smart ass. And there's a big difference between pussy and love. And I'm telling you now, this is deeper than sex. I can feel that this is right. You and me."

Then he bit her on the neck and sucked. Hard.

"Ah, god," she gasped.

Oooh, it was right all right. The way he suckled that spot as he pressed the thick ridge of his cock against her mound sent her up in flames.

"Fire, huh? Shall I let you burn?" he asked.

Oh my.

She obviously needed to shield her thoughts a bit better. With her sisters, there was a natural agreement to "knock" before entering each other's heads, unless they were on a hunt. Obviously, this human-to-shifter thing was a tad bit different given Austin didn't seem to realize what he was doing.

But he was hers. This bumbling-around-in-her-brain, beautiful, thoughtful, no-nonsense country boy was all hers.

Good god, she was getting hit on all fronts.

Outside—shared moans and tangled tongues, as if the most decadent treat was found in the touch of the other. Her skin heated and sweat gathered at the base of her spine.

Inside—pure emotion ebbed and flowed, crashed onto the shore of her mind. Wave after wave of carnality entwined with loving care, swirled through and around her. His intentions shone so clear, there was no room for mistaking Austin's true intentions. Actions could be faked, but this? Not so much.

The man kissed her as if she were his own personal antidote. Perhaps she was, if the way he made her feel was any indication. Hands skimmed over sensitive skin beneath her lab coat until he'd worked the thing halfway off her shoulders.

His fingers had been skating beneath her breasts, up her back and around her body. Her nipples were puckered tight in anticipation of the twists and pulls he would give them. Finally, he eased his mouth away from hers long enough to ask if he could touch her breasts.

Finally!

"Yes," she panted. "Please touch me."

"You know I'm big on consent."

"Yeah, fine. Hurry up."

"Bossy woman."

She chuckled then bit her lip as he threw her words from last night back at her.

Cool air met her stomach as he touched her everywhere his

hands could reach. Lab coat now on the floor, Austin unbuttoned her blouse and stared. Kory bit back a grin as he enjoyed the view—a pink bra with black polka dots and lace. The matching panties were slick and wet and she hoped that he'd get around to seeing those soon.

Soon, her blouse joined her lab coat, followed by the neat pencil skirt she wore. Next went the shoes as he sat her on top of her desk and stepped between her legs.

He stripped out of his ruined leather bomber and torn shirt. Koreas' eyes went wide at the sight of ten small cuts on his bare chest—one for each of her fingers.

"I love the bra and panty set, Ms. Pryde." He leaned in and kissed her again, this time down the side of her neck as he nuzzled an ear. "Mmm, you smell so good, Kory. I can almost taste your dew on my tongue."

He could smell her wetness? The shy part of her wanted to pull away and cover herself, but the horny, I-need-my-mate side wanted nothing more than to be devoured whole.

"How do you know I'm what you smell?" It was a reasonable question. After all, it could be her deodorant or body wash, right?

"After spending a nice bit of time devouring that sweet pussy last night, I'd know that scent anywhere. And god, it makes my mouth water. Lift up."

She braced herself on the desk and lifted her hips just enough for him to slide her panties off. When he stuffed her underwear in his face and made smacking noises, she shook her head at him as laughter bubbled up from her soul. Kory didn't think she'd laughed this much in the presence of a male that she was physically attracted to in...well, damn. She couldn't remember how long.

Guess Tara was right. I'm overdue for some fun.

Austin tucked her underwear into the pocket of his jeans as he made his way over to the first aid cabinet. He pulled open the glass doors and immediately grabbed what he was looking for. In moments he returned to her side, and without missing a beat, slipped a Chux pad underneath her bare butt.

"I figure you don't want the top of your desk wet, and I do intend to make you quite wet."

"Just what are you plan…oh my god."

Austin had leaned forward, spread her legs wide and dove into her, head first. His wicked tongue traced every dip and fold of her drenched sex. Her inner muscles groped for something that wasn't there until she was spasming with need.

Then kisses and touches just weren't enough.

"Austin. I want it. Please."

Austin looked up into her face, took one last long lick, then he kissed her again and lifted her off the desk. On her feet, Kory slid down his body, panting and groaning as the onslaught of sensations drove her to her knees. Literally.

And once she was there, she had one goal in mind.

Austin reached for her, tried to bring her back up so he could kiss her some more. He stilled when Kory growled low in her throat.

"Okay, okay," he chuckled. "Have your wicked way with me, darlin'. Just watch the claws."

Holy shit. She'd partially shifted yet again. With a deep breath, she retracted her claws, still amazed she'd lost control of her cat twice in barely twenty minutes. What could she say? The man was potent. The end.

Leaning forward, Kory rubbed her face over the granite bulge that was Austin's cock—the one he'd not allowed her to sample last night. The one her mouth watered for. Her sex swelled for. Her lioness hungered for.

She inhaled deeply and savored the masculine, clean scent of him.

"Mmm, you smell good, too." The words were muffled as she spoke against the denim of his jeans.

No response.

Kory looked up. Her womb clenched at the sight of Austin James, head thrown back, and his teeth bared on a swift intake of breath. She unbuttoned his pants, ridiculously pleased that he had no underwear on. Her kitty damn near purred in her head at the knowledge that her guy was the commando type who was clearly as hot for her as she was for him.

Again, Kory rubbed her face against him and savored the heat of his cock against her cheek. As his arousal skyrocketed— god, she loved *feeling* him, knowing that she pleased him in this way—his scent changed. It was deeper, muskier. Almost spicy. Her own personal catnip.

And she wanted a bite or five.

The man was thick, long and scorching in her hand. Without any warning, Kory swallowed him whole and inwardly grinned at herself at his near-shout to the rafters.

"Good god, woman!"

Mmmhmm.

She pulled back, licked around the engorged head, and then took him deep again. The man tasted so good. His unique flavor coated her tongue, sank into her blood, and ratcheted up her own arousal to a level she'd never experienced before.

Austin's fingers clenched and unclenched as he held onto the desk. Then those same strong hands buried themselves in her hair and tugged her closer.

A few more strokes of her tongue and Kory felt his cock actually twitch against her tongue. He tried to back away, but there was nowhere for him to go.

"Kory. Enough."

Well, she didn't think so. She ignored him, rode him with her mouth several more times before she found herself lifted to her feet and whipped around to face the desk.

Austin grabbed a handful of her hair, used it to maneuver her head where he wanted. Looking down at her bared throat, he said, "You may be the quiet one, but you are not the goody, goody. In fact..." He bit down on the sensitive spot where shoulder met neck. "Right now, you're naughty, naughty. And I have you just where I want you."

He rubbed the heat of his rod against her ass. Kory almost wept at the pleasure.

"Kory, I want inside."

She nodded her head but he didn't move. Her brain was functioning just enough to remember why he hesitated just as he asked the question.

"Consent, Kory. Do I have it?"

She nodded again.

"I want the words."

"Fuck me already!"

"Oooh, such a dirty mouth. And I love it. Is this your fertile time?"

"No," she snapped and then wiggled her hips, clearly in need. "Please."

Good. She was as far gone as he was.

Tucking himself at her entrance, Austin slowly eased inside, though it damn near killed him to do so. Even as slick and ready as she was, he was a large man and the last thing he wanted was to hurt her. So he forced himself to go slow while paying close attention to Kory's reaction.

Did she tense as he pushed further in? Were her moans of pleasure or pain? Was her body pliant or rigid?

He took it all in, tried to miss none of the clues as to what she needed, her pleasure his sole focus.

And at the moment he knew was right, he slammed home and rode her hard.

"Yes. God, yes," she panted as she pushed her hips back at him, begging for more without words.

His cock felt as if it were wrapped in indescribable heat, just as his heart seemed wrapped up in this woman. She was sugar and spice, heat that burned and soothed at the same time.

And the moment he felt just a smidge of a hint of concern on her part regarding their mating, Austin was determined to drive everything from her head other than what they were doing right at this moment.

He wasn't sure if he was doing it right, but Austin pictured a comfy blanket in his mind and pushed reassurance down their forming bond. Immediately he felt her relax, both inside and out, and her momentary lapse of worry dissipated as if it had never been.

He also knew she was very close to detonating all over his cock. And he couldn't wait to feel her milk him as he'd imagined since the moment he realized what they could be to each other —mates.

"Are you ready?" he asked, knowing she would understand what he meant.

"No. More. Fuck me more."

So he did, until she exploded around him, squeezed him tight within her body. Took his seed from him.

After catching her breath, Austin insisted on helping Koreas get dressed. It was a truly intimate moment, and he took each opportunity he could to drop a kiss on her forehead, cheeks and the lips, now plump from his kisses. He buttoned her blouse and helped her put her little leather flats back on her feet. Her skirt was a wrinkled mess, but she didn't seem to mind.

Her skirt made a swishing sound as she moved quickly over to the first aid kit mounted on the wall and removed a sealed container of cotton balls and a bottle of alcohol.

Back at her desk, which she would never see the same again, she motioned Austin to sit. He faced her with a wicked grin as she saw to the cuts she'd made on his skin. He didn't even flinch as the alcohol was applied because he was too busy being happy about the fact that she'd totally lost it enough to cut him in the first place.

"Thank you for a lovely morning, darlin'."

"Likewise. So, now what?"

"I hope to see you at dinner, then perhaps take a blanket down to the river and watch the stars, or something equally romantic and sappy."

She laughed. Couldn't help it.

"Fine. See you later then."

"Walk me out?"

"Sure," she said, and didn't even think to refuse when he stretched forth his hand in invitation. And they walked that way, hand in hand, all the way to the parking garage and parted with a kiss that lingered on Kory's lips long after Austin had gone.

Ladies and gentlemen, Austin James had left the building.

Thank ya. Thank ya verra much.

9

*T*ara grit her teeth as she stood in the middle of the floor of the space she shared with Kory. Her skin felt too tight as she flushed with heat from the scent in the air—sex. And if she wasn't mistaken, it had been good sex.

She almost laughed at herself as her face morphed from grumbles to grins and back. Peeling off her lab coat, she stepped into the private shower and set it on icy cold, careful to avoid paying extra attention to her sensitive breasts as she washed up. Dressed and ready to go, she snatched a light sweater off the coat rack and stood, arms crossed, near the door and glanced at her watch.

Five. Four. Three. Two...

And the doors eased open.

Kory walked through and slammed to a halt on a surprised gasp. Standing face to face, and almost toe to toe, Kotara shook her head at her sister, who was currently trying to wipe the goofy ass grin off her face and replace it with her typical calm-as-a-blank-slate expression. Only right now, it wasn't working.

Kory stepped fully into the room and headed over to the specimen table and took a seat on one of the tall metal stools.

And with her best "big sis" glare, Tara began the required interrogation.

"Koreas Lee Pryde, if you were supposed to be giving a tour of the Labyrinth, why do I smell Austin James all over both you and this lab?"

Arms crossed over her chest, she answered without hesitation, "Because, Kotara Ann Pryde, if you must know, Austin James *was* all over me."

Kotara bit her lip to keep from grinning in response to the glee that practically rolled off her twin. This was supposed to be a grilling. All sisters were required to give their siblings a tough time over their guy. It showed they cared for one another.

"Well, giving that this room reeks of sex, you'd better dish right now."

Kory hesitated. Tara moved in for the kill. "Dish, or I'm calling Neesia. Oh, and Niah is home today, too, so—"

"No she's not, but all right already!" Kory threw up her hands. "He drove me home from the pub last night."

"Last night? Kory, you went to the pub for *lunch* yesterday. Early, I might add."

"Yeah, well, day turned into night. We talked and—"

"That's a lot of talking."

"—and decided to start, uh, hanging out. And stuff."

"Hanging out and *stuff*?" Kotara tapped her foot impatiently. They both knew what was going on here—the out of control libidos complete with a case of horny-toad overload. Genetics didn't lie. Her sister had found a mate and Kotara was beyond thrilled. Even if that sister was currently playing coy while wearing a grin that matched her own. "Hanging out doesn't leave a man's scent on your skin, missy. So, kiss and tell."

"There's been some kissing...but I'm not telling," Koreas declared with her gaze still plastered to the results report she pretended to pore over.

"Really? Wanna bet?" Kotara didn't bother hiding what she

knew was an evil gleam in her eye. After all, she was a genius at pulling off the most original pranks. Sometimes chemicals in the hands of a particular smart-ass scientist was a bad idea...like the time she'd roofied their sister Niah's after-dinner drink to help Niah's mate, Lou, get her on a plane to Bora Bora. "May as well start talking, hon. Otherwise I'm headed to my private lab to cook up something just for you."

Kory's eyes went wide as she backed up a step and raised her hands in the universal I-surrender-please-don't-make-me-have-a-flaming-poo position.

"Something about him makes me go all soft and mushy inside. Makes me just want to do anything and everything. I don't think I've ever given that to a man, ever, but Austin makes me want to drop to my knees and just..."

Kory took a deep breath and let all her inner emotions—fear, happiness and sheer lust—wash through the special connection she shared with her twin.

The moment their minds touched, Tara's eyes widened and filled with tears. A thrilled wiggle filled her tummy and goose-bumps spread over her skin. In that moment, she understood everything that Kory couldn't quite put into words. It had been shared on a level so deep, there was no mistaking what she'd been trying to say.

Tara looked at her watch again.

"Crap, we're going to be late for lunch. Shower while you tell me the rest." With that, she herded a freely-gabbing Kory to the shower she'd occupied not long ago. Only this time, she set it to warm instead of to an arctic chill.

Sitting on the side of the counter, Tara asked, "So that's why you've been walking around all dreamy eyed this morning? Well, before he showed up at the labs, that is."

"I am *not* dreamy eyed." Her movement may have been swift as she swiped soap out of her eyes, but Kory's words held no heat. Not even enough to light a match. A tiny one.

"Oh, yes you are. No one else may have noticed but you can't fool me, sis."

And then Kotara proceeded to wring every juicy detail from her sibling, down to the last little bit of naughty. And it was immediately clear that her sister was experiencing something both freeing and eye-opening by simply admitting that Mr. Austin James had well and truly caught himself a lioness.

That spark of discovery was there in Kory's eyes as if she'd just discovered a new vaccine or breakthrough medicine. Excitement. Glee, almost. Why? Because she'd found a mate.

And that's what Austin James was to Koreas Pryde—a mate, one she'd never thought would ever manifest in her life.

Kotara was, in that moment, the happiest she'd ever been simply because she knew her sister was thrilled.

Now, if there was just something she could do about the universal horniness that accompanied these mating things. All three of Kotara's sisters now had honest-to-goodness, flesh and blood mates to scratch their itches. Kotara had a waterproof super-duper personal toy she called Mr. Hoo-ha and an endless supply of batteries.

Sigh.

Yep, she was definitely overdue for a sudsy bath with a couple of double A's. But first, she and Kory had a date of a different kind.

Sitting with Kory and Reya at a snazzy restaurant a hundred miles from Pryde Ranch, Kotara raised a glass with an easy smile. "Thanks for having lunch with Kory and me today, Reya. A toast to cool chicks with mad feline and geeky skills."

"To cool chicks," echoed around the table, along with salutes of mugs of bubbly apple cider. Yep, they were definitely forming a bond of friendship that Kory was sure only existed among shifter kind.

Kotara set down her mug and put on her serious face. "Food's here. Look out, you guys. This is going to be *so* not cute."

The local hottie server put the plates down, winked and then asked if they needed anything else. Kory bit the inside of her cheek when her sister's naughty reply hit the back of her mind. Yep, they were definitely sharing a case of horny-toad overload.

"Good lord," Reya muttered, "did they put the whole buffalo on the plate?"

"Are you complaining?" Kory asked, knowing she flashed a devilish grin.

"Hell no. But this much rare meaty goodness on one plate makes me want to yell, 'On your mark, get set, go!', then shift into my other form and dive in head first."

"Well," Kory said quietly, "we might not be able to shift in here, but there aren't any rules about diving head first into our plates."

The clattering of forks filled the silence as they enjoyed huge chargrilled rare steak and roasted sunchokes with rosemary and thyme.

After the main meal was done, Kory sat back in her seat and patted her tummy. "Wow, that was good. Almost as good as Neesia's."

"You'd better not ever let her hear you compare restaurant food to her own cooking. She'll skin you alive and then mother hen you to death while you heal."

The waiter set a carafe of coffee on the table. Kory grinned as she poured each of them a cup. "Good point, Tara. You never heard me say anything of the sort. In fact, I'm not sure what I just ate. Hell, I don't even know where we are, so I can't compare anything to Neesia's cooking, right?"

"I didn't hear anything," Reya chimed in.

"Uh huh," Tara chuckled and took a sip of steaming hot caffeinated goodness.

The meal had been fantastic. The company was awesome. Now, it was time to get some answers. Kory took a deep breath and jumped in head first. "Reya, I was hoping we could talk. Can I ask you some personal questions?"

"Sure, sweetie. Anything."

"How did you know Aaron was the one?"

Reya put down her cup and gave Kory her undivided attention. Her intense gray gaze reminded her of Austin's pretty eyes. And right now those eyes fixed on her, focused and fully alert on Kory's every word. It was like talking to, well, a doctor.

And suddenly, Kory was nervous, her typical calm was replaced by a swarm of nosey bumblebees that flit around in her gut. Ugh, what a foreign sensation. The whole stomach-twitching thing didn't make sense to her rational mind, but considering all kinds of strange emotional fluffiness had occurred since meeting—not to mention *doing*—Austin, Kory figured it was just part and parcel of the whole mate thing.

"Well," Kory continued, "When Neesia and Niah met their mates, their *shifter* mates, everything that followed made sense to me. I mean, all I know are shifter genetics and physiology." She paused and took a hearty swallow of coffee, and then decided she needed something with a little more kick for this conversation.

Waving over the waiter, she ordered a Long Island Iced Tea...this time *with* the Long Island.

"Anyway, this thing with Austin?"

Eyes wide with surprise, Reya's hands flew up and covered her mouth as she sucked in a huge gasp. "Oh my god! You and Austin?" Even though they were at a private table a bit away from everyone else, Kory was glad the other woman squeaked just loud enough for only their party to hear. She was also quite pleased that Reya was practically bouncing in her chair with glee.

"Kory, I'm speechless. I had no idea who you were talking about until just now. Just...yay!"

And now she was blushing and smiling and inwardly commanding her new friend—the tummy wiggle—to quiet down some. "Soooo...yes, Austin and me. I have no frame of reference for it. Didn't even think or consider the possibility of a human-to-shifter mating."

"I get you," Reya said. "And I mean totally. Biochem and genetics aren't my expertise, but as a doctor—"

"We've been meaning to ask what kind of doctor you are," Tara chimed in.

"After I earned my degree in medicine, I did a five-year residency in Colorado and some special respiratory stuff right here in Wyoming. Then I did some time as a trauma surgeon before I bailed and almost gave my Aunt Sulu a heart attack."

"Bailed? Heart attack?" asked Kory and Tara in unison.

Reya smiled. "I love the whole twin thing, you guys saying things at the same time and stuff. Way cool. Anyway, I went to Belize. My grandmother raised me on the serious down low. I mean, I knew who and what I was, but we were always in a city and away from other shifters. That story involves crazy fathers. I'll tell you another time. But anyway, my aunt was concerned I was throwing away my medical career by heading for Belize. She knows I love medicine. Always have, always will. So it was actually her idea to build both a medical wing and an eatery onto the B&B—"

"B&B?" Kory questioned.

"Bed and breakfast I own there in the jungle. Since I was headed to a jaguar sanctuary, it was a brilliant idea. No doubt someone would need a doctor at some point, given the danger inherent to the job, so adding a med wing made sense. The cafe-type eatery was a plus because the rangers and visitors to the park were an automatic customer base."

Reya didn't mention the fact that she was a jaguar who patrolled a jaguar sanctuary. Made sense, considering they were in public and all.

"Brilliant business strategy," Tara said. "I bet Neesia saw all kinds of dollar signs in her head if you told her this story. She manages the books and all the projects and such. Has the head for business."

Reya nodded. "Oh yes. I thought she was going to burst a blood vessel with excitement as we discussed some partnership opportunities for Pryde Industries and the Cockscomb Jaguar Sanctuary. Anyway, my aunt is brilliant, too. She was also happy that an old friend of the family went to Belize with me. In fact, Dr. Matons, the guy who helps me run my place, is the one who encouraged me to go for it. You know, live my dream and all. He was my rah-rah squad and cheered me through my internships when I wanted to quit. When I decided to focus more on jaguar-related things by aiding in their protection, Dr. Matons went with me."

"Wow, I didn't know that," Kory responded and waved down the waiter again as Reya continued.

"When I met Aaron, he'd literally crashed in my jungle. He was headed to Belize to work on some high-dollar swanky architectural project when lightening hit the plane he was piloting. I got him to safety and I've never been so grateful for my special genetics that allowed me to move that mountain of a man while he was unconscious in the dark."

Shifter genetics meant strength and speed that outmatched any human. But it also meant fast metabolisms, and lots of snacks between meals. Fries and more cider showed up and they immediately dug in without missing a beat in the conversation.

Koreas swirled hers in a special mix of horseradish,

ketchup and a splash of malt vinegar. She sighed happily as they got back to the subject. "Aaron wasn't hurt bad, was he? Must have been scary, in the jungle at night with a crashed plane."

"He got banged up pretty good but we have a nice layout in the B&B with lots of tech. Thank god for satellites, otherwise internet would be a challenge. But I have everything I need, and could do a fairly complicated surgery if I needed to. Luckily, my man didn't need it. Dr. Matons and I tended to him and he bounced back quickly. During that recovery is when we learned what we are to each other. Honestly, I was simply drawn to Aaron like crazy, and he to me. I don't say it was pheromones, hormones or any other 'mones."

"But did you have the crazy horny thing going on there?" Tara wondered aloud.

"Yep," Reya answered. "But honestly, I can't say it was because of some mate zing thing, or simply because the man is hot."

They laughed a bit, then Reya got serious again. "But to think of it, my understanding is that if there's a blood bond involved, it could certainly hit you like a shot of bottled lust."

Kory hadn't even considered such a thing. She looked to her twin. "So that's why you feel all hot and bothered right now. We have a blood bond, Tara, just by being sisters."

"If you take it one step further, all of the James boys have a blood bond with Jason, and Jason has one with Neesia and Niah, right?"

"Right," Kory and Tara said.

"Well, no wonder all of us are hot in our lady bits," Reya said.

"Wait. All of us? Do you mean...?"

"Yep," Reya said. "I've been horny as hell."

Tara jumped in, "And so have I. And if Neesia and Jason's more-than-usual disappearing acts have been any indication, so is our big sis."

"Wow. I'm not sure what to say. I almost want to say sorry, but if Austin is my mate, I can't really be sorry about that."

"Kory, listen. The most important thing is that you hit it off. So, if I may make a suggestion?" Reya asked.

"Please do."

"Just let it happen, Koreas. A scientist is who you are, and I get that. You want to have answers for everything, and I get that, too. But Austin is not a biotech project. He's a man, and as his sister-in-law, I can be honest in saying he's a very good man. Instead of researching and analyzing it to death, just enjoy it. Just...be."

It was the simplest, yet über-profound thing the woman could have suggested. Even without anything concrete, no statistics and no facts, it still made perfect sense.

"Makes sense to me, too, Kory," Kotara said. "Be right back. All this cider and coffee means I need to pee."

"I guess we're twins in more ways than one. I need to go, too."

"See you when you get back. Want another Long Island if the waiter comes by while you're gone, Kory?" Reya asked.

"Lord, no. Alcohol may not last long in my system, but it can be rather comical for the time it does stick around. A Coke is fine. And some water."

Kory and Tara rose as a unit and headed for the restroom.

Moments later, Koreas wished she'd held her damn pee.

Across the restaurant, just steps from the little alcove that led to the restroom, sat her man. And he was skinning and grinning at some chick who shared his table. Way the fuck out here. A hundred miles from Pryde Ranch.

And the two of them looked awful chummy.

He faced away from her and had no idea they were there, but that didn't last long. Koreas knew her shock hummed down their newly forming bond when Austin's shoulders and back tensed. He straightened in his chair as if he'd heard something but wasn't sure where or what it was. Shit.

The second he made to turn completely around and look their way, Tara growled and took a step toward the cozy-looking couple. Kory snatched her sister around the corner and hustled them both into the bathroom.

Speaking mind-to-mind.

"Oh no, he is not *sitting here with someone else when he was fucking wearing you on his skin not more than a few hours ago,"* Tara snarled.

"No. No. We are not doing this in a restaurant, Kotara Pryde. I'm just as pissed as you are, but we will totally not make a scene. These people know us. Know our family. We come here for special occasions often. Let's just use the restroom, get back to Reya, and get the hell out of here. Deal?"

"Fine."

"And stop snarling at me, Tara." Kory wanted to do some snarling of her own, but they couldn't both go bat shit crazy here. Someone had to remain rational.

"Well, it is your turn," Kotara snapped.

"Whatever. Now put the fangs away. No lion stuff here, remember."

"Grrrr."

After some morning quality time with Kory, Austin had returned to the main house to find everyone scarce.

Aaron and Reya had gone horseback riding—something Reya had never done before. Sure, she'd seen plenty of horses in Belize and at the family ranch in Colorado, but the kitty in her had never thought to go near one until now. Austin chuckled to himself at the thought of his feisty sister-in-law squealing on the back of a horse for the first time.

Anthony was stuck on a phone call regarding blueprints for an upcoming property and Jason had been deep into getting details on a possible hunt for the Shifter and Were Armed Tactics agency. Austin would never get over the fact that shifters had their own law enforcement flying right alongside humans for years uncountable. It was pretty damn cool, though unfortunately necessary.

Austin had been determined not to work while on vacation. Funny, Neesia didn't keep any adult beverages in the house and he'd absolutely needed a beer, so with a serious case of Koreas-on-the-brain, he'd borrowed one of the Pryde vehicles, used the navigation system to find the nearest high fallutin' restaurant and headed out.

An hour and a half later, Austin looked around the nicely appointed establishment and wondered yet again what he was doing here. He wanted to be wherever Koreas was, but she was out to lunch with her sister and he hadn't been invited.

He could have joined any of his brothers in their activities but he'd been determined not to work while on vacation. So instead, here he sat at a restaurant, alone and as far away from Pryde Ranch as he could manage to drive without stopping for gas. His stomach rumbled and he hoped the food was as good as Neesia Pryde's.

He picked up an ice cold glass of water and shook his head at himself. The way the condensation ran down the sides of the glass brought to mind the way Kory's sweet nectar dripped for him when she was all hot and ready.

Austin took a sip and set the glass back down with a cringe.

Damn. I hope the food is better than the mid-day entertainment. Not bloody likely since the person singing an oldie-but-goodie by the most fabulous Ella Fitzgerald brought to mind a cat with its tail stuck under a rocking chair.

So just why, exactly, was he out here again? Oh yeah. He was thinking.

Fact was, Austin was upside down over Koreas Pryde. He'd never been so focused on winning a woman in his life. It was kind of…scary. Not in a "run away" kind of way, but more of a "this is a life event of epic, but cool, proportions" kind of way.

He was going to go for it, and he had no doubts whatsoever. But after the earth shattering, soul connecting sex he'd shared with her earlier today, he needed a minute to get his shit together.

The woman totally wrecked him. Completely undid him. Made him want to find and conquer Mount Olympus for her and—

"Hey! Don't I know you?"

Austin looked up and came face to face with a pair of enormous boobs.

He leaned back to give himself a bit of room, inwardly shaking his head at himself. Just what he did *not* need. Some woman flirting with him in a restaurant where he couldn't be rude. Shit.

Quietly, he replied. "Uh, no. I don't believe we know each other."

"Are you s-s-shure?"

Good lord, the chick was hammered. Seriously, two sheets to the wind.

"Mine if I s-shit down, handsome?"

Really?

The houseman came over. "Sir, I'm so sorry. You asked not to be disturbed and we can escort…"

"Hey, I jez got here. And leggo of my arm," the woman said, a bit too loud. "I haven't even had an appatisher yet, damn it!"

Austin raised his hands at the houseman and said, "It's okay. No problem. Let her sit down. And bring some coffee, please."

"Are you sure?"

"You heard the man!" she said, only this time she was a bit

more quiet and fewer people swiveled their heads around to see what the hell was going on.

It was times like this that his parents' words came to mind—the very same words he'd repeated to his brothers during their growing up years. *Austin, you lose nothing by being nice. And sometimes, manners are all that are needed to diffuse a situation. Be polite. Be a gentleman. Be a James.*

The only time the family mantra didn't apply was if he and his bros were in a damn fight, and in that instance they were usually defending one another.

The woman sat down, almost missed the chair, but by some serious grace managed to land her ass in the seat rather than on the floor. Moments later, two cups of rich, black coffee were set in front of her.

After she took a couple of sips, Austin ordered his meal and then ordered for the mystery lady as well.

"I'm Austin. What's your name?"

"I'm Stay-shee. I'm know I'm drunk. I'm show shorry."

"Well, what brings you here, Stacy?"

"It's lunsh time. I'm not usually drunk by lunsh. I'm not usually d-drunk at all." Then she burst out crying.

Austin wanted to be annoyed, but he was honestly concerned for the woman. Obviously something was seriously wrong here. He wasn't a sucker for a woman in tears, but he was a sucker for a person who was in real trouble.

"So what's got a pretty girl like you into her cups at this time of day, darlin'?" And she was pretty. A long, curly ponytail of shiny auburn hair fell down her back. Bright green eyes were probably more glassy than usual, but her brows were perfectly arched. Somehow she'd managed to stuff a pair of double-D's into a baby blue linen blouse that fit tastefully everywhere except her breasts. A neat pencil skirt and a practical pair of flats, both in black, finished up her outfit.

Lovely, but not really his type. She was too...dolled up. Too much makeup, too much jewelry. Too much alcohol. Not enough natural beauty.

He couldn't help but compare her to his woman. Kory's skin was like cinnamon and silk. Her naturally curly hair fell in waves to her shoulders and was thick and shiny. Her eyes, a golden tawny brown, gave a hint of the animal beneath the skin. Gorgeous was too tame a word for the beauty of his lioness.

"Do you want another cup of coffee, Stacy?" Austin asked politely.

"No, I think I'm starting to feel more normal now." Just then their food arrived.

"Oh my goodness, thank you so much."

"You're welcome, Stacy. So while we eat, I'd love to know why you crashed my party."

Her face fell. "I'm sorry. I didn't mean to. I was a bit...out of sorts. You asked what made me get drunk at this ungodly hour of the day. Divorce. Plain and simple."

"Want to talk about it?" Austin asked, genuinely hoping he could be of help

"I don't know..."

"I'm not from around here so you can be sure your secrets won't get around town." Though if he had his way, he'd be at Pryde Ranch more than just this few planned weeks.

"Really? I don't want to bore you."

"Go ahead and spill it. Besides, if you were so upset before, it will probably do you good to get it off your chest. And if you don't want to tell your business to a complete stranger, perhaps you have a relative or someone you can call?"

"No. No relatives here. I moved here because my husband got a job in Laramie. I'm actually from Savannah. I, uh, I guess I'll be heading back home pretty soon."

Rather than push, Austin took a deep chug of beer and dug into his plate. After five minutes of silence, Stacy proceeded to talk his ear off. For the next two hours.

After the meal, she confessed that she did indeed feel better. And though her story was one of dysfunction and abuse, she was at least completely sober.

Though he was glad he could be of help, he was more appreciative of the Pryde dynamic. That family cared for one another. They talked and duked out their problems in a way that didn't cause damage to one another. They'd been raised in a house full of love and it showed. Anxious to get back to his woman and her pride, Austin took care of the bill, wished Stacy well, and broke the speed limit all the way back to Pryde Ranch.

10

"*L*ook, whatever you did to Koreas—"

"I swear, Jason, I didn't do anything." Austin raked his hands through his hair and walked around in a circle while Jason kept right on talking as if he hadn't spoken at all.

"Uh huh. Anyway, whatever you did to Koreas has all the women giving us the big freeze. I swear, I got icicles on my dick when I snuggled up to Neesia last night. When I asked her what was wrong, she cussed a blue streak, snarled something about how 'sisters stuck together'. Then went on a rant about idiot men and something about staking your balls to a rock, which would take quite a lot of pounding and—"

"Well, Reya suggested staking Austin's balls to a boulder, which is considerably larger than a rock," Aaron said. "And I got the same treatment from my lovely wife who threatened to shift into her magnificent jaguar self and rake her claws across all our asses. Problem is I've been on my best behavior since we got here and I know I didn't do anything."

"And I sure as hell didn't," Anthony finished. "I've been hanging out with Broglio. Seeing as how he runs the place, I figured it would be a good idea to check out how he does it, in case we ever have to build an estate like this one. Besides, I am very deliberately staying away from anything female, damn it. So," he said, stabbing a finger into the middle of Austin's chest, "that leaves you, bro."

"Damn, Anthony," Austin growled. "Even you're turning on me?"

"Turning on you? Dude, are you serious? You screwed the pooch some kind of way and I'd rather side with the ones who are going to come out on top."

"Come out on top? Who would that be, you assholes?" Austin wondered aloud.

Together, all three of them glared at Austin and yelled, "The women!"

Austin threw up his hands and walked away into the darkness. He loved camping, but right now it got a big "fuck you". He didn't really want to be out here cooking dinner over a spit, but the guys had all shown up at his door this morning, tossed his gear at him and declared they were headed out for a couple of days. Now he knew why—they wanted to get him the hell out of dodge to figure out what he'd done.

Only he didn't *know* what he'd done. And he hadn't seen Kory since the phenomenal sex in her lab. He had no idea where she'd scooted off to, but he did know one thing for certain—if he spent one more minute around that campfire near his brothers and Jason, he was going to deck someone square in the face.

As he eased his way through the waist-high prairie grass, Austin thought back on every interaction he'd had with Koreas that could have pissed her off. He came up empty handed. They'd seemed to be getting along just fine. No arguing. No fussing or fighting.

In fact, they'd had a great time together laughing, talking... kissing. God, that woman could kiss. His cock hardened just thinking about the way her lips molded so perfectly to his. How her breathing hitched in her throat when he kissed his way down her neck and nipped the tendons there. And the sex? Out of this world.

Add to that the fact that he genuinely cared about her—about her likes and dislikes, what made her happy and what pissed her off—Austin felt like the key to her lock. Like the hand to her glove. The jam to her jellyroll.

Koreas Pryde was a brilliant woman. She was also a powerful creature that could rip his head off if she simply felt like it. Yet she submitted to him in the bedroom, instinctively, without even thinking about it—naturally, beautifully. It was a gift, so precious and rare he couldn't form the words to express how much it meant to him.

It was bad enough to learn that the woman was unhappy, but it was worse knowing he was the reason for that unhappiness. It simply wasn't acceptable.

One way or another, he wasn't going another day without hearing Koreas' voice. Without her warm presence. Without experiencing the transformation of such a cool, quiet piece of perfection into an uninhibited sensualist as he peeled back her layers and exposed the freak underneath.

God, he loved freaks.

Correction, he loved his very own geeky *undercover* freak.

As soon as they got back to the main house, Austin was ending this. Even if he had to tie her to a tree and pray he could get her to listen to him. Before she shifted into a tawny-haired big ass lioness…

With very sharp teeth…

And claws…

Fuck.

Two days had passed since Austin had been spotted out with some woman. And two days for her to come to her senses, if she'd had any.

A part of her wanted to head out into the wild, find the man by scent alone, and wrap her body around his in wild abandon.

The other part still had an issue with the fact that he'd been giving big cheesy grins to some drunk-looking bimbo while out to lunch at one of the nicest establishments in this part of the state, all while he knew she was going out with her sister and Reya.

Considering that the man had come home to her rather than going with that woman, Kory was at a loss as to why she gave a rat's rear end. She knew he hadn't touched el-drunko either, because when he'd shown up at the main house for dinner, there was no scent on Austin but Kory's.

And that was the rub that annoyed the hell out of her—she wasn't pissed because he'd been grinning at the woman. She was pissed because she was *bothered* that he'd grinned like a fool at someone else.

Ugh!

She'd never cared about that kind of stuff before. Hadn't known there was a single jealous bone in her body.

But you've never had a mate before, either.

Right now, it felt like a part of her soul was missing without Austin around. Hell, she was a bad ass lioness with the ability to go after what she wanted. She could successfully hunt her prey for miles and miles if she needed to. It was why S.W.A.T. kept such close tabs on lion shifters—they were known to aggressively defend their territory for a hundred miles if not kept in check.

Well, this was her family's hundred miles and it was hers to roam as she pleased. The problem was that she *shouldn't* want to prowl. She was supposed to be puttering around a lab or have her head buried in a book, damn it. It didn't make any sense considering she'd only known Austin James for a mere blip in time.

Well, science can't explain how you change into a lioness with telepathic abilities, so why are you still struggling with the fact that instantly recognizing a man that is suitable mating material can't be explained? Goof ball.

Yay, Team Conscience.

Not.

When she thought of him, she wanted to smile and cry at the same time. Smile because he made her laugh, made her forget the hole that had existed in part of her heart for as long as she could remember—the one now filled with the presence of a mate. He understood what it meant that she was an introvert, even though he wasn't one. Understood when to back off and give her space, and when to push her just a bit.

And he was a master of the good ole slap-and-tickle—knew when she wanted it, needed it. Her body and mind missed him, and it made her want to bawl her eyes out considering she recognized him as a mate, yet he obviously didn't see her the same way.

An image of him smiling up at that flouncy over-abundance-of-tart at the only semi-swanky restaurant in Medicine Bow filled her mind. She could almost smell the odors of cheap perfume and too much beer as that woman leaned in and flirted shamelessly with Austin. And the man had smiled back at the woman and let her touch his hand. Next, she would have been rubbing her balloon breasts all over him and...

"Hey! Put those away and stop growling, Kory!"

She shook herself out of her musing and looked across the lab at her twin.

"What?" But it was an empty question. Sharp canines nicked her bottom lip and Koreas realized that she'd partially shifted. Unheard of for someone with her control, but there it was.

"Damn it, Koreas, will you just go get the man already?"

In response, Koreas snarled something even she couldn't understand.

"Why not? You know he's yours, even if he is human. Besides, after some thought, it doesn't actually sound like he did anything other than not be mean to an obviously drunk chick at the restaurant."

More growling.

"Don't take that tone with me, pipsqueak. Besides, you've done nothing but literally prowl around here and bite the heads off of anyone that asks you how you're doing. Given that everyone knows that I'm the snarky bitch and you're the quiet one, it's noticeable, Kory. I mean, *dayum!*"

The growling became menacing.

"You're being dysfunctional, girlfriend. No one here should be on your shit list because no one here has done you wrong. So stop taking it out on us."

The answer—glares, flared nostrils and a round of huffs and puffs. Next came a sigh because, after all, Kotara was right, damn it.

"Keep it up and I'll call Neesia on you. See how you like that. Now, go run it off, Kory!"

Tara may as well have doused her with a bucket of iced water and set her outside on the back porch to dry.

Grrrr!

Threatening to call in their big sister was like invoking the age old "I'm going to tell your father" adage. If she kept up her snarling and funky moodiness, there would be big trouble of the so-not-fun kind. And the words had the intended affect— Koreas snapped out of it.

After a deep breath and a few *woosahs*, she went for a relaxing run beneath the bright afternoon sunshine. And when that didn't take the edge off, she jumped in the river. Literally.

---

11

*A*fter her run, Koreas didn't bother going back to the labs. Sure, there were tests and formula tweaking that needed her attention, but there was always something to do. Work never seemed to end.

Right now, she was going to take her twin's advice and get her head together. A quick shower and a bite to eat would do the trick. Then she would head over to Neesia's gardens and eat some ripe tomatoes off the vine. Or maybe find some ripe melons or grapes to munch while she sat under a tree and enjoyed a good book.

Suddenly, her shifter sense went on full alert. Hair damp and skin wet, Koreas shot toward the door to her private rooms, yanking on a robe as she moved.

Before the knock could even occur, she threw open the door, planted her hands on her hips and glared for all she was worth. "Where have you been?"

Austin looked back and forth between her face and his loosely balled fist, which was still in mid-air and poised to knock on the door.

"Guess you knew I was coming," he said. The words were

laced with sarcasm as he lowered his hand and walked into her room. His cowboy hat was tossed into the nearest chair and then he turned on Kory and mirrored her stance.

"You already know where I've been, so the real question is, why are you asking me something that you know the answer to?"

Oooh, he was good. And she was busted.

"Fine. You were camping. What do you want?"

"Are you serious, Koreas Pryde? If I knew your middle name I'd throw that in, too. It's not a want for me, darlin'. It's a need. And you are going to fill it after you tell me what the hell you were so angry at me for, that my brothers had to drag me off to go camping just so they could ride my ass for two days over what was wrong with you."

So that was the reason they'd bailed and gone camping right after Austin's floozy-pa-looza in Medicine Bow? Really?

Before she could ask what in the world went on, he answered her question.

"Apparently, Reya snarled and snapped at Aaron because she was mad at me. And Kotara was giving the stink eye to all of us because she was mad at me. And Neesia told Jason to get to the bottom of whatever I'd done to you or he wouldn't get sex *or* food for a month. So, Koreas. What. The. Fuck?"

Damn. She'd known that her sisters and their new best friend, Reya, were upset on her behalf, but she hadn't known they'd been scaring the guys over it.

Ouch.

Kory sucked it up and told him the truth, after which Austin laughed like she'd told the biggest joke in the world. Cheeks heated and eyes tightened to mere slits, she fought to hold onto her temper.

Yet another new development since Austin James walked into my life—temper tantrums.

"What the hell is so funny?" she snapped through clenched teeth.

"Kory, I don't even know who that woman was. She stumbled into the restaurant three sheets to the wind, drunk off her backside. She sat at my table because I looked familiar. And she was rather loud about it, too. Instead of having her forcibly removed from the place, it made much less of a scene to simply tolerate her. We talked. That's all. She had coffee and sobered up a bit, then she called a cab and left. The end. Turns out she's recently divorced and is moving back home to...hell, I don't even remember. Back east somewhere, I think. I don't even remember her name."

"So you had lunch with a total stranger to avoid making a scene?" she wondered aloud.

"That's how it started. After getting some coffee into her, I continued with the meal because she started crying over the husband who just left her that she's still in love with. I was taught to be a gentleman to a lady. Especially one in distress. But being nice doesn't equal fucking her."

"I didn't think you'd had sex with—"

"Then what did you think that was horrible enough to have everyone mad at me?"

"I don't know," she shouted and threw up her hands as she stomped around her room. Well, she did know, but she didn't want to say.

"Well, you'd better figure it out because I'm not walking out of here until you give me a clue."

The man plucked her thoughts right out of the ether?

"Fine," she snapped. "I saw you with that woman and assumed the worst. Actually, both Tara and I saw you because we were dining at that same restaurant with Reya."

"So why didn't you just come over to my table and say something? 'Hello Austin' would have worked just fine."

"I don't know," she mumbled, feeling lower than the dirt the caretakers used out in the gardens—fertilizer and all. Her blush was a thing of the past as her face flamed hot enough to start a damn barbeque.

"So, is that the reason for the Pryde women's warpath? You were jealous?" he asked, with the smirk from hell plastered across his gorgeous mouth.

Bastard.

Koreas sucked in a breath and let it out on a huff as she stomped to her windows and looked out over the landscape. Soooo...had she been jealous? God, did she even understand what that word meant? It was tempting to hide behind the wall of her intellect and sort through her brain for the dictionary definition of 'jealous'. Then she turned around and looked at the gorgeous man standing across the room from her. He might have had a grin on his face, but his eyes told another story. Those beautiful gray orbs held a hint of uncertainty and more than a bit of vulnerability.

In that moment, she realized that she had the power to hurt this man, really gouge deep, and make his heart bleed. He'd just asked her if she'd been jealous, and she had a choice on how to answer the question—cold bitch or honest lover.

Koreas didn't have it in her to be cruel just because she could. And she didn't have it in her to lie to this man who'd come to mean so much to her in little-to-no time.

After a few moments, she finally said, "Yes, I was jealous, okay?"

"But, why?"

"Goddammit, Austin, I have no fucking idea!"

"Did you just drop an F-bomb, Kory?" She wanted to smack the grin off his face.

"Oh, shut up already."

He laughed instead.

"Is my kitty in need of some stroking?"

"I swear I will bite you in the ass, Austin James."

"Aww, don't be like that, darlin'," he teased as he stepped closer and eased his arms around her. "Here, kitty kitty.

"I fucking swear to god!"

"Whoa, two F-bombs in two minutes!"

His laughter was infectious and the next thing Kory knew, she was giggling at her own foolishness, with her man's arms wrapped around her body—damp robe and all.

Austin decided that his woman definitely liked make-up sex.

A gracious apology was given, and he readily forgave her. After all, though he was, as Kory described him, "a guy and all", he actually understood her frustration.

Here was a woman who was used to analyzing every facet of her life. Things fit into neat, tidy little piles, whether they were test results, statistics report, batch record data…or emotions.

What was she supposed to do with this out-of-the-blue, damn-near flammable attraction? Mating heat. Whatever.

"Believe it or not, I'm right there with you, Kory," he'd told her only moments ago. And he'd been completely honest. Neither of them had expected to find the love of their lives during a typical family vacation. Neither of them saw the other one coming, and they were both rocking back on their heels.

As far as Austin was concerned, the only difference between his woman and himself was that he didn't give a rat's ass about their biological differences, while those very differences were something she'd studied for years in her field of expertise. He could care less about what caused mating heat, but the lack of a plausible answers seemed to drive Kory up a wall.

The only thing Austin cared about, deeply and truly, was that this woman love him, accept him, of her own free will.

Never one to beat around the bush, Austin cut to the chase.

"Kory, I want more than just a physical relationship with

you. I'm pretty sure you know that. The question is, do you want me back or not? It's as simple as that. The rest of it, we can work through if we believe we're compatible enough both in and outside of the bedroom."

She was still wrapped in his arms. The moisture from her damp robe began to seep through his shirt. A tremor worked through her body.

"Are you cold, baby? Wait here. Let me get a fire going and I'll get you a dry towel out of the bathroom."

He took two steps away and found himself flying through the air. One second later, a flush-faced Kory was on top of him.

Amber eyes glowed like the setting sun. And her...fangs? Holy shit, were those fangs?

A grin kicked up on the side of his mouth and all he could say was, "Dayum, woman, that's hot."

She cocked her head sideways as if he were nuts. And maybe he was.

But all Austin James knew was that if this powerful, brilliant woman struggled to keep her human skin on, then he was under her skin. And he just couldn't see a downside to that considering he knew she would never physically hurt him.

Seeing those wicked fangs begin to recede into her gum line pushed at the natural dominant in him. He took a quick look around, still grinning, and said, "Well, we are in your bedroom, and I do believe I'm the boss in here."

Eyes flared bright orange.

Oh, was that a challenge? Hell, he almost rubbed his hands together in anticipation.

Flipping her off of him, Austin reversed their positions and relished the look of sheer surprise on Kotara's face.

And since she was wearing a damp robe that obviously needed to come off, he went ahead and divested her of it.

She lay on her back, writhing beneath his thorough loving. Each wiggle of her hips, each moan, each swift intake of breath sent Austin's need up a notch until his cock was as hard and hot as a branding iron.

But he didn't want to be simply aroused. He wanted to be *insane* with wanting her.

And if he was going to go crazy, he sure as hell wasn't going alone.

He feasted on her flesh, kissed her from neck to knees, and explored every bit of her smooth, delectable skin until he drowned in the warm, uniquely delicious scent. With lips, teeth, tongue and hands, Austin took his woman to a place so hot from their entwined need, that skin damp from her shower became downright wet with sweat. Moisture trailed down her temples and neck, to her clavicle, then down the valley between lush berry-tipped breasts.

Her head began to loll from side to side even as her hands swept up her body. Fingers circled the breast he teased as if to hold it more secure for him. Austin took advantage of it and sucked the entire crown of her areola into his mouth. He nipped with his teeth as she twisted and tugged her own nipples until they were diamond hard.

"Oh, please. Please give it to me, Austin."

On her back, she lifted her legs and let her knees fall open. Kory's short, trimmed nails sank ever-so-slightly into the back of her thighs as she reached down to tease her own slick skin where ass met thigh.

And then she opened herself for him.

The sight of her dewy flesh, dripping for him and no other, set Austin's libido on a crash course with oblivion. He knew before his cock ever got anywhere near her sex that this was a pivotal moment. Knew that he would come harder than he ever had in his life. Knew that tonight would seal his fate, bind him to Koreas on a level he couldn't yet comprehend, but wanted with every fiber of his being.

Her fingers scorched wherever she touched—pecs jerked

beneath the skin, stomach muscles rolled like the tide. He was like a bow strung too tight, so ready to be let loose. Austin headed into a mist of pleasure so thick, he knew he was lost, completely turned about and blind to everything but Kory. And whether she realized it or not, she was just as turned about.

Watching the reactions that he wrung from her body wrought such delicious agony, yet he still denied himself.

It will be worth it.

Kory's voice was in his head again. Whisper soft, yet solid. Firm. Sure.

And she was right—it would be worth it. Of that he had no doubt.

By the time Austin was done playing with Kory, sweat pooled at the base of her spine and dribbled seductively down her bare ass. In fact, she was drenched all over. The thick dark curls on her head were tangled and damp against her face and neck. Cheeks flushed with need. Plump lips parted and her tongue traced a path across them as she panted and growled.

He picked her up, flipped her over and let his lips blaze a trail down her spine. His fingers caressed her firm backside, then dipped into the dewy center until she panted. Moaned. Screamed.

Begged.

"Let me wrap my thighs around your waist. Please."

He didn't answer. Couldn't form the words, his desire too far gone. Instead, he shucked his pants, snatched his shirt off over his head and was back on her in two shakes of a bobcat's tail.

His cock pulsed in his hand as she pushed up onto her knees, then lay her chest on the cool linens on the bed. With his fingers pressed against her inner thighs, Austin spread her wide, kept her there a moment, and then took her hands and placed them where his had been.

"Now," he whispered, "when I tell you to assume the position, this is what I mean. Do you understand, Kory?"

At her gasped, "Yes," he positioned himself, ready to slip into heaven.

"Hold yourself open for me, baby."

And she did. But she was so wet, so sweat slickened, that she had to continually adjust her fingers as the flesh slipped out of her grasp. It was the sexiest damn thing he'd ever seen.

"Are you ready, love?" The words rumbled deep in his chest, asked more to himself than to her.

"Oh god, yes. Give it to me." When she began to chant two words—please and Austin—he couldn't hold back a moment longer.

He eased inside her ready sex, coated himself with her honey, and pulled back out just a bit. Then he pushed back inside, this time stretching wet flesh and parting slick muscles until he was seated to the hilt.

Kory was literally full of him.

"It's too much. I can't take it."

"You can and you will."

"What are you gonna do? Make me?"

"Do you want me to make you?"

Oooh. Perhaps she did indeed.

12

"*A*ustin James, just where are you going with that basket of yummy?"

Austin turned to meet the eyes of the spitting image of his woman.

"Good morning, Kotara."

"Amazing you can tell us apart already. I don't think the woman who had Kory and me in her biology classes through all four years of high school could ever tell us apart."

Austin couldn't explain how he knew who was who. It was just something about the way Koreas *felt* to him. It was as if her own special frequency was tuned-in to his. Loudly. And god, he liked it.

Kotara's jaw cracked as she yawned. He pictured a National Geographic lion special with a female lioness yawning, showing all those deadly teeth. Austin could swear she roared in a little spot somewhere in his head.

The thought made him smile.

Delusional. It's the only word that came to mind, though the smile didn't falter one whit.

"Where are you off to, Kotara?"

"Labyrinth." She yawned again as she shuffled along at his side down the hallway to the stairway that led down to the garages.

"Why so early? Better yet, why at all? Kory told me that your current project is delayed and that you two already finished some work-up thing for your next project." What was it with these Pryde women? They just couldn't sit still and enjoy the lives they'd built for themselves? Neesia was the most laid back of the four, and even she was still an all-out ball buster. And his Kory might be the quietest Pryde, but he could practically hear the thoughts flying through her head about this task or that job. Geesh.

"I thought you were all taking a day off since Niah and Lou are due back today?"

"That's still the plan. We're meeting them in Denver. I put some thawed proteins into the seed flasks to grow and I wanted to check on them before we go. They should be fine since it's a four day subculture process and the prototype flasks will auto-matically inoculate the bioreactor, but..."

His eyeballs must have started tracking to the center because Kotara blinked twice, stopped talking and laughed as she continued to walk toward the garage door.

"Oh," she said sounding concerned, "you'd better not let Neesia see you delivering that basket. If she gets wind that you fed Kory something that wasn't made in that ginormous football field-sized kitchen of hers..."

"I'm all covered. Neesia actually helped me put this together."

"Neesia is helping you woo Kory? Yep, I think you're family now." And she walked away while Austin went stock still just short of the door, with his mouth hanging open.

Part of the family? Say what?

Good thing it was still early enough in the season for cool mornings, otherwise he'd surely catch a bee or two between the teeth. In short, he was thrilled. While he patched together his outward calm, Austin headed to the Labyrinth on Kotara's heels and inwardly smiled like a loon at the thought of indeed being part of this fantastic pride. He might not be a shifter, but he knew a good thing when he saw one. To date, his sister-in-law, Reya, had been the most awesome female the James' boys had ever met. Now, he was sure that the Pryde women stacked right up there with her.

He caught up to Kotara next to one of the big all-terrain vehicles they preferred, glad to see that she'd actually waited for him. Her knowing smile made his own even broader.

They headed over to the far side of the property to the laboratories. Even in the dark of the early morning, he could tell it was going to be a beautiful day. Nothing but stars way out here and not a cloud in the sky. He liked that the Prydes were aware of their surroundings and took great care to ensure that their commercial activities didn't impact the environment too much. So no bright glaring lights on the Pryde properties...at least not up here. Once they descended down into the labs, it was an entirely different world.

In short, these ladies had built an incredible space where they discovered and created some of the most progressive medicines and vaccines for veterinary sciences in the world. There was a reason that many of the largest biotech companies contracted with the Prydes—they were fucking geniuses. The end.

Kotara slowed down and slapped her access card against the identification panel at what looked like a typical roll-up door. A few seconds after the panel flashed, "Access granted", the door rolled up and Kotara sped down a well-lit, but not glaringly bright, concrete drive.

Austin wasn't sure how far down they went, but it wasn't long before Kotara pulled into her personal spot in an underground lot. Austin hopped out of the Jeep and quickly retrieved the gift he'd brought from the back seat, and then walked around to Kotara's side of the vehicle. After all, he was a James through and through, and he and his brothers all had the need to open doors, pull out chairs, and stretch forth hands to assist the women they thought highly of—which happened to be all of the Pryde ladies.

Austin carefully put the huge basket down and opened Kotara's door just as she shut down the engine. Indulging him with a smile and yet another shake of her head, they headed for thick glass double doors that opened to a reception area.

Austin whistled and said, "Wow, this is right out of a Batman movie, minus the bats."

Once clear of security, Austin followed Kotara to the office she shared with his woman. The phone started ringing the second her butt settled in her chair.

She peeked at the caller id and said, "Nope. Not today. Send to voice mail, thank you very much." Austin thought it was adorable the way both Kory and Tara talked to their instruments and electronics.

But now it was time to get back to the house to finish up his arrangements. And once he was done, his woman would think this gorgeous gift basket was nothing compared to the surprise he had in store for her.

"So where's the best place to put this?"

"I'd suggest her desk, but it depends on how fun you want to make it."

"I don't follow," Austin replied, looking around the huge space filled with computers and equipment he hadn't known a single thing about until he'd shown up at Pryde Ranch.

"Well, if you put it on her desk, she'll see it right away. She'll be surprised and all, but she'll still see it the moment she steps into this room."

"Okay, so what do you suggest?"

"I'd actually put it in one of the sample rooms. She'll walk in, grab the samples off the table and walk right out. Then she'll pause and wonder if she saw what she thought she saw..."

Austin picked up where Kotara left off. "Then she'll turn around with her forehead all scrunched up and her brows pulled down into that adorable 'huh?' expression. And she'll be totally surprised considering there'll be a room full of lab techs who are all working and pretending as if nothing's there."

"You're a smart one, Austin James."

"It was your idea."

"Yeah, but for you to describe my sister that accurately, I mean down to her facial expressions, and you've only been hanging around her for a minute? Pretty impressive, dude."

"Well, thanks. She's worth noticing."

The phone rang again. Kotara still wasn't impressed by whoever was on the other end. "Nope. Don't care that it's noon in London. It's only five o'clock in the morning here, so voice mail for you, too. Anyway, as I was saying, dude, Kory is very much worth noticing. I'm glad you two are fixing your shit because if she'd remained heartbroken for much longer, I would have had to take things into my own claws. And I mean fully extended claws. You get me?"

Austin laughed, but it wasn't because he thought she was kidding. He laughed because he knew she was dead serious and the fact that she was straight up with him told him that she was on his side. If she wasn't, she'd just do him in and call it done.

This pride was fiercely protective of their family and took shit from no one. It still amazed him that there wasn't a single shifter on this entire hundred mile property that wasn't a Pryde. But he understood it—lions, even those in human skin, were fiercely territorial and a rival pride wouldn't stand a chance against these women and their mates.

"Can you run me over to this sample room you're talking about?"

Kotara's phone rang yet again. She looked at the phone and

sighed. "Sorry, I have to take this one. I'm okay with you running over there by yourself. Just go back out of this room, hang a right. You'll pass two hallways then make another right and you'll see it. It's room 10A and has a sign that says 'Large Molecule Pre-Bio Samples'. Head right out after so you don't get in trouble. You know, the whole 'authorized personnel only' rule."

"I can find it. And I'll make it quick. What time are you guys heading out to meet Niah and Lou?"

"Around ten o'clock. Funny how you knew Kory would come in here today knowing she's supposed to take the day off."

Austin looked down at his watch. "Actually, she should be stepping in here in the next forty minutes."

Shaking her head and smiling at him for at least the fifth time this morning, Kotara answered the phone while waving at Austin. She stood and walked toward one of the big silver cylinders on the other side of the room while she fussed in perfect Japanese at whoever was on the other end of the line.

He had no trouble finding room 10A given the lettering was printed in huge block letters on the glass wall. He stopped, leaned in close and noticed that the lights were on but there was no one inside. A little further down the hall was the actual door into the lab. Once inside, he found that he wasn't actually in the sample room yet, but in an outer staging area. The walls in here were glass like every other room he'd seen so far, but these were opaque white so you couldn't see in or out. Good thing, too, considering this must be where the scientists got dressed given the rows of neatly hung "bunny suits" along one wall.

Must be a busy place on a typical day to have such a large staging area. There were several doors in here, all clearly labeled. There were showers, restrooms and even lockers that looked more like swanky polished cedar drawers embedded in one of the walls. Austin's brows rose at the decontamination signs on two of the doors off to the right, but he wasn't worried.

If there was an issue, there was no way Kotara would have sent him in here alone.

Still he stood and listened a moment. No one around. None of the machines were running. Made sense considering how early it was. Then again, perhaps everyone was taking the day off since the Prydes were playing hooky?

Austin set the gorgeous, Neesia-inspired basket down on a stainless steel work table in the middle of the room and then turned to leave.

The tail of his leather jacket caught the edge of the table and caused it to wobble just enough to send a beaker crashing to the floor.

Shit. He hadn't meant to break anything.

Never one to leave a mess, he moved quickly to the various doors along one wall until he found one with cleaning materials. Figuring they must use the stuff to sanitize the lab, he carefully examined the different liquids neatly placed on several shelves.

He had no idea what it was, so he was careful not to touch it. He started to grab a bottle of bleach, but changed his mind. Even though the stuff he'd spilled looked like water and had no odor, he really had no idea what it was. Safer not to douse the spot with a chemical that might not interact well with it.

Kory's 'me-scientist-you-listen' lessons have been taking hold better than I thought.

"A pair of gloves wouldn't be remiss either," he grumbled to himself, annoyed that he'd broken the flask in the first place. He grabbed a bottle with "purified water" written in black ink, and a couple of nitrile gloves from a box on one of the shelves.

After sopping up the spill with what he hoped was a clean towel, Austin picked up as much glass as he could. Then he used another towel to carefully wipe up the pieces that were too small for his glove-covered fingers to grasp.

Satisfied that he'd gotten it all up, he disposed of the garbage using the sealed biohazard system built into the wall. Next stop, Kotara's office. Halfway down the first hallway, he changed his mind. Instead, he went to the nearest wall console and punched in the office extension. A few seconds later, Kotara answered.

"Hey, Tara, it's Austin. I'm all done and I'm headed out. Kory should be here any minute and I don't want her to catch me here. Mind if I take your Jeep back to the house?"

"Nope. Not at all. I can get a ride back with Kory."

"Keys?"

"It's unlocked. Keys are in the center console."

Hit with a sudden bout of dizziness, Austin asked, "Have any water in that cooler you keep in the back of the Jeep?"

"Yep. Always. You okay?"

"I haven't been drinking enough water. I think I'm a bit dehydrated. Easy fix, but thought I'd be polite and ask first."

"A James boy, polite? Say it ain't so."

"Smart ass," he said.

Kotara snorted. "Always. I thought you knew that by now."

"Good point. Catch you later. You guys have a good day."

"You, too, handsome."

13

*A*nthony James was freaking out. He hadn't heard from his brother since he'd called at o'dark-thirty and explained that he'd gone to the Pryde labs to drop off a gift for Koreas. The eldest James said he was going to change his clothes, go for a swim in the Medicine Bow, and then head back to the house to meet Austin for breakfast.

That'd been three hours ago, and none of the staff had seen him anywhere in the immediate vicinity.

His internal danger sense had moved beyond tingling to straight out screaming. Something was wrong, he was sure of it.

After alerting Broglio that he was headed out to look for his brother, Austin literally ran down to the Pryde's extensive garage and chose the fastest four-wheel drive he could find.

Half an hour later, after crisscrossing the prairie-grass covered terrain near the river, Anthony spotted what looked like an animal, washed up on the shore.

"Oh god, please don't be hurt. Please."

He slammed on the brake and slid to a screaming halt. Out of the borrowed truck in a flash, he ran down to the riverbank toward what he knew he'd found—his brother's prone body.

Unconscious, Austin was on his side in nothing but swim trunks. His chest was on the muddy bank, the chilled water gently lapped at his bare feet, and his skin held a freaky grayish hue.

Down on his knees, he gently tapped his brother's cheek.

No response—not a twitch, tic or spasm. Just...nothing.

"Aw, man. You've got sucky timing, big bro. You would go and get sick on the day that all the scientists and doctors are gone off to play." Anthony's heart lodged firmly in his throat, though he kept his voice even and somewhat snarky. If his brother could hear him, the last thing he wanted was for him to be anxious.

After carefully checking for wounds and injuries, Anthony sat back on his heels with a frown. There wasn't a single cut, bruise or break on his brother's body that he could see. So what the hell was wrong with him?

Just then, Austin's chest heaved and he began to make gurgling, choking sounds, as if he couldn't get enough air.

"Aw, fuck! Don't go turnin' blue on me, bro. Don't you dare."

Thankful for CPR training, Anthony tried to keep calm as he checked Austin's airways for obstructions. Again, nothing.

"What the fuck, Austin?" Anthony wondered aloud, genuinely confused.

The Prydes, Aaron and Reya were all up around thirty-thousand feet right about now, so a call directly to any of them was im-fucking-possible. What do to? What to do?

And then the lightbulb in his head flicked on. The Pryde estate had top of the line everything when it came to electronics and surveillance. Surely there was a way to reach that fucking plane.

Anthony looked down at his brother's prone body and felt his eyes go wide. In minutes, Austin's skin had gone from a pasty gray to icy blue.

Come on, come on, come on, come on became an impatient

chant as Anthony dialed Broglio and waited for the call to connect.

In seconds, Broglio forwarded the call to Harry—the man who typically piloted the Pryde jet. Harry connected the call to the radio frequency that allowed any air traffic controller to connect to the Pryde jet that Aaron and Jason were piloting today.

The moment he heard Aaron's voice, Anthony lit into him.

"Austin is sick!"

The moment he said the word 'sick', Reya was on deck. "Give me the phone!" she demanded, and must have grabbed the headset from Aaron, punched the off-speaker button and smashed the phone to her ear. "Tell me his symptoms. Don't leave anything out."

Anthony relayed all the details as quickly as his mouth could form the words.

"It almost sounds like he's been poisoned or something. Or like his body is rejecting itself. You guys, we need to go back and Austin needs a hospital right now."

"Should I move him? I don't know if it'll make him worse or what."

"No, don't move him."

"God, Reya, what the hell do I do?"

Anthony's already insane heart rate kicked up when Reya asked him to hold on a second. She demanded to know if Aaron or Jason could get a call through to the hospital from the jet. After an affirmative from Aaron, and an explanation from Neesia on the nearest hospital, Reya was back on the line.

"Okay, Anthony, the closest hospital is in Rawlins. Wait, Anthony. Neesia, does that hospital have an ICU?" Reya's words were muffled but that didn't mask the urgency in her voice one whit. Back on the line again, she said, "Neesia said the closest hospital with an intensive care unit is in Laramie."

Holy fuck. Intensive care? Then the rest of it registered. "Laramie?!" Anthony exclaimed, then repeated the question a bit quieter at his brother's gasped, strained moans. God, it was a pitiful sound that made the hair on the back of his neck stand on end. Not because it was loud...but because it *wasn't* loud. Barely a rasp. Fuck.

"Yes, Laramie—"

"That's ninety fucking miles away, damn it!"

"A helicopter can fly a hell of a lot faster than an ambulance can drive. He'll make it. Damn it, he'll make it. Jason is getting the hospital on the line on a different channel. Stay put."

Anthony stayed on the line and listened to Reya in full alpha mode as she demanded a helicopter be sent immediately to his exact coordinates. When they didn't seem to be moving fast enough, she provided her medical credentials and a quick rundown of Austin's symptoms, then demanded that they haul ass.

That's my girl.

"Okay, bro, sit tight," she said, "If you have a blanket, drape it over him and keep him warm. Watch for any deterioration in his symptoms, given we have no idea how long he's been out there."

"Got it. See you at the hospital."

Half an hour later, Anthony's family, both old and new, stormed into the emergency room at the hospital. Arms banded around each other, they sent up prayers and good energy for Austin James.

"Did they give you a report yet, Anthony?" Koreas asked quietly. All he could do was shake his head. "The medical techs tried to stabilize him as we flew to the facility, but I haven't heard a word since we arrived. They were expecting us, just like you said, Reya. They wheeled him away a half-hour ago."

Anthony sucked in a shaky breath. "H-he was unconscious, you guys. I can count the number of times Austin has been unconscious in my whole life. Zero."

When the doctor arrived moments later, Reya whipped out her wallet and showed the doctor whatever was in it. The expression on her face said that she would not be denied. And whatever she'd shoved into the doctor's face backed her up. Eyes wide, the doctor said, "Hi, I'm Dr. Grant. I assume this is the family." At Reya's very short 'Yes', he said, "Please follow me, Dr. Daines. I'll brief you on the way, then we can come back to speak with the family. Okay with you?"

With a curt nod, Reya said, "Be back shortly. Hang in there."

Aaron James watched his sister-in-law and Dr. Grant hustle down the hallway and through a set of gray sliding double doors that had 'To Intensive Care Unit' painted on them.

He pulled the youngest James brother into his arms and patted Aaron on the back as they both cried, and the Prydes closed ranks around them.

Several tense hours later, Kory sat in the small private waiting room off the I.C.U. with her hands balled into lethal fists. She fought to hold onto the change that wanted to ripple through her body. And if the expressions on her sisters' faces were any indication, they were all doing their best not to allow their inner natures' need to protect those who belonged to their pride, to burst forth. Two hundred and forty pounds of lethal, muscle-packed lioness would get Austin no closer to recovery, so cooler heads would have to prevail.

But god, it was temping to say screw cooler heads and let the anger and fear within, burning as hot as the caldera in northwestern Wyoming, flow forth and destroy everything in her path.

She took a deep breath in and let it out on a long slow huff. It didn't do a damn thing to calm her down.

Kory reminded herself that she was the calm Pryde, the chill and relaxed introvert.

But not today.

She needed a focus for her anger, and even now that they knew what had happened to Austin, Kory still had none.

Neesia chimed. "Listen, sweetpea, at least we know that he's going to make it. Remember that when Reya gave us the last report, she said that Austin's lung tissue is healing faster than..."

Kotara and Jason both hiked up a brow. Neesia's eyes went wide and she immediately clamped her lips shut. *"Sorry, almost slipped."*

Koreas was grateful that her sister was careful to continue the conversation along their telepathic bond rather than saying something that might be overheard in the supposedly private waiting room.

"Anyway, remember, Reya's primary medical experience is with humans, while ours is with felines. Reya said that Austin is healing faster than any human she's ever encountered. The other doctors are stumped, but Reya thinks it's because Austin has bonded with you, and that your lioness is giving him some of her strength."

Which actually made sense. Kory didn't bother saying that she and Austin had already been speaking mind-to-mind before he'd gotten sick. It was something that was expected with mates, so it came as no surprise that he was able to tap into other aspects of her feline nature. And for that, she was eternally grateful.

"Do we know how Austin got sick? Was he exposed to something, perhaps?" Jason asked.

"I'm not sure. He's been nowhere near the labs, and definitely nowhere unescorted. There are things that don't affect us that are lethal to others so we've been very careful," Kory said, the words a danger-laced growl even in her own mind.

"Wait, Kory. What about when he brought your big gift basket this morning? He left it in one of the sample rooms. I sent him along by himself because there should have been nothing, and I mean nothing in there. The room should have been clean because Erin..."

They turned and looked at one another, Kory with brows pulled down into a fierce frown, and Kotara's mouth wide open in an "a-ha" expression.

"Erin," they said in tandem.

"Hold on a minute," Kotara said, and snatched her phone out of her purse. "I'll call the lab and see who was supposed to enter that room this morning. If Erin left something out *again*, they'll have seen it." She stepped out of the ICU waiting room and out into the corridor. A few moments later, she reported that the lab tech who'd come into the lab right after Austin left confirmed that there was nothing left out anywhere.

"But that doesn't mean there wasn't something left out earlier," Neesia said. "Call Niah. She can remotely tap into the security feed and pull up the visuals from this morning from the hallways around your office as well as the sample room Austin went into. Kotara, what time did Austin leave your room to go to pre-bio?"

And with that, the call was made and Niah got to work. Within five minutes, she'd accessed the footage from five o'clock that morning to the time Austin had exited the building. And now they all knew exactly what had happened.

With quiet menace, Koreas made her intentions known. "I am going to tear Erin apart. That bitch is toast. And you know I don't like toast."

"Murder still isn't legal, even though we're all pissed, Kory. It was a careless mistake..."

"Don't fucking tell me about careless," she snapped between clenched teeth. "If Anthony hadn't gone out to find Austin, my mate might be dead. Dead, Tara!" Kory bit back her words. The last thing she wanted was to get kicked out of the ICU for being rowdy before she even got in to see Austin.

Kory's long fuse had been lit and the countdown to detonation was never a good thing. But it didn't matter right now—didn't matter that her anger seethed and churned. Didn't matter that it was justified. The only thing that counted was that she manage to hold herself together until this emergency was over. Austin needed her. Period.

Just then, the James brothers came into the room. "Okay, ladies," Aaron whispered as he reached the area where the Pryde women were speaking. "What the hell is going on? You four were huddled up over here when they took us back to see Austin, and you're still huddled up. So spill it."

With a tired sigh, Kory stood, walked over to Aaron and Anthony, and hugged them fiercely. When she opened her mouth to speak, the words came out on a broken sob.

Finally, she sniffled loudly and said, "It's my fault."

"What?" The word was echoed by every James and Pryde in the small private waiting area. When the surprised whispers died down from a roar to a dull buzz, Kotara stepped forward, yanked her sister to face her, and then shook her like a rag doll.

"What the hell is wrong with you? You didn't leave that flask out."

"Flask?" Jason wondered aloud. "What flask?"

"We were testing a new vaccine to battle the respiratory effects of certain stages of FIV, feline immunodeficiency virus. One of our process engineers left a flask of live culture sitting on a sample table. It wasn't supposed to be there," Kory said, sniffing loudly between every few words. "It's my responsibility to make sure the lab runs smoothly and that everyone is doing their job. We've had problems with Erin being forgetful before. I'm so sorry. I should have let her go sooner and..."

"*And* my ass," Aaron snapped. "If you're expecting us to turn on you instead of tearing a chunk out of the scientist who left that fucking flask, forget it, Koreas. We don't blame you for this. And Austin won't either."

At the whoosh of the almost-silent door sliding open, they all turned at once. "Speaking of Austin," Reya called quietly from the threshold, "you can come in and see him now, Kory. I'm sorry, but the rest of you will have to wait. And yes, they're keeping him for another day or so."

"Did they narrow down what's wrong with him, Rey?" Aaron asked.

Hands thrust into the pocket of a borrowed white smock, she came fully into the room. Mouth tight, eyes glittering, she took a deep breath and exchanged her "concern for a family member" expression and donned her "doctor's game face".

"Austin appears to have viral acute interstitial pneumonitis."

Kory groaned and burst into a fresh round of tears. She just couldn't help it. When it came to Austin James, her quiet, calm demeanor was moot. Interstitial...god, she couldn't even finish the thought.

Neesia pulled Kory back into her arms and tucked her head against her shoulder. Jason wrapped them both in his arms and said, "For us non-medical folks, can you explain what the hell that is?"

"The interstitium is a lace-like network of tissue that extends throughout both lungs and supports the microscopic air sacs that allow gas exchange between blood and the air in the lungs. A.I.P. is a sudden, severe interstitial lung disease, often requiring life support. Rapid progression from initial symptoms to respiratory failure is common, and the only known immediate cure...is a lung transplant."

Holy fuck.

"The median survival rate is 1½ months."

Oh my god.

"However, there's always a chance of skipping the transplant and recovering naturally, though it's rare. In that case, this disease is usually a one-episode event. Those who survive often recover lung function completely. The biggest problem with A.I.P. is, no one knows what causes it."

"So it could have been anything?" Kotara asked.

"Yep," Reya responded, "but I have a feeling you have an idea."

And the woman was right. They weren't related by blood or bond, so they couldn't speak telepathically. When Reya didn't press, Kory was thankful that the woman had sense enough to keep quiet about her suspicions.

A moment later, Neesia whispered into her head. *"Reya spoke to Aaron, and Aaron spoke to Jason..."*

"Aaron spoke to Jason? How?" Kory interrupted.

"They've shared blood, remember? Now hush and don't interrupt. This is important. Reya just told Aaron to tell Jason to tell me that usually it would take several days, maybe even weeks for a person to get well enough to come out of the I.C.U., but at the rate your mate is healing, he may be able to come off of the meds that are keeping him unconscious in a matter of hours. On the flipside, Jason passed on the info about the experimental flask that was left out. Reya agrees that your mate must have inhaled the particulates left behind."

Koreas heaved a sigh of heartfelt relief. Foolish didn't begin to describe how she felt about spending so much time worrying about Austin's humanity when she could have been loving him. Her insides still shook as she realized how close she'd come to losing what she'd just found.

Such needless time lost.

Carelessness was the reason her man was attached to a ventilator and fighting for his life, damn it.

"It'll be all right, Kory," Reya said. "They're keeping him unconscious for a little while just to make sure the medicines have time to work."

"Yes, I know. That doesn't make me any less angry. This didn't have to happen, Reya. At all."

"Go on, hon. Go see your mate." Neesia kissed Kory on the cheek and gave her a bright, but watery smile. "Harry has already gone to get Niah and Lou in Denver. Jason and I will arrange for a car to come and take us back to the airstrip so we can go home."

Spine straight, steely determination fully in place, Kory's tears became a thing of the past. "I'm not going home." She turned expectant eyes on Reya. "Arrange for me to stay the night, please."

It didn't sound like a request...because it wasn't one.

"I'll ask. I'm not on staff here so I can't make that call," Reya replied.

"So how did you manage to take part in Austin's care, get the helicopter, and all of that?" Kotara asked Reya.

"I told you that when I lived out West, I did some special respiratory stuff? Well, I was part of a team that discovered the reason behind a nasty lung infection whose cause, like Austin's condition, was previously unknown. My team's research led to a vaccine against that particular virus. The research and development was done right here. They, uh..." she paused, suddenly looking shy. "They call the virus Daines-Lass syndrome. Lass was a scientist on my team, and as you know, my last name is Daines. When I gave the emergency guys my information from the plane, I, uh, I guess they kind of recognized my name or something."

The other woman's smile was adorably sheepish. Kory was grateful for it. A bit of levity in a tense situation was usually good for all.

"So you're a fucking medical legend?" Kotara asked, mouth and eyes equally wide open with awe. Her sister rounded on her. "Kory, how did we not know we had a medical genius in our house? How is that even possible?" Her scary-but-awed expression was then turned on the men. "Ya'll were holding out on us!"

Kory shook her head at her twin, though she was just as impressed.

"Well, I wouldn't put it quite that way." Reya's sheepish smile became an impish grin. "I was a bit of a hellion while I was here. More hellion than genius, I'm sure."

Anthony groused, "Say it ain't so, sis." Reya promptly smacked him playfully across the shoulder.

Kory wrapped her arms around her new friend and whispered, "Thank you. If not for a bit of fame, we might not have been able to get a helicopter. We might have been too late."

"You're welcome," Reya said, returning the embrace. "Austin is my brother. I'd do anything for him." Then she whispered super-quietly into Kory's ear, "As for the reason behind his illness, you guys better make sure I'm nowhere around when the person responsible is dealt with."

Kory couldn't help but nod because she'd said the same thing to her sisters only moments ago.

And she'd meant every. Fucking. Word.

14

*K*ory sat in the fairly comfortable chair next to Austin's bed and let her feline senses remain at the forefront of her mind. Through her lioness—her true nature —she was connected to Austin on a level that had been unimaginable before she'd accepted him as her mate.

It was a deep thing, well beyond anything physical she'd ever experienced. Almost spiritual, it seemed.

Right now, he was unconscious but dreaming. She'd tried to talk to him, but right now his mind was off on an adventure of its own making. As she tagged along, Kory could somehow see what he saw in his mind's eye. And it was the most spectacular experiences she'd ever had.

The scenes in his head were so vivid, it was as if he truly lived them. In one scene, he hiked a snowy mountain trail with some men who were not his brothers. Fresh powder coated the leaves of a stand of aspens they passed through. It was early morning and the sun sparkled off of the terrain like diamonds, and the only sound in the high-country silence was the crunch of their boots in the snow and the quiet sounds of friendly conversation.

The scene switched to another where he was laying on his back looking up at the stars. So very many stars, it was as if someone tossed a bucketful of pearls over a velvet blanket. Just beautiful.

She saw him smile to himself and wondered what he was thinking about. And to her surprise, her image appeared in the sky! Austin was thinking, his head full of thoughts of her.

Instinctively, she reached out to him.

"Kory?"

Oh my god, he'd felt her? If he felt her, maybe he could hear her. She called out to him. He turned his head as if he searched for her, but couldn't see her. Finally, his image looked back up toward the stars.

"Kory, is that you?"

"Hi, baby," she said. *"How are you feeling?"*

"I'm not quite sure. My chest hurts. Where are you?"

"I'm here. You can't see me right now, but I'm right next to you."

"I..." In his dream, he sucked in a deep breath. A tear leaked from the corner of his eye. *"I can see your lioness in the stars. I can see the real you. You've never let me see you in that form before. I'm honored, baby."*

Kory knew that tears leaked from her physical eyes, but she didn't move to wipe them for fear that any alteration of her thinking would break the connection with Austin as he dreamed.

And she needed desperately to know that he was okay.

"I'm okay. And yes, I heard your thoughts. I've been getting pretty good at speaking into that brilliant mind of yours. But something happened to me, Kory. I think I blacked out or something. I tried to call out to you but it felt like...like I was drowning. Literally drowning."

She recalled how Reya had described the issue with his

lungs. They'd begun to fill with mucus as he'd lain next to the river. He had, in fact, been drowning in his own fluids. But she didn't want to send those thoughts to him, so she clamped down on them.

"*What else do you remember?*" she whispered.

"*I remember Anthony yelling at someone, and then the sound of a helicopter. Then nothing. I think some time had passed because I could have sworn I heard Reya, but I must have been hallucinating or something.*"

"*You heard her, baby. You got sick. Anthony found you passed out on the prairie near the river. You were airlifted to one of the premier hospitals in Laramie, Wyoming. I'm sitting in a chair next to your bed right now. You're in the I.C.U. but I think they'll be moving you soon.*"

"*But you were in Denver with your family.*"

"*Yes, I was. We turned around in the air and flew here to make sure you were taken care of.*"

His smile, beautiful and devastating, was mirrored on her own face when he asked, "*So, did you like your gift basket?*"

"*I absolutely did. It's beautiful. When they let you go home, you can share some of the goodies with me.*"

"*Home?*" he asked. "*I don't want to go home.*"

She was stunned. He didn't want…?

"*I don't want to go home to Colorado. My vacation isn't over yet at Pryde Ranch. Not sure it ever will be.*" He yawned and his eyes began to slip closed and the lines of concern etched across his brow relaxed.

The invisible fist that squeezed her heart suddenly released and in the moment, she knew that there was nothing she wanted more than to have Austin at her side. Wanted him, period. Yes, she knew he would heal, but there was more to it than that—she wanted to fall asleep with him, wake up with him. Learn him, inside out. And let him become part of her.

For the first time in her life, Koreas Pryde considered leaving her family.

"I wouldn't ask that of you, Koreas. I want you happy, baby. You're part of a pride, and you need that connection to thrive."

"But..."

"No but's. We'll figure it out. But for now, I'm sleepy. So very, very sleepy."

Arms behind his head, he continued to stare up at the outline of her lioness in the stars overhead. As his dream faded to black, she knew he slept peacefully with his thoughts filled with nothing but her.

Kory's tears, previously of rage and fear, were now tears of relief and joy.

15

*B*ack at Pryde Ranch, Austin James was in heaven. It reminded him of when he and Anthony had first met Reya in Belize. Not long after Aaron had been injured in a plane crash there, Reya had been mauled by a feral jaguar.

The first time Austin and his brother had met her, she'd been on bed rest as she recovered. It had been easy to cater to such a beautiful woman, not to mention piss off their little brother by giving his woman so much of their attention.

Now, it was Austin's turn. And he was being waited on hand and foot by all of the Pryde women.

In fact, when his brothers came up to Kory's room to sit with him, they spent half their time bitching about what a lucky bastard he was to have four beautiful lionesses and a sexy jaguar looking after him.

Grateful he'd only spent three days in the hospital, to the amazement of his doctors, Austin raised his arms over his head and stretched. A few more days of bed rest and he'd be up and about. He felt fine as it was, but he wasn't going to argue with three doctors telling him that they would skin his ass if he didn't follow the orders he'd been given when they discharged him from the medical center.

He rolled to his side and his gaze landed on the pillow next to him. A glance at the clock told him that after he'd eaten breakfast, compliments of Neesia Pryde, he'd promptly passed out and slept for another three hours.

Kory was long gone to the Labyrinth, but every time he moved, her scent wafted up from the sheets and bedding. He took a deep breath, drew it into his lungs and sighed happily.

At that moment, she rushed into his consciousness.

"Hey, how are you feeling today, handsome?"

"Like the luckiest man in the world. I'd be feeling better if you were here in the bed with me."

She chuckled into his mind and he could almost picture the expression on her face—a mix of shy and vixen.

"I hope I didn't wake you when I left this morning. It was still dark out."

"I felt you leave, but you didn't wake me. How long before you come home? I miss you," he asked.

"It's barely eleven o'clock. Not even lunch time yet," she replied saucily.

"Not for me, but definitely for you. Come eat with me while I watch? Tell me about your day?"

Just then, the door opened and there she stood. Koreas stepped into the room, closed the door, and unbuttoned her lab coat.

A whispered, "Holy shit!" was Austin's response as she dropped the garment to the floor. The woman was buck-ass naked, from her grin down to her perfect little toes.

"Uh, can we say instant hard-on, anyone?" he grumbled. His hand went directly to the piece of steel between his legs in an attempt to relieve some of the pressure.

She padded to the side of the bed and pulled the covers back to reveal his body...along with the boner from hell.

She whispered, "Good morning, love," and then leaned over his prone body until her beautiful bared breasts pressed against his chest. One of her slender hands took the place of his own as her fingers wrapped round his staff.

With a swift intake of breath that hissed between his teeth, Austin fought to keep his hips from rising from the mattress in rhythm with her lovely stroking. His arms automatically wrapped around her to hold her tight as she kissed him fully, passionately.

With one hand buried in her super curly hair, and the other squeezing a perfect globe of her ass, Austin groaned as she sank into that kiss, heart and soul. Tongues tangled, tasted…challenged.

"*Glad I brushed my teeth earlier.*"

She giggled, pulling back for a moment.

"Glad you think this is funny. No sex while I heal is killing me."

"Big baby," she teased.

He pumped against her palm. "Does this feel like a big baby?"

"Maybe. Maybe not."

"Maybe? How would you know what a big…" That was as far as he got because his woman took him in her mouth, got him wet in two strokes, and then had him clear to the back of her throat on stroke three.

"Oh my god," he growled. "Kory, should we? Holy fuck! Be doing…?"

She never took her lips from him as she said, "*Sex requires you to put your whole body into it. Reya said you won't be up for that —pun intended—for another day or two. However, she also said that cardiopulmonary exercises, such as deep breathing, is good for you. I think we can accomplish that, don't you?*"

"I can't answer questions right now. Feels too good." He felt his lungs working, reviving as they expanded and contracted with each deep breath he took.

His lids closed as his eyes rolled up into his head. His teeth clicked together with an audible "snap" when Kory's tongue made a swirly-circle pattern over the head of his cock.

God, the woman knew how to suck a dick.

"Glad you approve, handsome."

Austin knew he wasn't going to last long. The pleasure was too intense. And the woman delivering it was just too good. Too...right. Every time he was with her, it was like coming home. He'd never expected to find love on the Wyoming prairie. Never expected to become a mate to anyone, let alone a lioness shifter.

And when he exploded, he received the most precious gift of all since leaving home with his brothers to come visit Pryde Ranch.

"I love you, Austin James."

In this moment, there was nothing he was more proud of having done in his life, than pursuing Koreas Pryde.

SHIFTIN' SASSY

1

"*H*ave me out here riding like Evel Knievel, chasing your goofy ass through the mountains. Just wait until I catch you," Derria Sozi-Pryde snarled to herself, wishing the bad guy she was chasing could hear her inner commentary. She leaned into yet another curve and frowned at the force of the whipping wind as she straightened out her motorcycle.

Luckily her riding gear was heavily insulated but a quick glance up at the darkening sky warned that she'd need something a bit warmer, and soon. Thick, fluffy gray clouds and the dramatic drop in temperature over the last couple of hours warned of rain. Definitely not her favorite thing.

Derria thought she'd been everywhere, but she had to admit that this was the most curvy, lonely bit of highway she'd ever seen, let alone driven. No wonder they called this area the Tail of the Dragon.

This stretch of blacktop had so many twists and turns she'd had to disengage the helmet display for her GPS, or risk running off the road. Three hundred curves over eleven miles? Fucking insane. She would be sure to take the nerve-wracking ride out on her quarry when she caught up to him, the slippery bastard.

Since it was too treacherous to fly through the turns, the slower speed gave her the chance to see what would usually pass as a blur. She truly appreciated the nature of the place, despite the fact she was pissed off and chasing a rogue Were.

Both sides of the two-lane highway were covered with trees. As she chased the sunset, pink and orange reflected off soaring gray storm clouds. It caused a bit of glare in her mirrors, but the colors stretched across the sky were so beautifully brilliant that she didn't really care. Despite the looming storm, the distant skies reminded her of cherries and orange sherbet...which led to the realization that her last meal had been too long ago. Derria pushed her bike just a bit harder as the first fat drops of rain began to fall in earnest.

Derria's cousins owned Pryde Ranch and its subsidiary, Pryde Industries—the most awesome seventy-seven thousand acres of rolling prairie, groves and meadows off the Medicine Bow River in Wyoming. What most people considered "dark" was nothing compared to the über-dark out in the sticks. And this mountain road, like Pryde Ranch, certainly counted as the sticks. Usually she loved being in the middle of nowhere. But today, not so much.

Derria pulled over to the side of the road in a spot where she was sure she wouldn't be hit by any passing vehicles. Rather than taking her helmet off, she engaged the electronics embedded inside and tried to call her oldest cousin, Neesia Pryde. Neesia was just a few minutes older than her twin, Niah. Kotara and Koreas were the second set of twins, a few years younger than Neesia and Niah. All the mated women had been wooed by lion shifters, except for Koreas, who'd shocked herself by mating with a human—and a hot as hell cowboy human, at that.

Derria had just come to know them a couple of years ago

after learning, quite by accident, that her mother was the sister of the Pryde's long dead father. Neesia, Niah, Kotara and Koreas had lost both their parents when they were just little lionesses. Thankfully their grandmother had stepped in to care for them by bringing them out of Africa and over to the U.S.

Derria's family had already been in the States and didn't learn of the attack on their family's shifter village until after the girls had pretty much disappeared into thin air. Years later, Derria's own family had died in a fluke skiing accident. Unfortunately, the chain of circumstances meant some long-lost family had been floating around out there thinking they were totally alone—namely Derria.

She spoke the control password into the concealed microphone in her helmet. Nothing happened.

"Show signal strength." A grid popped up on the visor display.

Zero bars. Great.

She unzipped a side pouch on the gear bag strapped to the back of her bike and pulled out a mini-satellite dish. Once she unfolded it and hit the power button, she said, "Switch from mobile to satellite." A couple of beeps later, she turned to the southwest, held the unit up toward the sky and hoped to get a signal somehow.

Yes! Thank goodness for Niah Pryde's amazing inventions. That woman was a genius when it came to all things electronic, hence Derria being on this hunt with military grade everything. After all, what good would it be for Niah to provide services to the government on behalf of Pryde Industries if she didn't keep a little something special for their own little pride? And right now, the voice activated encrypted software system embedded into her helmet was one of her favorite toys.

"Call home."

Neesia Pryde answered on the second ring. "Hey, Derria!"

Her words were bright with genuine welcome. "Everything okay?"

Derria explained the issue with the GPS display on her visor, which was probably due to all the damn curves on this road.

"The signal must be terrible out there," Neesia said. "I actually lost you a couple of times."

"Lost me? Why were you tracking me in the first place?"

"I'm your liaison on this hunt, remember? And before you get all snotty, let me tell you that I just got some new information from the agency. You're not going to be happy about it, because I sure as hell am not."

"Okay, lay it on me." Derria felt the snarl building in her throat as her annoyance at this mystery information grew. Considering she didn't even know what it was, she chalked it up to a long day.

"Find a place to hole up tonight, then tomorrow you need to check in with the locals," Neesia said.

"The local what?"

"There are multiple shifter populations near you. In fact, you're in an area that's considered neutral and it sits between various territories."

Derria bristled. "I'm in a neutral zone? What is this, Star Trek? What are you going to tell me next, Neecie? That I need to look out for Romulans and Klingons?"

"Smart-ass. Don't take it out on me because your rogue gave you the slip. Now, what you need to look out for are the various clans who live in that area. Checking in with their council members is a must if you expect to pass through their territories."

"And why are we just hearing about these clans? They're not under S.W.A.T. jurisdiction?"

"Nope. Those communities predate S.W.A.T. They opted out when the organization was first formed ages ago. Bunch of old guard, stuffed shirts are determined to keep their people in the dark ages."

"Are they going to interfere with me once they know why I'm here?" Like, hiding the person she was looking for, or warn him that she was hot on his trail?

"No, but you still need to check in with the Elders of each territory you pass through."

Then the "nosey" in Derria perked up its head. "How are they surviving with no new blood? Inbreeding?"

Neesia said, "Actually, there is no inbreeding. In fact, there's no breeding at all. When it happens it's rare. For some reason their fertility rate is so low that extinction is a true possibility."

"Interesting." Derria paused and let this new information sink in. So not only were there several communities that weren't under her agency's jurisdiction, but they were in danger of disappearing as well? Instead of voicing the slew of questions flying through her brain, she said, "Let it go on the record that I am totally pissed that S.W.A.T. just now chose to share these little details after I'm already out here in the boonies." Derria kicked a big rock as hard as she could, and then winced as it went flying high up into the air and landed on the other side of the highway in thick bushes.

Damn thing was denser than I expected, ow!

"There would have been no need to know this stuff if you'd caught your guy in Tennessee," Neesia teased.

"If I could voice an eyeroll, I would, Neecie,"

"I'm with you there. When I tore them a new asshole about leaving out such important details, the powers that be said it was on a need to know basis, and obviously they felt as if we didn't need to know until now. Bastards."

"Indeed. So how do I know when I'm in clan territory? And how do I know which clan belongs to which part of this windy ass mountain range?"

"Well, according to the system you're in Nantahala."

"Nanta-who?" Derria wondered aloud as she looked around. She's been riding so fast for so long, she couldn't remember the last road sign she'd seen.

"Nantahala. You're just North of the national forest, Dare. Hold on, I'll send the deets to your GPS unit so you can see exactly where all the lines and borders are. The satellite signal should be strong enough to handle the data dump."

In seconds, the bits came through and Derria's eyes grew wide.

Holy shit! There were several species of felines, including cougar and jaguar, as well as psychics and magic workers.

"Neesia, did you look at this shit? I have to deal with witches? And fucking mages? Seriously? Next, you'll be telling me that there are demons and vampires, damn it." Pacing back and forth next to her motorcycle, she fought to hold in a deep snarl.

"They're not witches, but they do have various psychic abilities. But so what. Think of it this way," Neesia said. "None of us shifters are supposed to exist so why would it be so strange to learn that there are all kinds of other folks out there that we didn't know about?"

"Are you saying there are vamp…"

"No, but I'm making a point here, cuz. Just roll with me."

"Hell, I'm tired of rolling. My bike needs gas and my ass needs a break. I could do with some food and a good night's sleep. Looking through the data you sent, I don't see any hotels close by. Aw, hell."

"What?"

"It's starting to really rain. I need to get moving."

"Keep heading southeast for another couple of miles. There's a little town called Stecoah. Stop there."

"Fine," she grumbled.

"Derria, you're a kick ass bounty hunter, but diplomacy is not your strong suit. Think you'll need any help?" Neesia asked.

"Niah and Lou are out of pocket, but my mate is out on a hunt not too far from you."

"Nah, I've got it, Neecie. If I need Jason, I'll call him, but I don't think the big guy is necessary for this. It's supposed to be a simple smash and grab."

"Where's your quarry?"

"Now that I've got a signal, I'll send you the coordinates. That way we both know where he is since he's tagged." Her bounty had been shot in the leg with a high-powered rifle that contained some very special ammunition. The bullets contained non-metal nano-trackers that split away from the slug when the ammo hit the body. Even if the guy managed to get the bullet fragments out, and then shift to accelerate his healing, the tracker would remain inside him.

Genius, if she could say so herself. *All hail Niah Pryde!*

Derria pulled up the data feed with a word and smiled. "He's no more than half an hour from me. Looks like he's gone off-road." Since the little red dot that represented him wasn't moving, he'd probably forced a shift and hunkered down somewhere to heal and get out of the weather for the night.

Speaking of weather, it was time to go. Her bike was modified for her needs, but the last place she wanted to be was on a slick road. In the dark. Sure, as an African lion shifter, Derria had exceptional eyesight, but no lioness in her right mind enjoyed being out in an ice-cold downpour at night.

"Okay, Neesia. I'm out of here and headed to Stecoah."

"Good. There should be at least a bed and breakfast or something there. If not, there's a pub with a hostel. It's called Deep Blue Ridge. Word has it that they may have a room or two available."

"Got it." Derria climbed back onto her bike. "I'll check in with you one more time before I hit the sheets." With her typical request that Neesia deliver a somewhat grumpy hello and long-distance hugs to Derria's cousins and their mates, she signed off.

With the mini-satellite dish secured to its "cup holder," Derria checked the strap of her helmet. She revved the engine once for good measure, flipped on her headlights and rode hell for leather for the town of Stecoah with one prayer.

Dear God, please don't let me roll into town and find that the only place to stay the night is owned by a tobacco spitting, moonshine swigging, banjo playing toothless wonder whose favorite pastime is carving himself new teeth...or carving up intruding lioness shifters from Wyoming. Amen.

Kerr Blackstone couldn't believe his luck. He'd been shot by the most beautiful bitch he'd ever seen. He pushed his bike as hard and fast as he could, making his way toward his clan's lands. He knew this winding road like the back of his hand and he hoped he'd made a clean getaway into these mountains.

His pack had been declared renegades by their bass ackwards, ancient as dirt Clan Corwyn council leaders for wanting to live in the modern age. Though they'd walked into exile together to form their own pack, Kerr wasn't stupid enough to think that all Blackstones were good guys. Some of his brothers and cousins were fucking scary ass bastards, and the last thing a smart man did was tell crazy shifters where he would hole up in times of trouble.

He'd turned off the main road some time ago and carefully rode at a speed that wouldn't kick up dirt and gravel and leave a glaring trail directly to him. He maneuvered his bike into a dense spot of brush and stopped at the bottom of a sheer cliff. Finally, just as the sun was setting, he reached his own personal little hidey-hole.

With the push of a button, the solid-looking rock face slid open to reveal what looked like nothing more than a cave.

Holy shot-in-the-ass, Batman, he grumbled to himself. Hell, he wished he had been shot in the ass. Less blood loss. In fact, he hadn't realized he'd lost so much until his vision began to waver and his limbs refused to work properly.

Oh, and the pool of sticky cooling fluid that gushed out of his boots as he tried to balance his bike was a slight indication of a small problem. Getting shot in the leg isn't so bad...unless the bullet nicked an artery. It might explain why he should be healing, but his body wasn't cooperating. There was no way in hell he should be losing steam like this, and he wondered for the billionth time what he'd been shot with.

Once inside, he quickly shut off his ride, secured the door and activated both the alarm system and the dim lighting. He stripped as quickly as he could, and then forced his animal to the fore. His wolf was sluggish and that worried the hell out of him. After a bit of coaxing, his beast responded, and the buzz of magic filled the room as the change rippled through his body.

Born a shifter, he usually felt very little pain when his body rearranged itself. Right now, it hurt like hell. He lay there on the polished stone floor. Shallow pants and a few moans were all he could manage. Even after the shift, the typical burst of energy from taking on his natural form was absent. A quiet clink of something hit the floor—a bullet. He rolled over with a groan, thankful that his body had at least rejected the slug he'd been carrying for the last however many hours as he'd run like hell from whoever was after him.

The Blackstone pack possessed some of the best trackers in the shifter world. And if this chick who was after him had half his skill, she'd be on him within forty-eight hours in his current weakened state. All he could do was remain as limp as a ragdoll on the floor, and hope to god that whatever was wrong with him would wear off quickly enough for him to keep himself alive.

What he couldn't figure out was why he'd been shot in the first place. And why the hell was this bad ass woman after his ass? He hadn't done anything lately. Well, not that he could remember.

But there was nothing he could do about it now but rest.

Sometime later, Kerr rolled over on the hard floor and hissed.

What. The. Fuck?

He'd shifted back to his human form in his sleep?

Snatching up the pants he'd left in a messy pile near his head, he retrieved his phone and gasped. The thing claimed it had been several hours since he'd passed out. Even though he'd shifted and his body had rejected the bullet, the site where he'd been struck was still red, puckered, and stung like hell.

And now he had to pee but didn't have the energy to get up off the floor.

Maybe he'd been tranquilized? Nah, that would have simply knocked him out rather than sapped him slowly, right? Maybe he should go see the doctor that some of his cousins had kidnapped from Clan Corwyn? Simone-something-or-other, he thought her name was. Maybe the doc would know what was going on with his whacked-out body.

He dragged himself across the smooth tamped earth, glad no one from his pack was here to witness this. A strong alpha wolf crawling across the floor, bare-assed naked with his balls swinging in the wind? Fucking insulting.

Finally, he made it to the staircase that led up to the small living area of his special little space and, one step at a time, hauled himself up on his hands and knees.

By the time he reached his bed, Kerr was exhausted. But it didn't stop him from cussing a blue streak, laced with vows of revenge as he again slipped into oblivion.

He didn't expect to dream, but he did...of a tawny-eyed goddess with the biggest fucking gun he'd ever seen, aimed right at him...and all he wanted to do was kiss her.

Yep. He'd lost his mind, along with pints of blood somewhere out on the highway.

Lakota Phillips walked out of the Deep Blue Ridge roadhouse
shaking his head at himself. How the hell did Aldin always
know shit that he shouldn't? How did he know to call Lakota
down here to meet a person that no one should know was
headed their way? In fact, Aldin wasn't even in town right now,
so how the hell had he known that a bounty hunter would be
riding in within the next five minutes?

Derria Sozi worked with the Shifter and Were Armed
Tactics agency...but not a soul within five hundred miles of this
place should know such a thing. The moment he'd received
intelligence that this *Derria* was indeed a real person and a
fellow agent, he'd requested details on her assignment, as well as
authorization to assist as needed.

Part of him was peeved that he'd learned through back chan-
nels that an agent was headed his way. On the other hand,
perhaps Aldin had served as his "heads up." Either way, Lakota
couldn't decide to fume or tilt his head in bewilderment, as the
conversation he'd just had spun crazy circles inside his head.

Ten minutes prior...

*Lakota stared at his phone, then put it back to his ear. "You called
me to arrange a meeting with some woman?"*

*Aldin's deep laugh boomed through the phone as Lakota sat in his
favorite spot in the Deep Blue Ridge roadhouse. The bartender had slid
a cold mug of beer his way. It stopped right in front of him without a
single drop spilled.*

*"This particular chick," Aldin said as he suddenly sobered, "you
definitely need to meet. Never seen or heard of her before, but from*

what I understand, she's got shifter written all over her. Rides a bad ass sport bike, too. A real crotch rocket."

"So?" Lakota responded and took a sip of dark ale. Reminded him of tar.

"So, I have a feeling she's the snooping kind. I was hoping, given your special line of work, maybe you could find out who she is."

Now that took Kota aback. Special line of work? With another swallow of his beer, he'd forced his body to remain loose and his voice even, though the other man had thrown him for quite the loop.

"Special line of work?" Kota asked.

"Well, it's technically a secret." The words were delivered with enough snark to choke a stand-up comedian.

And then the other man rocked his world with no hesitation. "I know you work for the Shifter and Were Armed Tactics agency, man."

Without confirming or denying the conclusion, Lakota stood, left a tip for the bartender and headed out to the parking lot. No way he wanted any of the rest of this conversation overheard. Damn shifter hearing.

Aldin repeated, "You're with S.W.A.T., Kota."

Still, Lakota kept quiet and waited for the other man to give him an idea where this was going.

"No one in the Gorge knows but me. And it'll stay that way," Aldin said.

"As long as...?" Kota asked.

"No conditions. I'll take it to the grave. But I still want to know who this woman is that's rolling in as if she's the mistress of Hell itself. From what I understand, she gives off the same vibe you do."

"And what vibe is that?"

"The cop kind."

And all those close to Aldin and his band of miscreants knew that the last thing anyone wanted nosing around was an outsider shifter cop, regardless of species.

As he finished up the strangest conversation he'd had lately, came the deep rumble of a powerful engine just as the sun sank below the tree line.

Now here he stood as he came face to face with who must be Derria Sozi. And the woman looked pissed.

Lakota had to be nuts, considering her expression promised death to whoever she was after. And it flipped his switch like a strike of lightning to the brain. Shaking his head at himself, he made his way over to the sexiest woman he'd seen in an age as she straddled a machine that any biker would orgasm over.

Still waiting for a response to his request for information from his superiors, Derria's purpose might be unknown, but her presence here was not. If Aldin and Lakota knew she was here, he began to wonder who else was aware. And more importantly, how was that possible given the security protocols in place at S.W.A.T.?

Lakota smelled a rat...and the stench wasn't coming from the piece of perfection staring at him as if he'd grown a horn from the middle of his forehead.

2

*D*erria shut off the purring engine of her custom ride and hopped off. She grabbed her gear bag and headed toward the front door of an old, two-story, wooden building with a worn sign that read "Deep Blue Ridge Roadhouse." The place looked like a tornado-tossed barn from the old television show, *Wild Wild West*.

All she wanted was a hot shower and a bed, to go with the delicious smelling baguette and roast beef she'd managed to grab from the local bakery in town. She'd happened in right as they were closing and totally lucked out. The owner, a cheerful woman named Sierra, mentioned that she had some leftover cold cuts from the lunch crowd that she'd have to throw out unless Derria took them off her hands.

Starving and chilled from the rain shower she'd ridden through, Derria didn't need to be asked twice to accept such hospitality.

Unfortunately the little bed and breakfast she'd passed was booked up, but thankfully Neesia had already told her about the Deep Blue Ridge. Hopefully she'd luck into a room for the night.

As she headed for the front door, she expected a man with a

cowboy hat and a banjo to run out and greet her. Once she was closer, it was a surprise to hear the blare of some serious old-time rock-n-roll. Maybe it was her kind of place after all.

Off to her right, the man who'd been watching her as she'd pulled into the parking lot began to move her way. She hoped he wouldn't harass her because she wasn't in the mood for any bullshit. One wrong word and she'd just have to kick him in the brain and go on about her business.

She took a deep breath, released it and prayed for patience. The man was now right behind her as her hand closed over the door handle to the building. She turned to give him the stink eye and went still. The moment her gaze met his, the hair on the back of her neck started doing the hustle.

What the hell?

She sucked in a gasp and hoped it didn't sound as shocked as she truly felt.

"Good evening," the guy said as he flashed a smile that was both friendly and strangely smoldering. How did a man even do that? Her lioness suddenly sat up and paid very close attention indeed. This guy had said all of two words to her, yet the timbre of his voice echoed in her head. He moved like a shifter, all graceful and shit, but most shifters, in her experience, couldn't tell one of their kind from a human unless that particular shifter had gone rogue. And when that happened, they called Derria and her cousins to round them up or put them down.

The stranger held out his hand. She looked down at it, then back up at his face. Her ability to paint on a cool demeanor served her well just now because the intense expression in the greenest eyes she'd ever seen sent a wiggle down her spine.

It wasn't fear she experienced. No, this was something else. A *something* she'd never encountered before that made her antsy for no apparent reason.

Suddenly she wondered what he smelled like.

Girl, what the hell is wrong with you?

Thankfully he stood downwind, otherwise if she'd caught his scent just now, she might just drop her helmet and gear in the mud and start sniffing him about the collar.

Good grief, Derria, get your shit together.

He still held his hand out to her as he said, "I'm Lakota Phillips, Clan Hollen and council liaison."

Okay, so her thoughts of him being a shifter were confirmed as soon as he'd said the word "clan." But how in the hell did he know to share such a thing with her? She could have been a human for all he knew.

She took his bare hand in her gloved one and shook it once, twice and then pulled away.

"Derria."

"Nice to meet you, Derria. Buy you a beer?"

"Nope," she said, intending to leave him standing there. Suddenly her mouth said, "But I'll take a hot toddy. It's cold as hell out here."

He motioned toward the front door she still hadn't managed to open, and they headed inside.

It turned out the place wasn't as big of a dump as she'd expected. They'd missed the memo on dark wood being out of style, but otherwise, it was clean and neat. A couple of pool tables were off in a far corner, and there were plenty of places to sit and eat at the tables spread about.

Derria immediately spotted the bar in the dim lighting and headed for it. Hyperaware of the presence of Lakota next to her, she ordered her toddy with extra lemon. It arrived in a thick, warm mug with steam wafting upward. Smelled like maybe there was a hint of ginger as well. After a couple of sips of the spicy, perfectly blended mixture of honeyed whisky, she turned to see Lakota handling a beer.

"Have you eaten?" he asked.

"Nope. Dinner's right here." She held up her baguette and meat-in-a-bag and plopped it on the counter. Thankfully, Sierra had thought to put her paper bag inside a plastic one to keep the rain out.

"I see you found our little bakery in town. Sierra makes a mean muffin."

"It's just bread and meat. I caught her as she was closing," Derria said, and wondered at herself for falling into such easy small talk with a stranger.

To her surprise, he snatched up her bag off the bar and tossed it into the air. The guy who'd made her toddy caught it as Lakota said, "Hey, Cage, mind turning that into a hot sandwich?"

"No problem. Want fries with that, ma'am?" Cage asked, looking at her with the same warm smile as Lakota's...minus the whole "I might want to lick you" thing.

"Fries? Hell yes," she replied, genuinely thankful to get her fried-food fix. It wasn't something Neesia did at home very often. Another sip of sweet whiskey goodness and she turned her attention back to Lakota. "Thanks."

"No problem. Southern hospitality is second to none."

"So are you the liaison to all the clans, Lakota?"

"I am. I spend a good chunk of my time here in the Neutral Zone playing middleman between outcasts and their former clans, when needed. Sometimes I do have to run interference between the councils themselves, or my Guardian..."

"Guardian?" she asked.

"Yep. The enforcers of the law for Clan Hollen."

Perfect. Exactly what she needed. But she had a question first.

"So how did you know to share your status as a shifter with me? I'm just some chick off the street."

"But you're not a *human* chick off the street, are you?"

"Not human? Says who?" she demanded, as her voice dropped an octave and pushed the words out as if she hadn't a care in the world.

"Your scent tells me exactly what you are."

Da fuck?

"What do you mean by that, exactly?" she asked, sounding more bored than she had a moment before.

"You're a lion shifter. We can tell up here in the Gorge."

How. In. The. Hell?

"And," he continued, "there are no humans in here. Didn't you know?"

No, damn it, she hadn't.

Okay, Dare, note to self—tell Kotara and Koreas that the shifters up here can smell non-rogues.

Every shifter she'd ever met outside of these mountains was indistinguishable from any other person. It was the reason that shifters ran in such tight circles. Keeping their status hidden from humans meant some serious discretion. And those who outed another of their kind would find S.W.A.T. agents on their ass in a blink.

A shifter walked into a bar...

Here she was, in the middle of nowhere and the first person she'd met knew exactly what she was packing? She needed to control and contain this situation, and quickly.

"I'm here in an official capacity. I need a place to sleep for the night as well as a guide who can take me to pay my respects to your elders. Can you help me with any of that?"

The man took a sip—the *only* sip—of his beer, and set it down with a quiet thunk on the top of the highly polished bar.

"I can surely help you with that. Mind if we take this elsewhere for a bit of privacy?"

Her brows dove down into a frown as the suspicion radar in her head beeped like crazy. But before she could begin to ask questions, he cut across her.

"I'll get all of your questions answered, but trust me, you don't want that to happen in here. Room first, then talk."

In that moment, Derria knew this was more than just any

liaison to some council. This guy was either a spy or a cop. She had better figure out which one quickly, because the last thing she needed was for her quarry to get wind that she was already close on his literal tail.

With the key to her room in one hand, and her gear in the other, Lakota led Derria upstairs. He almost felt bad about pushing her buttons downstairs, but his training as an agent meant he had to discern her weaknesses and strengths in the most pragmatic manner possible.

He knew that outside of this place, most shifters couldn't tell one from the other. Being able to scent one's species seemed to be something very specific to the Nantahala Gorge. If she couldn't, it was a weakness that made it dangerous for her to hunt here. Other shifters would know in a heartbeat exactly what she was, while she wouldn't have a clue what she was dealing with unless it was a rogue.

And now her thoughts spun at a mile a minute. He practically felt them boring into the back of his head as he led her to where she would crash for the night. It was almost as if her mind was just on the other side of a thin veil that he was trying to peer through...which made no sense whatsoever.

He'd just met her, but something about this woman was indescribable.

Outside in the wind and rain, he hadn't been sure. Inside at the bar, he'd caught a whiff of her distinct fragrance, but cooking oil and wood smoke competed with his nose.

But now, in the clean hallway that led to the private rooms, the woman's scent hit him hard. She was salted caramel, overlaid with cloves and cream.

Mate.

He stopped so fast that Derria ran into his back.

"Hey, you okay? Something wrong?" she asked.

"Uh, no. I'm, uh, fine."

"I know I just met you, but you don't sound fine, dude."

He'd been around shifters all his life. Hell, he even worked for an agency that was responsible for shifters that weren't under the jurisdiction of the councils here in the Gorge. But Lakota had never had the natural odor of a woman pull on his insides until it felt like he'd been punched in the gut repeatedly…and he liked it.

I'm a damn sadist.

Moving on down the hall, he stopped at her door and handed her the key.

She looked down at the little piece of metal in her palm and back up at him. Just that little bit of connection, of their gazes taking in one another, brought gut punch number two, three, four and five. Left him almost breathless.

Holy shit.

"I thought we needed to talk about plans for tomorrow?"

"Something's come up," he lied. "I've got to run. I'll pick you up in the morning for breakfast at seven."

And he was gone.

But not before her whispered, "What the hell was that?" reached his ears and made him smile.

Breakfast had been a quiet affair. Derria and Lakota had inhaled their meals while a busy Sierra ran back and forth serving bakery customers. A strangely tense Lakota hadn't done any of the talking he'd said they needed to do before they headed over to the first council meeting.

Her brain had kept shorting out, overloading on brief flashes of…something. She hadn't been able to tell if it had been thoughts, emotions, or what. But one thing she'd been sure of—

whatever caused the constant buzz had lit up her inner cat. And that made for a super restless agent. The longer they'd sat at the bakery, the more she was convinced that the bolts of energy emanated from Lakota Phillips. The man had been hiding something, Derria had been sure of it. The question was, did she want to know what it was?

Nah.

Now, as they stood before the council of Clan MacRowan—the resident mages in these parts—and Derria wished she'd just stayed at the bakery in Stecoah. She would have happily continued to inhale Sierra's awesome pastries and breakfast fare.

Why?

Because this fucking sucked.

Here she stood in front of a bunch of crotchety, set-in-their-ways, no-care-for-the-present-or-future men who didn't appreciate the reason she was here.

They even sat up on a dais, for cripes sake. Really? A goddamn dais, as if they held court in the days of Henry VIII?

Condescension didn't begin to describe their behavior, and she wondered that they had a clan at all. Who in their right mind would put up with this bullshit?

Even as she asked herself the question, she already knew the answer—people stayed because they knew nothing else. And if the choice was to leave their families and their safety nets, or stay here and take this crap, most would choose this dysfunction over loneliness and uncertainty.

Then came another thought—where were all the women? There wasn't a single one in this room. In fact, she hadn't seen any on her way in either.

After taking in a subtle breath, she let it out deliberately, slowly. Then did it again. And again. She might be the feistiest of all her cousins, but only when she was at home. Derria could usually pull her calm around herself like a cloak during a hunt.

In fact, of the younger twin set, Kotara and Koreas, super-genius scientists extraordinaire, Koreas was the quiet, no bull-shit twin. It was hard to out-focus that woman. But Derria even had Kory beat with a focus that was unflappable on a hunt.

Until today.

In went another breath.

Woooosah, Derria, woooosah! You can't lose it in front of these people.

She opened her mouth and explained yet again why she was here. "As I said before, I am here on behalf of the Shifter and Were Armed Tactics agency. You are not under their jurisdiction, so this is a courtesy call. I'm here on a sanctioned hunt. I don't need any help and I will keep this as quiet as possible. But I don't need your permission, either."

Shit. She hadn't meant to say that last part. It was true, but the last thing she wanted to do was push anymore buttons than she already had.

After the grumbling died down, she finally said, "The name of the man I'm looking for is Kerr Blackstone."

The council members all looked toward Lakota with raised brows, as if addressing her directly would break some kind of law, or perhaps give them cooties. "Blackstone? Aren't they wolves? Correction, *exiled* wolves?" asked an ancient, gnarled man that reminded her of a saddlebag with eyes.

At Lakota's confirmation, an elegant, gray-haired male sitting next to Mr. Saddlebags steepled his fingers and looked pointedly at Derria. "Then why are you here?"

Derria wondered the same thing. Dusty old farts. She gave zero fucks about their snooty sensibilities, but she'd play along for a moment longer until she got what she needed.

"This is a courtesy call," she said...for the fifth time. "Since I may need to do some surveillance in your territory, it is very important that you know I'm here. However, I don't want anyone else to learn of my presence. If word gets out, my quarry may run."

"Surveillance? On MacRowan land? Why would that be necessary, little girl?" asked yet another member, this one a bit younger looking, yet older sounding, than some of the others.

Wow. She'd heard the expression "sucking down vinegar" to describe puckered up sour faces, but she'd never actually seen such a face until this asshat damn-near spat the word "wolf." And she wasn't even going to touch the equally funky assed "little girl" comment.

Derria bit her tongue as a slew of emotions whirled through her body, as powerful as a Pacific typhoon...but the feelings weren't hers. Keeping her gaze forward, her mind sought out her escort just off to her right. Anger vibrated off of him in deep waves so strong she could almost put a color to them. Odd. What was he so pissed about? It's not as if the backward thinking asshats were being condescending to *him*.

Even still, he gave the silent impression that if she needed him, he'd have her back. And in all her years as a hunter, that was a feeling she'd experienced only recently, and solely with her cousins and their mates.

And this *knowing* was kind of...nice. She'd never been the fluffy bunny type, but there was no denying that some serious warm fuzzies were traipsing up her spine right now. And it was the fault of the man standing just slightly behind her—Lakota Phillips.

Turning her inner attention back to the council, she said, "Sir, I'm aware my bounty is a wolf. Wolves can run. That means they're mobile. Mobile means they can cross invisible boundaries and pass in and out of territories. You know, kind of like I did when I came to see you."

"Who would dare?!" Mr. Vinegar sputtered. "No wolf would ever..."

"Look, my bounty is a bad guy, and right now he's more

concerned about me than any sensibilities or boundaries of yours."

"So you believe you're so much of a threat that you can make a mangy wolf cross into our—"

Derria didn't bother letting him finish. "Yes, I do believe I could, because I am a bad ass bitch who has probably bagged and tagged more rogue Weres in the first three months of this year than you ever did at my age. And I'm guessing that was a long, long, long, long, looooong time ago. Now, my courtesy call is done. Bye."

With a slight nod, which was all the deference this bunch was going to get, Derria did a perfect about face and headed toward the door.

She didn't even need to look Lakota's way to know he wore the smirk from hell. And she refused to question just how she knew exactly what he was thinking right now.

Nope. Not going to question it at all.

Why? Because she never asked questions that she didn't really want the answers to.

3

*D*erria's head whipped a hard left as she turned to pin Lakota with a glare. He glanced her way.

"What?" he asked.

Holy crapdoodle! I can smell what he is. Can tell as easily as if he'd told me himself, as if I've had the knowledge this whole time. "You're a jaguar!" she blurted.

"Yep. I thought you weren't able to scent a species."

"Normally," she said, "I can't. And I mean, at all."

But now that she thought about it, she'd noticed an odd sensation in her olfactory system when she'd gotten up to pee in the night. And this morning when she'd walked into the main dining and hang-out area of the Deep Blue, she'd picked up some scents that hadn't made sense. One of the staff had walked by her and the way he'd smelled had made her trouble radar scream "big *big* threat" and go full-tilt. Yet the guy hadn't said or done anything, except whistle as he'd swept the floor and opened a few windows to air out the place. At the time, Derria had chalked it up to just being tired, and had headed on out to meet Lakota in the parking lot.

He'd stood there looking all kinds of edible in an all-black outfit—tactical pants and boots, and an evaporative cooling tee-shirt, like the ones she wore under her motorcycle jacket.

With his deep golden hair pulled back into a thick ponytail, his dark brows and lashes totally set off a bright and intelligent pair of brilliant green eyes. And the moment she'd stepped out the door, his gaze had pinned her, made her feel like a butterfly on a piece of Styrofoam.

He'd motioned to the Jeep and informed her that he'd be driving her today; and then suggested that she move her bike to the back lot, where she'd picked up even more odd scents.

She was a fucking lion, so of course she could detect things with her nose. But she'd never been able to detect another shifter before. Ever. But that's exactly what her nose had told her she'd caught wind of—shifters. Half-breeds, to be exact.

Hell, she'd never known there was such a thing. After she'd covered up her bike in that rear lot and made her way to Lakota's Jeep, her mind had spun a mile a minute and hadn't managed to stop twirling, even now as they left the clan leaders meeting.

So what the hell is going on?

She had no idea, but this, this *whatever* it was, had become stronger. Stranger.

So would her senses become even more acute the longer she hung around here? Was it something specific to the Nantahala Gorge? Something in the water, in the air? In Lakota's pants?

Oh shut it. Do the job and leave Lakota and his pants alone, Derria.

But her womb didn't agree. And the more she thought on the man next to her, the more his scent seemed to imprint itself on her brain. It was like someone had blown an aphrodisiac into her face and then rolled up all the windows in the Jeep. She wondered if...no, couldn't be. Could it?

She pulled out her tracker and switched it to communication mode. While penning a note to Pryde Ranch, Derria told her breasts and ass to stop tingling. God, it was like her whole body fixated and reached for the man sitting behind the wheel.

She hit the send button, and prayed she'd get a response from home quickly while her body, mind and—as tough as it was to admit—her cat fixated on her escort.

Switching the tracker back to GPS mode, she watched the little blue unmoving dot. She sighed, wishing she could go after her quarry now while he was just sitting there. But not yet.

"So, what's a full-blooded jag doing hanging out on the Island of Misfit Toys?"

Jaguars shouldn't even be in the North Carolina area or anywhere on the North American continent. Unlike lions, they were jungle cats. Then another thought occurred to her before he could answer her first question. "And how does a jungle cat get a Sioux Indian name? The Lakota are a Northern Plains tribe."

"I'm assuming you know this from your line of work?"

"Kind of."

He raised a brow but said nothing as he obviously waited for her to continue.

But she didn't. Derria didn't know this man and just because he smelled like heaven and made her skin tingle didn't mean she would spill everything about herself.

Finally, Lakota said, "Well since you're not elaborating, I'll just say that shifters of my species have a distinct advantage to non-shifting jaguars."

"Yeah?" she asked. "What's that?"

"We can get on a plane and go wherever the fuck we want."

"Smart ass." She'd snarled the words but knew her own grin belied the growly quality in her voice. Lakota's smile was blinding and made the hard lines of his face morph into an almost boyish countenance.

"So," she said, "now that we've visited the Clan MacRowan asshats, where to next?"

"Clan Hollen, and then Clan Corwyn."

"So cats then wolves. Got it."

Lakota put the Jeep in gear, turned and headed back to the road that would take them away from the MacRowan's lands.

"That was fucking horrific," Derria said. "Almost the worst meeting I've ever had regarding a hunt."

Lakota pulled off the road and slammed on the brakes. Without another word, he pulled out his phone and dialed.

At her puzzled expression, he held up one finger and gave her the universal "hold on a sec" signal, accompanied by a secretive smile. So she watched, listened, and waited.

"Hey, it's Kota. You know the guest I'm supposed to bring to see you on business? Her name is Derria Sozi and we just had a less than pleasant meeting with the MacRowan council. No way am I going to let her go through that hell twice more." He paused and listened to whoever was on the line, then said, "Yes, it's a law enforcement issue and she wants to talk to you before she hunts in your territory. It's a sanctioned hunt, though I don't know the circumstances at the moment. We also need to talk to Cage, alpha of Clan Corwyn. You up for a neutral location in, say, an hour? Sweet. Thanks, man. I'll call the other... Ah, gotcha. Okay. See you in an hour."

"Your clansman?" At his nod, she asked, "What did he say?"

"He'll be there, as well as make the arrangements with the wolf alpha. That way, *they're* arranging this meeting instead of *us*. Keeps us off the shit list of the other two councils because they will definitely be pissed that they were excluded. If they find out, that is."

Then her brain backed up a step.

Had he really declared that he wasn't going to "let her" do something? Derria didn't particularly care for the whole "Me, man and me no let you!" thing, given she needed no one's permission to do a damn thing. But Lakota had just proven to be gorgeous and brilliant—a rare and attractive combination. After all, his bit of high-handed good intention did get her off the hook of having to both arrange a meet and broker a deal with anymore of those council people, so…

"Thank you, Lakota."

"Call me Kota. All my friends do. May I call you Dare?" At her nod, his smile was as brilliant as the sun that had finally risen high enough in these mountains to chase the chill from the air.

"So, I'm a friend now, Mr. Kota?" she teased and wondered where this flirting woman who was masquerading as Derria Sozi-Pryde had come from.

The man turned and gazed at her as he put the Jeep back into gear. "I'd hope so. And I'll stop right there because the rest of what I hope for would send you running back home, woman."

Derria gave him a look as smoldering as the one he was giving her right now.

"Was that a dare, Kota?" Oh god, her lioness was purring. Actually purring! And she hadn't even done anything…yet.

"You have to play if you're going to win. So, if I say yes, will it make you want to?"

She cocked her head to the side. "Make me want to what?"

"Play, Derria."

"Most likely," she said.

"Then yes. That was definitely a Dare. Or should I say, Derria?"

She laughed. "Did you just make a pun out of my nickname?"

"Totally." He stretched out his hand and gently smoothed the back of his index finger across her cheek. Derria leaned into the subtle contact—it seemed her body knew what to do even if the rest of her threatened to combust from the sheer smoldering gaze sent her way.

They got back on the road. Both of them smiled like loons, but as the tension ratcheted, neither spoke another word.

An hour later, they were deep in the southern part of the Neutral Zone. It was a quiet spot well off the beaten path, and away from Stecoah or any border zones. Derria and Lakota entered one side of a bright grass-filled glade, surrounded by trees. Moments later, four others emerged from the opposite side.

The two alphas had brought their mates—Neko, a female cougar was mated to Rafe, the Corwyn wolf alpha—which blew Derria's mind. And Jaz was a, wait for it—a fucking witch?!—and the mate of Klyne Hollen, the Guardian of Clan Hollen.

A few introductions and handshakes later, they sat down in the grass and got down to business.

Very careful to keep her personal life separate from her work life by super-wide margins, Derria stuck to facts, answered questions, and appreciated that they didn't bombard her with their private life history unless it was related to why she was here in the first place. Honestly, time was of the essence and this hunt had to be wrapped up as soon as shifterly possible. Pun intended.

They listened to what she had to say, and afterward, promised to keep her business to themselves in hopes it would help her catch her bounty without interference. But when Rafe stated that neither he nor their clan's council had any idea of why this particular Blackstone was wanted, Derria was alarmed.

With a fierce frown that made the skin between her brows bunch together, she put out in the open what they were all thinking anyway.

"That makes no sense. No one knows what the man did to warrant…well, a warrant?"

Rafe's long legs stretched out in front of him. He appeared

relaxed as he leaned back, resting on his palms in the thick green grass. But Derria knew better. All of these people were on alert. What in the hell was really going on up here?

"While it's true that the Blackstone pack split off to themselves, it's also true that they kidnapped my omega and friend, Simone. She was working on trying to solve our fertility problem. She's also the only damn doctor in this area."

"And now the Blackstones have her," Neko chimed in.

"Fertility problem?" Derria asked. She was up here because of a fertility problem?

Though Neesia had already given her the heads up, Derria listened to them confirm the details on the seriously low birthrate of shifters in the Gorge. She filed the info away and made a mental note to pass the new details on.

As to her hunt, usually it took some serious murder, or eating a human or something to get a shifter onto the S.W.AT. radar, and this Kerr guy was on that radar in a big way. Hell, Derria even had a kill order that gave her permission to "disappear" his ass if he chose not to come along quietly.

She voiced her concerns to Lakota—pardon, Kota—as they headed back toward Stecoah.

And suddenly the alert signal on her GPS went nuts.

She yanked it out of her bag and grinned. "Kerr is on the move."

"Which way?" The strong lines of Lakota's face became sharper angles as he concentrated on her directions.

"Fifty meters. Hang a left."

She held on to the leather strap attached to the steel frame of the door with one hand and the GPS with the other. As she navigated, Kota drove like a bat out of hell. Bouncing over the rugged terrain as they doggedly followed the signal from her tracking device, Derria was oh-so-thankful their vehicle had a four-wheel drive. Her motorcycle was a solid piece of work with special engineering to look sleek, yet still take on rough terrain, but no way in hell would it have survived off-road through this thick brush, forest and rock.

So, thank goodness for Lakota and whoever had put him on her trail.

No, she hadn't missed the fact that nobody here seemed to know why she was really after Kerr, yet Kota had been waiting in that parking lot to meet her when she'd arrived.

His vibe was pure and seemed free of malignance...but it didn't change the fact that there were way too many questions than answers...and Mr. Kota the Gorgeous' was one of them.

The signal halted and so did they. Derria unholstered her weapon, clicked off the safety and sprinted off, following the silent beep of the little blue dot as it moved across the GPS display.

Nothing but a swift yank on her arm kept her from tumbling headlong off of a sheer cliff that hadn't been there only moments ago.

Note to self—be sure to make it up to Lakota that he didn't let you pitch yourself off a cliff and leave your brains splattered all over the rocks below.

4

"*D*amn it, this doesn't make any sense. I don't see or scent him anywhere."

"You're sure this is where he's supposed to be, Derria?"

"I'm positive. Even if my electronics were malfunctioning, which they're not, I can always scent a rogue shifter, but…"

"You can't scent him?"

"Nope. Animals, trees, fauna." She turned her root beer gaze on him. "I even smell you." She flashed her most saucy grin. Just couldn't help it. The man was like her favorite ice cream—she saw it on a shelf and knew she shouldn't…but also knew she would anyway. "I smell…something." A wolf, in fact, but she kept her mouth shut in case her new-found ability was a total fluke. "But a rogue it is not."

"What does it smell like? A rogue, I mean?" he asked.

"Like a deep-seated sickness. Almost like a rotten carcass. One whiff and you never forget it."

"Well that sounds delicious and appetizing," Lakota said with a disgusted curl to his lip. "Maybe the tracker is faulty?" But Derria doubted it considering the one she'd quietly attached to the inside of one of Kota's back pockets beeped exactly where it was supposed to—four feet to her right.

And her quarry? Well, his little blue dot was stationary again. Right where she stood.

With the adrenaline from the hunt still coursing through her veins, she turned and kicked the nearest tree, then turned and stomped back to the Jeep.

"Looks like I need to stick around town a little longer. You mind dropping me at the Deep Blue so I can pick up my bike?" she asked Kota from the passenger seat just as the phone rang.

"Where are you heading?" Then he looked her way and asked, "Do you need to get that?"

Nope. No way in hell was she answering her phone right now. One glance down at the tech that doubled as her tracker and communicator had Derria's gut in a free fall.

"Nah. I'll get it later. It's just my cousin," she said, blowing him off. "I'll head back to Stecoah, I suppose. I can check to see if a room has opened up at one of the bed and breakfast spots."

"I have a better idea. Why not hole up where you are? You know, extend your stay if your room is still available?" Besides, it would keep her closer to him. And that was something he needed in a way that was as urgent as it was unexpected. Yes, he knew what this beautiful, strong woman was to him...but that didn't make it any less of a shock.

"Nah. There's a lot of construction going on right now. I'd rather not."

They pulled into the back parking lot right next to her motorcycle. But before she could hop out of Lakota's vehicle, he gently put a hand on her forearm. "Wait a sec. Let me check on something."

He pulled out his phone and hit the speed dial. "Hey, Klyne, this is Kota. Thanks again for today, by the way. Look, I hate to bother you this evening, but I need a favor. You met my guest earlier. If Neko's former place isn't occupied, mind if

I put her there? All right. Where's the key? Okay, thanks, man.
"

He disconnected the call and turned his full attention on Derria. Not like he'd ever taken his focus off of her in the first place. "All right, you have a place to stay for as long as you need it. In fact, you have a whole house."

"Excuse me?"

"Neko was supposed to move in there not long ago, but as you know, she mated and then plans changed. So it's vacant and you're all squared away."

"That's awesome!" Derria beamed. "Thank you so much. I really appreciate it. Or at least I think I do. It's not a shack is it?"

Lakota laughed and assured her it was quite a cute little cottage and Derria's smile lit him up from the inside out. He doubted she realized that this was a totally selfish move on his part considering he was just a few doors down. But even if she'd known, he had no shame.

Without a doubt, she was his, and it made him thankful for his shifter genetics. Genes that allowed a solitary creature, like a jaguar, to change his typical behavior and take a mate.

One step through the front door, Lakota dropped Derria's bag while she stood there and shivered. The thunder showers hadn't stuck around, but the chill in the air certainly had. Now that evening approached, it seemed warmer outside than it did indoors.

Lakota ducked out the back door for a few moments and came back in with a big plastic tub filled with firewood. After starting a blaze in the fireplace, he grabbed her duffel again and headed toward a surprisingly wide staircase.

"Show you around?"

At her nod, he said, "May as well start up there."

The cottage was airy and spacious with bright, yet neutral colors that lent an airy quality to the space. Glad she'd kicked off her shoes at the front door, Derria was sure no one had ever lived here because despite the cream carpet and white walls, there wasn't a spot anywhere.

Upstairs boasted two huge bedrooms and two full baths. The master bath sported a sunken jetted tub that she was definitely going to have an affair with tonight. The thought of affairs and getting wet brought with it another—doing that with the man right next to her. The one practically sizzling with need and not bothering to keep it to himself? Yeah, that one.

Royal blue blackout drapes and wood blinds covered all the upper windows. And downstairs—which was warming nicely thanks to Kota's quick handling of the fireplace—was filled with comfy-looking furniture arranged around a nice, wide open den.

And then she stepped into the kitchen and gasped. She was sure even Neesia would approve. The matriarch of their little was a top notch chef with a professional kitchen the size of a football field. Though this spot was considerably smaller, the highly polished wood floors, granite counters, and stainless steel everything was pretty darn nice.

A little breakfast nook, a wrap-around porch, and lots of light-colored wood blinds made the perfect mix of contemporary comfort and country charm.

Then her stomach rumbled. Loudly.

"The place was prepped for Neko, but she never lived here," Kota said. "Anyway, the freezer is fully stocked. All the meat you can eat."

"How do you know I eat meat? I could be a rabbit or a deer shifter for all you know."

"I told you before that I scented your lioness, beautiful."

Ignoring the little thrill that skated up her spine at his words, she turned away and turned to peek out of the nearest window. "I'm still amazed that a feline shifter mated with a wolf. I didn't imagine that, did I?

Kota laughed and shook his head. "Nope, you didn't imagine it."

With genuine awe, she said, "Wow. Go figure." Kotara and Koreas would give their canine teeth to be here. The two braini-acs, both premier bio-geneticists in the veterinary and bio-shifting sciences, were no closer to pinning down the secret switch/trigger/*whatever*, to mating heat. It annoyed them that the key to what should be a straightforward hormonal event eluded them.

With so many scientific conundrums, K and K, as they were lovingly known by their family, would be itching to solve them all. The fertility issue here was a strange one, considering that three of Derria's four cousins were mated *and* pregnant. No muss, no fuss. And definitely no problem.

They'd also be super-excited to jump into the question of the cross-breeding of species. Feline and wolf? Da ferk? It boggled the mind, but she said, "I guess Mother Nature doesn't really care."

"I hope that's the case, Dare." And the look he gave her was enough to melt paint off the walls. Two steps brought the man within touching distance. And Derria was surprised to find that she did indeed want to touch.

She blinked.

So how did one know they were being affected by mating heat, rather than plain-old lust? After all, every female on the planet had a fertile period, whether they were human, shifter, mated or not.

And she still had no idea what the hell was happening with her nose, but as soon as Kota headed out, she'd be on the phone with Niah to hopefully find out. She'd never had this kind of malfunction on a hunt. But Lakota's scent brought with it more information about him that she'd ever experienced before. It was insane...and kind of cool.

Would it wear off when she went home?

The thought of leaving this stretch of beautiful country added a certain blue tint to her thoughts. But there was no time to dwell on the why of it, so she pushed it away.

Instead, she acknowledged what else was going on in her body. The thrill of the chase had fired her blood. Adrenaline still coursed through her and caused a flash of heat. Skin felt too tight; body taut with need. The scent of her own arousal only made the dew gather more swiftly between her thighs. And if she could smell herself, then Lakota was getting a nose full.

She went still when his irises began to swirl until his gaze held a glow of otherworldly magic. Shifter magic.

Fight or flight? Fuck or flee? Well, neither of them was the fleeing type.

Her guts bubbled again and they both broke out in genuine laughter.

"It's been a hell of a day," she said. "I at least owe you dinner, and since the freezer is full, how about a steak? I thought I saw a grill out back through the window of the kitchen door."

He stepped forward. When she remained still, he moved deeper into her personal space. Derria looked up into those beautiful eyes that still held the glow of a man wrestling with the beast inside. And it was a turn on like she couldn't believe.

With a gentle touch, his fingers stroked just beneath her chin.

"Please tell me I can kiss you, Derria. I've been holding back all damn day."

Something rushed forward inside of her. Broke, like water over a sea wall. Flashed through her until she damn near shook with need.

Oh dear god!

Derria grabbed him at the back of his neck, pulled him into a fierce embrace and kissed him with all the pent-up passion that bubbled inside her. It started out wild. No way it could get any wilder, right?

Wrong.

It was as if they were two famished people getting their first drink in the parched desert. And Derria couldn't get enough. When she came up for air, she realized that they'd moved from the entrance to the kitchen and fully into the living room. Sure, shifters typically ran hot, even when resting, but Kota's touch sent her up in flames from scalp to baby toes. Even in the chill of a house that hadn't been lived in all winter and into late spring, it was almost too warm.

They took each other down to the carpet and scrambled for purchase. One moment he was on top. The next second, she was over him grinding away, knees to either side of his waist.

Then her legs were wrapped around his back as he settled between her thighs. And back and forth they went. They weren't competing so much as complimenting, and it was fucking glorious.

When had her shirt disappeared?

The moment the thought filled her head, he whipped his own over his head and tossed it behind him.

The rasp of his belt passing through the loops made her moan. And when she palmed her own breasts through her bra, it was his turn to make that magnificent soft growly sound of a large feline ready to take his fill.

He leaned over and held himself up on his elbows as he buried his face in the crook of her neck. He inhaled, sighed, and then did it again.

"You smell so fucking good. I can't help it, but I need you. If you want me to stop, Derria, now's the time to say so."

And then he nipped her in *that* spot—the one between the tendons of her neck and shoulder. The one that made her writhe and sent a frisson of pure unadulterated lust down her spine. Rather than warn him off, she arched into his body, breast to breast, skin to skin, wanton and unashamed.

Still in his black tactical pants, he ground an impressive-feeling cock against her core as he kissed her senseless. He tasted of wind and water, vine and tree—the very foundations of the wild jungle beneath a thick canopy. He may live in the Great Smoky Mountains now, but his birthplace, the lineage of who he was and where he'd come from, was evident in every breath that fanned her skin.

Once she was completely breathless, and needier than she could ever remember, he eased away, unzipped her pants and took them with him as he leaned back.

His fangs were visible now, as were the sharp claws that shredded her damp panties. Derria nicked her own lip as she demanded what she wanted.

"Fuck me, Kota."

"Only if you need it as badly as I do."

She closed her eyes and writhed in agony. "Please."

"You know what we are to each other, don't you, Dare?"

She started to deny it, but rather than lie outright, she simply stared at him and repeated her plea.

This time he gave her an even deeper growl—one that made the hair on the back of her neck stand on end with anticipation as he flipped her over onto her stomach.

She landed on her hands and knees, and pushed desperately back against him.

Fingers buried themselves into the thick natural curls of her head and pulled until her neck was bared to him.

"You're mine, Derria Sozi. My mate. But I won't take what is not freely given, won't mark you without your consent, no matter how badly I want to."

But it didn't matter what words she denied him—she knew what was real and what was imagined. She'd felt the connection long before now. Even when she'd read Niah's response to her text—a simple "Call me asap"—while they'd been tracking their quarry, she'd had a clue.

Mate.

It was the only thing that explained the crazy hunger for Lakota Phillips…and the innate knowledge that if necessary, she would fight tooth and claw to defend him as he would her.

"I hope you like it rough," he rasped into her ear.

"You have no idea," she hissed back.

With one hand still buried in her hair, he pulled even tighter as he guided himself to her sopping wet core. He teased her just a bit with only the tip of what felt like quite a wide cock. In two strokes he was buried to the hilt. Thick and long, he filled her completely. The sugared walls of her sex stretched just short of the point of too much, yet it was nowhere near enough.

Was she going insane? If so, it was an awesome way to go!

Lakota rode her until her pants turned to moans, and her moans became screams. And she was so close to an orgasm she could damn near taste it.

"You feel so fucking good. I'm not going to last much longer. Reach down and make yourself come, Derria. No way in hell will I blow first." The words were clipped through gritted teeth, even as his movements in and out of her body became erratic and all she could do was sink her fingers into the carpet and hang on.

"Do it, Derria. Now."

She reached down and stroked her clit. The bundle was swollen, sensitive and reaching out of its hood for completion. And she would certainly oblige.

In no time, the energy of her climax tingled in her scalp, and worked its way down. In her mind's eye, the lioness that shared her body took up the same position—on her belly, surrendering completely.

And in that moment, ecstasy rolled through her—an orgasm so powerful, it brought a sob to her throat as it overflowed in wave after crashing wave. Moments later, he joined her with a genuine roar that told her that she'd pleased him as much as he'd pleased her.

Both their knees gave out and they landed in a replete heap of arms and limbs in front of the fireplace. And there they lay, laughing quietly together as each poked fun of the other's purr.

---

5

*T*he steaks they'd finally gotten around to were delicious. Nothing quite like meat grilled to rare perfection and shared, bite by succulent bite, with a new lover. Dinner had proved to be as delicious an affair as the sex.

After eating until they were stuffed, Kota had carried her up to her bedroom. "One for the road," he'd said, followed by a kiss so tender she'd been tempted to ask him to stay. With a promise to catch up with her tomorrow after taking care of some clan business, he'd left.

Since Kota had rocked her world and then helped her with the dinner dishes, there was nothing for Derria to do but wash up and then hit the sheets.

Skipping the jetted tub for tonight, she hopped into the shower. As the water sluiced over her body, her mind relived every touch and caress. Lakota was what she called a "whole body lover." There wasn't a single bit of her body he'd left untouched. Titillated her outside, then filled her inside.

Just...*dayum!*

Turning off the water, she grabbed one of the fluffy towels she'd found earlier in the linen closet and used it to lightly pat her oversensitive skin. Back in the bedroom, she kicked her gear bag aside. Grateful didn't describe how she felt that Kota had brought it up and set it at the edge of the bed earlier while showing her around. *Yay* on not having to expend energy dragging the damn thing up the steps. Energy she totally didn't have just now.

Retrieving her tablet, she set it on the nightstand just in case she was needed in the night. After all, when out on a bounty, important details could come through at any time. No one wanted to "get dead" from turning off their comm device because they didn't want to be disturbed in the night.

Sheets cool and crisp against her skin, Derria settled beneath the blankets with a satisfied sigh.

Just as she reached for the switch on the lamp, her tablet beeped. A special tone told her that a message had arrived on a coded frequency.

Derria sat straight up in the bed, snatched the sleek piece of hardware off the nightstand and input her private code. As soon as the confirmation popped up on the screen that the encryption was in place, she attached the mini keyboard and accepted the connection.

The ID came through. It belonged to Niah Pryde.

"Well this can't be good," she typed.

The response was immediate. *"It all depends on how you look at it considering you didn't answer my earlier hail,"* Niah responded. Derria chuckled, knowing the message had been sent with snarky, dry humor.

"I thought you and your mate were out on a hunt, Ni?"

"Tagged 'em and bagged 'em. Got back this morning just in time to get your intelligence request. Got to work on it right away, since it was you and all."

Derria smiled, like she always did when she heard from any of her cousins. It had been a total fluke when Derria learned of the Prydes via an overheard phone conversation. Oh hell, who was she kidding? She'd totally been eavesdropping that day at the agency.

She'd overheard Captain Johns, the H.B.I.C.—Head Bitch in Charge—talking about the Prydes as she jogged down a private stairwell that Derria wasn't supposed to have been in. Captain Johns had confirmed to whoever she was talking to that the Prydes had just taken down number six on the S.W.A.T. "Twenty Most Wanted" list.

That little shortcut in the stairwell that she wasn't supposed to know about had changed Derria's life.

After hearing her own family name, one that hadn't been spoken in more years than she could remember, she'd done a bit of snooping through the personnel files. Sure, Derria was a fellow agent of the Prydes, but for safety's sake, she'd always used her grandmother's last name, Sozi.

She was typically assigned cases that required not only a competent fighting ability, but a high level of technical expertise —better known as hacking to some, snooping to others. Either way, she was good at it. Very good.

She'd learned that no one, including herself, was supposed to know about the Pryde sisters. A few discrete phone calls later, Derria had found herself in Wyoming, hugged from one end of the vast Pryde estate to the other by a group of women who looked eerily just like her.

From their caramel skin and bright amber eyes, to their shapely curves and sharp wit, there was no way they could deny they were related, even if they'd wanted to. Four months later, she'd secretly moved to Pryde Ranch.

S.W.A.T. still didn't know the link between herself and the Prydes, and they'd all agreed to damn well keep it that way. Out in the wild, lions were the most territorially aggressive animals and tended to expand their holdings like crazy if left unchecked. Shifters were no different. For this reason, the organization took the control and, if necessary, the containment of lion shifters very seriously.

But that wasn't a worry for her family—they owned a hundred square miles on the Medicine Bow River in Wyoming. There was plenty of room to work and run safely in their pelts on the fully self-sustaining estate.

"So what's up?" Derria asked, typing as fast as she could, given that her eyes were trying to close without her permission. Damn she was tired. Guess a combo of adrenaline laced post-hunt energy followed by bone-melting sex kind of did that to a girl. *"You know I'm two hours ahead of you and you wouldn't hit me up this late unless it were important. So lay it on me."*

"Pick up so I can tell you this bit. It's too much to type."

"Okay," Derria typed back.

"One sec while I put the protocols in place."

Derria slipped her microphoned earbuds in and waited for the whir-clicks that told her it was safe. A moment later she was voice to voice with Niah.

"First off, you're just weird," Niah quipped. "You sent a note from your comm unit asking about mating, but when I told you to call me asap, all I got was crickets. You're lucky I love you, weirdo."

"Yeah, yeah." Derria yawned and snort-giggled at the same time. "So what's what, cuz?"

"Let's start with the first question on your list," Niah said.

Derria waited, biting her lip as she tried to ignore the anxious flutters in her gut. Why? She already knew what Niah was going to say. Hell, Kota confirmed it himself as he was laying the sexy on her.

"Well, Dare, sounds like you have yourself a mate, chick-a-doodle. It would explain the tight skin and the hot, nervous belly jiggle thing. Oh, also the ability to scent him like no other. Does it feel like someone is burrowing into your head just so they can infuse you with sex hormone or something?"

"Uh huh."

"Might throw you into heat, as well. As the bond forms, you'll be able to talk with him telepathically both in and out of your pelt, just like you do with us. He will, in essence, become family," Niah said, matter-of-factly.

Wow. She sat stunned for a moment. Then she squealed like a kid at Christmas morning, and just as quickly, shut that shit down.

It was the happiest and most fucked up moment of Derria's life. Someone all her own, in mind, body and soul. And a *hot* someone, at that. But what the hell was Mother Nature thinking to pair her with a mate in the middle of a hunt, damn it?

What a craptastic time to be distracted. What if something happened to him? Or to her? Or them?

Gah!

"For your second question, I discussed the issues with all my sisters. None of them have a clue about why you suddenly can scent other shifters who are not your mate. But whatever it is, we hope it hangs around. It would give us an amazing advantage on hunts, plus would help us understand why shifters outside that area have lost the ability to do what comes so easily to those from the Gorge. You'll have to be our guinea pig for now, so put a drop of blood in the scanner. Let me know the second it's there. Koreas and Kotara can start the sequencing from here."

Derria hopped out of bed, unzipped her bag and grabbed the med scanner and a sterilized suture kit out of the first-aid pouch Niah designed for them to carry on hunts. It was cool, spaceman type shit that even sterilized itself after use.

A little prick on the finger, which hurt like hell, and she quickly dropped a single bit of blood into the little chamber. The press of a button closed the sample slide inside of the scanner.

"Okay, it's done."

A second later, a bunch of numbers and scientific calculations started scrolling across the screen.

"Okay, the information is being automatically sent to K and K." But Niah wasn't finished. "Now, as for the guy ferrying you around, Lakota Phillips? He's S.W.A.T."

"Excuse me?" Derria snapped.

"I said, he's S.W.A.T. I put his name and picture into the database. Smart of you to take a pic of him on the sly and send it to us because his name alone wouldn't have done the trick. And don't worry, I ran the search in such a way that the agency won't notice I was digging around."

That's my girl. Hackers of the world unite!

"It was slower than I would have liked, but the information did finally come back. He's definitely one of ours."

"The warrant claims the guy I'm after killed someone in Idaho, and that's firmly in S.W.A.T.'s jurisdiction. But he's obviously from here. These people rejected the agreement with the agency and aren't under our jurisdiction. Don't they have their own law dogs?"

"Yep. And you met them earlier today. Looks like each clan has its own arm of enforcement, so to speak," Niah said.

"And you're right, I did meet them, but I was hoping like hell you'd have some different information for me, Ni. It's strange that the people who should know why I'm here don't have a damn clue. None of the folks I've talked to so far know anything about why S.W.A.T. was called in to apprehend Kerr Blackstone. Why didn't they just have Kota find this guy? A warrant *and* a kill order?"

"I agree that it doesn't add up, Dare. Just be careful and keep your eyes open. Something stinks about this hunt."

"No kidding."

"Oh, and from the information I've gathered, your guy is a good agent. And don't be pissed because he didn't tell you he's one of ours."

"Why not?" she asked, though it was a dumb question fueled mostly by the still-unfamiliar restlessness to hunt down Lakota and jump his bones. Again, and again. But in addition to the physical attraction, it was the oddest thing to have a deep care for a man she'd just met.

Sigh. Yep, definitely a mating thing.

"Well, if you hadn't been ordered to check in with the elders and tell their emissary that you were an agent, would you have told Lakota?"

"Oh, shut up."

"Yeah, that's what I thought," Niah laughed. It was a marvelous sound considering she did it so seldom. Miss Serious Pryde was more of a dry English humor kind of gal.

"Have you heard anything from Kotara and Koreas on the lack-of-babies issue?"

"They're working on it. They said you can share the information with the alphas as they pass it to you, if you want. They only ask that the alphas keep it to themselves. They don't want to deal with any council politics if they can help it."

"I don't blame them for that one. Pass something else to them, will you?"

"Sure. What's up?"

When Derria added the fact that she'd met the alpha pair of the Corwyns, a male wolf and a female feline, Niah's amazed whistle filled the line. With a promise to pass the information on to the evil genius twin scientists, Niah disconnected the call.

Derria sat a few moments and let her thoughts run amok.

There were more mysteries in the Gorge than she cared for. And while she might be a bounty hunter trained in the arts of espionage and double-o-seven undercover type stuff, she preferred to be the one in the know. And right now, she didn't have that assurance.

Someone was playing games. Unfortunately, in this business, games could get you very dead.

As the sun began to rise, Lakota lounged on a thick limb high up in a huge old maple tree. Yesterday afternoon, he and Derria had stood up on top of the cliff that this tree overlooked and wondered what in the hell was going on. The tracker had beeped continually, but there'd been nothing and no one anywhere around. It hadn't made sense then, and it didn't make sense now.

Derria's words echoed in his thoughts. *"Maybe, just maybe, I'm not looking for what I originally believed?"*

Hidden by branches and thick foliage, Lakota's tail flicked in agitation as he waited for the Blackstone wolf to pass him by.

Soon enough, moving silently, a huge grey wolf with cream socks eased its way through the brush. The wolf paused, looked around and sniffed the air. Relieved that his perch wasn't down-wind, Lakota watched who he believed was Kerr Blackstone swipe a spot on what looked like a sheer wall at the base of the limestone cliff.

Why would a wolf paw at a rock wall?

Then to his surprise, the rock moved aside just enough for the wolf to slip through the opening, then closed again.

No wonder Derria's tech seemed to believe that the Blackstone wolf had disappeared into thin air. Because he had.

Moments later, a muscular gold and black jaguar jumped down out of its hiding place and loped away.

Derria had just poured herself a steaming cup of coffee when her sixth sense came fully alert. She stood at the kitchen window and stared past the grassy expanse of yard that ended where the forest began. The high humidity and cool overnight temperatures had caused a shroud of low fog to float just above the ground.

Though the mist appeared undisturbed, something was out there.

Squinting into the morning sun that streamed in through the glass panes of the back door, she waited.

Come on, you bastard. Show yourself.

Moments later, a beautiful gold jaguar, with perfect black rosettes along its body, loped out of the trees, across the yard, and up onto the back porch.

It sat on its haunches and waited. Its gorgeous green eyes were...

Green eyes?

She yanked the door open and inhaled deeply. Yep, it was him. "Lakota Phillips, get your ass in here before some human driving through the Gorge sees you. Crazy cat."

His paws made no sound on the wood floor of the kitchen and she had to smile at how light he was on his feet. It was no surprise that he was a big jaguar—that subspecies was, after all, the third largest feline in the world, right behind lions and tigers. Shifter genes tended to make them all just a bit larger than their natural cousins, no matter what kind of shifter they were.

With a thickly muscled body, big paws and a heavy jaw, he was a killing machine. Heavy enough to take down large prey, yet light enough to get up into trees, unlike lions who were less than stellar at those kinds of moves because they were just too damn heavy to climb well.

She poured him a cup of coffee and followed him into the living room. She shivered as the ripple of his shift float through the air and wrapped around her like a caress. She hadn't even made it all the way into the room, yet she knew she'd find him back in his beautiful human-looking skin.

The man was quite the specimen, all the way around. Hair,

wild after his transformation, was a lengthy riot of soft-looking, dark blond curls all over his head and just a bit down his back. His skin was silky smooth, as gold as morning sunshine in mid-summer, and his eyes were as beautiful as the rarest jewel. A muscular, but not overly bulky build, looked as if he worked out every day, then ran miles and miles on top of that. Stamina. Oh yes, that's what he made her think of. Oodles and oodles of stamina.

She handed him the steaming mug and waited. While he sipped the black brew, she watched his strong profile as he stood in front of the blazing fireplace, buck-assed naked with not an ounce of concern. Tall, dark and handsome described him perfectly. Her gaze started at his calves and made the tour up his body. Sure, she'd seem him last night as they had hot and delicious sex, but she hadn't taken the time to savor the package. And what a nice one it was, too.

He turned and set his cup on the mantle above the hearth.

"Derria, stop looking at me like that or I'll be on you before I have a chance to tell you what I found."

So, he'd picked up on her ogling, eh? She should probably be a little embarrassed, but nope.

"So, about those biceps and forearms that look like you lift weights without even trying? How can you be a fucking lumberjack and have a runner's build at the same time?"

He laughed and shook his head at her. "Well, I'm glad you appreciate what you see."

"Considering you're standing naked in the living room, if you turn a bit more, I can appreciate it a little better."

"Woman, what am I going to do with you?" he asked as he moved toward her and pulled her into his arms.

"You have to ask?"

She lifted her chin and when he was a hair's breadth from meeting her lips with his own, he rocked her world.

"I found Kerr Blackstone."

"What?" Her head tilted a hard left and a riot of fluffy curls came loose from the messy bun on top of her head and fell into her eyes.

Deadly and adorable? What a combination in a female.

"I said, I found—"

"I heard you, but how? Where?"

"I had to go out and serve a warrant at the edge of Corwyn land early this morning. On the way back, I took a detour to that spot where we lost Kerr Blackstone yesterday. You were right. He was right in the spot he should have been."

She motioned for him to talk faster.

"He was under us the whole time."

She shot to her gear bag that was sitting near the bottom of the stairs and yanked it open. Back at his side, she pulled out her tracker and said, "Show me."

"Right here. There's a cliff, remember?"

"How could I forget? You kept me from flying over it."

"At the bottom of that cliff, Blackstone has a hidey hole. You wouldn't ever know it was there, even if you were standing right next to it."

"So how the hell did I scent him, then?"

"I'm guessing that since his hidey hole is in the rock, there are some small holes or something for ventilation. But again, very hard to detect.

"You," she said as she pulled him into a hard kiss, "are awesome! I'm out of here in twenty minutes. Do you think he'll still be there?"

"I don't know. Let me grab a bite and I'll go with you."

"I don't need back up, Kota. I've got it. You go ahead and do your liaison thing and I'll catch up with you after I have him in custody. I have a kill order, but I'd rather question him. Where

348   T.J. MICHAELS

can I take him? Neko told me that there's a human sheriff in Stecoah, but I'd rather not use his jail in case things get bloody. Besides, he's none the wiser to the fact that there are shifters all around him."

"Where can you take him? You're not taking him anywhere without me."

"Excuse me, but I don't need any interference. I was instructed to do my little courtesy song and dance to the councils and alphas, and I've done that. You were a huge help, but I'm not asking for, nor do I need any help for this. It's what I do."

"And I'm still going."

"Whoa, wait a minute." She took a few steps back, looked him up and down with a curl to her lip that made him wonder if he smelled like shit or something. "Are you assuming that because we had sex that you're the boss of me?"

"What? No!"

"Good. Because this task is my responsibility. And you've pissed me off, so screw leaving in twenty. I'm out of here now."

"Damn it, Derria, you have no idea what you're getting into!"

"Right now, I don't give a shit about anything except the fact that you're yelling at me and telling me what to do. Or in this case, what *not* do."

"I don't mean to yell, but it doesn't change what I said. The Blackstone pack are a bunch of exiles. They owe allegiance to no one. They're mangy ass wolves who'd sell out their own mothers for a can of fix-a-flat. They tried to kill Sierra when she first came to us. Word is they kidnapped the only doctor in the area, right out of her office on Corwyn lands. They. Are. Killers, woman."

"And?" she asked. Based on her "what's your point" tone, he obviously wasn't making his case very well.

"Gloriously stubborn ass woman," he grumbled under his breath.

"I heard that," she snapped. Damn shifter hearing.

But he wasn't budging on this, not one single inch. Just the thought of having the Derria-sized spot in his soul suddenly become empty sent a rush of panic through him. No way in hell was it going to happen.

"No fucking way am I going to let you just walk—"

He should have just stopped talking when her mouth fell open in shock, but he cared too much for this beautiful scrappy female to let this go. He had to make her see how dangerous this was.

"Let me? *Let me?* Who the hell do you think you are, and what illness do you have that's given you delusions that I need your fucking permission to do my job?"

"Dammit, Derria, I mean it!"

"Fuck. You. I had a life before you, Lakota Phillips. I was kicking ass before you, and I'll be kicking ass and taking names after you."

"After me?" he bellowed. "I swear to god, Derria Sozi..."

"Pryde, you numbskull."

"Pryde? Your last name is Pryde?" He wasn't sure why that name rang a bell, but he instinctively knew to keep his questions to himself just now. She'd snapped her mouth shut and pinned him with a mutinous glare. But, damn it, this was his mate, and over his dead body was she going anywhere far away from him. He'd ask her about the name thing later. Besides, they were in the middle of a fight. And it was one he intended to win. "Whatever. There will be no 'after me' bullshit."

"Oh yeah?" She stepped right up to him, put the tips of her steel-toed boots up against his bare toes and slammed her fists onto her hips. "Try to control me, mate or not, and I will drop your ass like a bad cold."

His cat panicked at her words. Would she leave him? Could he lose his mate, whether she went into this fight or not? The energy of the change charged forward. It took all his considerable skill and strength to control it and keep it at bay.

"And don't you dare do that glowy-eyed thing at me either," she snapped as he struggled to maintain the slim hold on his jag.

She sniffed, turned and began to walk away.

He had to make her face him. Had to make her see.

Lakota's hand landed on her shoulder.

The only warning he got was a flash of energy that sent the hairs on his arms scrambling. And then Lakota was flat on his back with the wind knocked out of him. The three-inch canines of a snarling majestic lioness were mere inches from his nose.

Holy hell, she was big. And beautiful. And a good three hundred pounds—or at least that's what she felt like—she braced her front paws squarely on his chest. He almost chuckled at the remnants of the tee-shirt that hung around her neck in tatters, like a not-quite-thought-out piece of Christmas garland.

Forcing himself to slowly suck air back into his lungs while lying completely still, he opened his mouth to speak.

She roared in his face.

Ears ringing, and sure she'd been heard at least a good five miles away, he decided to change his tactics.

Doesn't she understand that both man and beast are concerned for her well-being?

She roared again.

Well, obviously not.

But Derria did know. She *did* realize. As soon as the threat to leave him had left her mouth, the lioness within cringed and then clawed to get out, reaching for its mate. She understood Kota's struggle because she was having the same trouble. But regardless of the pain it would cause her to pull up stakes and high tail it back to Wyoming without him, she would do exactly that if he forced the issue. Heart in her hand and her soul bleeding out, she'd walk just the same.

"Derria?"

Slowly raising one hand, he eased it toward her flanks and gently stroked her fur. Suddenly everything he couldn't quite articulate rushed like flood waters down their newly forming bond. It was such a bombardment of care and fear it caused her to suck in breath after breath. Then came understanding of how deeply he believed in her—in her ability to take care of herself and handle her business. Then, there was love. True, deep, abiding love.

For her.

One moment they were in a heated argument, and the next she felt everything he couldn't quite say. Her cousins had told her about the bond that formed between mates. They'd said it usually took some time to solidify, but this had all seemed to slam into place out of nowhere.

Fur and fangs receded as the change rolled over and through her. And then Derria was back in her human form as fast as she'd shifted out of it. Tremors wracked her body, but not because she now lay on top of Kota as naked as he was.

"Oh my god, Kota. I didn't know. I didn't realize how you felt." The words came out in a rush even as his emotions continued to swallow her whole. Sprawled across his chest—a chest that sported ten claw-sized cuts across perfectly formed pectorals—she didn't hold back the tears that fell in fat droplets and splashed on his skin.

Keeping her gaze glued to his, she asked the one question that truly burned in her soul.

"Can you feel me, too, Kota?"

"Yes, baby, I can feel you. I'm not typically the sappy type, but damn, it's beautiful what we feel for each other. I..." He swallowed hard, took a moment to pull it together. "I don't quite understand what the hell just happened. It came out of nowhere and..."

And then he rolled, taking her to her back.

The moment her thighs parted in invitation, his thick cock plunged deep into her weeping pussy as he covered her mouth with his. They expressed, without words, what they meant to one another, what they needed, and what they were willing to give.

He took her fast, hard. Rough. But she sensed it wasn't quite enough.

"Dare, I'm aching."

She opened her eyes and gazed into his glittering emerald eyes. "What do you need, baby?"

"My fangs…"

Her eyes went wide at the partial shift of his teeth and gums, thankful he was both skilled and strong enough to keep the rest of his body from succumbing to his beast.

After a few deep breaths, his canines remained extended.

Finally he said, "I need to mark you, bite you. Fuck, my fangs ache, I need it so bad."

She pushed gently against his chest until he eased back and pulled free of her body. On her knees, ass up and head down, she opened for him. Welcomed him. Offered herself to him. A low growl sounded deep in his throat as he slid back home and began to fuck her in earnest.

"Oh my god," Derria moaned. "Oh yes, Kota. Fuck me."

And he did. Thoroughly. The sound of his flesh slapping against hers, combined with the scent of their sex and the wicked sensation of his cock stretching her, all combined to send Derria out of her mind.

"'Kota! Oh please. Please," she begged, needing to come so badly she could taste it on her tongue.

One hand on her hip, the other tapping at her clit, an orgasm flew out of left field and blew her apart. It left behind a smoldering need for a repeat of that particular performance. And it was on its way, beginning at the crown of her scalp.

Fingers buried in her hair, Lakota pulled her back towards

him until she sitting back on her haunches, her back against his chest. She knew what was coming.

Marking wasn't necessary, according to her family, but Derria was all in. She would hold nothing back from this man, and offered her whole heart, in addition to something that she knew *he* needed. "Mark me, Kota. Make me yours."

Her lioness was so very close to the surface, yet seemed content to hang right there on the edge of ecstasy until...

BOOM!

The moment his canines pierced the sleek muscle where neck met shoulder, Derria detonated, followed closely by Lakota. Vision blurred, skin heated and sex dripped.

And a little part of herself that had always been uniquely hers began to fill with her mate—a *winded* happy mate, who rolled off her and then pulled her into his arms.

Panting in cadence with Kota's gasping breaths, Derria poked him in the ribs. "You're sweaty."

He swatted her butt and said, "So are you. I think I like it."

She chuckled, glad that the tension of earlier had not only dissipated, but it was as if it had never been.

"Hold on a sec." He got up and moved quickly to the small bathroom between the living area and the kitchen. A few moments later he returned with a blessedly wet and warm towel.

"Lay back for me?"

She did and he cleaned her up as gently as if she'd been the one handling the task. Back on the carpet, he lay next to her. The silence was comfortable, pleasant.

"You know, I've never really thought on this much in my life. Just always saw it as the way things are, you know?"

"What are you talking about, Dare?" Lakota asked on a loud, totally manner-less, post-sex, man yawn. She bit back a smile.

"I'm glad that in this moment, I'm not human. When I was a little girl, I used to want to be one of them. Wanted to fit in, and not have to hide my true nature while walking among them. When I got older, I stopped caring and chalked it up to the fact that I'm an example of Mother Nature doing whatever the hell she wants."

"Why are you glad?"

"Because if we were human, we'd be wondering if we'd lost our minds by deciding to do what is kind of like marriage in their world, and if not marriage, it's still one hell of a commitment. We'd be wondering how we could love this fast, and whether we'd made a mistake," she said.

"True, but shifters go through that as well, don't you think?"

"Sure we have the choice to mate someone other than our true mates. We also have the choice to skip waiting for them to appear. But it doesn't change the fact that we know when we've met him or her. I think that it's a blessing to have our beasts looking out for us. We know our a suitable mate once we've come across them. Without a doubt, we know. "

"True. So you accept me, completely?" he asked, pushing up on one elbow so he could meet her gaze as she reclined.

She reached up and touched his cheek, his jaw, traced his bottom lip until he nipped her finger. She grinned. "Yes, Lakota Phillips, I accept you."

"Good," he said, getting up off the floor and reaching down a hand to help her up. "Now, about our earlier conversation."

"Aw man, do we have to do this now?" she grumbled.

"I have no right to tell you how to do your job, but woman, you are my mate and I can't turn off my protectiveness of you any more than you can turn off being who you are."

"Then I guess we'll just have to figure this out. But it won't be today, Lakota."

"Fine. Go do your thing. Just promise to call me if you need me."

"I promise. Now go shower. You smell like me."

"And that's a bad thing?" He nipped her nose, smacked her playfully on the butt, and then ran up the steps two at a time.

With the memory of Lakota's perfect ass imprinted in her brain, she grinned, snatched up her gear bag and pulled out a change of clothes. Derria was dressed and out the door the moment she heard the water turn on upstairs. After she secured her duffel in the saddlebags and put her helmet on, she stilled.

Lakota.

He was just out of reach, then suddenly rushed into the forefront of her mind. He'd blown her the equivalent of a mental kiss from inside the house.

With a smile, she climbed on her bike and pressed the ignition button. With her intuition screaming some serious warnings, Derria headed toward whatever destiny held for her.

Dear God, please let it be something good.

Her thoughts drifted back to the wonderful man she'd shared her time, her bed and would spend her life with.

Okay, that was pretty good. Let it be even better, okay?

6

*K*err knelt in the shower in a mixed state of confusion, relief and blinding anger. Why wasn't he physically back to one hundred percent lethality? It wasn't as if he hadn't taken a bullet before, but since being shot by beauty bitch, sluggish had become his middle name. He took in a deep breath and tried to relax as the soothing mist of the shower chased off the morning chill but did nothing to reduce his fury. One thing had become quite clear by the near-misses he'd had over the last few days— someone was setting him up.

"Who would benefit from having you out of the way?" he wondered aloud. An old enemy? No, that couldn't be it—to his knowledge, he hadn't left any of them alive.

Someone filled with blind ambition?

Maybe. Though exiled for their anti-council sentiment, the Blackstone pack was technically still part of Clan Corwyn. He'd not only told them that he didn't give a rat's ass about their wish to remain in the stone age, hidden in these mountains, but he'd then packed up his shit and left town for a month.

Just before he'd left, he'd spoken, quite strongly actually, against kidnapping the doctor who'd been trying to solve the low birth rate of their kind. That alone had earned him plenty of new enemies, but was it enough to put him on the radar of a bounty hunter?

He thought through the list of possible suspects. Who had enough power to pull something like this...or who was low enough? After all, if a coward wanted to increase his standing in the pack or up his chances of winning an alpha challenge, Kerr would have to go.

If the Blackstones left the Gorge all together, or claimed a bit of territory of their own in these mountains, Kerr would be at the top of the contender list for alpha. He wasn't just a big wolf; he was cunning with alpha in his blood. There were several packs in Clan Corwyn, and Kerr could trace his roots back to the first wolves who'd ruled here. Unlike many others of his kind, his family hadn't immigrated. No, his ancestors were born on this continent, had ridden in war parties against invaders whether they were native or those who'd trespassed from overseas.

He may not have cared enough to challenge the current alpha for leadership of the clan, but he belonged to this land. And he'd be damn sure no one would run him away. Ever.

So who'd brought this trouble to his door, dammit?

Shutting the water off, Kerr shook his head like a...well, a wolf and sent water droplets flying across the wide stall. Snatching a warm towel from the rack, he wrapped it around his waist and stepped out onto the cool stone-tiled floor.

He needed help with this problem. And he knew exactly where to go—to the Neutral Zone to find Aldin. Sure, the man's primary role was to keep an eye on the hybrids and outcasts who'd been banished by their clans, but anyone with a little common sense knew that Aldin had his hands into...other things. That shifter knew sneaky people who knew other under-the-radar people. It was as good a place to start as any.

Clicking the light off, he moved through the darkness, down

the stairs and toward the living area. Before he got to the threshold, he scented—a lioness? In a wolves den?

Insane.

Tempted to drop his towel and shift, he forced himself to wait. With a little patience he might just learn who was turning these wheels.

Get some fucking answers, Kerr, before you start tearing chunks out of things.

The light came on and Kerr froze.

Her eyes went wide for a moment, then narrowed with a fury that burned as hot as his own.

"You?!" they snarled at each other.

The change rippled through him, but she didn't react. In fact, she sat, legs crossed as if she were right at home, in *his* favorite chair. Even as fangs exploded in his mouth and his body reshaped itself so fast he bounded toward her in a blink, she looked fucking bored.

Kerr hadn't thought it was possible to get any more pissed.

He was wrong.

Didn't she know that he was the epitome of the big bad wolf?

Kerr sprang with a snarl and landed inches from her.

Holy shit!

Paws slid on the smooth wood floor and he came to a halt with his wet nose smashed up against the barrel of a big ass gun.

When he shifted back, water still formed pearls on his deeply tanned skin. His chest had a light smattering of dark hair, barely there but not sparse or patchy. She wondered briefly if it would be as soft against her skin as it looked. Kerr's face was all angles and lines, including the unique shape of his crystal-slate eyes.

Tipped up at the sides, he looked more like a gray-eyed,

native warrior, complete with powerful build, long beautiful hair, and sleek body composition. With dark, wet locks plastered against his head, he stood and never took his eyes off the barrel of the gun that had just been pressed to his muzzle.

Dear God, he's so beautiful, please, please don't make me have to put a hole in him. Again. The thought turned her guts inside out and back again so fast, it was a marvel she didn't blown chunks all over the floor.

And then their gazes clashed, but not with the rage of emotion she'd expected. No, this was something deeper, darker. Hotter.

She sucked in a shocked breath that brought a big whiff of his scent.

Suddenly she vibrated from the depths of her soul, as if this man had struck a huge gong in the pit of her stomach that rang out, *"MATE!"*

Oh good grief, not him, too!

This couldn't be happening. Maybe her nose was totally haywire along with the rest of her body? She was supposed to take this guy in as a prisoner, not fall for him, damn it. So rather than voice how the edge of his sultry-feeling energy rode across her skin, she did what she did best—Derria got back to work.

"Why don't you smell like a bad guy?" she demanded.

"You shot me, woman!" then he paused and regarded her. "What do bad guys smell like?"

"They smell like *not* you. What did you do to be tagged for a sanctioned hunt?"

"Tagged by who, is the real question, beautiful."

His ragged snarl made her belly quiver even as the hairs on her arms and neck stood at attention. Derria, the perpetual smart ass who could usually turn her emotions off like a fucking light switch, suddenly wanted nothing more in the world than the man in front her...just as much as she wanted the one she'd been with this morning.

Sure she was a liberated sexual being, but she'd never been into more than one guy at a time. Suddenly, in her mind's eye she couldn't see herself without Kota...or Kerr.

"How did you find me?"

Whoa! Suddenly his nose was pressed against the back of her neck.

"How do you move so fast?" she asked on a swift intake of breath.

"Oh that was nothing. I'd be even faster if you would undo whatever you did to my body when you shot me a few days ago."

Was she worried? Nope, because when he'd moved, so had she, and her pistol was now jammed tightly against his crotch. But that didn't stop the shiver that skated up her spine as he buried his nose into the soft curls at her nape.

As for what she'd shot him with? No way in hell would she reveal that secret. Not quite yet.

The man didn't touch her with any other part of his body—just his nose. Such a shifter thing to do. But then partially shifted fangs made intentional contact with her skin and she froze.

"Who do I smell on you, woman?"

"Excuse me?" was all her warring brain could come up with. Part of her wanted to lean against him as he teased her skin. The other half wanted to be shocked and outraged. Her lioness was...*oh dear god!*

Kerr lightly nipped her skin and her knees almost gave out. Suddenly the floor looked like the perfect place for some raunchy "nice to meet you" rolling around...literally.

Wait, what the hell was she thinking? She had a mate now. This was ridiculous. Wasn't it?

"Tell me who I smell on you. I won't ask again."

This man oozed alpha. In fact, it was oozing through her pores and causing a lick of electric flashes just beneath the flesh.

Holy hell, even with Lakota, the lust hadn't hit her this fast. Maybe she'd been thrown into heat? Did that mean anyone could scent her? Everyone would be attracted to her?

No, Niah had already explained how it worked, but her head seemed to have trouble holding on to a rational thought for more than a moment at a time. It was like she'd overdosed on caffeine and male pheromones.

"You scent my mate on me," she gasped.

"Impossible," he growled low into her ear. "My wolf is howling loud and clear that you are ours."

He nipped her again, right on top of the marks Kota had left this morning.

All it did was increase her need for them both.

Suddenly her phone rang. She tapped the little receiver hidden inside her ear and answered the call.

"Derria! I can feel you, woman. I'm on my way to see Rafe and had to pull the Jeep over. Are you okay? I can't tell if you're on fire and need me inside you, or if you're literally on fucking fire and I should be calling the fire department."

"I-I'm fine." Yep, totally on fire. "I have Kerr."

Or did Kerr have her?

"He doesn't seem to be a danger to me."

The wolf licked along her neck, just at the juncture of neck and shoulder. Kerr lapped at her skin as if she were his favorite dessert, but the moment he'd heard Kota's voice, a low menacing growl began to hum in the back of his throat.

"Tell him," Kerr demanded. A single finger tickled down the back of her arm. It was the first time he'd touched her, and oh what a sizzling trail he'd left behind.

"'Kota, he says he's my mate."

"What?! Let me talk to him."

"What for?" Talk to Kerr? What an odd request. An odd silence filled the line, but the newly forming bond with Kota was anything but quiet. Derria went stiff as a board. If these two alpha males thought they were going to decide her fate, they were deranged as hell. As for Lakota, she wouldn't use the bond against him. No, instead she'd give him a chance to reverse direction and back up using the foot he was about to put in his own mouth.

"Answer me, Kota. Why do you need to talk to Kerr? What needs to be said to him that you can't say to me?" Even though he wasn't here, the tension crackled between them.

"Because I want to know if you're safe with him."

"Are we going to have a replay of our little lover's quarrel from earlier this morning? I just said he's no danger to me."

Kerr raised his voice so he could be heard through the little microphone in the wire attached to her earbud. "Besides, the bad ass woman has a mean looking SIG Sauer gun jammed into my nutsack. I'm pretty sure I can't make her do anything that she doesn't want to. But," he drawled as he nibbled the lobe of her ear. When she sucked in a deep breath, Kerr said, "If I were you, I'd get here quickly, all the same."

"Derria, I'll be there in twenty."

"Okay, see you," she said, then tapped her ear rig to disconnect the call.

She turned to find herself wrapped up in Kerr's strong arms and her lioness wasn't trying to break free of him. At all.

Instead, the damn feline was rolling around in her mind as if she were in—aw hell—heat!

"So, your name is Derria?"

Oh lord, yes!

But instead of screaming those words, she turned on as much 'cool' as possible. "So I assume you're not an outlaw?"

"Not to my knowledge, though I've certainly done my share of uncouth shit. And you still shot me, Derria. I haven't been one hundred percent since."

Again, she ignored his mention of the bullet she'd shot into him that deposited the tracker beneath his skin. "Tell me how I could possibly be mated to a jag and a wolf at the same time?" she asked. "I'm not from around here. This is new for me and I need to understand it."

He tightened his arms and buried his nose in the top of her head and inhaled deeply. They moved as if some sensual music had come on in the radios of their minds, inciting them to sway and move together as he spoke right into her head.

"There is a tale among my people, the first ones to roam this land, that sometimes the Universe would designate more than one mate to a female of the warrior class. All females of my people were and continue to be precious, but those of the warrior mind even more so. These women need to be protected...and satisfied."

"I don't need anyone's protection."

"I said protected, woman. Not saved. There is a great difference. Now listen."

To her surprise, she found that she automatically gave him what he wanted simply because she lost nothing by doing so. It was a give and take for them both, and she sank right into it as if she'd known how to do this mating thing all her life.

Weird.

"So," he continued, *"it is said that this type of woman had great sexual need. The more bad ass the woman, the more intense the need—hence two mates to sate her. The warrior would go off to fight, and the woman, being completely unbiddable, would go with him whether he wanted her to or not. She watched over him, and he over her, and their additional mate watched over them both."*

She scrunched her brows into a tight frown, not sure she liked where this was going.

"They were all equal in the relationship. Though all alphas, no one was above the others. Well matched. Well suited."

Kerr, having dropped his towel as soon as he'd shifted and charged, was completely naked while Derria was fully clothed. Still slow dancing to music unheard, she pondered his words... and the swelling cock that pressed against her belly.

Speaking aloud, she asked, "But it's just a myth, right? I mean, how many times have you seen this triad mating thing happen in your lifetime?"

"Among my people, I have seen it several times since I was a small boy. I may be part of the Blackstone pack now, but my family did not originate in these mountains. We are from the northern plains. Many migrated here and managed to stay out of the mainstream of things long before the Civil War, when the Union soldiers of the North herded our people onto reservations. Those who didn't comply were hunted until our tribes were practically extinct.

"Your people? Native Americans? As in Northern plains? As in Sioux?" At his nod, she added, "You mean, Lakota Sioux?"

"Indeed."

She laughed out loud. Just couldn't help it at such a turn of irony. Then the giggle died in her throat as Kerr's mouth covered the super-sensitive spot on her neck and sucked earnestly.

"Oh my god!"

Her arms twined around his neck as her head fell back. Derria's body rolled against his—seeking, needing, wanting.

And then just as suddenly, she was across the room, holding her hands out in front of her to ward him off.

"No, wait. I need to wait for Lakota. We need to figure this out. I can't be unfaithful to a mate I just accepted."

Yet, according to his story, she wasn't being unfaithful.

But still.

Kerr Blackstone, a man with a kill order on his head, a man who was supposed to be so dangerous she could drop him without even having a reason, stepped back and went still. "I will honor your wish." A moment later, he looked toward the entrance to the surprisingly large den. Nostrils flared a moment, then Kerr disappeared down the wide hallway that led to the front door.

The layout was brilliant. When she'd arrived, Derria had hacked the security on the stone door outside and then stepped into a large foyer where Kerr's motorcycle was parked off to one side. The foyer led to a hallway, and that hallway led to this absolute man cave. To her surprise, the rock walls were smooth and covered with some kind of rubbery compound. She imagined it was sound insulation or something. The foyer and hallway walls were a pitch black, but this room was a bright cream color, edged in shades of blue and gray. Comfortable oversized loveseats and chairs were arranged around thick sheepskin rugs that chased away the chill of the surrounding stone. She'd also discovered that Kerr loved his electronics, such as the huge television, satellite access and a workstation with a state-of-the-art computer system...which she'd dug around in while he'd been in the shower.

The man was a total geek with a game console fetish. Yep, had all the makings of a rogue Were. *Not.*

Right now, a nervous Derria left the living area and ducked into the small bathroom on the other side of the full kitchen.

When she returned to the den, Kerr joined her, along with a pissed off jaguar.

The man stood naked, unmoving as his gaze took her in. It must be raining outside—he was soaked, and the water mixed with the natural oils on his skin to create a fragrance that wound its way into her lungs. His body glowed like a bronze god under the soft lighting from the sconces embedded into the walls. That glow seemed to float from his fingertips and away from his body like tendrils of incense made of sex and magic.

Kota had been irresistible before, but now her attraction to him shot into the stratosphere. Like the lift-off of the space shuttle—the higher it went the more powerful and unstoppable it became. Forcing herself to remain still, every muscle in her body fought with her head until she thought she might just crack into little pieces of needy woman.

Then she made the mistake of glancing at his amazingly fine and über hard cock. Derria's insides melted and pooled into liquid longing. The aching lips of her pussy swelled even more, and he hadn't even touched her.

Three steps across the threshold, Lakota paused and held out his hand to her. Without hesitation, she walked into his arms and let him engulf her in the safe cocoon of his body.

Derria's swift intake of breath mirrored his own. Lakota was stunned. She could feel it deep inside herself. His energy was wild and flaring and seemed to be everywhere at once.

Even still, she had no doubt that this man was meant to be hers. Derria has seen Kota in action from day one in the Gorge. He'd watched her back at both the MacRowan's and the Clan alphas meetings. Had taken care of providing a place to stay. He'd even played escort and driven her around, as well as fed her. The crazy attraction to him had only been heightened by his own need to take care of her. In a short time, she'd began learning Lakota, understanding him, knowing him...yet Kerr was already there. That knowledge brought with it a strange sense of guilt that burrowed around in her gut.

"This can't be true...can it?" she asked quietly, the words spoken against his chest as she tried unsuccessfully to calm all the myriad emotions assailing her just now.

"What can't be true, Dare?"

"I can feel him, Lakota. But I swear I didn't—"

"Stop it, Dare. Right now," he growled. Derria snapped her gaze up to his as he said, "No one is at fault for this turn of events. There is nothing for you to feel guilty about. And I can feel him, too, Dare. Can damn near hear his voice inside my head, right along with yours."

Speechless was a state she rarely experienced, but right now, not a single word popped into her head nor came to her rescue.

"It's like the both of you are starting to burrow...no, more like *meld* into me. He's your mate, Derria." Lakota paused.

"But how can you be sure, Kota?" she asked, though she already knew the answer.

"The same way I was sure the moment I met you. Because he's mine, too," Lakota stated matter-of-factly.

She backed away from him. When Kerr stood at Lakota's side and they both regarded her with concern, she backed up even more.

Point of fact—she was on the verge of freaking out. All she'd done was walk out her door to do her job like she'd done a million times before. But this time she'd stumbled into a small town where shifters ruled, but not particularly well. Her bounty wasn't a rogue, but he and the man asked to escort her around turned out to both be her mates.

'Overwhelmed' didn't begin to describe her state of mind.

And for the first time in her life, Derria wanted to run. Far. Right now.

But they were closing in on her.

"Back up."

They didn't.

"Back the hell up before I lose my shit!"

They paused, looked at each other, and then took a single step her way.

Well, she'd warned them.

Kerr heard Lakota yell, "Down!"

Instinct kicked in and he hit the floor as the roar of his fully shifted mate filled the air. Kerr's mouth fell open as his very own red-gold lioness pounced at the nearest body, which belonged to the man who'd had sense enough to yell a warning. Bounding over Lakota's crouched form, Derria shot down the hallway to the exit and was outside before either man could get up off the floor.

She'd run from them! Didn't the crazy woman know not to run from big bad wolves? They had to go after her, had to protect her. She had no idea what was out there, and couldn't possibly...

"Oh, you have no idea," Lakota said, interrupting Kerr's train of thought. "Derria is one of the most capable women I know. If she could get here and ambush you alone, trust me, she'll be fine."

Kerr paused on his way toward the hallway and turned back to regard the man that fate had delivered right into his den—also his mate, along with Derria.

"Besides, the newly healed claw marks on my chest from just this morning are a reminder that when I get the urge to try to control her, it's best to change my mind."

Eyes closed, Kerr sought his woman along their newly forming bond, and that bond immediately responded. Lakota was right. She needed a moment to get her thoughts together. Her entire life had just changed and she was a bundle of "what ifs" and no small amount of concern for all involved. Suddenly, as if she'd figured out he was eavesdropping, the bond went dim, but not before she sent him a bolt of ire.

A moment later, she spoke.

"Will you please get my motorcycle and put it next to yours? I saw your bike in the foyer so there must be a way. I have a feeling I'm going to be there for a while after I get back from running off some steam. I'd prefer my ride not be left in the forest."

In the forest? She must have ridden it as deep into the wild as she could, shifted and run the rest of the way, and then still had time to change her clothes. And all while he'd been in the shower? Impressive.

"Show me where it is," Kerr said.

A few quick mental images later, and he knew exactly where to find the machine that he'd seen all too recently in his rearview mirror, as he'd hauled ass while bleeding out. And he still didn't have the answer to the question of why she'd been hunting him.

But they would get to that later. Lakota was right. Derria needed partners, not babysitters. The woman was resourceful, smart and strong...and right now, very vulnerable.

"I'm sorry for shooting you, now that I know you're not a bad guy," she whispered into his head.

"Oh, I am definitely a bad, bad man, Derria. Just not one that should be on a bounty hunter's radar."

"Okay, you can get out of my head now," she said.

"But what if I don't want to? I like hearing what's going on in there," he teased.

Kerr had felt Lakota ease gently into the telepathic conversation a moment ago. Unsure of how much he'd heard, he told the other man about Derria's request and what she'd done when he'd been caught snooping.

"Tattletale," she snapped and then went dark again.

They threw their heads back and laughed because this time the message had been delivered, loud and clear, to them both.

*a*n oversized black and gold jaguar loped alongside an equally immense charcoal gray wolf as they appeared from out of nowhere and took off into the surrounding trees.

They reappeared a short distance from Lakota's Jeep which rested at the top of the cliff. Glad he kept his vehicle stocked with a few changes of clothes, Lakota immediately took on his human body and tossed Kerr a pair of sweats and a tee-shirt before dressing himself.

On the way to find Derria's motorcycle, Kerr shared the myth of the warrior woman, just as he'd shared it with Derria. Lakota had never heard anything quite like it, yet something about it resonated within his soul. Just out of sight of the den, Kerr stopped and waited for Lakota to pull up alongside him.

He shut off Derria's bike, put it in neutral and hopped off. Just ahead of Lakota's vehicle, Kerr pulled on the limb of what looked like a jumble of bushes and brush to reveal a space large enough for anything he needed to hide.

"Pull on in and put it in park. We want this place to remain hidden from my crazy ass pack mates, so we'll need to speak through our bond...which shouldn't even be possible if you think about it. We're not

going in the same way we went out. Den's a mile and a quarter that way," he said, and motioned toward some rolling hills off to the west.

Lakota nodded, and did as the other man asked, but all the while, his brain flew along at a mile a minute. Kerr was right—none of this should be possible. They weren't related, and they didn't share a pack. Hell, they didn't even share a species, yet they'd been walking in and out of one another's heads from the moment they'd come face-to-face.

As they walked toward the foot of Kerr's cliff, Kerr asked, *"How do you see this working, Lakota?"*

"Just Kota is fine. Well, I can't say the story is bullshit considering most of the world believes that shifter legends are utter crap, yet here we are."

After giving his shifter-PC—politically correct—answer, Lakota paused and considered how to answer what Kerr *really* wanted to know. *"Look, Kerr, I have no idea how we're going to handle a triad of alphas. Derria alone is a handful."*

"I can imagine. When I saw her sitting in my living room all I could think was that she was the bitch who shot me in the leg and almost caused me to bleed out. I shifted before I realized I'd done it and came to a fucking skidding halt at her feet with my nose pressed into the barrel of a gun."

Yep, that sounded like his Dare, all right. And given that Kerr had a smile as wide as a bridge spread across his face, it must sound like his Dare, too.

"I believe Derria is the one," Lakota said. *"I want her, and you want her. I'm pretty sure we both ring her particular bell. But understand this, Kerr, she and I are already mated. She has to accept you into our mate bond. If she does, I will, too. She's my focus. It's all about her."*

"Then we're of like mind. So, a gentleman's agreement?" Kerr suggested.

"Of what kind?"

"We agree on a united front. To take care of her together. Gang up on her, if necessary. No rivalry. No jealousy."

Lakota listened, nodded his head, but managed to keep a few of his thoughts to himself.

Why? Because Kerr's solution sounded fucking impossible. Didn't it?

Back inside the den, he followed Kerr to the kitchen, happily accepted the tall can of beer tossed from the fridge, and then plopped down at the small dining table. Thoughts tumbled one over another as he realized one thing: He was way out of his league.

Unlike most S.W.A.T. agents, he'd been born in a place where there'd never been a need to hide his true self—right here in the Gorge. Grew up knowing truly what it meant to be what some called a "two spirit" or "skin walker." A shapeshifting human with the spirit of the jaguar. But he'd never heard of a triad before outside of fairy tales, yet Lakota knew he was being offered a rare gift.

Thankfully he and Kerr seemed to be on the same page. They wanted nothing more than to know and love Derria, to keep her happy until they took their last breath and kicked the bucket.

Strangely enough, he felt not a twinge of jealousy at the thought of sharing his woman but was rather taken aback by his muted attraction to Kerr. Tipping up his beer, Kota suddenly had nothing to say. His first impulse was to clam up tight and pretend that it wasn't there—no attraction, no quiet hum of awareness, no mate.

"Well, this isn't working at all," he mumbled to himself.

Kerr brushed against his mind, seeking entry rather than demanding. Asking rather than attempting to order.

Seeing that this man, who was just as much of a leader as he was, was willing to humble himself even in this small way, was all the assurance Lakota needed. He let himself fall open to

Kerr's polite 'knock' and, completely at odds with his typical self, held nothing back. Not the uncertainty, the worry...or the literal animal magnetism.

Kerr sucked in a deep breath. "I understand, and man, I admit that this is tough. But I'm willing to do it," he said.

Lakota cocked his brow. "For who? For Derria, or for yourself?"

"For all three of us. We need each other, I can feel it."

Jealous, yet grateful, of the fact that Kerr was so calm and deeply in tune with his inner self, Lakota silently acknowledged the truth of the other man's words. Then he said, "Well, I have no doubt I can do the job, but it would sure as hell be easier if there was some kind of instructional manual for this mating shit."

Kerr looked at him with an expression of pure puzzlement. With laughter reflected in his crystal gray eyes, he said, "A manual? What for? We're men. We don't read instructions anyway."

Lakota laughed and raised his brew toward Kerr. "To Derria, and us."

"Cheers!"

"Here she comes," Lakota said.

"Yeah," Kerr said as he turned toward the main hallways. "I feel her. Seems a bit less chaotic than when she left, but not by much."

"Hmmm. I think we need to get her focused on something other than her current state of mind."

"Agreed," Kerr said as he rose to his feet.

Derria stalked into the foyer and was relieved to see her bike there, just as she'd asked. Through the hallway and into the den she moved. Hmmm, though she sensed they were here, neither of her men were in sight. On her way to the stairs, she caught something in her periphery. A quick glance to the left and her eyes went wide and her mouth fell open.

Lakota had Kerr pushed up against the kitchen wall, kissing him with all the pent up passion she'd felt wrapping around their bond.

It was the hottest damn thing she'd ever seen! They broke apart, each panting wildly, keeping their gazes on one another. She couldn't move. Couldn't get her legs to obey her commands as the fantasy of where this could lead played out in her head.

Without giving her time to react, Kerr and Lakota walked right up to her.

"Do you accept me, Derria?" Kerr asked.

She looked to Lakota, who said, "It's your decision, Derria. Kerr and I agree that we can make this work. But the call is yours."

Turning her gaze back to Kerr, she still hesitated.

"We won't move forward without your consent. It doesn't matter what Lakota and I think. I asked if you accept me because you are my primary concern. I've already told you the story of the warrior woman and her mates, and you understand that you're the lynch pin to all of this."

She did indeed.

"Then come to us of your own free will." With a snarky and evil-ass grin, Kerr walked three steps past her and then turned to say, "No pressure."

And then the two men headed for the stairs, shoulder to shoulder. They seemed to instinctively reach for each other to take those first steps hand in hand.

And they left her standing there? Seriously?

She couldn't decide whether to be pissed and stand stubbornly where she was or run after them. The sound of water had her bolting for the stairs.

Though it was her first time upstairs, she followed the awareness of her mates directly to the bathroom without error.

She couldn't help but admire the den that Kerr Blackstone had built given the engineering marvel was inside of a huge cliff-side cavern. The room was painted in various hues of blue, with an ombre light-to-dark effect that was quite eye-catching. Wide and spacious with rugs strewn about, one side sported a big white claw-foot tub, an oversized granite vanity and a water closet. On the other side of the space was a shower worthy of one of those television shows that featured the rich and famous.

Large enough to comfortably seat—yes, *seat*—six people, it was a circular glass enclosure with tiled benches set into the walls. From where she stood, it appeared they had the water running, but there were several other nozzles that weren't turned on. Steam and massaging jets, perhaps?

She headed toward her men. They stood soaping each other, but the emotion flowing down the bond was one of friendship and camaraderie with an easy buzz of attraction. Yet when they turned their gazes her way, that damn bond flared with a strike of blatant need, blanketed by a deep abiding care for her.

It was impossible not to notice how beautiful they looked next to each other, their differences as sexy as their similarities. Lakota was beautifully tanned, like raw almonds and cream, while Kerr was closer to her own salted caramel tones, but deeper, darker with a hint of red. Kerr's jet black, bone-straight locks complimented Lakota's blonde waves. Where one was leaner and taller, the other was broad and stocky. Both equally muscular.

And packing some seriously hard equipment in the sex department.

Oh my!

Having experienced Lakota's brand of rough-and-ready loving with that tool he called a cock—thickly veined and long —she wondered what it would be like to have Kerr's hardness riding her. The man's dick was made like a soup can—super thick and as stocky as the rest of him.

These two might be a study in opposites when it came to their bodies, but in their hearts and minds they had a singular goal—claim her by any means necessary. And they weren't attempting to hide it at all.

"And we never will," they echoed in her head.

Kerr held his wet hand out to her. Their gazes held and she moved, this time without any hesitation or freaking out. That wild need to run, to seek her own space, dissipated with each second that passed.

Instinctively, she eased between them, inhaling their natural scents as they mixed with the warm mist of the shower and whatever soap they were using. Lakota's strong fingers began a lathered journey from the base of her back and up along her spine. Kerr turned so she could suds up his shoulders and back.

As one, they did an about face and Derria found herself now washing Lakota's back while Kerr finished up hers.

A thought flickered into her head. *"What about our fronts?"*

With that, Lakota faced her, placed his hands on her shoulders and gently pushed her backward. Derria found herself sitting on Kerr's waiting lap, his cock pressed firmly against her ass.

One thing was sure—she was going to have to learn to shield her thoughts sometimes.

If she'd looked down, surely there would be arcs of electrical current moving over her skin in all the places on her body where she was connected to these two men.

There were hands everywhere—a cloth slid up and down her arms, a sponge worked her breasts and stomach, arms, legs and feet, all tackled. Even as she leaned back, eyes closed and body completely relaxed, her gut danced with an unexplained sense of urgency. No danger, or fear. Just...necessity.

Suddenly the water switched off and she found herself

wrapped in a thick towel—correction, two thick towels. One patted her front, the other her back.

"I just can't resist," Lakota said as he dipped his head and suckled a dark nipple and then pulled it deep inside his warm mouth.

"I'll keep my hands to myself. For now," Kerr said as he did just that.

"Hey!" Derria yelped.

"Nobody said anything about mouths, love." The man nibbled and licked the sensitive spot along her shoulder muscle on the left, then he sucked and laved the little stings away.

The combined sensations sent trembles from her baby toes clear up to her crown.

They stood in the steam of the shower for long moments as Derria held Lakota's head to her swelling breasts with one hand, while the fingers of the other hand stroked Kerr's cheek as he tasted her from behind.

Derria didn't have a poetic bone in her body. If it didn't have to do with technology or fighting, she didn't typically have much to say. But the things her mates made her feel? God, she could write odes about them—chapters and chapters of odes.

Hips began to seek. Breath went shallow. Body overheated.

"Oh my god, that's so good," she whispered. "Bed. Now. Please."

Kerr lifted his head and went still. Lakota backed up a step and Derria wanted to scream for them not to stop. But that wouldn't happen until one last bit of business was handled.

Kerr's deep rumble of a voice caused the hair at her nape to rise, a replay of the first time she'd laid eyes on him. "Look at me, Derria."

"No wanna," she grumbled.

Lakota's hands landed lightly on her waist and the man proceeded to physically turn her around to face Kerr. The only way she could avoid his gaze was to stare mutinously at the tiled floor of the shower stall. But given she had no desire to be a complete five-year-old brat at the moment, she conceded and gave Kerr what he'd asked for.

Once their gazes met, he crossed his arms across his Conan the Barbarian-esque chest, his expression soft but no-nonsense at the same time. "I will not coerce you, Derria. I absolutely will not have you without your consent."

"But I'm standing right here, aren't I?" she challenged.

"Not good enough. Give me the words."

And she found that she wanted nothing more than to give him what he'd asked for. But first, she asked, "So why doesn't Lakota have to give you any fucking words?"

A soft puff of breath fanned over her skin as Lakota stepped up behind her and said, "I already did, Dare. And Kerr gave them to me, as well."

Her mouth fell open and for a moment, she couldn't speak, couldn't form a thought as the enormity of what these men had pledged sank into her soul.

And all for her.

Kerr stroked the edge of her jaw just beneath her ear. Derria leaned into his touch and put her heart and soul into the pledge.

"I accept you, Kerr Blackstone, with all my soul."

That last piece of the bond sprang into position with such force Derria swore she'd almost *heard* it snap into place.

In seconds they were breath to breath, his mouth on hers with an easy coax of lips and teeth that set her insides to dancing.

The kiss started gentle enough, then his arms tightened around her until she felt the bulge of his biceps beneath her shoulder blades. She could tell he wanted to crush her to him and that the effort of not doing so pushed him toward the edge of some unseen peak.

And that kiss, that trading of breath and longing, went on and on...until Derria inhaled sharply at the buzzing charge that flashed through her belly. The cause? Lakota's erect cock pressed against the crease of her butt. Hot, thick, hard. A mix of velvety smooth skin stretched taut over solid steel.

Lakota's arms came around her body, one hand landed on her hip, and the other on Kerr's as he pulled them all into a firm embrace. Skin to skin, mind to mind, there was one thing that they all needed right now.

Each other.

In the bedroom, Kerr turned on and then dimmed the lights with a remote mounted on the wall. Easing the covers back on the big bed, he stepped aside so Derria could climb in, while Kota moved around to the other side.

Fitting their bodies against hers—curve to curve, dip to dip —Derria was surrounded by two six-foot-something packages of *irresistible*. Kerr pressed against her front, Kota against her back.

As her wolf pressed his lips to hers, one arm pillowed her head as his fingers gently burrowed into the thick curls to massage her scalp. The other hand eased beneath a swelling breast to weigh and squeeze, to roll her nipple between insistent fingers, tugging them until her breath had trouble choosing whether to sough in and out, or remain stuck in her lungs.

It was almost overwhelming, yet so very good.

"Lakota, roll to your back and take Derria with you."

And just like that she was stretched out as if the man was a big firm pillow. Without another word, Kerr arranged her so that her legs were outside of Kota's thighs. As if on cue, her other mate bent his knees to raise and part her thighs to the perfect angle. Her mind reeled with the possibilities now that Kerr had complete and easy access to all her cocoa-pink parts. And one part in particular wept until she felt her own cream run from her pussy, down the crack of her ass, no doubt leaving a trail of dew clear down to Lakota's ball sac.

The jaguar crooned softly into her ear. "Damn, woman, you feel so good against me. Wiggle that ass against my cock, lovely." Then soft, juicy licks fell on her lobes as Lakota tasted his way down the side of her neck, sucking and nibbling.

Derria let her head lull in whatever direction it wanted while obeying Lakota's command. Hell, she couldn't help it. The way these men played with her body made it impossible to stay still. A sharp nip at the cords of her neck had her making a few demands of her own.

"Lakota, oh god, please. Mark me again."

"Where, lovely? Here?" He licked just below her ear.

"No." She was panting now. "Lower."

"Here?" Lakota bit down on the tendon where neck met shoulder. Derria shivered violently. But that wasn't the spot. Wasn't the spot that made her stomach clench so tightly she thought she'd come just from him kissing her there. He was playing with her, but she wanted to feel his bite so badly she didn't want to take the time to get mad. *God, please let him find it again.*

"Here?" Lakota sank his teeth into *that* spot. Derria's fingers found the sheets and tugged. Hard.

"Oh god, yes. More. Please."

Her whole body got in on the action as Lakota's hands explored her body and his mouth left his mark on her flesh.

"Mmm, that's it, Derria," Kerr crooned. "Enjoy this. Revel in it. Take what you want and tell us what you need."

Need? Well that was easy. "More. Just, more."

"That we can definitely do."

Kerr touched and teased her with the backs of his hands, with wrists, knuckles and fingertips. He caught her nipples in the webbing between his fingers. An indelicate moan turned into a needy plea when he tensed his hand and gently pulled it away, taking her nipple and areola with it.

The scent of Derria's pussy reached up, grabbed Kerr by his neck and pulled him toward it. Mmm, she smelled so good. Her body was ready for him, he knew it. Could see the honey dripping, especially with her laid out on top of Lakota with her legs open and inviting.

Lakota sucked on her neck like a starved man. Derria's whole body hummed and writhed. It was a beautiful sight. But an image flashed into his mind that was even lovelier—his mouth on that hot pussy while Lakota was buried balls-deep inside of her.

"Derria, look at me."

She lifted her head and looked down her body and directly into his eyes. She looked sleepy-eyed, her lips parted just a bit as she breathed roughly through them.

"Lift your hips just a little bit."

Kerr reached underneath her ass and wrapped a hand around Lakota's cock. It was the first time he'd ever touched a man in such a manner. Lakota met his gaze with a smirk and that was all the permission he needed to continue.

He tucked the head of Lakota's cock at the entrance of Derria's soaked pussy and her lids slipped closed on a delicious moan as Lakota surged forward.

"Do you like it, Derria? Does it feel good?"

"Oh god, yes. Need. More. Harder."

"You like it rough, lovely?" Lakota asked.

"Please. Oh please."

The cock of his new mate plowed away and Derria went mad. But it was nothing compared to her reaction to Kerr's tongue lashing her clit as Lakota fucked her deep.

"Kerr, my god, I'm close."

Lakota had readily agreed when Kerr asked him to join in Derria's pleasure. The other man knew that Derria was Kerr's heart, just as she was his own.

"Come on, little kitty cat. Come for us."

Derria would come first this time, and every other time. But their woman wasn't the only one close to blowing. The sight of Lakota's cock shuttling in and out of Derria's plump, ready flesh caused the skin to literally tighten all over Kerr's body. The pleasure on the woman's face, the tautness of her limbs, the arch of her spine as she strode toward her climax. The unashamed and unrestrained heated words that flew from her mouth trashed his self-control.

She told him she liked it. Told him she wanted more. That she wanted *him*. It was almost enough to make him come without anyone laying a finger, tongue or anything else on his cock.

"It's too good. I'm gonna die, Kerr."

With a firm hand, Kerr stilled Lakota's thrusting and put all his concentration on Derria's clit. Flicked it. Swirled his tongue around it. Spread her juicy lips and flat out ate her as if she were one of those delicious cranberry tarts from the bakery in town.

Derria came on a scream.

"Fuck! Her pussy is so tight. I swear she's milking my cock," Lakota ground out.

"Now, Lakota."

With that, Lakota pulled out of her still pulsing pussy, flipped her over and then thrust into her mouth as she landed on the bed on her knees. Derria wrapped her lips around his throbbing cock and he came on a shout just as Kerr deep-ended Derria's lovely pussy.

Ass up, head down and hands tearing at the sheets, she was close to coming again. Kerr could feel it. Could feel her pulling at his inner-beast just as her flesh pulled at his cock.

The silky hot slide of sleek inner muscles caressed him as it parted her sugared walls. With each stroke she bowed and arched, pushed back on her knees, sought more of the exquisite sensation.

The ridge of his cock stretched the tight opening of her pussy as he pulled out enough to stimulate only the band of muscle and flesh just inside of her gate. And that's all he would give her. Just that little bit.

"Stop teasing me, Kerr. Give it to me. Please."

But he couldn't. If Kerr gave her anymore he would lose it.

"If you don't fuck me senseless, I swear I will slash the tires on your bike and push it off the nearest cliff!" she yelled. Actually yelled. Wow.

He couldn't help but grin. Obviously, he was doing something right. But then again, he needed to make sure she understood where he was coming from. He needed to hear her say she wanted him again.

"Derria, do you want me to pull out so Lakota can make you come?"

"No."

"Are you sure?"

"Yes! Right now I *need* you. Now enough talking, more fucking."

"Bossy," he said, unable to keep the smile out of his voice. "You already came once."

And she was peaking again if the squeeze of her creaming sex all around his cock was any indication. "Come again. Then two more to go," he promised.

She blew. And he followed her into oblivion just as he sank his fangs into her shoulder to join his mating mark with that of Lakota's.

8

"*We* have a problem to solve," Derria said around a jaw-cracking yawn. They'd kept her up most of the night, but did she have any complaints about being half zombie-brained just now?

Nope.

"My problem is that you're not wrapped around my cock," Kerr rumbled against her neck.

She was a lion sandwich, pressed between her men.

No, not just men, but mates.

The thought brought a smile to her lips even as her fingers drifted to her neck to trace the mating marks left there. They'd sucked on damn near every part of her body until she felt like one big sensitive hickey.

Lakota's quiet, yet satisfied groan hummed in his throat as they both reached for her. But she knew where this road led.

With a burst of speed, she took herself and the covers down the middle of the bed and hopped off the end. Standing there wrapped in a mass of blankets, she glared at the two most gorgeous, but currently laziest men she'd ever met.

"I repeat, we have a problem. And, Kerr Blackstone, unless

you want your head and your cock mounted on a wall somewhere, we need to figure out who in the hell is trying to have
you killed."

With an annoyed huff, Kerr sat up and looked at Lakota.
"Well, it looks like there will be no morning pussy for us." He
stood, cock waving in the wind. "You know what they say about
all work and no play, right, Derria?"

Seriously?

"You two are the greediest coochie hounds in all of the
universe," she laughed as Lakota beat Kerr to her side and
engulfed her in a big, warm hug. And he smelled so good. And
his morning wood was all hot and hard as it pressed into her
side.

"Are you complaining?" Kerr challenged around a yawn of
his own as he joined in their enticingly warm group hug.

*Nope. Not going to be distracted by scents and hands and lips and
cocks. Nope, nope, nope.*

She hugged them back, pushed away and headed for the
shower. When they started to follow, she dropped the covers,
grabbed her gear bag from the foot of the bed and held out a
hand to ward them off. "You two wait your turn. I'm showering
alone this morning. I need to call in anyway."

"Call who?" Kerr demanded.

Eye roll.

"Home, Kerr. You know, the people who may be able to help
keep you from getting 'disappeared' off the planet, courtesy of
whoever reported you to the agency I work for."

They looked like a set of twin bookends as they crossed their
arms over muscle-packed chests and...pouted?

She tried to appear stern and down-to-business, but it was a
tall order when all she wanted to do was preen. These handsome, strong, down-to-earth men weren't hunting for sex. All
they wanted was her—no one else, just Derria Sozi-Pryde's love
and happiness.

The sex was a bonus. And it was one hell of a dividend, if she could say so herself.

Out of the shower and dressed in tactical pants and shirt, she awaited her two mates downstairs in what she now knew was Kerr's favorite chair.

With that thought, the man descended the stairs, laughing as he came down with Lakota right behind him. She looked up with a smile. A single dark brow hiked up as he tilted his head just a bit.

Without a word, he walked over to her, picked her up as if she weighed nothing and then sat down in the loveseat next to *his* chair and arranged her in his lap. All the while, the two men kept chatting as if nothing had happened.

Kerr planted a kiss on her cheek with a murmured, "You smell like us even after your shower. I like it."

She kissed him back, got up and gave Lakota the same peck on his cheek and then she headed for the kitchen toward the sanctuary called "coffee."

As she searched through the most logical places for her liquid morning wake-up, Derria called over her shoulder.

"Kota, how did you know I was coming to town?"

He answered as he and Kerr joined her in the kitchen and sat down at the table. "I got a call from a friend of mine that you were headed our way. He knew I was S.W.A.T. and hoped I could learn who you were."

"Question one, how did *he* know you were S.W.A.T., and question two, who told him that I was coming to town?" she asked.

"He's a good friend, a shifter. I don't think he set these wheels into motion, but he won't give up his underground contacts unless he learns that they screwed us all over."

Derria had no doubts on that score—the pooch has been screwed royally and without any lube.

Kota continued, "I had no idea who you were. In fact, I submitted a query to S.W.A.T. about one Derria Sozi, and asked if I could have authorization to assist you on your hunt." He cocked his head to the side and appeared to sink deep into thought. A moment later he said, "Now that I think about it, I've been so caught up in this unexpected mating business, I forgot to share the outcome of that request. I was denied any information about you, or why you're here."

"Who denied you?" Kerr asked. "And what is S.W.A.T. doing here anyway?"

Derria chuckled. "Good question considering we're shifter law enforcement all over the country, except for in these mountains."

"Makes sense. Those in the Nantahala Gorge have always resisted outsiders, and that includes you, as beautiful as you are. It was clear when you shot me that you were hunting me," Kerr said. "But none of us know much past that?"

Lakota stood and paced silently across the polished stone floor that was surprisingly warm against her bare feet given they were literally inside a mountain. "As for who denied me, I'm not sure. The message came through on a coded frequency but there were no IDs, names or rank attached to it."

"I think I definitely need to call home again," she said. "And you two need to be part of that conversation. Oh, but before we do that," she got up, retrieved her bag and pulled out a piece of equipment.

"Whoa," Lakota said. "Did you steal that from the set of Star Trek? It doesn't look like standard issue."

"Because it's not. It's one of the benefits of being a Pryde. I'm related to the premier innovators of high tech security equipment and biotech compounds, for both the military and the private sector."

Both men whistled as she kneeled next to the chair that Kerr was sitting in.

"Kerr, I need to see where I shot you before." Without hesitation, he stood and dropped his pants. A semi-hard cock bobbed in front of Derria's face.

"You're incorrigible, I swear," she snickered.

He indicated the spot where she'd shot him days ago. There was the slightest bump there. She only noticed because she knew what she was looking for. "Okay, hold still please."

"What are you doing?" Lakota asked.

"When I shot him, the bullet left behind a tracking device. It's how we were able to find him. This…" she said as she held up her little space-aged thingy, "is going to get it out. Or rather, the vibration of the device will break the nanotech and their bioagents down to particles small enough that Kerr's body will be able to expel them."

"Bioagents?" Kerr asked. "That's why I didn't heal right away even after I shifted?"

"Yep."

With that done, she sat in the chair next to him and tapped a code into her comm device. Moments later a male voice came on the line and said one word.

"Key."

Derria tapped the buttons on the device again, and then she spoke. "Hey, Jason, I need an emergency conference call. Is everyone home?"

Kerr whispered, "Who is that?"

"My family," she whispered back.

"Are they all shifters?"

"Yep, a whole pride of lions. And my cousin-in-law, Reya, is a black jaguar."

A few moments later, Jason was back on the line. "Okay, Dare, we're all here. The line is secure."

She was already happy, but it overflowed into her smile as she greeted her family. It was the same smile she reserved for her mates.

"You are so beautiful when you smile, Derria," Lakota said. *"I promise to make you do that often."*

She winked at him and said, "Meet my mates, Lakota Phillips and Kerr Blackstone. Lakota and Kerr, my family, the Prydes."

"Your family is named Pryde and it's a pride of lions?" Kerr thought it was the funniest thing in the world. "I love irony."

"You mean, kind of how you're a Lakota Sioux who has a mate named Lakota?" she asked. A ton of snark laced her words.

The shit eating grin fell from his face as he grumbled, "Damn. Hadn't thought about that one."

And that opened the door for her family to welcome Kerr and Kota in their own special way.

Let the games begin.

Neesia Pryde, the matriarch, made the introductions.

"First, let me say we're thrilled to meet you, and my sisters and I are kinda jealous that Derria gets two mates. Ow! Damn it, Jason, don't nip me like that."

But Derria knew better. She knew how Neesia typically responded to her mate's nips, and it was along the lines of 'do it again.' Actually, now that she had mates, she could totally relate.

Neesia went on, "As you know, we are part of S.W.A.T., but there are things that S.W.A.T. doesn't know about us Pryde's and we'd like to keep it that way. We'll get into that later. I'm mentioning it now because it's my way of letting you know that we are willing to trust you with sensitive information, just like we trust the rest of our family, unless you give us a reason not to."

"I'm honored," said Kerr.

Lakota said, "Understood."

"I'm Neesia Pryde, and these are my sisters. My twin is Niah, and then there's the twins, Koreas and Kotara." All of the women spoke up with welcoming hellos, which was a relief to Derria. "The mated pairs are Jason and myself." Jason greeted them all. "Niah and Lou, and Koreas and Austin James. Austin is the only human mate so far, but I'm pretty sure he was a feline in another life or something." More hellos and a few chuckles.

Niah chimed in. "I've already shared all the weird shit that's going on in North Carolina with the family. And we all agree that we need to get you all out of there until we figure out who's yanking our chain."

Jason joined the conversation. "I'll make a call to Captain Johns. She'll be interested to know that we might just have a mole in S.W.A.T. That will piss her off, and a pissed off Johns is a thing of beauty."

"And," Neesia hopped back in, "I'll arrange for Harry to meet you. The closest airport is GSP, Greenville Spartanburg International. I think it's the only one close enough that can handle the size of the jet."

"Jet?" Lakota and Kerr asked in unison.

"Yep, jet," Neesia Pryde replied. "By the way, you can bring one vehicle a piece, if you want. Otherwise, we have plenty of stuff here to keep you mobile. But our primary goal is to keep you safe while we figure out who wants Kerr dead."

"And why are you doing all of this?" Kerr asked. "You don't know me, or anything about me."

Niah, who Derria likened to the female version of Spock from the Star Trek franchise said, "Because you're mated to Derria. That means we're actually doing it for her."

"Well, Dare," said Neesia, "pack it up and come on home. We've got a mystery to solve."

With a sparkle in her eye, Derria looked at both her mates as she asked her cousin, "How much time do we have to prepare?"

"We can have the flight arranged in a couple of days. I'll send you the flight plan and itinerary via your comm device. Work for you guys?"

After replying in the affirmative, Derria said her "love yous" and "see you soons".

The moment the call disconnected, she stripped while yelling, "You've got two days to do your worst!"

Shifting mid-stride, she headed toward the hallway.

As she flew out the front door, she felt the breath of her two beautiful shifter mates fan across her heels as they chased her toward their destiny.

WINTER BLUES: KOTARA PRYDE

1

---

*K*otara paused outside of her cousin's suite. Derria Sozi-Pryde and her two mates were like bunnies when it came to sexing. Once she was sure that there was no moaning, screaming or pleading, she knocked on the door.

"Come in," Derria called.

No way in hell. There were way too many sex hormones in there. The last thing she needed was yet another cold shower from all the "gimme some" those three gave off.

It still amazed Kotara that Derria had gone on a typical bounty hunt for the Shifter and Were Armed Tactics agency, also known as S.W.A.T., and come home with not one, but two mates.

Lucky bitch.

Moments later, Lakota Phillips opened the door. Kotara breathed a sigh of relief. At least he was dressed this time. Shifters were the most immodest of creatures when it came to nudity. She was glad that they had a healthy sense of self, but for a single female in a house full of mated shifters, life in the horny department could be a bit trying.

"Didn't you hear Derria say it was okay for you to come in?"

Lakota asked, with a typical twinkle of mischief in his eyes.

"Yep. And for the millionth time, I am not coming in there," Kotara declared with a grin of her own.

"I know, I know. Too many pheromones."

"Damn right. Now if you guys don't mind, you, Kerr and Derria are wanted downstairs. Library in ten minutes."

She did a smart about-face and left him standing there looking all gorgeous and puzzled. She almost chuckled as she hit the staircase at a brisk walk, but the reason they were being summoned was no laughing matter.

She ran her fingers over the thick swirls carved into the polished bannisters. Gaze drawn to the Persian-style designs woven into the rugs, Kotara released a semi-contented sigh as her combat boots made no noise on the plush wool carpets.

From the fourth floor down to the first, the beautiful paintings of various cultures and their animal spirit guides called to her. Her thoughts fell back to when she and her sisters were building this place. It was important that they be good stewards of their lands. It was the reason the research laboratories, lovingly called the Labyrinth, were all underground with rolling prairies covering their existence.

Each log for the chalet, every tree in the orchard, the plants in the gardens, and the water features—everything had been chosen with care because the design of the estate was meant to fit with the surrounding acreage of the ranch.

In the end, the Pryde's chalet-style mansion was a luxurious, but homey place.

Down on the first floor, Kotara headed straight for the library. In the center of the brightly lit room was her favorite piece of equipment—a table made of highly polished aspen. With one tap of the remote embedded in the center, the thing transformed into a literal King Arthur-style Round Table. Thanks to Niah Pryde, it had all the electronic bells and whistles that allowed them to coordinate missions out of this room.

Kotara took a seat closest to the wall of windows that looked out onto the vast snow-covered prairie. She closed her eyes, took a deep breath and simply bathed in the sun, appreciating and loathing this place all at once. Moments later, her family began to stroll in—all hunters, the lot of them...and so much more.

Neesia and Niah Pryde were the oldest twins. Neesia was the matriarch and Niah was the technical genius. Neesia and Niah sat near Kotara while their mates, Jason DiCaplis and Emmitt Lee Lewis—Lou for short—settled in next to each other.

Pryde Industries' security division existed solely because of Niah, and the scientific division was all on Kotara and Koreas Pryde, nicknamed *'K-and-K, the mad scientist wonder twins'*.

Derria and Lakota strolled in with their graceful feline steps in sync. Next came their mate, Kerr, the only non-feline, non-hunter in the pride. Koreas entered last, minus her mate. But Kory brought just the slightest hint of him with her, given he was imprinted on her skin.

"Where's Austin?" Kotara whispered into her twin's mind.

"Fishing down at the river. You know he hates these briefings because it usually means we're headed out to chase bad guys. I think he's becoming more of a mother hen than Neesia."

Kotara smiled. *"You and I both know that's impossible."*

Looking around the table, Kotara smiled. She loved her family, loved this place—all seventy-seven thousand acres of it.

And for the first time in her life, Kotara Pryde wanted to be anywhere but home.

Every person in the room was an agent for S.W.A.T., except for Kerr Blackstone, Derria's second mate. He wasn't an agent, but his entire pack—or rather, *former* pack—were expert hunters.

It's what they, the most ruthless wolf shifters that hailed from the North Carolina mountains, were known for.

Kotara braced herself for the coming conference call. In front of the video screen sat Jason, Neesia, Derria, Lakota and herself. Everyone else remained off-screen for their own safety. The Shifter and Were Armed Tactics agency might make the safety of shifters their top priority, but it was still a bureaucracy. And everyone, shifter or not, knew such organizations eventually became corrupted. So the Pryde's kept their family and their secrets close at all costs.

Jason jumped right in. "Johns called this meeting. I don't know why but I believe it has to do with Derria and her mates."

Kotara cut him a hard glance. She might not have seen that coming, but thankfully there was very little that eased by either Jason or Neesia. Ever.

"Okay, let's get down to business," Jason said as he hit the speakerphone button and the tone of the speed dial filled the large, bright space. The small talk ended, and the room went quiet. They all knew the drill, but that didn't make the instant anxiety dissipate one bit.

On the video screen appeared a stern-faced woman. Dark hair was pulled back into a French braid so tight, Kotara often wondered how her eyes weren't stretched to mere slits, especially when the woman wore a perpetual scowl.

This was Captain Lola Johns, the crankiest badass director S.W.A.T. ever had, who luckily believed that the Prydes were capable of reeling in the worst of the worst of the shifter world's offenders.

And she wasn't wrong. The Pryde's were very good at their jobs. Very good indeed.

"Captain," Jason greeted.

With a slight nod, she gave her typical response. "DiCaplis."

"So what's going on?" Jason asked. "It's been months since Derria chased Kerr all the way to the mountains of North

Carolina. Surely the trail is completely cold by now. We've researched everything we could get our hands on and come up empty on finding whoever set up Kerr."

"Until now," Johns replied dryly.

Kotara looked from Neesia to Jason, glad to see their eyes were as wide as her own. Johns spoke into the silence.

"We have a lead, though a rather reluctant one," she said.

"Reluctant? Why?" Derria's words were pressed through gritted teeth. Kotara didn't blame her at all. Someone had done a hell of a job putting her on the trail of her mate in hopes that she'd kill him. And she almost had. Thank the universe for mating pheromones, otherwise her cousin's hunt would have turned out quite differently. Derria would have executed an innocent man.

"He'll be reluctant because he's human and has no idea he's about to become the focus of a S.W.A.T. investigation," Johns said.

An eruption of questions, queries and outrage followed the good Captain's declaration.

"What the hell do you mean?" growled Derria.

"Human? Are you serious?" Jason.

Kotara sucked in a breath, while Neesia glared daggers at the screen.

Johns, ever unflappable, waited. Finally, she dropped the real bomb.

"We occasionally work with the human military when it furthers our own cause. No different than Pryde Industries managing several contracts to provide superior technology to the military and world-class solutions to global biotechnology manufacturers. The only difference is that the assets we manage wear skin—namely *our* shifters and *their* military humans."

So while S.W.A.T.'s job was to keep humans in the dark and safe from rogue Weres, they were working *with* the humans on the down low? Holy hell, what a bombshell.

"What exactly do you mean by *'the assets you manage wear skin'*? You all just check us out like library books or something?" Kotara flinched when Neesia's foot made contact with her shin. After all, Kotara hadn't meant to say that out loud.

Ignoring her snarky-assed question, Johns continued.

"The military somehow failed to mention that one of their own happened to see Kerr in Idaho. Saw him ride in. Saw him ride out. This human is the one who reported a murder by a rogue Were. He was the one that found the body that was supposedly left to rot by Kerr. But the story around how that body was found doesn't add up now that we've heard Kerr's side of things, and the evidence doesn't seem to point to him at all."

"Dammit, Johns, this just makes it worse," Derria fumed. "So, someone unknown to S.W.A.T. dropped Kerr's name and we didn't bother to investigate whether the lead was credible or not? What kind of shoddy police work is that? Someone can accuse a person of murder and they can be declared the perpetrator without any evidence at all? Just shoot first and ask questions later? Or worse, don't ask questions at all? This is some foul-assed bullshit!"

Kotara looked over at her cousin and wondered if Dare's head was about to pop off. The natural hue of her skin combined with the blush of anger made the woman look like a caramel apple ready to blow.

"I agree. We dropped the ball on this one—" Johns admitted.

"Dropped the ball? I almost killed my fucking mate, and that's a hell of a ball to drop. And now you're dropping a bowling ball of a bomb on us just weeks before the winter holidays?"

Ignoring Derria's outburst, Captain Johns tossed out another grenade. "I'm going to do something I've never done before in my history at S.W.A.T. I'm putting this in your hands to investigate in whatever way you deem best. My only order," said Johns, "is that neither Derria nor Lakota be allowed on this hunt simply because they might be recognized. And of course, Kerr can't go as he is not part of the agency and is the center of this mess. The rest, you can decide on your own. The human is a man named Harrison Blue. The details have already been transmitted to your comm units. Johns out."

The screen went black and Johns was gone.

Neesia Pryde looked around the table. "Well, holy fucking hell."

Yep. That summed it up pretty well.

———————

Two days later, Kotara pulled off the main road and onto the trail to Alice Lake in Idaho. The sky was crystal blue and the day super bright, due to the reflection of the sun's rays off the thick pristine snow. The stark beauty of the Sawtooth Mountains struck a chord in her soul. To her surprise, the energy of the place reminded her a lot of home.

She cranked up the heat and then tapped her password into her portable comm device. Within moments a familiar voice filled the cab.

"Hey, how are you doing up there? Niah had to duck out so I'm your liaison on this hunt," Derria said.

"I'm fine. I'm rolling up on the coordinates Niah sent to my comm unit earlier."

"Uh, Tara, I'm showing you're on a hiking trail," Derria replied. Sounded like the woman was trying really hard not to laugh.

"That's because it *is* a hiking trail, Dare."

"Kotara Ann Pryde!"

"What? You're acting like normal people don't take their four-wheel drives on hiking trails or something."

"Tara?!"

"Oh, pipe down, Derria. The weather is crazy right now, so

this particular spot is closed anyway." After a few more minutes of friendly bickering, Kotara slowed the monster she called a truck down to a crawl. "Okay, Dare, I can't go any further in this ride. The drifts are so ridiculous that I can't tell what's trail and what's going to take me off into a ravine or something. I'll have to pick my way on foot."

"That's probably the best option anyway. Captain Johns said that we occasionally work with the military, but she made it pretty clear this mark doesn't count. We don't want the guy to get wind of the fact that you're near. If he knew enough about our kind to call in a hit to S.W.A.T. and blame it on Kerr, who knows what else he's aware of."

She knew Derria was right. They didn't know if they were dealing with a matter of a little espionage or simple stupidity. Regardless of the current conundrum, she still didn't want to leave the warmth of the oversized cab of her ride to romp around in the freezing cold.

But there was no help for it. According to their calculations, she'd have to head into the Sawtooth Mountains and make her way around to the spot where the protected forest bumped up against private property. It might look close on a map, but it was at least ten miles away.

Luckily, that was nothing for a lioness. Her chilled paws wouldn't thank her, but she'd get the job done anyway. Completely off the trail now, she eased behind a small stand of trees to hide her vehicle. Snow was falling again in earnest, so she wasn't worried about covering tire tracks.

Kotara hopped down to the ground and turned slow circles. The terrain was amazing. Sure, she was familiar with snow— after all, she lived on the plains of Wyoming where they received plenty of the white stuff every winter—but this took the concept of snow to a whole new level. In fact, this was damn ridiculous.

"Whoa! Is that a glacier?" she wondered aloud. "Holy shit!"

She really was in the middle of nowhere, in the middle of winter, in the middle of icicle hell, barely a week before the holidays. Had she truly signed up for this crap? Just how was she going to find a human way out here anyway? Surely the guy had more sense than to camp out among nothing but trees and glaciers, right?

Well, only one way to find out.

She yanked her gear bag out of the back seat, walked a short distance and dropped it on the snow-covered ground. Off came one boot, followed by a thick wool sock. She forced herself not to hop around on one foot as she removed the remaining one. Shoes and socks were carefully placed into her bag on top of her weapons, electronics and gloves. Next, off went snow pants, silk thermals, jacket and heat-regulating top that she would need to protect her from the cold after she got to her destination.

Kotara strapped her gear bag loosely to her back and fell to her knees. With the power of the change rippling through her being, she ceased to feel the acute cold that had snapped through her body when she'd removed her clothes.

A powerful shifter, as all Pryde's were, Kotara relished the flash of unexplainable magical energy that lit the blood in her veins. As her body lengthened and reshaped itself, the muscles burned with an ecstasy that was just short of an intense high. She loved who she was, what she was. And right now, she would do what she did best.

Hunt.

Moments after stripping naked in the mountains of Idaho, a three-hundred-pound lioness loped off, headed toward the asshole that made it necessary for her to be out here in the first place. In her mind's eye, she imagined what she would do when she caught up to him. Yep, a bite in the ass was definitely in order.

2

*T*his was the right path; she was sure of it.

The terrain here was steep and craggy. Moving carefully from rock to rock, Kotara avoided several spots where the snow had drifted to make the trail look solid, when in fact it dropped away into deep pockets. The last thing she needed was to break her neck by stepping into thin air.

At this rate, she wouldn't make it to her destination until she'd grown old and gray. And the only way to get new coordinates would be to engage the GPS on her comm unit, which required her to shift back to her human form.

The sun was setting quickly, and she might not have a choice but to shift back, dress quickly and figure out how to get out of here before nightfall. No way in hell did she want to be out in the open given the only thing she *didn't* have in her gear bag was shelter.

This is not my best day ever, damn it.

Moments later she spotted the human mark's nicely hidden spot off in the distance. Shouldn't be more than a couple of miles now. Perhaps her timetable wasn't totally blown after all.

Now, to find a way down off this damn ridge.

Arms full of firewood, Blue could have sworn he heard a...a roar? Impossible way out here. But then again, after what he'd learned from that S.W.A.T. agent who'd recently passed through his town, he shouldn't be surprised about anything. Not anymore.

The question as to whether humans were alone on the Earth had been answered, and the answer was a resounding "fuck no". And it wasn't an alien or ET type of thing that had taken up residence on this planet. It was shapeshifters. He didn't know much about them other than the fact that a shifter had committed the one and only murder in their little town in years. Killing didn't happen much up here, people were too busy trying to stay alive through the winter. Who had time to slaughter, decapitate and skin a man?

Shivers threatened to overtake him that had nothing to do with the weather. Just the memory of what had been done to that body he'd found was enough to make him want to blow chunks right there in the wood pile.

Unbidden, his brain extracted pictures in his head—the bites, the claw marks, the blood. The ripped and torn flesh. And a missing head. Not even in all his tours of war had he ever seen a body destroyed like that.

Must be a shifter thing.

He went still as a sound that raised the hair on the back of his neck once again ripped through the still evening. Whatever made that noise must be wounded and he could almost picture it stuck in the snow out there somewhere.

The doctor inside of him rushed to action. Saving lives was his specialty, or at least it had been at one point. Either way, Blue had never played favorites with a life. Shifter or human, people couldn't choose what they were born as.

He ran to the house, dropped the pile of logs in front of the fireplace, grabbed his rifle and was out the door before he'd even formed a plan, or conjured a true reason to head out into the growing dark after whatever-it-was.

No worries. He could always talk himself out of it as he went, right?

Right.

He attached the specialized trailer to the back of his snow-mobile, jumped on and headed towards the sound, hoping he could pick up some tracks or something. Seconds later, the whole ground shook, followed by an earthshattering rumble.

"Oh hell!"

Yes, he knew this music. They didn't get avalanches often on this side of the valley, but he sure as hell knew what one sounded like.

The rushing power of quickly moving snow echoed from the other side of the rise. As he pushed his snowmobile as fast as he could while still maintaining control, Blue hoped he made it in time. And if whatever he found was still alive, he only hoped he didn't end up getting his ass chewed off in the bargain.

Kotara opened her eyes and saw absolutely nothing. *This* was dark. Even with her enhanced vision this was, like, out in the sticks, middle-of-the-desert dark. Though her eyes were useless just now, all of her other senses seemed fully intact. Her ears picked up the quiet but deep breathing of someone next to her. This someone had a unique scent that wafted up from whatever covered her body. It was warm, enticing and smelled so good she had to have more of it. It was like being surrounded by the cool woods in springtime—pine and mint overlaid with some-thing musky.

She took in a deep breath.

Holy hell, that hurt.

"No," a deep male voice demanded in the dark. "Don't move. You were injured pretty badly in the avalanche. I almost didn't get to you in time."

Avalanche? Is that what they call it when the earth falls out from beneath your feet on the side of a mountain? Guess so.

Oblivious to the conversation going on within her own mind, her rescuer asked, "Are you safe?"

Was she safe? The words rumbled in the chest of the person next to her and held the slight slur of someone who'd obviously been sound asleep in spite of asking such a question. It took three tries for her to moisten her throat enough to reply. And even then, all she could squeak out was a simple, "Huh?"

"You've been out of it for two days."

Two days? What? She sat up…or tried to anyway.

A strong but gentle pressure held her in place via an arm that suddenly banded around her body. To her surprise, Kotara was so wiped out she didn't have the strength to push it away.

"Wait. You're not well. Drink a bit of water and I'll fill you in on what's what." He eased his arm from around her sore body and reached for something behind him. A moment later, he said, "Here. Drink."

A straw was pressed between her lips and her mind raced like mad as she sipped, then coughed and sputtered. "What in the world is in this? It tastes like boiled ass."

And he laughed, actually *laughed* at her in that deep rumbly voice of his. "Amino acids and electrolytes," he admitted through his chuckles.

Now she understood why her family literally snarled at her when she fed nasty-assed, good-for-you things to them.

But back to her interesting and not-fun predicament. Bottom line—she lay somewhere in the dark with an unknown man close to her very vulnerable body. And if the burning in her chest, stomach and thighs was any indication, she was severely injured. Kotara drew on her shifter energy as strongly as she drew on the straw in her mouth, but got nothing.

Damn. I'm totally depleted.

With an annoyed huff, she pushed the water away. "Why are you in bed with me?" she snarled.

"I only have one bed, and the couch isn't suitable."

"Something wrong with the floor?" she asked.

"Yep. I'm not sleeping on it. I spent enough time sleeping in inhospitable places. My home is exactly that—mine. And I sleep on the floor for no one."

Well, all righty then.

Kotara almost smiled because honestly, that was how she'd feel about the situation if things had been reversed. Only difference was there were plenty of rooms in the estate on Pryde Ranch to stick a healing person.

She tried to stretch but the pain was so intense, her breath stuck in her lungs. *Pant*, she told herself. *Pant, woman. Breathe. Holy shit.*

After a few very tense, silent moments, she managed to drag enough air into her lungs to talk. "So what's damaged?" she asked between shallow breaths.

The doctor part of herself grumbled as he described what she'd already ascertained for herself. Several broken ribs—thank goodness she wasn't blowing bubbles through her lungs—but there was no telling whether anything else had been punctured. The lacerations across the stomach and the muscles on her back and legs burned as if shredded. It was all knitting slowly, thanks to her shifter genetics, but damn, the healing hurt almost as much as the injuries.

Now back to his original question.

"What the hell do you mean by 'am I safe'?"

"Are you planning to eviscerate me?" He sounded completely serious.

"Why would I do that?" Kotara really was confused, then the

lightbulb in her brain began to turn on as she became more and more awake. When she'd fallen, she'd been *fully* shifted.

Well, fuck-a-duck.

"When I found you, you looked like one of those beautiful lionesses from big cat week on that television channel where they have all the animal documentaries. No way in hell an African lion should be in these parts, right? When I dug you out, you started changing in my arms."

After a few moments, she finally replied, "Am I safe? Hell no, but I mean you no harm. Move your arm, please. Help me sit up."

The moment the covers slipped, she wished she'd remained snuggled in. It was cold as all get out. No surprise for Idaho in the middle of winter. Once in a semi-sitting position, Mr. Deep Voice shoved some pillows behind her so she could sit unaided. Then he rolled away from her and clicked on the light.

Their gazes met and the growl deep in her throat was full of deadly promise. "I may have to change my mind on that whole *mean you no harm* thing," Kotara said.

"Why?"

"Because," she said quietly as she pulled back a bandage and inspected a wound. "You're the person I came up here to find."

"Me?" he wondered aloud.

"Yes, you. Nice work on the stitches, by the way."

"You're welcome. I think."

Inspecting the next sore spot, she said, "I'm Kotara. Kotara Pryde."

"Harrison Blue. Nice to meet you."

"Uh huh. You a doctor?" She'd read everything she could get her hands on about this man, both classified and not-so-classified. A first-rate trauma surgeon, he'd been awarded the Medal of Honor for saving countless lives on and off the battlefield at great risk to himself. He'd even performed a surgery under mortar fire, for crying out loud. It was pretty impressive. She also knew he'd retired barely a year ago and was much more handsome than his photographs. But right now, all she really wanted to know was if he would tell her the truth to her very simple question.

"I am indeed a doctor. Or I used to be when I was in the Navy. Why would such a beautiful woman be looking for me? Don't get me wrong, I couldn't be happier to have a lovely lady in my bed but considering you could shift and tear me to pieces, it makes me wonder what you're doing here."

Although the man's fists settled on a pair of slim hips, he had the body of a warrior. Up north were ripped abs, perfect pecs and shoulders, and buffed biceps. South were thick thighs and powerful looking calves. And the package covered by a pair of silk boxers was nothing to sneeze at though he was nowhere near aroused.

Yep, absolute warrior all right. She hoped she wouldn't have to shoot him.

A stitch stuck to the bandage she inspected. "I'm here," she gasped on an agony-filled breath, "trying to solve a riddle."

He replaced her hands with his own and eased the bandage free. "I'm not good at riddles," he replied in a perfect bedside-manner voice—not too loud, not too soft.

"Then it's a good thing you're not the one that needs to solve it."

He pried at the edges of one of the deeper wounds across her ribs. Pain slammed through her torso and another gasp caught in her throat. Kotara's eyes shut without her permission and the last thing she remembered as she passed out was a whispered, "Bless your heart," as the bed dipped next to her.

3

What in the hell am I getting myself into? Blue wondered to himself. *She's a shifter. Could split me open from neck to knees with no effort, yet here I am nursing her wounds and watching over her in my bed.*

And fighting the insane need to hold, help and take care of her. Which made no dang sense considering he'd just met the woman. Correction, he'd actually met a big ass lioness out in the snow drifts. This woman, this Kotara Pryde, had shown her true self just a little bit later as the beast faded and the female came to the forefront.

And he'd been instantly snared by her beauty, both in her animal and human forms. Captured by her vitality, even though it was currently hidden beneath her unconsciousness.

Their short conversation before she'd passed out told him that when she came awake again, she'd be a handful.

Blue smiled at the thought. Actually *smiled*. Maybe he really was crazy.

Out of bed, he grabbed a flashlight, a stethoscope and his blood pressure kit. Moments later, he climbed back into bed with a deep feeling of profound relief at her solid vitals.

Maybe this was the first stage of some kind of post-trau-matic dementia where he'd become all angsty and crotchety?

And attracted to a total stranger?

Yes, that was it. He was bonkers. Nothing much in the way of partners way out here, unless you counted bears. Maybe there were sexy bear *shifters* he just hadn't discovered yet, now that he thought about it.

The idea made him shiver, and not in a good way. Yet when he looked down at the lovely creature in his bed, even in the dim light of his room, all he could do was wonder what in the hell was going on…with *himself.*

This is more than hormones, Blue. If your libido was the issue, why are you hoping she regains consciousness again so you can make her pancakes and feed her breakfast?

Did post-traumatic issues involve bacon and talking to one's self?

Maybe lions didn't even like bacon. He hoped that wasn't the case. Dislike of bacon was a serious character flaw. But regard-less of Kotara's dietary needs, she sure was nice to cuddle with especially with the blustering wind and chill in the air. He'd had a lot of quiet holidays in his life. Perhaps this one would be a bit livelier…if he didn't get eaten. Literally.

"Owww," Kotara heard herself moan in her rapidly departing sleep state. A deep breath in told her olfactory system that she was alone in the room. Along with that information came a quiet ripple of awareness deep in her gut at the scent on the bedding of the man who called this place home.

She'd been too out of it the last time she woke to realize that the current of energy she'd noticed was more than just her muscles knitting back together. It was deeper than that. More acute. More…intimate.

Kotara cracked her lids open and blinked against the bright winter sunlight that streamed through the bank of small windows on the other side of the room. Sitting up carefully, there was no help in giving an appreciative whistle at the layout of the place.

The bed was strategically tucked into a corner on one side of the long rectangular room, protected by three walls. The windows looked more like a bookshelf with thick panes set into each block. It was the only point that exposed exactly how thick the walls were—a good one and a half feet thick? Who was this guy expecting to come calling?

Then again, he'd gotten himself ankle deep in shit by reporting a false claim to the Shifter and Were Armed Tactics agency.

The short answer—*she'd* come calling.

Though she was healing much more slowly than she should, Kotara didn't worry about it. As a scientist and doctor in tune with her body, she knew a bit of food, some more rest and a shift into her alternate form would kick start her metabolism. Many didn't realize that a fast metabolism not only helped a girl keep the weight off, it also determined how quickly one healed.

The bedroom door stood wide open. Kotara's mouth watered and stomach growled from the scent of bacon and coffee that wafted in. Keen hearing picked up the sounds of the front door opening and closing, followed by footsteps and the sound of wood being gently tossed onto a hard surface.

Wood smoke joined the other enticing scents floating in the air.

Kotara swung her legs over the side of the bed and breathed a sigh of relief at the steadiness of her knees. Pain was still a present bedfellow, but considerably less than before. Moving silently, she snatched up a thick robe that lay across a chest at the foot of the bed and slipped it on over her chilled body.

She spotted her gear bag and headed directly for it and...

"Ouch! Son of a bitch! Toe, meet gear bag tucked next to that very solid chest. Gear bag, meet toe."

After wriggling each digit to make sure she hadn't damaged yet another part of her body, she knelt, disengaged the locks on the bag and checked the contents. The batteries on her comm unit and med devices were at three-quarter's power and her pistol and ammo cartridges were just as she'd left them.

Everything was there that should be, and nothing was there that shouldn't—meaning her guest hadn't slipped any surveillance transmitters into her stuff while she'd been knocked out. Well, that ruled out his trying to sabotage her mission. Any true agent or spy would have certainly taken advantage of her injuries by now.

So, if he wasn't a bad guy, then who the hell was this man who'd rescued her, stitched up some spectacularly nasty wounds with an expert hand, and then tucked her into bed naked without attempting to violate her? He'd still accused an innocent man of a ghastly crime, so what was his deal on playing nice? After all, he was responsible for setting up her brother-in-law, and something had to be done about that.

Walking into an unknown situation wasn't her most favorite thing ever, so Kotara drew on her shifter genetics and hoped they would answer her this time.

It was almost like coming home, the music that sang through her body as her lioness responded. She was nowhere near one hundred percent, but she could shift enough to elongate her claws and canines just in case she had to defend herself.

But for now, she would accept what appeared to be his good will, which meant walking out of this room unarmed.

Following her nose, Kotara headed for the kitchen and hoped her good luck held out during the coming conversation with Mr. Harrison Blue.

She came upon him in a kitchen that screamed bachelor. Not because it was small, but because it was a beautiful wreck.

The beautiful part was spacious and full of top-of-the-line, all black and stainless steel appliances, cream cabinets trimmed in sea blue, and sealed, shiny-looking stone countertops in a complimenting dark hue.

The wreck? One side of an oversized double sink looked as if the man had used every utensil, pan and bowl available just to make breakfast. Egg shells made a gooey mess where they sat on the gourmet block. Milk, flour, sugar and all the ingredients for pancakes and oatmeal were spread across the counter next to an impressive gas stove.

A giant bag of roasted coffee beans sat open next to a sleek-looking burr grinder. Her gaze homed in on a full pot of coffee. Kotara almost smiled at the fact that the man had a huge mug of the brew close at hand. Another ceramic mug sat empty nearby with three kinds of flavored creamer, all ready for use. Considering she'd dropped in quite unexpectedly, one thing was obvious—the man liked his coffee.

Keeping her distance, she poured herself a cup and sipped immediately. Her sisters called her lava mouth because she loved her brew strong, black and scalding hot.

"Mmmm, that's good." And...odd. She was on a high priority hunt, standing in the kitchen of the man she was looking for, wearing his very good smelling robe, in her bare feet. Yet, in spite of all of that, Kotara felt totally at home.

Maybe she'd knocked herself in the brain when she fell off that damn mountain during the freaking avalanche? Or maybe it was because the man who'd rescued her stood in a messy kitchen, making what she assumed was her breakfast, in nothing but a pair of flannel pajama bottoms.

She tilted her head as she took Harrison in. In addition to an amazing upper body, she was impressed to see that he was well armed—which made him smart as well as gorgeous. A double shoulder holster on a wall peg near the stove sported one exquisite handgun. The gun that should be in the empty holster slot was near his left hand on the counter. He might be flipping bacon and scrambling eggs as if this were a sunny Sunday brunch, but Harrison Blue was ready for action.

If she wanted to, she could be on him before he moved his hand from the spatula to his sidearm. But this situation warranted a little bit of tact.

"So, what's with the red plaid jammies? Are you pretending to be Santa Claus?" she asked.

Well, so much for tact.

His answer was a wink and a mega-watt smile before turning back to his current duty of *not* burning the trough of bacon he was flipping.

And how the hell did he have tanned skin in the middle of winter? Maybe he was a shifter after all? Well, part animal or not, the man was ripped and toned as if he worked out every day. Both his chest and head looked as smooth as a baby's bottom, but he was obviously a red-head, if the trimmed goatee and mustache were any indication. Kotara found herself wondering if he shaved his chest, as some men did. Even with a chrome dome, he still managed to appear tousled, red tartan jammies and all.

"Thank you for the coffee, and for hauling my frozen butt out of all that snow."

He smiled but kept his eyes on his task. "I could actually see a hint of your bag poking up out of the snow. The rest of you was buried pretty good, though."

Wow, what a lovely southern drawl. It reminded her of her brother-in-law, Lou. That particular lion shifter was as country as sweet tea and hot water cornbread, and he loved the ever loving stuffing out of her sister, Niah.

Family. It meant everything. Every year they had a huge event at Pryde Ranch. The place would be full of relatives and friends, food and fun. Kotara almost wished she were home to watch them begin the holiday preparations. Almost. But the bottom line was, she was lonely. What better way to keep her mind off of that than work?

"So," Mr. Harrison Blue said as he piled several platters with meaty-and-carb-laden goodness. "Are you ready to tell me why you were looking for me?"

Her stomach rumbled. "Can we discuss it over breakfast? I'm so hungry I could gnaw off my own leg."

Yep, tact to the rescue, without a doubt.

Settled directly across the dining table from her host, Kotara served herself as much as her plate could hold. For a while, silence reigned as they both stuffed their faces with what turned out to be a delicious meal. Finally, she slowed down enough to turn her attention to her host.

"Okay, Captain Harrison Blue—"

"Just Blue is fine."

"Okay, Blue," she said without missing a beat, though her gut wiggled around as if permission to use his nickname was a special gift. Besides, it was the holiday season, and she *loved* gifts. "You reported a crime to the Shifter and Were Armed Tactics agency. I'm here to, uh, interview you about it." Then she painted on the cheesiest smile she could muster.

And he gave her one right back as he said, "Really? Well said. Glad you used interview instead of interrogate. What else do you know about me?"

"What else?" she asked.

"When you woke up in the night, we introduced ourselves." He leaned forward, elbows on the table as he held her gaze. "As polite as we were to each other, I'm sure I didn't tell you my former rank in the Navy. So obviously you've studied me, yes?"

"I wouldn't be a good bounty hunter if I hadn't." He kept his body relaxed as he leaned forward, but his gaze screamed "danger, Will Robinson". She continued, "I'm telling you my profession because you've given me no reason not to. You've taken pretty good care of my wounds and if you wanted to hurt me, you could have done it by now."

He nodded but didn't reply.

"By the way, I'd rather do the interview thing," she said, "but I can interrogate you instead, if you want." Another piece of bacon met its end. It was perfectly crunchy, and as delicious as the coffee she chased it down with. At this rate, she'd inhaled two plates of maple syrup-covered pancakes, a bowl of oatmeal and a trough of smoked deliciousness.

Surely she would have to crawl back to bed to finish healing because her stomach would weigh more than the rest of her body by the time she got up from the table. And with the intense look Blue was giving her, shifting right now was out of the question. She could let her lioness do the talking, but she'd rather gain this man's trust than scare the ever-lovin' shit out of him after the murder he'd witnessed.

She looked up and caught Harrison's gaze again.

"Is there a reason you're smirking at me?"

"I don't usually have such an enthusiastic breakfast partner," he said. "Glad you like the food, and I'm not being passive aggressive about it. I *really* am glad."

"You know what I am. I need the calories to complete the healing process."

"So how does that work? I'm a mix of fascinated and terrified. But you haven't skinned or bitten me, so I guess that will wait until later?"

"So you want to be interrogated and bitten?" She laughed. "That takes extra energy so I'm going to need another pancake." Kotara moaned for the millionth time around her fork. Was there anything sexier than a man who gave off the vibe of both bad ass and good cook?

"Will I turn if you bite me?" he asked.

"Turn? Into what?"

"You tell me." He took a final sip from his mug and set it on the table. Sitting back with arms crossed over a sculpted chest, he appeared to wait patiently for her answer, but the zing of his own distinct energy filled the air. Someone wasn't as calm as they pretended to be.

Deliberately ignoring his question about turning, she said, "You reported the murder of a man and claimed to have seen the shifter who did it. In addition, you identified the perpetrator by name. Or at least, that's the story we were told."

"You're way prettier than the last S.W.A.T. agent I met."

The last agent? Kotara had no idea what he was talking about. Meeting another person from her agency was nowhere in the reports that Captain Johns had sent to her pride. "Do go on. Tell me what happened from beginning to end, with as much detail as you can remember."

4

*T*his woman turned into a lethal killing machine that outweighed him by at least a hundred pounds. Though he was well armed, he'd be a fool to believe he had a chance against her if she decided to stop being nice.

Just then, he caught her gaze. Eyes of such a clear amber, they brought to mind his grandpa's aged sipping whiskey. She gave an encouraging smile and tucked an errant curl behind her ear. He loved that she was a natural beauty. Her hair, thick and long, was pulled up into a messy pouf of a bun, but a few tendrils had escaped and corkscrewed around her face and nape. His fingers itched to play in it. Naturally curly locks complimented a honey-brown complexion. He shook his head to clear the wayward thoughts from his mind, but the thoughts weren't listening.

Fine. He had a story to tell anyway.

So she wanted to know about the kill he'd stumbled upon just outside of Sawtooth? It was an easy task for two reasons. One, unfortunately, he remembered the incident as if it were just yesterday, and it was never far from his dreams. And two, he had nothing to hide, so spilling his ever-lovin' guts to the beauty across the table wasn't an issue. She was law enforcement for her kind...which brought to mind another thought.

"You're the first law enforcement officer to come up here to investigate the event."

Her brow pulled down into a disbelieving frown and Blue felt a punch to his gut that seemed to come from outside of himself. From...somewhere else.

"So," he continued, "it makes me wonder, why look into it now? What took so long for someone to check it out?"

A manicured brow winged upward as she pinned him with what must be her "Uh huh, on with the story, buster" expression. A smile bloomed on his face without his permission as he took in her disgruntled bedhead, yet alluring posture. "Well, I'm just saying."

Kotara winked at him.

And something inside of him shifted in response.

He'd had his share of spiritual-type experiences all the times he thought he was going to die overseas, but considering his life wasn't in danger just now, this was a deep knowing that he couldn't explain. As a doctor, he liked facts, statistics and stuff that could be proven. Yet here he sat with a female whose species shouldn't exist...just like the memories of his last encounter should never have been formed.

With a long intake of breath, Blue began.

It was late spring, and Blue had already been working through his to-do list in preparation for the winter months. No sane person who lived this far out in the sticks waited until fall to prep for the snowy season. Sure, tourists came through here to enjoy skiing and such, but they went home after a week or two. When you made your home in a place like this, your options were a bit different.

All his hunting, butchering and curing were done, and now canning and freezing were in full swing. He'd just put away several cases of goods down in the root cellar and had run out of pickling salt. He was a planner, and a list-maker, and it annoyed him that he'd miscalculated and now had to take time to make a run to the grocer in town.

As a person who preferred a solitary existence after what had seemed like a lifetime of death and battle, Blue found that spending time outside and keeping his body in tip-top shape by using nature helped him remain grounded. To make sure he wasn't as surly when he got to town as he felt right then, he'd decided to work out first.

The meadows had looked like a river of green, and the trees were heavy with leaves. Blue headed to his favorite spot that overlooked a small lake in the forest, just off of one of the walking trails he'd cut himself.

More than a time or two, he'd had the feeling of being watched, but rather than pay attention to it, he'd done some deep breathing exercises and chalked up his twitchiness to the stress of getting his household chores done on the ridiculous timetable he'd set for himself.

His first stop in town was the little pharmacy because he'd done his pull-ups by climbing into a tree and using a strong limb. Since he'd forgotten his gloves, he'd soon sported several nasty splinters. Reminded him of an old boxing movie where the guy got in peak fighting shape using the natural landscape of what looked like the heart of Siberia come winter.

The sky turned gray, ushering in a blustery wind and the deluge from hell, but there was still plenty of light left in the day and Blue had planned to take advantage of it.

After his errands, he'd pulled off the main road headed back to his place. A set of thick, deep tire tracks stretched out before him in the mud. Someone in a large truck had been up this way, which was odd considering there were very few homes up here. The neighbors who lived a half-mile from him on either side had been spotted in town...so who?

The tire tracks continued, but Blue slammed to a halt. Something in his periphery had caused him to brake hard and pull over to the side of the road.

Out of the cab in a bound, taking his meager first-aid supplies with him, he'd run over to what turned out to be a body. A badly mutilated, shredded and quite dead body. Blood soaked the green grass beneath and was splattered across the wildflowers. Deep slashes through muscle, clear down to the white of the bone were across the chest and ribs, as if the person who'd done this wanted to make the body unrecognizable. His experience told him that it was a precision job made to look like a messy accident. And where the hell was the head? Even in war, with the beheadings and charred bodies, he'd seen nothing as gruesome as this. Nothing quite this "up close and personal".

"Holy hell," he'd whispered to himself. "What in the ever-lovin' hell could have done something like this?"

Just as Blue removed his phone from his jacket pocket to call for help, the rumble of a big engine had sounded just up the road.

He'd jumped to his feet and waved down the motorist, who'd stopped and come running.

That motorist had told him that he knew exactly what had done this—a wolf shifter. Blue had looked at the guy and bluntly asked him if he was off his medication.

"Medication? That's cute. No meds needed. I'm an agent for the Shifter and Were Armed Tactics agency, also known as S.W.A.T. It's a top secret organization, but since you've already seen this mess, there's no harm in telling you as long as you keep it to yourself."

"I'm former military. I understand protocol."

"Good."

"But I've never heard of your agency. Shifters? Weres? Sounds like too many fiction novels and late night vodka to me."

"I can prove it to you, but you can't freak out. I'm a wolf."

"Uh huh."

And then the man had changed, right there on the spot, and Blue had literally pissed his pants as the creature pounced, landing on his chest. It, he, snarled right in Blue's face as he lay on his back wondering if this would be the last breath he took.

And then, the beast simply dismounted, moved a few feet away and changed back.

"Did you do this?" Blue asked.

"No, but I know who did. I was chasing him in these parts and lost him. But his scent is all over this body."

"I don't smell anything," Blue said.

"I don't expect you to. I'm going to have to call this in."

"Uh...okay." Those were the only two words Blue could manage to form around the lump in his throat as adrenaline tore through his body.

"What's your name?"

"Blue. Harrison Blue."

"I'm John Green. My people will be here soon to take care of this. I don't want to pull a human into our mess, so get on out of here. I won't tell anyone that you were here. Remember, this is top secret."

"Got it."

And he'd hauled ass and never looked back.

When he finished relating the tale, Harrison Blue was on the verge of being physically ill. His brain was full of all the various colors he'd seen that day—the green of the grass, the gray of intestines, the red of muscle and blood, the white of nicked, exposed and broken bone.

He watched for body language and cues as he spoke, and Kotara Pryde was very good at keeping her expression relaxed and somewhat cool, though he knew he'd surprised her at least a time or two with his tale. The problem was, he had no idea what he was dealing with, no idea why she would be surprised at anything he had to say if she worked for the same agency as the guy he'd met on the side of the road that day.

The man was visibly shaken as he finished his story. The raw emotion, anger and confusion of what in the hell had happened that day took up residence in her head as if she owned those emotions, experienced them. Hated them.

They sat in silence a moment, then she asked, "Blue, you served several tours in a warzone, yes?"

As he nodded, it was obvious that he was trying to push those memories back where he kept them sealed away. To his credit, the distant expression she expected when a person was lost in their past never appeared on his face. Instead, Blue was coping, doing a series of breathing exercises right in front of her with no shame whatsoever. She was glad for that. Impressed, actually.

"Do you have PTSD?"

"After leaving the service, they gave me the all clear. Technically I don't have PTSD, but sometimes I swear I want to lose my shit at certain triggers."

"Like what?" she asked, genuinely curious.

"Well..." he paused, seeming to think about how to phrase his thoughts. "I don't do well with people running up into my personal space. I'm all right with loud noises, but I loathe big fireworks shows. They sound too much like battlefield artillery fire."

Understandable.

"I can usually handle my memories better but reliving all that blood and gore, giving a voice to it, made other instances of bullshit surface. I hate blood and gore. Hate. It."

"So is that why you were wearing your guns when I walked into the kitchen for breakfast?"

"Nope. Last night you said you were looking for me, then you passed out. These babies," he said as he patted his hardware, "had everything to do with the fact that you were a relative unknown. I had no idea how you would respond to my presence once you woke up and were in full control of your mental faculties."

"God, you sound so much like a doctor. I wonder if I sound like this all the time when I talk. All clinical and shit."

He burst out laughing. She liked what the sound did to her tummy. In fact, she kind of appreciated the little twitch behind her kneecaps, too. And just like that, the tension of his reliving of the past was broken.

"Wanna take a break?"

"Are you patronizing me?" he asked bluntly.

"Nope. I just want some ice cream. Plus I need to check in with my family before they all converge on this place."

"Holy hell, I hadn't even thought about that." Then he gave her a lopsided grin. "I've been a bit preoccupied with my current patient." He rose and crossed over to a chest freezer tucked into a corner on the other side of the kitchen. "You look good in my robe, too. And yes, I'm totally flirting with you."

Now it was her turn to laugh, but it was accompanied by a blush. She wondered what would make this man blush in turn. "Watch it, bub. I hear my type has sharp claws."

A couple of bowls from a cabinet joined what looked like an entire shopping cart worth of ice cream on the counter. Blue said, "You have very nice claws, if you don't mind my sayin' so, darlin'. You're kinda heavy, though."

Good lord, she was a goner, a total sucker for that country drawl. And those eyes. And that body. And the strength of character she sensed in him.

In an attempt to change the subject, she said, "Well, I'd like to sink my claws into…well, what have you got ice cream wise?"

"I've got butter pecan, chocolate peanut butter chunk, a coconut pina colada-like thing, cherry and walnuts with these little crispy wafer things in it, and a light raspberry sorbet. And if you don't like those, we can ride into Stanley and find whatever it is you do like."

A man who knew his way around his ice cream? Oooh, well all righty then.

"You pick," she countered.

He stared at her with an unreadable expression, but the zap of energy that came with it was unmistakable. And that expression screamed, "Me wants!"

She stood and uttered a single word.

"Uh, change clothes." Okay, that was technically three words.

And with an unexplainable lump in her throat, she turned on her heel, headed back to his bedroom, and took her flaming cheeks and screaming lioness with her.

Behind her, his words filled the growing space between them.

"Soooo, I guess I'll just dish something up, then."

he change rode Kotara hard as she did something that she didn't even think was in her vocabulary—she retreated. Her dual nature, her lioness, wanted out so she could play with the flirt she'd left in the kitchen.

She slapped her hand over her mouth with a gasp at the first purr that rumbled in her chest as an image filled her brain—her lioness wrapping herself around Blue's body, rubbing like a kitty cat sliding itself around its favorite scratching post.

Kotara loved strength—both in body and character. Harrison Blue appeared to be a strong man in every sense of the word. She couldn't think of anything more difficult for the mind, body and spirit than performing the duties of a doctor on the battlefield. Watching comrades die. Seeing innocent bystanders get caught in the crossfire. In war, everyone was a victim, both young and old. And Blue had seen and endured it all, over and over again, both physically and mentally.

Yet here he was, giving to a total stranger and asking nothing in return.

Kotara sucked in a breath and commanded the tears that threatened to fall to remain hidden. Not bothering to pretend she didn't know what was happening, she embraced how she knew things about this man that hadn't been in his file.

Mate.

Back in his room, she shucked off his robe and immediately missed his scent wrapping around her. Rather than linger, she slipped into a pair of sweats and a loose fitting t-shirt. Changing her mind, she called out.

"Hey, do I have time for a quick shower?"

She wasn't sure why she was asking. Typically, she'd just do what she wanted considering this was her interrogation...er, interview.

"Sure. Go ahead," he called. "Bathroom is off to the right. Your bag is at the foot of the bed."

Yeah, her toe still ached a bit from *finding* it.

Moments later, Kotara stood under a fall of barely lukewarm water, hoping the lack of temperature in the chilly space of the bathroom would cool her skin. Five minutes later, she gave up on achieving her goal of getting rid of the instant heat that sprang up in her body. Washing quickly, she dried off and jumped back into the sweats and t-shirt and then shrugged Blue's robe back on.

Grabbing her gear bag again, she retrieved a pair of warm socks and added it to her oh-so-fashionable wardrobe choice and then sat on the floor. She slipped the earbud for her comm unit into her ear. As soon as the connection was made, Kotara braced herself.

"Where the fuck are you!?" Derria's voice snapped through the earpiece.

"I made contact with the subject," Kotara responded calmly, though a piece of her flinched at her choice of words.

"You've been silent for three fucking days, Kotara! What the hell? You know you're supposed to check in when on a hunt! I ought to fly up there and kick your—"

"I was injured, you loudmouth. But I do appreciate your

concern." And she did. Her family meant the world to her. But she often felt like the third wheel among all her mated sisters and cousins.

"Injured? Holy hell, Tara!?"

"Girl, will you let me tell you what's up?"

With a snarly huff, Derria piped down. But Kotara knew it wouldn't last long if she drew this out, so she got right to the point. "I was making my way around the back of one of these god-forsaken mountains and fell off a cliff into some snow." She didn't bother getting into the whole 'avalanche' thing, knowing it would just make Derria and all the others worry. In the end, she was fine and there was no reason to make everyone panic.

"How bad are you hurt?"

"I'm actually good. Blue found me and—"

"Blue? Harrison Blue? And why does his name sound all breathy rolling off your tongue? He's the subject of an investigation."

Well, she couldn't ever say her cousin wasn't observant.

"So anyway, Derria," she hedged, "the subject saved my ass and dug me out. I've been recuperating at his place for the last couple of days. And since I'm where I was supposed to be anyway, no worries, right?"

"Wrong, dammit. We were worried sick about you." Koreas Pryde was now on the line and Kotara felt her heart tug at the sound of her twin's voice. "I couldn't feel you, Tara. I couldn't feel you at all. It was the scariest damn thing I've ever experienced."

"Aw, Kory, I'm fine, sweetie. Honest."

"Yeah, well I didn't miss the fact that you blew off Derria's question about the whole breathless sounding name-rolling-off-your-tongue thing."

Yeah, she wouldn't have missed that.

"Kory, I need to speak with you in private for a moment.

Derria, I'll have an update on the case shortly, but I need to ask the subject a few more questions first."

The moment Dare dropped off the line, Kotara lost it.

"Oh my god, Kotara, you're crying?" Koreas asked. "What the hell is going on? I'm flying up there right now, damn it."

"No, Kory, listen. I think Blue is my mate. But don't tell the family yet because I don't know. I want to be sure. Can you run some tests on my blood? You know which ones."

"Of course I can, you big goof. And I'll respect your boundaries in regard to keeping this all hush for now, even if I don't think you should."

"Well, just because I feel all googly about him over breakfast doesn't mean he's mate material. It could be that he's simply hot as hell and I had a head injury."

"I understand, Tara. But the whole mating thing is pretty hard to mistake. Do you have your field kit with you right now?"

"Yep. I'm poking my finger and inserting the slide into the tech now."

A few tense moments passed. As soon as Koreas said, "I've got it. Initiating sequencing." After a few moments, Kotara let out the breath she didn't realize was stuck in her lungs. Listening to the tap-tap-tap of the keyboard sounding through the earpiece as Koreas worked, Kotara waited for her sister to speak.

Finally, Koreas said, "I remember when we did this blood test for Derria. It was pretty exciting to measure her hormones and things. We finally have some kind of proven method to detect mating heat, even though we still have no idea what causes it. That part is annoying. Hey, Kotara, I have an idea, if you're up for it."

"What?"

"Do you think you can get Harrison—?"

"Blue, Kory. Just...Blue." And there she was, doing the whole sighing-his-name thing.

"Uh, okay," Koreas said. "Do you think you can get Blue to provide us a bit of his blood? I'm curious as to whether there's something about the males that push the females into heat."

"He's human, Kory."

"So. We're scientists. Since when does species matter to us when it comes to research?"

Good point.

"Fine. I'll ask him. When will you have my results?"

"After you get me a sample of Blue's blood."

"Are you blackmailing me, little sister?" Kotara demanded with a chuckle in her voice.

"Little sister by a few minutes, and damn right I'm black-mailing you."

"What if he doesn't want to?"

"Kotara Pryde, I have a feeling that he'll agree to just about anything you want right now. Remember, if it's mating heat, it goes both ways."

And if it's not, then make the most of it while you can, she told herself.

"All right, Kory. I'll check in with you later. Love you, sis."

"Kotara, are you okay?"

"Absolutely." Not.

During some delicious ice cream—correction, homemade ice cream—Kotara listened to Blue's story again. By the time they were done, she felt as if she'd been the one put through the ringer.

She'd never been super empathic before, except with Koreas. As twins, they had an unshakeable connection, just like Neesia and Niah did. At times that connection could be a pain in her ass but today, it was Blue that seemed to bleed right into her consciousness until Kotara couldn't tell what was up and what was down. As he'd told his story, deep-seated emotion that ranged from care to molten hot anger whooshed around the room, kicked her in the face, and then took off again.

It was exhausting.

Finally, she said, "Okay, I need a minute."

He sat back in his chair and sucked in an exasperated breath of his own. Then he said, "Want lunch first?"

"Lunch? We just ate breakfast."

"Uh, that was four hours ago, Kotara. We've been at it for a while."

"Four hours?!" Genuinely shocked, she immediately felt awful. Sure, she was a hunter, but four hours without a break was a long time to ask someone questions…and sit there while your brain is bombarded with everything they're *not* saying. "I'm sorry, I didn't realize."

"No problem. I was in the military, remember. I can withstand prolonged questioning."

But she felt bad none the less.

"Thanks for the offer of lunch. I think I'll have a nap. Maybe lunch later? Okay with you?"

"Absolutely," he said around a big yawn. He stood and stretched and, to her surprise, held out his hand.

She looked at it.

"What?" she asked.

"You said you need a nap. So let's go take one."

She sat stunned for a moment, then a wide grin spread across her lips.

"Fine. A nap. But that's all, mister."

"Hey, you slept naked in my bed for two days without raping me," he said as her mouth dropped open. "I think I can trust you to keep your hands to yourself, woman."

Snapping up his holsters, he said, "Since we've gotten to

know each other a bit better, I don't think I really need these. Do I?"

She burst out laughing and followed him to his room as she shook her head and said, "I think you're safe with me."

Blue tucked his hardware into the nightstand, then motioned her into bed. Since they were both dressed, or semi-dressed considering Blue was in jammie bottoms, he pulled the covers back and neatly rolled them at the foot of the bed. They climbed in and pulled up the sheet.

A moment later, Blue's feet hit the floor again. "Crap. I forgot something."

Kotara didn't want him to go.

"I need to set the fire in the front room or it'll be freezing when we get up."

"Can I help?"

"Nah. It doesn't take two to add wood to a fire. Be back in a few."

When he returned, he smelled faintly of wood smoke and pine. She inhaled deeply and let the familiar comforting scent— one that reminded her of home—lull her into a sense of peace.

He climbed into bed and she automatically turned toward the warmth of his body. Arms came around her and she instinctively nuzzled his chest, inhaling the natural clean scent of his skin. The man was everywhere—the pillow she rested her head on, the sheet over her body, the linen beneath her.

And it was the most heavenly thing she'd ever smelled in her life. It was something she wanted to pull inside of herself. Roll around in. Drown in.

Kotara sucked in a deep breath.

And then another.

"Uh, Kotara?" Blue said.

"Hmmm...?" Kotara rubbed her cheek against his pectoral muscle. She giggled when the muscle jumped, so she did it again.

"You're making some seriously sexy sounds. I only have so much self-control."

Another deep inhale. Mmmm, he smelled so good. Fingers joined the foray across his bare skin, then she remembered her manners.

"Do I have your permission to touch you, Blue? I can't seem to help myself, but I'll stop if you want me to."

"Stop? Hell no, don't stop." His words were deep, growly, and almost guttural. Kotara lifted her gaze to his face and saw that his midnight blue eyes were closed tight and his jaw was clamped as if he were trying to keep still.

Still sliding her jaw back and forth across his pectorals, she added a hand to the play and traipsed her nails across his stomach. The muscles rippled and he grunted as if she'd just punched him in the gut. The more she played with him, the stiffer he got.

Was he afraid that she might show her claws? No, that wasn't it. No fear rolled off of him. This was something else. Something he was trying to compartmentalize and keep hidden. Whatever it was held a hint of delicious darkness.

There was only one way to find out what it was.

"What's wrong, Blue? You're stiff as a board. And don't lie because I've been picking up your emotions all damn day long and I believe I'll be able to tell if you're less than truthful." She hoped.

"I..." And then he went quiet, eerily still. The man needed a minute and honestly, so did Kotara. She had a feeling why the urge to rub all over this man was so strong, but she didn't have any proof. So she wouldn't go there. Not yet, anyway.

Finally, Blue spoke. "This is going to sound totally cliché, but I feel absolutely drawn to you. It's not something I expected when I dug you out of the snow."

Tell me about it.

"I'm human. I don't even know if this is supposed to happen

or how I'm supposed to feel. My only experience with shifters has been less than wonderful."

She looked up at him again and said, "Until now?"

His bold gaze met hers. "Yes. Until now."

"Blue, I'm as drawn to you as you are to me. I'm just going on instinct here, which isn't something I typically allow myself when I'm on a mission. But I can't seem to help it, which kind of pisses me off. At the same time, I like it because it's been a long time since I've been drawn to, let alone touched a man. Any man."

Blue's burst of pride rolled off of him and lit up her insides, so Kotara decided to share a bit more.

"I'm not just a S.W.A.T. agent, by the way. I'm also a doctor. A scientist, to be exact."

"I know. Pryde Industries scientific division won an award for finding a cure to FIV in felines. I'm impressed that you run the division by yourself..."

Which wasn't true, but she sure as hell wasn't going to tell him about Koreas or any of her family. Not yet.

At her inquiring look, he said, "I looked you up while you were sleeping."

"Looked me up while..." She paused and thought on it. "You got out of bed without my noticing last night?"

"Yep. No surprise. I got up this morning without you noticing as well. You were sleeping deeply, and I made sure to leave you that way. You needed it to heal."

True, but still, it was rare that she slept so deeply as not to hear someone moving around in whatever space she was in. Even at home, with all the superior sound-proofing on the rooms and such, she could still sense when someone was two floors down, walking through the wide hallways of the giant log chalet-styled mansion that was the showpiece of Pryde Ranch.

Kotara was sure that snoring while Blue moved freely around had more to do with feeling *safe*, than anything else.

"So, tell me why you're holding yourself all stiff. If we're drawn to each other, do you really care that I'm not fully human?" she asked and forced herself not to hold her breath as she waited for an answer.

It didn't matter that she was a self-made millionaire, ran businesses with her family, and was a bad ass hunter. Kotara didn't care whether this was a biological reaction or not—something about Blue pulled at her insides. And in spite of her independent nature, it would hurt if he rejected her because of how she'd been born.

In the end, she wanted him. Period.

"No, I don't care if you're not fully human, Kotara. I know you're strong, even if you are still healing. But I don't want to hurt you, physically or in any other way."

"So kiss me instead," she whispered against his skin.

With a hungry groan, Blue eased his fingers into the hair at her nape. It seemed as if time slowed down as his mouth eased towards hers. By the time their lips touched, she was so ready for it that her body trembled.

It was a gentle meeting of mouths, yet Kotara felt Blue's restraint. He nipped and nibbled and teased until she grabbed his sexy bald head and said, "Let go. Please."

Blue shuddered and let out a shaky exhale.

Next was a blur of movement and she found herself on her back with an aroused Harrison Blue taking her mouth with a need that rivaled her own.

Fingers sank into her hair, positioned her head the way he wanted. Licked at her mouth. Moaned against her neck. Suckled the spot right below her ear. Devoured her mouth as if she were his favorite taffy.

"Mmmm, I like that," she whispered. "I think I could get addicted to kissing you."

"Yeah? Then have a little more."

And she did. She kissed him until she was needy and writhing and wet and wanton.

He broke the delicious contact, rolled to his back and took her with him as he sucked in breath after breath.

"Hey, what gives?" she snapped, wanting her new favorite toy back where it had been moments ago—namely him on top of her, kissing the wind out of her sails.

"Nap time," he said. "You need it." Oooh, he oozed alpha from his very pores, and it tripped her not-often-flipped submissive switch.

"Are you seriously telling me what to do right now, Blue?"

"I am. Nap while I get myself under control."

Well, shit.

Kotara found herself rolling over with a huff as she gave him her back, and then sighed at the markedly stiff cock pressed against the crease of her butt. "I'm never going to get to sleep with your erection teasing me from behind."

"I'm not even going to tell you what your words made me think just now. I'm supposed to be behaving."

"I thought I was the one who's supposed to be behaving," she shot back, but the chuckle in her voice tipped her hand that she was trying unsuccessfully to be mad.

"Fine. Lay back and let me check your wounds." He was clinical in his removal of her bandages, followed by poking and prodding. "These are almost completely healed. I don't even think you'll have a scar.

"So does that mean we can play a bit more?"

"Come here, woman." He gathered her into his arms and settled his chin on the top of her head. When she grumbled, he said, "Count sheep or something."

"Fine," she said. "One. Two…"

She made it to seven.

Blue still felt Kotara's kiss clear down to his toes. In fact, it *curled* those toes. The dark side of him clawed to get out. The need rode him hard to mark and bite, not in anger or rage, but in pure, unadulterated lust. He wanted to wrap his hand in her hair and pull her head back to expose her neck. To run his blunt nails down her back, over her perfect ass and down the back of her thighs with just enough force to sting but not break the skin.

He wanted to make her his. And it made no sense whatsoever to need a woman with such blinding intensity from out of nowhere.

Blue's natural dominance was something he typically kept leashed, but this thing with his little S.W.A.T. agent was... primal. Some women were afraid of a man who enjoyed things hard and rough. He had a feeling Kotara wasn't one of those women, but he couldn't be sure.

Could he?

She was sound asleep now. He should get up and go do something, *anything* other than lie here with his arms wrapped around her.

The heat of her skin scalded his bare chest, even through her t-shirt. It was as if he'd become attuned to her from moment one. It was downright unsettling given he hadn't had this connection to anyone, patient or fellow soldier, in all his years as a doctor.

Yep, he should get up.

But he needed to hold her for just a few more minutes. Why couldn't he let himself have this, even if just for a little while?

"Because you're damaged goods, and you know it," he whispered to himself, so as not to wake Kotara. Then his own voice sounded in his head.

Damaged? Says who? And who made the rule that you don't deserve love, or that you aren't allowed to have it?

How many times had his therapist told him that since

returning stateside? How many times had he sat and meditated on loving himself, healing the damage to his psyche from war? Focused on what he wanted, rather than what he didn't want in hopes of attracting it into his life? Maybe those post-combat counseling sessions had done him some good after all because he sure had a piece of perfection right here, right now.

Nose buried in her soft, natural curls, Blue did something he hadn't done in the middle of the day for as long as he could remember—he fell asleep. And his dreams were of a beautiful, tawny-eyed beauty who offered herself to him with utter and complete trust. And when he hesitated in taking her, she took him instead.

6

*W*hen Kotara awoke, not only was she fully healed, but she found herself sprawled across the chest of a snoring Blue. Two reasons to be ridiculously happy. She giggled at how her whole body rose and fell with each one of his deep breaths. He really was a magnificent specimen of a human male—stocky with a wide chest, serious guns for biceps and, if the growing ridge beneath her stomach was any indication, an impressive package.

"I can't believe I slept so long in the middle of the day."

The words rumbled beneath her ear as he came awake with an almost lion-like yawn. Maybe he was a shif... Nah. Impossible. If he was a shifter, he wouldn't have been so shocked at discovering one in town during that whole murdering incident.

Blue sat up and took her with him. "Get dressed."

She stretched and yawned. "No wanna."

"It should be illegal to be so cute, Kotara."

"Cute? I turn into a three-hundred-plus pound lioness with three-inch canines, and you're calling me cute?"

"Absolutely. Especially when you snore."

"I do not snore!" All she could do was shake her head. The

man was adorable in a pain-in-the-ass kind of way. "So, where to?"

"To get whatever vehicle you drove to get here. Leave it too long this time of year and the next time you head to the other side of the mountain, you might not be able to find it."

"It snows that much up here?"

"First avalanche advisory was early November. It'll be Christmas soon and it just gets nastier. Hey, what's wrong?"

Though she knew her face held no expression, at the mention of Christmas, she'd crumpled in on herself as sadness flared through her heart. Kotara hadn't meant to let her emotions get the best of her but the holiday season was fully upon them, and there was no ignoring the fact that she was the only one without a mate now. And she was away from home to boot.

Her entire immediate family was mated. Neesia and Jason. Niah and Lou. Koreas and Austin. Even Austin's brother, Aaron James, was mated to a lovely jaguar named Reya.

Sigh.

The sizzling chemistry between Blue and herself didn't mean he was her mate any more than he was Santa Claus... unless Santa was ridiculously hot, loved bacon, and had a wicked sense of humor. He might just be her very own jolly Saint Nick.

Her chuckle drew Blue's eye.

"How do you go from giving me the stink eye for nudging you to get up, to as sad as sad can be, to laughing? And all without a word?"

"I'm a scientist. We're quirky like that."

Except when it came to other people's mating. In the case of her sister's brush with the dreaded, yet anticipated mating heat, Kotara had convinced her bone-headed twin that Austin James, a human, was indeed hers for the taking. In that case, she hadn't needed scientific evidence. The signs had all been there, not to mention Kory and Austin's insane attraction for one another.

And the pheromones that made the entire household instantly horny.

Nope. Can't forget the blasted pheromones.

But in her own case, nothing less than proof would do. She'd rather keep her expectations to nil than convince herself that Blue was hers, only to learn later that he really wasn't.

And where the hell was Koreas with the results of her blood test, anyway? Oh yeah, blackmail—her results in exchange for a bit of Blue's blood. Kotara thought proudly that her sister could sure be a real piece of work.

The sensation of fingers traipsing up her arm pulled her out of her current train of thought. Blue. The man's touch was electric. It was damn ridiculous the way he made her feel with no effort. She looked up into his midnight blue gaze and was snared. There was no other way to describe it.

"So, may I kiss you again?" he asked.

She swallowed. The image of a cartoon character gulping in surprise with big googly eyes filled her head. All Kotara could do was nod as anticipation bloomed deep in her belly.

As she sat on the edge of Blue's bed, the man knelt in front of her. Suddenly she was falling—into his kiss. Into his caress. Into what felt like the very center of the man himself.

He moved into her personal space and she inhaled deeply, letting his scent settle into her lungs. As the body moved air into the blood through the little sacs in the lungs, Blue seemed to slide right into her bloodstream. The more he touched her, tasted her, the more he filled her senses.

And then his lips were pressed to hers. Kotara readily opened to him and reveled in his taste on her tongue. Blue's fingers sank into the thick curls at the same time he deepened the contact. Fingers tightened and then pulled—he seemed to do that each time their lips met...and she liked it.

In between kisses, he rubbed his face along hers.

And Kotara was snared in that moment. Heat gathered low in her belly and radiated into her sex. At this rate, she sped towards arousal until she was damp with need in no time flat. She wanted Blue. Wanted him inside of her, joining with her in sating the most basic of needs.

She opened her mouth to ask him for what she needed. To demand that he strip her naked and have his delicious way with her. Just as she began to form the words, a little piece of Blue took up residence in the smallest part of her head, just out of reach. She was so stunned, she froze.

"You okay? I wasn't too rough with that kiss, was I?"

"Oh god no." She was breathless, stirred and needy. Blue looked as shaken as she was. He backed off and in the next moment, was clear across the room. Kotara blinked. The man was nowhere near as fast as her, but still had a speed and grace that made no sense for a human.

Her mouth fell open. "Blue, are you a shifter?"

He looked over his shoulder with genuine confusion. "Me? No. I'd never heard of shifters until that whole man-turned-wolf, post-evisceration thing."

Interesting.

Dressed for the weather, they were out the door ten minutes later.

Blue navigated the ice and snow covered terrain expertly on a snow mobile made for two. Considering he was single, Kotara found herself wondering who he'd been thinking of when he'd purchased the thing. For all she knew, the man had a girlfriend somewhere. Just as the thought cleared her brain, his head swiveled her way and he pinned her with a glare.

"What?" she asked, a bit alarmed.

But he only shook his head and said, "Nothing. I think I'm just tired...or nuts." But he wouldn't say another word.

Banishing the thoughts from her mind, she took in the land

around her as they moved through trees, over trails, up hills and over dales. This was some seriously pretty country...but it wasn't Pryde Ranch.

No matter how much she felt like the oddball out, family was everything. And she had to admit that the thought was driven home every time she left on a hunt for S.W.A.T. or a business trip for Pryde Industries. And even now, as she sat behind a man who rang her bell, she still missed home.

"What's wrong?" Blue asked, engaging the audio system in the helmets they wore.

She tapped the side of her headgear to engage the mic and lied through her teeth. "Nothing. I'm fine. Just a little tired is all. I need to shift, too. I'm all healed now, but I'm just now getting enough energy to pull it off."

"It takes energy to shift?" he asked.

"Yep. Quite a bit of it, actually."

"Is that why you eat so much?" She tried to poke him in the ribs through his thick ski jacket and smiled when he laughed at her.

"Give me the skinny on shifter stuff. So far, you've avoided every question I've asked you."

"Have not," she protested, but knew she'd done exactly that.

"So, biting? Not biting? Turning? Full moon crazy stuff? What?"

She was laughing, genuinely cracking up.

"Uh, dude, this is nothing like the movies, okay?"

"I happen to like the movies. Well, most of the time. Can't blame a guy for being curious given my limited experience with your kind."

Her eyebrows crashed together at the words "your kind".

"Wait, that didn't come out right. What I meant to say was that the only shifter I've ever met scared the shit out of me and claimed another shifter killed a long-time member of the local community here."

"Can't blame you for being a little skittish, Blue. Honestly."

"But I'm not skittish around you, and I'd like to understand that as well."

"You have a problem *not* being skittish around me?"

"Not at all. In fact, I think I like it. Now, spill the beans already. What am I getting into?"

"Getting into?"

"Oh yes, darlin'. Definitely getting into." He glanced back at her just long enough for her to catch the gleam in his eye. It set off a sizzling chain reaction that traveled from the spot where the hair stood up on the back of her neck, clear down to her little pinky toes.

Clearing her throat once, then again for good measure, Kotara gave him a history lesson in shifter genetics. And to her great pleasure, he looked at it like any peer would—as a physical and physiological phenomenon rather than something freaky or weird.

She left out details about her family, hoping against hope that Koreas had good news. Some things just weren't shared with a person who wasn't a mate.

Dear Santa, please, please let this gorgeous, generous man be my present this holiday season...

Blue unhitched the trailer attached to the snowmobile and connected it to the hitch on the back of Kotara's monster truck. Once all was secured, he drove the snowmobile up onto the transport.

Since he knew the roads and trails much better than she did, Kotara asked him to drive. In no time, they were headed back to Casa de Blue.

The ride back was filled with a mix of comfortable silence and the kind of chit-chat that happens when two people are getting to know each other. In the middle of explaining why disco music and roller skates should make a comeback, Kotara's comm unit buzzed.

"I don't mean to be rude, but I need to take this. It's my sister."

At his nod, Kotara keyed in her access code and sent a message letting Koreas know she was not alone. An acknowledgement came through followed by a note that made Kotara bite her lip to keep her mouth from falling open.

"*Your blood shows elevated levels of mating hormone! I couldn't keep you in suspense. Now, what are you going to do about it? Does he know? And I still want that blood sample of his.*"

Kotara fingers flew over the touchscreen as she typed her reply. "*Oh my god, really? Kory, I wish I could tell you what I'm dealing with. I asked him point blank if he was a shifter because of the way he moves, and he's not. But there's something about him I can't pin down.*"

Until recently, it had always been their experience that shifters couldn't tell one of their kind from a human unless that particular shifter had gone rogue. Then all of their lives had changed when Derria had chased one of her mates, Kerr, to his home in the North Carolina mountains.

There she'd met the two men who were now both hers—Lakota Phillips, a gentleman jaguar shifter, and Kerr, a grumpy but gorgeous wolf.

While hunting, Dare had suddenly developed the ability to literally sniff out others of their kind, rogue or not. In fact, that whole area where Lakota and Kerr were born was full of felines, wolves and psychics that could not only discern if they were hanging out with other paranormals, but could even nail down what kind of para they were dealing with. The question in Kotara's head was, why there but nowhere else? Or at least nowhere else that they knew of.

Since returning home to Wyoming, Derria's new instinct

was still firmly in place. Thanks to that little debacle of a bounty hunt, Pryde Industries had more medical mysteries to solve than they could shake a stick at. If there was one thing that Kotara and Koreas Pryde were good at, it was chasing down scientific weirdness.

"By the way, is Derria's super Spidey sense wearing off yet?" Kotara typed.

"Nope. I think it has to do with her mating with someone from that part of the country. It's like she's taken on some of their traits or something."

"Interesting. Well, I have some information to share. As soon as we get back to Blue's place, I'll call in with a situation report."

"Got it. Congratulations, though, Tara. Mating is awesome."

"Thanks, Kory. I love you, sis."

"Back at you. Be careful and we'll see you soon?"

"Yep."

Even as the thought of going home cleared the ether of her mind, Kotara already dreaded leaving this place because there was no guarantee she would be leaving with her mate. Or alone.

"All right, time to report in," Kotara said as she hauled her gear bag to the kitchen and pulled out an electronic notebook. As she set up her tech on the dining table, Blue came up behind her and slid warm hands over her back and around to her belly. Soon, she was wrapped up in his embrace and her body immediately warmed. Her hair was up in its typical poufy bun, which gave the man plenty of room to play with several sensitive areas all at once.

As a soft kiss landed on the back of her neck, Kotara shivered. It wasn't just her body's reaction to Blue that blew her mind, but her *mind's* reaction to him. It was like hanging out with an old friend, as if he'd always been there rather than just arriving in her life mere days ago.

The question was, did he feel the same? She'd grown up learning about mates and the life of a part-woman, part-lion. This man would know nothing about what to expect. And unfortunately, what she knew of humans was that they typically resisted what they didn't understand, no matter how well-meaning and open-minded.

Sigh.

"You can worry about whatever is on your mind right now, or you can kiss me," Blue whispered in her ear and she giggled.

"That tickles," she said, easing away from him.

But with every backward step she took, he took a forward step until her back ended up flush against a wall next to that oh-so-lovely freezer she knew was full of homemade ice cream.

"Ice cream or me?" Blue asked.

"Damn, that's hard. Can't I have both?"

Kotara eased her arms around Blue's neck and she could swear his eyes literally sparkled as he lowered his head and kissed her.

His taste rushed through her and infused her head, then streaked through the rest of her body like a shot of adrenaline. So unique and delicious was that kiss, Kotara leaned in for more. Sweet and seeking became wild and wanton. Blue pressed fully against her, moaning into her mouth as she was flattened against the wall. The man had her so fully surrounded, she couldn't move...and didn't want to. He bent until he could loop his arms behind her thighs, and then lifted her clean off the floor. Kotara's knees were in the crooks of his elbows, legs spread wide as he pressed his swelling cock flush against her warming center.

Blue ground until she was simply so close to coming, even her lion roared in her ears. And then they were moving together.

Grinding.

Growling.

Moaning.

Begging.

"Oh yes, I want it. Want you," she breathed in between nips and licks of his talented tongue against hers. She inhaled his scent at the crook of his neck, then bit that same spot. Blue hissed and did a rolling-rocking motion that made her imagine him sliding deep into her body, where she wanted him most.

"And I want to give it to you. Do we have time, Tara?"

"Time? Time for...? Aw, hell. I totally forgot about calling home."

"Just that fast, woman?"

"Yes, just that fast. Your fault." Then he damn near preened. "Good grief, save me from the egos of men."

He dropped a quick peck on her lips then lowered her to the floor.

With a huff that sounded as frustrated as she truly was, she headed back to the table and started the con call with Blue seated right next to her.

The screen lit up and she entered her access codes. The next thing she saw were the faces of her entire family, which was unusual.

S.W.A.T. kept close tabs on lion shifters because they were known to aggressively defend their territory for as much as a hundred miles, if not kept in check. To keep their family safe and under less scrutiny, S.W.A.T. believed there were only two Pryde sisters, Neesia and Kotara. No one, *no one*, outside of family knew there were four bad ass African lionesses, and their equally dangerous mates, roaming the plains of Wyoming.

Even the human scientists who worked in the Labyrinth, who knew all of the Pryde family, had no knowledge of S.W.A.T. or that the Prydes moonlighted as bounty hunters.

The fact that Koreas knew to expect a call for a sit rep, and the *entire* family was present meant that the beans had already been spilled and her nosey pride wanted to get a peek at her possible mate.

After introductions were made, rather than wait for her family to start asking questions, Kotara launched right into the issue at hand—Blue hadn't set up Kerr. He was innocent.

"We've got a bit of an urgent situation here, guys. I need Kerr to be fully onscreen. I can only see part of him with all of you gathered around."

A moment later, the handsome face of Kerr Blackstone, grumpy wolf extraordinaire, filled the screen.

"Blue, look carefully at the image that is coming up on the screen. Is this the man you saw commit the crime?"

Without hesitation, Blue said, "No. Like I told you before, I didn't see who committed the crime."

The line went quiet and Kotara knew they all reeled with this new information, just as she had when she'd first heard it.

"Go on," she encouraged.

"The guy who came along right after I found the body said he'd been chasing someone through these parts. He gave me a description and said he knew for sure who'd killed the victim."

Derria jumped into the conversation. "Then why did you report the crime to S.W.A.T. as if you'd seen who'd done it?"

"I didn't report any crime," Blue snapped. Kotara couldn't blame him. What honorable man would appreciate being accused of something he hadn't done? "After coming across the corpse, I didn't know what to do or who to call. The other S.W.A.T. agent said he'd handle it, so after I got home, I just kept my mouth shut and ordered extra ammo in case one of those things," he looked up at a scowling Kotara. "I mean, another shifter came calling."

"What else did the other man say? The one who claimed he knew who'd killed the human?" Jason asked.

"Said the murderer's name was Kerr Blackstone and that he

needed to call it in. I have to admit, I didn't believe the whole shifter thing until..." Blue paused a second and looked toward Kotara. She nodded, encouraging him to go ahead and spill it all.

"Well, the guy said he was an agent for a group called S.W.A.T. and he asked me if I saw the dead man shift before he died. He wanted to know if he'd said anything to me before he lost consciousness. I didn't answer. Instead, I just looked up at him confused, because honestly, I was confused. Then he...changed."

"Shifted? Right in front of you?" Niah asked.

"Yep. Turned into the biggest snarly wolf I ever saw."

"How did you know he wouldn't attack you?" Jason asked.

"I didn't. I may not be in the Navy anymore, but I'm certainly not stupid. After getting out of the military, I maintained my concealed carry license. The .45 caliber pistol I keep on me ensured I'd have at least a fighting chance if the wolf decided to try to tear my throat out."

Neesia summed it up neatly. "Bottom line is, people, we have a very good impersonator on our hands. First, whoever this bastard is pretended to be an agent of ours as he talked with Blue. Second, our mystery man called in the murder to S.W.A.T. claiming to be Blue while blaming Kerr. And our agency, one of the most sophisticated and competent in the world, missed all of this." Neesia sounded pretty pissed, which was understandable because Kotara was pretty pissed herself.

"So now what?" Kotara asked. "We have no way of knowing—"

"Wait. Blue, what did the man look like who gave you Kerr's name?" Neesia asked.

"In which form," he asked. Smart man. Very, very smart.

"Human," the entire table yelled all at once.

"Hey, don't start hollering at Blue," Kotara snapped. "He's trying to help us, dammit."

He whispered, "You don't need to protect me from them, but I must admit, it's pretty sexy when you get all riled up."

Her cheeks immediately felt as if they'd been lit on fire... especially after he leaned in and nipped her on the jaw. In front of everyone.

Now the silence was one of thrilled expectancy rather than outrage.

"Uh, Tara?" Neesia spoke into the pin-drop quiet of the moment. "Is there something we should know?"

There was no way of wiping the damn grin off of Blue's face any more than she could reach through the screen and smack her sisters, who were all cheesing equally as much as Blue.

"Can we just get back to business, please?" she grumbled.

As Blue gave the description of the man who'd caused him to piss his pants when he'd turned into a wolf, Kerr and Lakota both shot to their feet with equal amounts of cussing and threats.

"Uh, I assume you guys recognize the description Blue just gave?" Niah asked.

Kerr spoke up while Lakota growled low in his throat and sounded like the very dangerous jaguar that he was. "We recognize it all right. Same idiot who was the mastermind of a recent kidnapping. He's a Blackstone, and as quiet as it's kept, he's related to one of the council members of my former pack."

"But your pack was banished and separated from the others," Derria pointed out.

Kerr pinned his mate with a hard glare. "Guess blood is thicker than water."

"So now what?" Niah asked in her typical calm, logical timbre.

"We give the details to Captain Johns and let her run it down. Our job was to find Harrison, get some details on the incident he supposedly reported and get out. So technically,

Tara is done with her mission, and just in time to get home for Christmas. Blue?" Neesia asked.

"Ma'am?"

"If you don't have plans to visit your family during the holidays, you're more than welcome to accompany Kotara home. We would love to meet you."

"Yeah and feed you until you pass out or die," Koreas whispered, but not quite quiet enough for a room full of people with super sensitive hearing.

Neesia threw a balled up piece of paper at Koreas's head while the rest of the family quietly chuckled, looked up at the ceiling or whistled little tunes that said they knew better than to talk just then. After all, Koreas was right—Neesia Pryde took great care of her family and loved to feed them. Only their genetics kept them from turning into stuffed, overweight turkeys themselves.

"Thank you kindly for the invitation, Ms. Neesia."

Kotara turned and regarded him carefully. A very polite "thank you for the invitation" was not the same as "yes, I'll be there", and far less than a commitment.

"Tara, when are you coming home?" Koreas asked.

She felt Blue stiffen beside her, but there was nothing she could do about what she was going to say next.

"I'll head out day after tomorrow. I'd like to spend a day with Blue convincing him to come home with me."

7

*A*fter the call, she retreated to Blue's bedroom to put her gear bag back at the foot of the bed, where it had been since she'd landed in the Sawtooth Mountains. She felt Blue come in from the kitchen before she saw him. Brilliant and smart was the man who brought a girl butter pecan ice cream after such a stressful, yet relieving conference call.

She spooned up a bit and moaned. It was so, so good. A few bites into the creamy deliciousness, Kotara remembered something else she needed to do.

She set the napkin Blue had given her on top of the sturdy wooden chest she'd sat down on and her bowl followed, still half-full.

"You know I'm a scientist, right?"

"Of course." Blue licked his spoon and winked at her.

"Well, I have an unusual request. My twin and I are on the trail of figuring out how mating heat works."

"Mating what?"

"Mating heat. It's a biological reaction we have to a person who has the genetic predisposition to mate with us. My sisters are all mated to other lions, except for my twin. She's mated to a human."

"Really?" His beautiful deep blue eyes were round as saucers, but she sensed a mix of both fascination and something less than fear, but more than a passing concern.

"Yes, really. I think part of why we're so in tune with each other, and attracted to each other, is because we're mates. Or we can be if it's something you can accept." She sucked in a deep breath and looked him straight in the eye without wavering, no matter how much her stomach jumped around beneath the skin. "I believe you're mine and I'm yours...but the question is, why? Would you mind giving a sample of a drop or two of blood so we can run some tests for our research?"

"Tests? What kind of tests?"

"Hormone levels and the like."

"Hormones? So you think I'm on my period?"

A laugh burst out of her chest before she could stop it. It was pure unadulterated joy at the snark and humor of this man. Yep, they were made for each other all right. They should get t-shirts that said, "Snark One" and "Snark Two".

He reached out and pulled her into his embrace, then tickled her until she cried for mercy. Between giggles, trying to catch her breath, and twisting and kicking, Kotara had to rely on her shifter genetics to actually get loose. Wow, the man was strong. When she was finally free, she danced out of reach and tossed a few choice words his way.

"You kiss your sisters with that dirty mouth?" he teased.

"I sure as hell do."

"Good. Glad you're this way all the time. Or I'm assuming you are. Now, about the whole period thing."

"As you know, Doctor Blue, men and women secrete different kinds of hormones. We're sure it plays a part in mating heat—"

"Heat? I like that word."

"I bet you do, cowboy. So anyway, we've never taken a sample of blood from the male mates and we're trying to learn if that's where we're coming up short in figuring this out."

"Makes sense. So, how do we do this blood thing? I don't have the proper equipment here."

"No worries. I have what we need. I only need a few drops, and I have some tech that's integrated into my field med unit."

"Sounds high tech. Why are you telling me about it?"

"Because you're mine."

His grin lit up his eyes like fireworks on New Year's Day. "I'll ask about that field med thing...after."

"After? After what?" Then she practically purred as her lioness rolled around deep in her consciousness, tongue lolling as if she were completely sated. But Kotara wasn't sated at all. She wasn't sure she ever would be again.

This wasn't just sex. This was deeper, as in down-to-the-marrow-of-your-bones deep. Blue seemed to touch every part of her all at once. When he slid his fingertips along her biceps, warmth sank beneath her skin, set her muscles a-tingle, and infused her blood.

This man was like a shot of aged whiskey laced with his own special brand of liquid horny. Honey spilled from her channel as her sex caught fire, along with the rest of her.

"It's been a long time since I've been this turned on with a woman," he whispered into her ear. "Actually, I don't think I've ever been this far gone. What have you done to me?"

"When I figure it out, I'll let you know. In the meantime," she panted, then lost her train of thought as Blue kissed a trail across her hip, and then inhaled deeply.

It was such a primal thing to do, as if he serenaded her with nothing but the wafting of breath over her skin.

"Damn, I love the way you smell, Kotara. Is this normal for a human to be this attracted to a shifter? Or is it part of the mating heat thing?"

Now that was a question she should ask her sister, Koreas, or her sister-in-law, Reya. They'd both mated humans and this was just so unexpected and what if he didn't want to…?

The flared head of Blue's cock pressed inside, just past the strong ring of muscles at her entrance.

Then he paused.

"Hey, come back here," Blue demanded with a whisper.

"Huh?"

"You slipped away for a moment. If I can't keep your attention, then I'm not doing it right."

"Oh, you're definitely doing it right, Blue."

Blue's cock was perfect—just long and thick enough to make her feel the stretch of her honeyed walls, but not so big that she couldn't take him deep. Sure, she enjoyed the occasional rough play…okay, fine, she enjoyed rough play period. But that didn't mean she wanted her pussy to feel as if she were being split apart. In that case, she'd rather masturbate and get herself off.

No, this man was well-endowed, but he knew exactly how to work with what he had.

She swiveled her hips, trying to take him deeper, but he simply held her gaze as a mix of pleasure and frustration wrapped around her consciousness. And she knew he was holding back.

"Oh no you don't," she snarled.

His eyes widened, but it wasn't fear. It was a challenge.

And she was up for it.

"Don't you dare hold back, Harrison Daniel Blue."

"Did you just say my whole name, woman?"

"I sure as hell did."

"Well, in that case, tell me how you want it, baby."

"Hard. Fast."

"Rough?"

"Hell yes," she panted.

Something seemed to unravel from around him in that moment. It was as if he'd wrapped himself up in a coil of rope for ages and was just now figuring out how to unwind it.

A whispered, "Oh thank god," was followed by Blue sinking balls deep, then deeper still as he rode. The pleasure sank into her muscles, down to the bone until she felt as if she was drowning in it.

"Tara, I feel you. I can actually *feel* how good this is for you."

She was streaking toward orgasm and let her emotional and psychological walls crumble and fall until her entire being was wide open. There was no desire to keep any of herself separate from Blue.

"Holy fuck! That's hot. It's like your mind is naked to me," he gasped.

Because it *was* naked to him.

"Ah, I see," he said, just before he angled her just the way she liked it. There was a lot to be said for the whole mind-meld mating thing. His strokes were long, then shallow digs that left her panting. And when she was sure she couldn't take anymore, he flipped her over and dove in from behind.

Sweat gathered at the base of her spine and formed rivulets down the backs of her thighs where his legs rubbed sensually against hers. A hand wrapped in her hair and pulled her back hard against him, even as he surged forward.

Her orgasm ran toward her like a pack of mustangs, wild and unrestrained. And she welcomed it with open arms as her man pushed her toward it. Muscles went taut. Scalp tingled. Toes curled. And Kotara yelled her pleasure to the rafters.

Blue's cock pulsed deep inside her soaked channel as he joined her in the ultimate, most intimate of expressions, complete with a mind altering climax.

It was as if he were made just for her, and she guessed he

was. And true to his word, he allowed Kotara to take just a few drops of his blood...after.

When she woke from a post-sex coma, she rolled over and immediately missed Blue's body warmth. She closed her eyes again and listened. He wasn't in the house, but something delicious wafted on the air that made it clear she'd slept so hard, he'd not only gotten out of bed without disturbing her again, but he'd made dinner, too.

"Some bounty hunter you are," she grumbled to herself. Sitting up, she then noticed that the little message indicator light on the comm unit she'd left on the nightstand was flashing.

The message from Kory simply said, "Call me right away."

Since Blue wasn't in, she slipped in a pair of earbuds and initiated a voice-to-voice call. Koreas practically screeched with delight as she said, "I have some interesting news. Your guy has recessive shifter genes."

"What?!"

"Yep. You mentioned to way he moves. The way he smells. Well, it may have something to do with why he seems to move faster than a typical human, as well as your attraction to him. He's emitting hormones that he probably doesn't know he has."

Holy cock-a-doodle on a cracker!

"This is huge, Tara! I really can't wait to meet him now. I'm wondering if we'll all have the typical reaction to your mating since he has..."

"We're not mated, Kory. I've explained it to him, but he hasn't agreed."

"What do you mean he hasn't agreed?"

"Just what I said. We get along well enough, but we haven't discussed where this is going."

"So he's not coming home with you to meet us?"

"I don't know, sis. I really don't. I grew up knowing who and what I am. And you must admit, his introduction to our world was less than stellar. I don't expect him to just accept all of this because I say so, Kory."

"Kotara, please don't cry."

"I'm not crying, damn it."

"I'd be crying if it were me. And I hear you sniffing and snotting and trying not to bawl. I'd think you were crazy if you weren't concerned about it."

And then Blue was there in her head. He'd obviously been close enough to feel her sadness because a second later, he not only bulldozed into her emotions, but he flew through the door. Just like a true mate would.

"Baby, what's wrong? What's going on?"

She looked up and her mouth fell open. The man was covered with sweat and bare-chested in a pair of stretchy pants that left absolutely nothing to the imagination.

"I was outside working out when I felt you...crack. Like something inside you was broken or wrong. What the hell, Kotara?"

"Koreas, I'll call you later."

"Listen, Kotara, just talk to him," her sister said.

"I will. See you soon."

"Did your sister upset you, baby?"

"Nah. It was something else."

"Tell me."

When she just looked up at him with tears in her eyes, he walked over to the bed, picked her up and headed for the bathroom.

"What is your deal with picking me up and carrying me around?"

"I like it. Have a problem with that?"

"No, not really. Was just wondering."

"Good. Shower with me so I can warm up while you tell me what's wrong."

He stripped her with efficiency and set her into the over-sized stall.

"Okay, spill it."

"Wash my back first," she said.

The second his hands touched her skin, they both went up in flames. Her pain was forgotten, his worry receded. Instead, they explored each other's bodies until the heat of the shower was nothing compared to the scorching need they had for each other.

Kotara needed him to mark her, to take her like a lion takes its mate. And given his shifter genetics, which she and Koreas agreed to keep to themselves for now, he seemed to know exactly what to do.

"Hands on the tile," he said. "Bend at the waist."

"Hurry. Please."

"Say it again," he whispered against her ear.

"Please."

With that, he sank into her drenched heat and slid home in three strokes. Once seated, he gave her exactly what she needed, even if he had no idea why.

Blue zeroed in on the super-sensitive patch of skin where neck met shoulder. The moment his lips covered it and he sucked deeply, she knew he would leave a bruise. But when his teeth sank into that spot, Kotara's knees went out from under her and she came on the spot, even as Blue held her on her feet.

As she pulsed around him, he joined her with a shout to the rafters.

8

"*B*lue, are you coming home to meet my family?"

"I don't know. I'm having a tough time reconciling this shifter-to-human thing. This is a bit fast for me, Kotara."

"You care that I'm a shifter?" she asked, incredulous.

"Not at all. It's just that you've spent your whole life understanding that when you met a man of mating material, it's normal to make a decision on the spot. This is new to me."

"I understand that. To put your mind at ease, we may be in mating heat right now, but the bond doesn't solidify unless both parties want it. I would never tie someone to me who didn't want me back."

"It's not that I don't want you, Tara. It's just that…"

Suddenly, it was all right there at the forefront of his mind. He was struggling with whether he was worthy of her or not. It was a holdover from his military days—the thought that his hands were so bloody that he didn't deserve love.

"You know," he spoke into the darkness of his bedroom, "I really thought I was past all this. Past the worry and doubt about who I am, the things I've done. I'm a pretty level-headed guy, but I guess I have this little part of me that wonders whether I can truly make someone happy."

"I don't need you to make me happy. I already love and like myself. It's a matter of whether you're willing to take a chance."

He pulled her in tighter into his embrace as if he were trying to imprint himself onto her skin, yet inside he seemed to distance himself at the same time. It was…odd.

"We don't have to stay in Wyoming all the time," she said. "My sister, Kory, goes with her guy to his family's home as often as he and his brothers come to ours. We're a family, and we enjoy being together."

Harrison Blue had never experienced anything like what she was talking about. Couldn't find a thread of experience to relate. He'd grown up in his grandparent's care, if you could call it that. Born to his mother later in life, his grandparents were damn near ancient by the time he'd come along. Neither of them had relished taking care of a small boy during the years they should have been relaxing and enjoying their golden years. Not wanting to be a burden, he'd joined the military as soon as he was old enough to go.

Even in the service, he'd been tight with his brothers in arms, yet never expected any of them to keep in touch once they'd parted ways. Besides, who would give up their lives to join him in his solitary existence, especially after surviving the hell of war? Not a soul.

Except the woman next to you, idiot.

Into the still of the night, Kotara spoke again. "I'm going home in the morning."

Blue jack-knifed in the bed, full of a snarly rage he knew he had no right to.

"So if I'm yours and you're mine, then why the fuck are you leaving me, woman?"

"I'm not leaving you. Well, I am, but I don't want to. It's just that my family means everything to me. I want you to be a part of that, but you won't even come and meet them. You just want me to hole up here with you and pretend that my life, up to this point, never happened?"

"Maybe it's because I wish the rest of *my life* had never happened, Kotara!"

"I'm not responsible for your emotions or dysfunction, Blue. As much as I love being with you, I can't heal you. I can't make you ease out of your comfort zone. I..." Her voice broke. "I can't make you love me."

With the full moon's glow casting shadows in the darkness of the winter night, he watched the misery etched into the lines of her beautiful face. Something inside of himself cracked like the hairline fracture on the shell of an egg—barely visible, but there none the less.

Each crease between her brows held a story, every spark of fire behind her eyes told a tale. But right now, she was eerily silent as he refused to give her what they both needed—a chance to be together.

"Okay, then. I have your answer," she said. A single tear slipped down her cheek and Blue's gut did a free fall as his emotions morphed from abject resolution to outright horror.

"God, Tara, please don't cry." He reached for her but she moved out of range.

"No. Don't. If you touch me right now, Blue, I'll shatter."

He lay back on his pillow, pulled the covers up, but felt no warmth whatsoever. His insides seemed as frosted over as the ground outside. But he still said nothing.

"I'm going for a run."

"Kotara, it's dark and..."

"Don't worry. I'll be back soon. I just need to go. I need..."

What she needed was the man in front of her. Both she and her lioness were steeped in anguish over the thought of leaving here without him. But if he wouldn't budge, then there was nothing she could do about it. Better to keep him tucked into the little part of her soul along with other fond memories. The decision was his and there was no way in hell she would force a man to be with her that didn't want her.

He sat up and looked at her as she got up and moved over to the wide swatch of moonlight streaming in through the window. Kotara let the magic of the change rush through her body. His expression moved fluidly between awe and dread as he proceeded her out of the room, and to the front door. He opened it for her, and she could have sworn she heard him whisper her name as she bounded out into the snow-covered terrain and away from what she'd hoped had been her destiny.

9

*B*lue missed Kotara more than he thought possible. He imagined her drowning herself in bacon at his kitchen table, moaning as she caught the hint of chocolate he'd put into her coffee. Kotara's scent lingering in the bathroom after a shower. Kotara tucked in his bed. Kotara underneath him as he rode her into oblivion. Kotara on top of him as she rode him.

The woman was everywhere. It was as if he nursed an abscessed tooth—it hurt so bad he wasn't sure he could bear it, yet there was nothing he could do about it.

You could go see her, you moron.

She was probably so disappointed in him, surely she wasn't interested in seeing him again. Besides, he'd been calling her since she left and she wasn't answering the phone or returning his messages.

Oh well. He'd royally blown the chance to be with a woman who was invigorating, brilliant and a total smart ass.

Mate.

He'd always loved living in this house, on this land. But right now, it felt so empty and bereft, it was all he could do not to put his hands over his ears and yell to the top of his lungs about what an idiot he'd been.

His mate had gone home.

The physical exercise that usually centered him, had done exactly jack shit since she'd left, but he would go and work up a sweat anyway. Stripped down to his underwear and a pair of snow boots, Blue tossed a few logs into the coals smoldering in the hearth and then headed out.

He opened the front door, took two steps and froze.

Less than ten paces from where he stood were two male lions in their prime, and two lionesses by their sides.

***

Blue was blowing up her phone. Again.

Kotara had tried her best to ignore him. It was for the best, after all. She allowed herself to grieve because she missed her mate to the depths of her soul. She missed him so much it was as if she had a defective, bloody and torn limb—it would hurt until the healing process was complete. The end.

Preparation for the holidays were in full swing. The guys had gone off hunting a few days ago and come back with a beautiful venison that Neesia coo'd over. The thing was so big it would need a trough full of marinade, but it would be delicious.

Lou had just returned from the high country with a gigantic ten-foot-high tree. The family had spent last night decorating it, and the staff was constantly in the kitchen with Neesia preparing all the dishes for their holiday celebration dinner.

They'd also just gotten word from the council elders of Kerr's former pack. The councilman and his nephew, who'd set Kerr up, had been quietly dealt with. Captain Johns was working with Jason and Lou on figuring out who the mole in the agency was. There was no way a kill order should have been shuffled through and approved solely on the word of a virtual unknown. That meant someone else had to be in on it, and they would indeed learn who.

In the meantime, Kotara would do what she did best—bury herself in work and solve everyone else's problems.

After yet another sleepless night, a quiet knock sounded at her door. She'd finally passed out from sheer exhaustion and been dreaming about riding on the snow mobile with Blue. Running through the forest doing parkour with Blue. Eating pancakes with Blue.

Blue. Blue. Blue.

Hell, he was making *her* blue, damn it.

The knock came again, and she rolled over and looked at the clock. Six thirty in the morning? Who the hell was bothering her this early, and on Christmas day? If it was Broglio, their facilities manager, coming to bug her about the New Year's lab cleaning schedule, she was going to skin him. Twice.

Knock, knock, knock.

Kotara grumbled a few choice curse words. She was tired and annoyed and didn't want to be awake this time of morning. Not to mention that her delicious dream had been interrupted, damn it.

"Come in and this better be good!"

And then it hit her. A scent she hadn't expected to ever catch again. *His* scent.

Covers forgotten, she jack-knifed into a sitting position just as the door opened. "Oh my god!" she squealed as Harrison Blue walked into her room, right up to her bed and dropped to his knees.

"What the hell are you doing here?"

"Merry Christmas, Kotara."

"B-but how?"

"I was fetched," he said with a grin.

"Fetched?"

"Yep. Two of your sisters and their mates came to get me,

and I'm glad they did. I've been wanting to chase you down since…well, you know." And he had the decency to blush clear up to his bare scalp.

She probably shouldn't have been so happy that he looked as tired and miserable as she did, but she didn't have time to question it.

"I've missed you like crazy," he said. "And I'm the biggest idiot in the world for thinking I could go a single day without you. I'm down on my knees asking your forgiveness, Tara."

Kotara bounded out of bed and landed square in the middle of Blue's chest. They rolled around on the floor, a tangle of arms and legs, kisses and laughter, as they promised to ring in this holiday season, and every future one, together.

ALSO BY AUTHOR T.J. MICHAELS

Carinian's Seeker, Vampire Council of Ethics Book One

Serati's Flame, Vampire Council of Ethics Book Two

Hatsept Heat, Vampire Council of Ethics Book Three

Seeker's Solace, Vampire Council of Ethics Book Four

Silk Road, Seals of Destiny

Spirit of the Pryde, Pryde Ranch Shifters

Niah's Pride, Pryde Ranch Shifters

Pursuit of Pride and Pleasure, Pryde Ranch Shifters

Shiftin' Sassy, a Pryde Ranch Shifters/Southern Shifters Crossover

Winter Blues, Pryde Ranch Shifters

Jaguar's Rule

Forever December

Egyptian Voyage

On the Prowl

Entwined Hearts

Shards of Ecstasy

Caramel Kisses

Hide No More

Juicy, Twilight Teahouse Book One

Luscious, Twilight Teahouse Book Two

Succulent, Twilight Teahouse Book Three

Gathering of the Storms Vol 1, Wind and Fire

Gathering of the Storms Vol 2, Reckoning

Some Naughty, None Nice

ABOUT THE AUTHOR

T.J. is an award-winning author of several romance genres, including paranormal, fantasy, sci-fi and urban fantasy romance. Writing like a madman, T.J. hasn't lost steam. Her mind? Yep, that's gone, but steam there is a-plenty.

No matter the genre T.J. is penning, her favorite thing to do is build worlds. To take you somewhere extraordinary. To transport you to a place where you can close your eyes and slip into your fantasy...

Visit T.J. Michaels online at her website
www.tjmichaels.com

www.ingramcontent.com/pod-product-compliance
Lightning Source LLC
Chambersburg PA
CBHW051532250626
47157CB00001B/20